THE
AGE
OF
THE
CHILD

~ A NOVEL ~

KRISTEN TSETSI

THE AGE OF THE CHILD

Book cover design by Kat Mellon

ISBN-13 978-0692992432

for danielle

my strong, brilliant, inspiring,
and dearest friend

cheers

PART ONE

ONE

Katherine had never been this close to an abandoned. She had seen them from her car, and occasionally one wandered past her store window, but the distance had always allowed her the convenience of assuming she was imagining the worst. The children were simply walking home, she could tell herself. The babies had been set on the sidewalk "just for a second" while their parents ran inside for some forgotten thing.

There was no pretending this baby was there for any other reason than that someone had fully intended to leave it there.

Above the shaded entrance where the car carrier sat on a WIPE FEET HERE mat, a second-story banner declared THIS CLINIC STAYS OPEN in futile defiance of a thick iron chain looped in a taut lemniscate through the metal doors' handles. (Katherine had hardly expected the *Daily Fact* article about the clinic's chained doors to be quite so literal.) Graffiti, some old and veined—*Adoption is a loving option!*—and some new, bold, and bright—*The future children of this great nation have prevailed!*—decorated exterior walls and fresh wood panels nailed over the first-floor windows.

Not only had no one run inside this building for anything, but one half of a legal sized envelope—what could it be but a note?—poked out from behind the baby's large head, which swiveled this way and that in a scan of the world and the two women standing over it.

"What should we do?" Margaret said.

Katherine looked again at the locked doors and felt physically ill.

She focused instead on the miniature t-shirt printed with green frogs and red daisies, at the plump legs with undefined knees poking out of a plain white diaper. A drop of water from the previous night's rain fell onto the tiny stranger's wrinkled neck. The baby opened its eyes and stretched one leg. Katherine tried not to imagine the moment someone had set down the carrier and walked away.

She stepped over the baby and pulled the chain, then yanked it hard.

Could they really have left no one on staff when there were still appointments to honor? Was that professional?

The padlock connecting the end links clacked hard against the door. She only half heard Margaret telling her it was useless as she tugged, her fingers wrapped so tight around the cool metal her skin burned. She dropped the chain and pressed her hands and face to the glass.

"Maybe you can find someone else to do it," Margaret said. "There has to be someone, doesn't there?"

A pamphlet on the vestibule floor promised *Safe Sex, No Regrets*. Narrow window panels cut into each of the interior doors allowed a fractured glimpse into the waiting area: an unmanned reception desk, empty lobby chairs, and a short magazine stack on an end table.

The sound of a vehicle passing on the rarely traveled industrial road carried over the tall wall of barberry bushes that obscured the clinic's entrance. Margaret bent to reach for the baby, but Katherine held her back.

"No touching," she said. She listened until the engine faded. Her neck started to sweat.

The baby made a sound that could have been a cry, and Margaret reached for it again.

Katherine grabbed the back of her shirt and pulled. "No touching, Margaret. They have a task force."

Margaret straightened and slipped her hands inside her skirt pockets. She looked down at the baby, and Katherine did, too. Its mouth puckered and twitched.

Margaret said, "How do they operate?"

"I assume they look under a microscope at skin and clothing and grasses, and such."

"I know what a task force does." Margaret kneeled beside the baby. "It's a robot baby, then? An android?"

"A what?" Katherine looked at Margaret long enough to establish that she was genuinely confused. "The babies are not a task force, Margaret. The police have a task force. To catch the people putting them out."

Margaret's face turned red.

Katherine looked away to give her a moment.

"But we didn't leave this baby here," Margaret finally said. "Why don't we just bring it to the police?"

"Were would you say we found it?"

"Right here. It's not illegal to walk by, is it?"

"Do you think they would believe we were just walking by?"

Whether they believed it wouldn't matter, Margaret said, because a simple DNA test would prove neither woman was the parent, and the results would clear them with either the police or the vigilantes.

Katherine looked at Margaret the way she always did when Margaret's refusal to read the *Daily Fact* left her ignorant of yet another critical piece of information or current event that could have a devastating impact on her future.

"If we bring this baby to the police," Katherine said, "we risk exposing ourselves not only to vigilantes, but to vigilante police officers.—Yes, some police are members, too. Margaret, if you would please just read—"

"But we're completely innocent," Margaret said.

"Innocent of leaving the baby, yes, and we might be allowed to prove that. But where we found it will be more than enough for anyone wanting to accuse one or both of us of hoping to find the facility open."

Margaret rubbed her nose. "One of us was."

"Margaret."

The baby made another crying noise. Its doughy skin was starting to develop a sheen in the humidity. The awning provided shade, at least, and the frog shirt appeared to be cotton, which was helpful, but the awning was narrow and the forecast had predicted rising humidity and a temperature in the nineties.

Margaret said, "Oh! See! There, under the leg. Is that a pacif—"

Katherine held up a hand at the sound of an engine on the other side of the barberry bushes. She clutched Margaret's wrist, said, "Sh," and crouched at the base of the hedge to peer through the loose mesh of low branches. A burgundy van with dark windows idled on the street beyond the parking lot.

Just one car, Katherine's, occupied a space.

The van turned into the lot and rolled toward Katherine's car. It halted in front of it, driver's side facing the clinic.

Margaret stooped beside her and told her they had to stay completely still, now. Her book research had taught her that was how soldiers and animals survived.

"What if they get out?" Katherine said.

"If we have to move, we will, but not until then."

Behind them, the baby squawked and then whined, its short, shaky protests building into howls.

Katherine and Margaret looked back at the baby, and then through the hedges.

Over the crying, Katherine heard the door on the opposite side of the van slide open with a dull grind. Artie Shaw's "Temptation" played to the lot. The baby screamed. Margaret spun to reach for it, and Katherine pushed her a little too hard before she could make contact, knocking her sideways onto the concrete path.

"You are one of the smartest women I know," Katherine whispered, pulling Margaret back to her crouch, "but I sometimes think you intentionally repel common sense. Are you all right?"

Margaret swept a hand over her still-flat abdomen.

Katherine whispered, "Margaret, I am so sor—"

"Don't be silly. I'm fine.—Kat, it's fine." She put a finger to her lips.

The people in the parking lot must not have been able to hear the baby over the music, because no one materialized around either side, and the faint shadow of the driver's head moved only slightly behind the window. At "You were born to be kissed," the sliding door slammed shut and the van peeled out to the street.

Katherine and Margaret waited one full minute before standing. The baby continued to exhaust itself in the shade.

"We can call the police for it from a gas station," Katherine said.

They crept from the barberry bushes to a line of oaks and ran from there to the car. Katherine plucked a folded piece of paper from under the windshield wiper and slid behind the wheel. She pushed START, unfolded the note, and read it aloud while Margaret, who was more familiar with AVs, programmed the GPS.

"'We came to collect some of our personal items but changed our minds when we saw your car.'" Katherine said, "Why do you suppose they wanted us to know why they were here?"

"They probably don't want us to be scared," Margaret said.

"'If you're here to cause harm or damage,'" Katherine continued reading, "'please know you've already won. There's nothing more for you to do. If you're here for help, please know how sad we are that we can no longer help you.'"

Margaret pressed the BEGIN circle on the monitor. The car eased out of its space.

"What will you do now?" Margaret said. "Tell him?"

Katherine watched the steering wheel turn on its own. She followed the green line on the map from the clinic to Margaret and Ernie's house, and from Margaret and Ernie's house to the much smaller Newchester house Katherine and Graham had owned for two years.

She had meant to tell him four days ago, on the day of her appointment. That morning, she sat at the kitchen table with coffee, a muffin, and the newspaper spread in front of her, just as she did every morning. She intended to read, as she always did, while waiting for Graham to come downstairs for the coffee he consistently filled with an inconsistent amount of creamer. *I have an appointment*, she was going to tell him once he set down his mug. *It should be no surprise to you, considering, but I thought you should know.*

She tried to read, but her prepared words repeated and repeated, blurring the headlines. The speech itself, succinct and harmless as it was, was making her needlessly nervous. Of course Graham would agree. Of course he would. Of course. She smoothed the soft crease in the paper's center and tried again, getting no farther than the second sentence before spontaneously vomiting her first bite of cranberry muffin and a sip of coffee onto the lede:

> NATION—In a long anticipated but hard fought move, the country's five holdout reproductive health clinics will chain their doors today in compliance with federal laws enacted under the pro-creation Citizen Amendment. Anti-abortion and pro-creation activists who together have waged a decades-long battle for the protection of unborn citizens call the clinics' closings "an epic victory"...

The *Daily Fact* was a carefully gathered wad in her hands when Graham finally sailed chin first into the kitchen and sucked up the air with flared nostrils. Polished Italian leather shoes bought on their Austrian vacation dangled from his fingers. After a look at Katherine, his eyes went to the paper, but he said nothing as he sat at the table and set his shoes at his feet. He fluttered his eyebrows at her, then frowned as she left the table with the *Fact*. When he asked what had happened in the world—"Can I read it before you throw it away, next time?"—she told him what little she knew.

"Ah, well," he said when she finished. "I know you must be upset about that—and you should be! We all should be—but it was bound to happen. Do you know, I've been thinking about changing my mind about all that. Babies. Fatherhood. Motherhood, for you." He winked and smiled and put on his left shoe. "Just thinking." His right foot slipped into the right shoe. "Hey! You're still in slippers. Aren't we going in together?"

Katherine, stunned vapid, only shook her head. Graham's revised perspective on their future was—surely inadvertently and wholly unconsciously—a threat. She immediately rethought her once deeply held belief that they should always be completely honest with each another.

She had stayed home from the store that day, and for two days after that.

"No," Katherine said to Margaret. "I think not yet."

TWO

Katherine found herself on the map and looked at the time. Charlene had warned her not to be late, so Katherine had given herself twenty minutes to spare. "Three sets of knocking, and say nothing," Charlene had said. "They won't answer the first two times. Listen, now. If they do, it isn't them."

Katherine thought it sounded risky, but she trusted Charlene, a tall, thin banker in her sixties and Katherine's first customer when Oxford Spirits opened two weeks after the ratification of the Citizen Amendment. It was also the only underground clinic Charlene said she trusted, and Charlene was the only person Katherine knew who knew of an underground clinic. (Many people could direct her toward black market birth control—all of them customers—, but very few were aware of, or would admit to being aware of, an abortion provider. Were black market birth control more reliable, and less frequently a pink vitamin B12 pill or a condom made in someone's home kitchen, Katherine might have opted for it in favor of the rhythm method that had proved powerless against the charms of Austria and a blindingly beautiful husband.)

There were other options, of course, but she had carefully thought through each one and had ranked them from most to least pleasant. She would turn to the alternatives only as they became necessary.

By force of habit, she hovered her hands near the steering wheel as the car navigated itself away from the liquor store. ("You're taking the AV?" Graham had smiled at her from the vodka aisle. "Where're you going?" He'd looked down, then, distracted when their customer crouched to investigate a lower shelf, her tangled red hair blanketing her shoulders. "Margaret needs me," Katherine had lied, turning to leave before he could ask anything else.) When the car reached a steady speed on Tinytown's Main Street, straight road for a mile and a half, Katherine relaxed her hands in her lap and looked out the window.

Even with the increasing attention law enforcement was paying to abandoned children, discards still sat in doorways every several blocks. Some wore signs around their necks: FREE TO A GOOD HOME, read one hanging from a child who looked old enough to ride a bike. A little girl in a frayed dress wore a small whiteboard reading POTTY TRAINED, a rainbow and sunshine doodle crammed into the top right corner. Others had no signs, but huddled on stoops with bottles they may or may not have been able to manipulate themselves, stuffed animals that fell and rolled away, or toys Katherine had seen more than one child drop on the sidewalk and then promptly jam into a dirty mouth.

Discarded coffee cups, fast food containers, used pregnancy tests, and pint-sized liquor bottles also dotted Main Street's once pristine sidewalks. When traffic slowed to maneuver around a drunk pedestrian, Katherine found herself at pace with a bearded man in a business shirt collecting trash as he came to it, his arms loaded. When he glanced up and caught Katherine watching, she turned forward and concentrated on the road. One car ahead, a brightly-fingernailed hand popped out of the passenger side window to toss a soda can. It bounced into the gutter in front of the man, who lost a beer bottle picking it up.

Traffic picked up speed, and the man became a small figure in the side mirror. Two blocks later, a red light created another standstill. It was the only major intersection in north Tinytown and the final light before the highway turnoff. Consequently, semi-regular protests had taken shape on the high-traffic corner early in the debates over the Citizen Amendment, whose supporters and opponents waved and shouted at rush hour commuters pretending to be distracted by their dashboard screens. Those semi-regular protests had over time become a weekly gathering for anyone who wanted to stand in support of or opposition to nearly anything.

This week, the focus of the protest was children. A sign reading BABIES AREN'T TRASH bounced in rhythm with steps taken in a tight circle. IF YOU CAN'T DO THE TIME, DON'T DO THE CRIME, read one side of a large poster. It spun to flash CLOSE YOUR DAMN LEGS on the other. A woman wearing a mask of some kind—she was three vehicles ahead, so her back was to Katherine—jumped out of the front car in the right turn lane and plopped a baby at the feet of a protester carrying a sign reading THINK OF THE CHILDREN. By the time she returned to her car (it was a gray seal, the mask she wore) and the driver sped around the corner, the protest group had managed to shuffle ten or fifteen feet away from the baby left squirming and crying on the warm asphalt. Katherine watched to see whether one of the protesters would turn back to pick it up, but none did. She was reaching for the door handle when the man who had been collecting trash sprinted by on the sidewalk and scooped the baby into his arms. He held it to his chest while shouting and gesticulating at the backs of the protesters who stepped farther away, signs bouncing in exclamation.

After half an hour, much of the drive along a curving, tree-lined county highway, Katherine's car parked itself at a convenience store on the outskirts of a small town. She locked up and hurried across the street. Sweat collected under her chin and trapped stray hairs against her cheeks and forehead before she reached the opposite curb. By the time she made it to the red house half a mile away, her shirt pressed flat against her rib cage.

She scanned the sidewalk and the street, saw no one, and turned into the gravel driveway narrowed by tall hedges and reaching vines. Small rocks crunched under each step she took toward the house. Its upstairs windows were dark cutouts in thick, curling ivy, and blue glass beakers on the bottom floor windowsills glowed bright against the white curtains closed behind them.

She stopped.

The beakers struck her as odd.

What respectable underground abortion clinic would advertise as a laboratory, or as a scientific or medical facility of any kind?

Charlene had cautioned her about the knocking, but going all the way to the door to announce herself now seemed like a reckless idea. The police could have set a trap. So could the vigilantes. Prison for attempted murder on one hand, a potentially fatal beating on the other.

Katherine watched the house—the beautiful, old red house that just seconds before had promised her freedom—as she backed away from it, each step a grating that traveled the length of her legs to grind at her abdomen. When she reached the sidewalk, she was almost certain the left window curtain moved an inch or two to one side. She ran for the convenience store as fast as she could for as long as she could.

The pharmacists standing behind their white counter made no effort to pretend they were uninterested in Katherine's study of the vitamins and herbs in the natural health aisle. She fingered through the vitamin A, B12, and D. There was no vitamin C.

"Help you?" the woman pharmacist called.

Katherine asked sweetly where she might find the vitamin C.

Both pharmacists looked her over. Katherine imagined what they saw: Clean, intact shoes, pressed mid-lengths, and a crisp black shirt. Shiny blond hair and—she smiled at them—remarkably unstained teeth. A large box of "All natural! 100% Organic!" diapers tucked under her arm.

The male pharmacist said, "You know the law's this close to changing. I suspect you don't want to get caught up in that."

Katherine said, "Law? What law is that?" She knew precisely what law. Time was critical.

"Stop making accusations, Bertram. She probably just has a cold, the poor thing," the woman said. "C is for cold." She laughed at her own joke. "Is that right? You have a cold, hon? We keep all the C behind the counter, these days. You never can tell with some people."

"That's exactly right, June."

"Oh, Bertram." She pointed at Katherine's diapers. "Can't you see she already has one?"

"Doesn't mean she wants another one," he muttered.

"Come on over, hon. I have some C right here. How many milligrams?"

The seasoning aisle was next, and it had a supervisor, as well, this one wearing a white shirt, black slacks, and a red MANAGER tag. Katherine dropped as many containers of curry, onion powder, and rosemary in her basket as she did cinnamon. Now and then, as the manager inched closer, she struggled with the diapers to draw attention to them.

"That's an awful lot of cinnamon, ma'am," the manager said.

He stood so close behind her she could feel her shirt sleeve touching some part of him. She turned to face him and checked his neck and wrists for tattoos. Some vigilantes had them, but most kept their participation hidden until it was time to, as one member had phrased it for the *Daily Fact*, "administer justice."

"Is there a limit per customer?" She spoke sweetly. She twirled her hair. Graham said men liked that. Katherine never understood why.

"That all depends," he said. "What do you need it for?"

The Fourth of July, of course, she said. She twirled her hair again and tilted her head. She cooed, "Do you enjoy a party?" When he smiled that way and let his eyes fall down her neck to the last open button of her shirt, she nudged him with a shoulder and said, "Graham—my husband—always prepares a delightful pasta salad."

He pulled away. "That's fine, ma'am. Have a nice day."

Katherine avoided Margaret's calls for the next two weeks. It was easier to pretend there was no pregnancy if she could escape talking about it, and Margaret would want to talk about it. Although Margaret might think Katherine's absence made her a terrible friend, Katherine had to risk the misconception for now. In truth, she was there for Margaret in her own way, listening to every single voicemail she left.

Margaret was excited—not only about her own pregnancy, but about (what she believed would be) their shared due dates. Their babies, she predicted, were "destined to be best friends," and she hoped that would comfort Katherine as she settled into her "…um…situation."

Margaret had chosen names. Elmore for a boy and Lenore for a girl. "Have you thought about names?" she trailed in a small voice.

Margaret was convinced she could feel every extraordinary moment of her baby forming itself from her own blood and tissue.

Margaret was drinking Rooibos tea and working on her eleventh novel, the activity in her uterus making her feel "so optimistic and creative" she had half considered beginning a new series.

Katherine, meanwhile, was doing her best (and mightily succeeding) at ignoring whatever activity she had going on in her own uterus in between as yet ineffective doses of this and that. When she worked, she worked late, her undivided attention on the second store's final, pre-grand opening touches, various employee concerns, and Graham's plans for opening day (Katherine would not attend; Graham was a natural at social gatherings).

The days she stayed home to experiment with herbs and spices, Katherine found many ways to occupy the time spent waiting (hoping) for cramping. When she was confident Graham had driven far enough away to not turn back for something, she switched on the television news and listened to the all but intolerable voices in the background while straining to lift impossibly heavy furniture. ("You're seeing the true animal nature of human beings," said the blond male opinion generator one hot July day. "Pest status, here we come. Correction, correction: here 'they' come. I don't want to speak for anyone else, but me and the wife, for one—or is it for two? Ha! Ha!—aren't mindless breeders like…Hey, what's another nuisance breeder? Mice? Yeah? Mice? What about sunfish? Most of their eggs die, did you know that? That's why they have so gosh darned many of them. Natural population control at work with those sunfish. What say you, audience? Is it time we start looking into some kind of human population control? If so, what's your proposal? Chemtrails? Something else? You're invited! Come fight it out at YouGuidetheNews.com.")

The day Katherine left behind cinnamon, parsley, and vitamin C (in all of its incarnations), she committed as soon as she got out of bed to a blend of black cohosh and pennyroyal. Graham got ready upstairs and she let the herbs do their work while skimming the headlines at the kitchen table, making tic marks beside selected *Daily Fact* articles.

She read the newspaper for Margaret nearly as much as she did for herself. Not talking regularly to Margaret meant not keeping her informed as well as she would have liked, and although Margaret did claim to spend plenty of time reading relevant discussions on social media, Katherine thought it critical to send her clippings to keep her apprised of the issues not making it into blogs or online meeting sites—at the very least those issues that might be easily misunderstood, misrepresented, or blatantly manipulated with an edited word here and a misquote there. Margaret granted too many interviews and attended too many signings and book launches to be as uninformed about the world's "negativity" as she would like to be. (And Margaret had more than once thanked Katherine for having somehow selected just the right current events to help her better navigate the intolerable world of small talk.) Katherine did, however, do her best to respect Margaret's wishes and rarely sent her anything that would upset her.

Katherine would unquestionably include the top two front page stories in her weekly news update envelope, the first for its documentation of an extraordinary moment in history:

Citizen Amendment proponents overwhelmed by babies
STATE—Opposition to the Citizen Amendment continues to escalate, with an increasing number of lawmakers and residents finding infants and toddlers on their front porches, lawns, and in some cases in front of their places of business.

Governor John Santoro, perhaps most widely known for his repeated declarations on the dangers of birth control, said babies left outside his private gate eleven times in the last week have made it a "real chore" to leave his house.

"You have to go out and you have to move them, first, otherwise the gate will scuttle them across the driveway. It isn't a soft, smooth stone, like slate. We have cobblestones, authentic. Ripped straight from the streets of Munich," Santoro said.

Santoro is one of at least four hundred politicians nationwide reporting the presence of uninvited children, but until recently the phenomenon had not significantly affected the northeastern region. State representatives Alice Charles and Chadwick Allen, staunch opponents of the Citizen Amendment and in particular the June shuttering of the Eighth Street Reproductive Health Clinic, have argued the uptick in doorstep babies is a direct and clear response to the clinic's closing. Haverton selectwoman Frances Platt, who also opposed the Citizen Amendment, hesitates however to credit the loss of the state's holdout clinic with the rise in what many are calling shocking demonstrations of animosity.

"People are tired of not having sex, so they're having it. These babies are in many cases an inevitable result," Platt said. She added that while parents have options, such as putting children up for adoption, "My guess is they figure these people they're leaving them with will want them, and it's a lot easier than going through that whole process."

Politicians aren't the only targets of those seeking alternative permanent childcare. Tinytown resident Albert Griffin, 20, filed a police report Monday claiming he tripped over a toddler asleep on his door mat. Windbury resident Zelda Knightly, 60, last week reported finding a young girl sucking a watermelon wine cooler from a child's sippy cup on her back porch swing. Police estimated the girl to be two years old.

Both Griffin and Knightly say they were openly supportive of the Citizen Amendment but that they don't know who could have left the children outside their homes.

Santoro, who said he spoke on behalf of all Citizen Amendment supporters, condemned the behavior.

"Are the babies precious? Well, of course they're precious. Every child is precious. But I'll tell you what, they aren't mine to treat preciously. Is it so wrong to want to be able get in my car and go out for some milk once in a while?" Santoro said.

The second story would be light fodder for party conversation:

Baby Stuffs to add fifty new links to its chain
NATION—Baby Stuffs will add fifty new stores over the coming year, executive vice president of corporate affairs Danielle Marias announced Thursday.

The big box retailer's surge in popularity follows 32 years of disappointing sales that reduced the once booming retailer to fewer than 100 stores nationwide. Marias said that although precise locations are to be determined, she expects the bulk of the stores to open in the higher-than-average birthrate regions of the Northeast and Midwest. Marias said she could not be more excited about the store's success.

"Three years ago I was mainlining Cabernet in my office bathroom. I was just waiting on word that I was out of a job, you know? Tip Top One Stop already had my resume," she said. "But then everyone started having all their babies, and boom!"

Statistics compiled by the Centers for Disease Control reveal a marked spike in the nation's birth rate, previously holding steady at 5.1 million. One of the authors of the report, Hazel Schnyctic, said she is astonished by the figures.

"In the last four years we've grown by at least an additional half a million annually," Schnyctic said. "Five hundred thousand one year, then five hundred seventy five, and we expect this year to top out at about six hundred fifty thousand. These are all extra, you understand." Schnyctic added that the CDC's projections for the next ten years are "astronomical"...

Katherine cut and folded the articles and slipped them into the yellow envelope before turning to page two.

Lice no longer the only daycare strain
TINYTOWN—Daycare providers face new pressures as enrollment continues to exceed available accommodations.

Facilities already over capacity struggle with the challenge of understaffing, tearful brawls over inadequate toy supplies, and employees traumatized by the number of children left behind by their paren—

"Staying home again?"

She looked up from the paper. Graham, wearing her favorite of his sports jackets, stood in the space between the kitchen and living room. The ends of his hair just touched the collar. He was beautiful.

"Yes," she said. "I think so."

Rather than walk toward the coffee pot to fill his travel mug as he did every morning before leaving, he raised the cuffs of his pants to show her his platform shoes. He winked an eyebrow.

She suspected the sight of the tan leather lace-ups he'd bought in Austria should have transported her directly to their small, pink hotel room overlooking the Salzach River, and to the uncommonly dizzying sexual connection Salzburg had always inspired in them. Instead, she thought of abdominal intrusion and unbearable weight. Of old age and Salzburg's penetrating rain. Of prison.

"Oh, Graham. You know it was never the shoes." She reached out to him. "The time. You have to open. Customers will be waiting."

He tapped his watch. "I'm early. On purpose." He posed in his jacket. "Ten minutes, Katie."

"This exhaustion..."

He let her hand hover between them. "You've sure been tired a lot, lately," he said. "What's going on?"

"Nothing. Nothing at all." She hated to lie, and lie again, but it was the only way. If she told him the truth now, which she believed she could safely do with the miscarriage so imminent and irreversible, he would still feel betrayed by the decision she had made without him. He would almost certainly stop trusting her. And then stop loving her.

"Nothing," he said. "That's the whole problem. Even on the days you don't stay home tired, there's nothing. It's been months, you know that?"

It had not been months, but it had been a long five and a half weeks since they had last engaged in almost any form of intimacy, she realized as he stood there in masterfully unveiled sorrow.

"It has not been months," she said quietly.

He took her hand, finally, and got on one knee in front of her. He kissed her knuckles and then slid her robe aside and kissed her breast. She wanted so much to appreciate the kiss for what it was, and for a brief, blissful moment it did clear her mind of anything but the pure physical sensation, but the vision of a suckling baby fast replaced the reality of his mouth and she nudged him away.

Graham adjusted his crotch as he stood. "You used to like sex you didn't know was coming." He shook his hair out of his eyes and smiled. "If it worked with the calendar…"

"Is that what this is about? Graham, you have to allow me to not always want—"

"Sex? You think this is about sex? Only sex, I mean? Katie, if that's what you think, how could you even love me?" He dragged a chair around the table and sat close enough to touch her arms under the wide sleeves of her bathrobe. "Katie. Katie, we…We planned the whole second store in the middle of the night, standing out in the weeds. Remember we used to get drunk together?"

He slid his hand further into her sleeve and cupped and stroked her elbow. They used to make dinners together, he said. They used to have sex after the morning alarm and then share the newspaper. They used to talk in the car on the way to the store.

He scraped a fingernail against her forearm, over and over again in the same spot until it itched. She moved his hand so she could scratch.

"You used to like being around me," he said.

"Five weeks ago, Graham?"

He looked at her, cold. "Not long enough? Well, Katie, you let me know when I can officially start missing you, and—"

She pulled him close and whispered in his ear, with full sincerity, "I love being around you."

He held her tight and whispered back, "I know how you can be around more of me."

She laughed and squirmed away, wanting but very much not wanting. "The grand opening." She wiped her eyes. "Lout."

"That's exactly what I'm—"

"The store, Graham. The opening." She tapped her bare wrist.

"Oh! Yep, yep, I guess I should get." He hopped up, adjusted his crotch again, unhooked a pant cuff from the heel of his shoe, and smiled dazzling eyes at her. "Sure you won't come?"

She was tempted to, now. She promised herself that if the herbs performed early enough, she would do her best to make it. To him she said, "Tell me about it tonight, and please kiss me hard before you go."

She would have continued reading about the troubles of lice after he was gone had she not been distracted by another headline (one she was appalled that the *Fact* could for one second believe was a page-two story):

Miscarriages will be investigated, lawmakers say
STATE—Governor John Santoro signed into law Thursday a bill requiring that all miscarriages be investigated by a state appointed physician.

Effective immediately, the law previously adopted by 23 of the 50 states applies to women who admit themselves to hospitals for treatment following a miscarriage. The law also applies to those whose miscarriages are otherwise brought to the attention of medical or legal authorities. The decision follows months of often heated debates that notably included Senator Betsy Knoell at one time throwing her briefcase at Representative Victoria Larsen.

Knoell called Santoro's refusal to veto the bill "diabolical."

"This is absolute insanity. Absolute insanity. That's all I can say," Knoell said.

Larsen acknowledged that it was a tough loss for Knoell and her supporters but praised Santoro's decision.

"The Citizen Amendment leaves no room for a gray area. We outlawed birth control to ensure right to life, so why on earth wouldn't we protect any and all existing life? Look, a person conceived in the United States is a United States citizen, and United States citizens are endowed by their creator with certain inalienable rights," Larsen said. She added, "We investigate the mysterious deaths of our post-uterine citizens, so it only follows

that we would investigate the deaths of our youngest, most
vulnerable citizens."

Tinytown councilman Jerry Deutsch said that at the core of his
support for the law was the protection of women who have been or
could become the targets of pro-creation vigilantism.

"Women have died because there was no real system in place
to determine the authenticity of these 'miscarriages.' It breaks my
heart that some of those beaten and murdered women had valid,
unintended loss of uterine life," Deutsch said. "Now, someone—
not me, but other people—might also say some of those women
had it coming. Murder will always, always have a price. That's just
the way it's always been and it's the way it'll always be. But
without a proper investigation, we really don't know that it's
murder, do we? To the vigilantes I say, job well done, but your job
is done. We'll take it from here."

An unidentified woman present for Deutsch's comments
kicked Deutsch in the shin and shouted, "I hope you get syphilis!"
before police escorted her out of the building.

Those found guilty of a self-induced miscarriage, including
any person found to have been complicit in the act, will be
considered abortionists and as such will face a life sent—

Katherine ran to the bathroom.

The old phone's ring was so loud, the tail of the rapidly clanging bells so
high a pitch, that she could hear it with her head surrounded by porcelain.
The last time the bells had tormented her under such uncomfortable
circumstances had been the day her mother brought home the Western
Electric. Katherine was twelve and sick with a virus, vomiting in the toilet
as her mother demanded each of her friends call her to test the antique
phone's ability to receive calls. It rang and rang, pounding Katherine's head
already strained from heaving. Her mother, resistant to the change, had
complained loudly and at length to everyone who had undoubtedly
expected to donate only a minute or two of their time.

"If they want to force us to return to land lines," she had spit, "I'm
certainly not pumping money into any business hoping to profit from such
an infuriating law." Instead, she told them, she had found a phone
manufactured by a company not in operation anymore, a phone that was
also, incidentally, "every bit as archaic as the feeble-minded, paternalistic
ideals driving the inane decisions endorsed and approved by those
cowardly, misguided, power-blinded politicians." (Ironically, in their quest

to protect people from the smart phone distractions that had caused innumerable deaths and immobilizing learned helplessness, the government had unwittingly led thousands accustomed to constant aid to their demise during the transition period.)

The ringing stopped, and Katherine removed her finger from her throat long enough to hear the message. Margaret said she was worried and needed to know Katherine was alive.

"At least give me a call and leave a little message, will you please? I promise not to pick up."

At the click of the answering machine, which had taken hours of online antique store searches to find, Katherine pressed as far back on her tongue as her index finger would reach. Nothing, this time. She tried again, and still nothing. Small, dark bits of leaves floated in the water under her nose. She flushed the toilet and brushed her teeth, gagging at the bits of cohosh and morning muffin cranberries dislodging from her molars.

She bared her teeth in the mirror and used the bristles of her toothbrush to flick out dark remainders. Cohosh and pennyroyal, the least pleasant and more dangerous options on her list, had also been the last. Had the mixture not worked (her intervention notwithstanding), and had the miscarriage law not passed, she wondered: would she have been prepared to throw herself stomach first onto the kitchen's stone floor? It was, admittedly, a relief to not have to answer that question, but she was disappointed by what the relief said about her commitment. Surely it was possible to miscarry and survive without medical assistance.

She put down her toothbrush and rinsed and gargled.

On the other hand, exposing herself to that kind of risk would mean she found the possibility of death or life imprisonment more tolerable than the physical experience of gestation and childbirth. She would have to be to some degree suicidal to invite either outcome. And because she was in no way suicidal, it only followed that she was also not a coward to allow the pregnancy to go forward. She was, instead, a pragmatist. Yes. Therefore, Katherine decided (as it were), whatever she did next was ultimately her choice. And her choice (she had to believe) was that she would let it grow until it was time for it to come out, and when it did, she would find someone who wanted it.

Katherine called Margaret, who was either not home or was, as promised, allowing the ringing to go on until the message prompt.

"Alive," Katherine said. "And…and still pregnant. Please, Margaret, never ask me about it."

All that was left to do now was tell Graham.

THREE

Katherine and Graham sat in hard, high chairs at a tall table in a dim, expensive restaurant. Graham rubbed his eyes, two fingers on each eyelid. He said, "Marriage isn't fun right now."

There was nothing she could think to say that would make him feel better. She bit her cinnamon biscotti and tasted nothing. She forced it down with a drink of water and said, "Have you considered a dog?"

Graham put his chin in his hand and looked out the window. Cars drove by in the rain. They had never been to this restaurant before, but Katherine had always wanted to try it.

"I don't really want a dog," he said.

"Well, that should settle it for you. If you would shy away from the responsibility of a dog, how on earth could you handle a child?"

"I didn't say I couldn't handle a dog. I said I don't want a dog."

"Oh, thank goodness. I like them just fine—Margaret's dog is lovely—but one of our own? The fur everywhere, and all that mess and walking. Who would do it all?"

Graham nodded. He smiled the saddest smile Katherine had ever seen him smile when the server delivered their second round of drinks. Katherine adjusted the napkin on her lap, sipped her fresh water, and when the server left she held Graham's hand across the table. Black glass sucked cold at the tender skin of her forearm.

"I guess that explains why you've been so tired," he said.

"I guess it does." She stroked his fingers. "It was never the plan," she said.

"Plans can change." Graham drank his ginger beer and licked the foam from his upper lip.

"I cannot imagine why you would think that."

"Yeah, well, I 'cannot' imagine why I wouldn't."

Katherine wanted to tell him that when she closed her eyes, she saw nothing but teems and teems of babies cocooned in blankets, streaming out hospital doors by the millions in tightly packed schools while fertile bodies continued without consciousness to create, create.

"Are we ocean sunfish, Graham?" She detested that blond television idiot. "Are we mice?"

"What?"

"If you love me," she said, and when Graham released her hand, she crooned, "as I love you. My galaxy."

"But you won't do this for me. This one little thing."

"Oh, Graham, no." She moved aside the thick curl of hair that always threatened to sneak inside his ear. "But if you need to have it, you should. If you want to raise it alone, or…or even find someone to do it with you, I would never try to keep you."

"Why are you being like this?"

"I am being nothing but sincere."

"Yeah, well," he said, "the only way anyone is leaving anyone is if you're the one leaving me." And quietly, his beer glass hiding his mouth, "You know, they only stay until eighteen."

"Oh, is that all?"

The next morning, both were tense and quiet after having pretended to sleep at the end of a clumsy sexual effort during which both seemed to have forgotten what the other liked or how to do it. Graham sullenly agreed over coffee to officially agree to adoption when the time came, in whatever way such an official agreement was made.

The time came three months later when Katherine collected Graham from Oxford Spirits II to bring him to sit at a polished marble desk across from an adoption counselor and a notary. In yellow wingback chairs much too large for the space, they leaned forward to read the contract and sign their initials beside arrow-shaped tabs to confirm both consented to all components of relinquishing "the child" at birth.

The adoption would be closed (this clause required their initials, unless they preferred it to be open), and no, Katherine said, they did not wish to participate in the selection of the parents (initials required here, as well).

"Why don't we wish to participate in the selection?" Graham said, pen held over the blank line.

"Because the decision is not ours to make. How can we behave as her parents one moment, concerned over who will take her, what their treatment of her will be—"

"Her?"

"An arbitrarily chosen pronoun." She urged the tip of his pen to the blank line. "We either are or are not the parents, and we are not. This child should go to its new parents with as much random chance as it came to us."

Katherine would not dare tell him that it would be too much to bear to wonder year after year whether they had chosen the wrong guardians. If the new parents presented ideally on paper but let the diaper sit full for hours, or if they shook her—or him—Katherine would never forgive herself for having said, "Those people. They look perfect." That she would never know the level of parenting they, the people she had handpicked, were achieving would only add to her anxiety. If she expressed her fears to Graham, he would latch onto her concern and insist, smiling and stroking whichever part of her body was closest to him, that it was a sign she wanted to be a parent, and from that moment until the day her body split open, he would peck and peck and ever so charmingly peck at her until she either walked away or relented.

"Initial there," Katherine said, and Graham scribbled *GJH* on the short line beside *Adoptive parents will be chosen at the discretion of the Happy Baby Agency*. "And there," Katherine said, having only just read the line, herself. It was in a smaller font, an obvious afterthought, squeezed tightly between paragraphs as if to retain the contract's original page count, which was exactly four full pages: *The Happy Baby Agency cannot guarantee placement of your child and reserves the right to revise and/or terminate the contract up to or beyond fourteen (13) days prior to or following the child's birth*.

"Is it fourteen days or is it thirteen?" Katherine said, showing the contract to the middle-aged man behind the desk.

"That's a typo."

Graham said, "It's one day, Katie. What difference does it make?"

"It took exactly nine minutes to make this difference, Graham. Now, which is it? Whatever it is, please cross out the incorrect number, write in the correct number, and initial it."

The counselor crossed out the number thirteen, wrote in *14*, initialed the change, allowed the notary to pound a tiny seal into the page beside the initials, and returned the contract to Katherine.

"Will your notary be with you if you do decide to revise the contract up to or beyond thirteen-slash-fourteen days?" Katherine said.

"Every change and every signature is verified and validated. Can't have people claiming they didn't know this or that or never signed this or that line. Makes a bit of a jumble of things."

"Natalist Net said you were the top child placement agency in the state. We waited three months for this appointment," Katherine said while initialing with *KBO*. "I did not expect to be forced to accept that you anticipate likely failure."

"We don't like to anticipate failure, Ms. Oxford, but you were the first appointment of the day. And you were a legitimate appointment."

"What has that to do with anything?" Katherine signed the final line.

"You'll see."

And they did. When Katherine and Graham stepped out of the elevator, they confronted a double-wide line stretching from the reception desk to the glass doors and out onto the sidewalk. Everyone inside the doors, their coats draped over their arms and their bodies sagging in the warm lobby, turned to look at Graham and Katherine. They did not look away after a second or two, as Katherine had expected they would, but lingered on their once-overs. Graham placed a protective hand over Katherine's protruding abdomen.

"What are you doing?" She plucked it off.

The teenager at the reception desk screamed at the crowd that he was doing his best, but that there was no time between appointments to see anybody today.

"Anyone without an appointment and who has more than seven months left on your pregnancy, move to the back! I'm not saying it again. I don't care how insulting and offensive you are, I will not put you on the wait list if you're up front and I can't see a bump. Move to the back!"

Necks craned to get a look at the end of the line, but from the inside, there seemingly was no end. People fell out of their places—some only feet from the desk—and made their way farther back, greeting each person in line with, "How far along?"

Katherine and Graham shoved the glass doors against a steady, cutting wind whipping bright scarves and long hair into the faces of taut, shivering strangers. Most were bundled in that year's trendy faux fur hats, the expensive and the inexpensive easily distinguishable by sheen. They wore tattered polyester, suede leather, or puffy cotton-blend coats, most of them ankle length and some straining at the midsection. The men wore platform shoes ranging from brand name to generic, shiny to torn, their soles so high the shortest man was as tall as the tallest, high-hatted woman.

Katherine was suddenly aware of the feel of her own hat on her forehead. It was the best faux available, and the first time she had been able to afford something so ridiculous. It was also every bit as warm as advertised.

"Nice hat," someone said.

"Oh, thank y—"

"I'm kidding, you elitist cunt. Why don't you buy one of us an appointment?"

Katherine felt Graham's hand close around hers. Too many women for her taste looked at her.

"Look at them," one of them muttered. "If me and my husband looked like that I bet we'd walk confident about our baby's chances, too."

Katherine wanted to say something, but what? She could hardly say what she wanted to say, which was that she hoped the woman was right. Odds were that a baby she and Graham made would indeed be, at least, aesthetically superior. Even if it were…well, an intolerable nuisance, no one would know or care until it was too late. People took babies home because they wanted a baby. While some undoubtedly favored a particular skin color, eye color, or something else, they did not take them home because they liked them for who they were. (Katherine made a mental note to write that in a message she decided at that very moment to have the agency deliver with the baby: *I never knew you. It had nothing to do with who you might have been or who you might become. It was nothing personal.*) She found herself, then, scrutinizing the women. What if there were no opportunity to leave a note? Which of those women might ruin her chances by having a baby more attractive than her own? The one with dark brown eyes and delicate hands? The one with full lips and high cheekbones? Probably not the one who muttered at her, but babies sometimes looked surprisingly unlike their parents. It could, therefore, be any one of them.

An unnerving flutter thumped low in her throat. She pulled at Graham's arm and rushed him across the street to the car.

FOUR

With the stores closed for the holiday, Katherine and Graham slept late on the morning of Margaret and Ernie's Christmas dinner—Graham a bit later, because, Katherine guessed, no one was pressing every available appendage against his insides.

She looked out the kitchen window at the purple, early morning landscape while waiting for the coffee to percolate. It had been unusually warm for weeks. Warm enough for snow, falling now as it had off and on for days in flat, wide flakes that covered their four acres of weeds (which until recently had been only one acre of weeds). Bare trees normally passed by for their dull brownness stood in proud, naked glory under the building layer of white.

For as long as Katherine could remember, winters had been painfully cold and, but for a tiny flake here and there, free of snow. (As a child she had had to scrape and scrape to gather enough snow for one small, tight snowball, which she had thrown at her mother when she stepped outside to take a picture of Katherine in her knit cap and mittens. The snowball—no larger than a rock, and almost as hard—made it into the photograph before pelting Katherine's mother's face the second she lowered her camera, "yet another expense, not to mention another piece of clutter" caused by the smart phone ban. Katherine's mother had henceforth forbidden her to make snowballs.) The intermittent snow had so enthralled Katherine for the last several days that, until this morning's intrauterine abuse, she had managed to completely forget she was pregnant.

"Merry Christmas," Graham said behind her. "Where'd you go?"

"Right here."

"I thought maybe you'd stay in bed."

"Why?"

"Christmas."

She had considered it. She missed their closeness. In the months since her abdomen had taken on more girth, however, Graham had started paying it more attention. Taking off her shirt only drew his eyes to it, and being naked beside, on top of, or beneath him meant being close enough for him to touch it. He would heed, but soon forget, her well-intentioned lies about sensitive skin and slide his palm over her before she could turn away or hold him off. It was easier to not be physical at all.

Graham rubbed her behind on his way to the coffee pot. He filled a mug, twitched in a drop of creamer, and carried it to the living room. He was a gorgeous morning mess sitting on the couch in his loose, partially open blue robe, his wavy hair tousled from having been pressed against his pillow. In the gold dimness of Christmas lights, Graham's lips looked full and dark, his eyes warm and focused on nothing but her face. He smiled his slow smile at her, and she drifted automatically to him and sat on his lap and kissed his neck.

"Merry Christmas to me," he said.

"This is for me."

"It's been months."

"This time, it has."

"I thought you stopped loving me again."

"I never did."

"Or, that you—Oh…That's nice—that you, that you resented me. I've been thinking about that, you know, and I know it isn't my fault, what we have here, but I'd understand—"

"Kissing, Graham."

"Yes, I feel that. But, um, Katie, over—over the last few months you have to admit it's been a little—"

"My love." Katherine stopped to look at him. "You are so handsome."

He wrapped his arms around her waist and looked up at her with the vulnerability of a virgin. "You haven't said that in a long time."

"So handsome." She pushed his hair away from his face and kissed him, and he said nothing else.

In keeping with the uncharacteristic temperature pattern since the snow had begun, precipitation stopped soon after the sun came up. Roads cleared within an hour, and by mid-afternoon trees under sixty-degree sunshine dripped the last of their covering onto thin, white slush. Katherine drove to Margaret and Ernie's with the AV on MANUAL to avoid any thick pockets that might pull the tires, a hazard her particular model had not been designed to sense.

"We should probably do as much of that as we can in the next three months," Graham said, tapping Katherine's thigh. "Sex."

They passed a restored Victorian home with a sign out front reading NEWSOME LAW OFFICES. A figure in a gray winter coat lifted a blanketed baby carrier from a dry corner of the covered entry. Katherine watched in the rearview mirror as the woman, she saw now, stepped through slush to the sidewalk. She looked right and left before hollering something at the surrounding small, single-family A-frames.

"Watch it!"

Katherine's body yanked against a hard correction when the car lurched left and missed sideswiping a van parked at the curb. Graham released the wheel to Katherine. She glanced again at the rearview mirror and saw the woman marching away with the carrier.

"Nervous about seeing Margaret?"

"Hm?"

"It's been a while," he said.

"What has?"

"Since you've seen Margaret."

"Oh. Yes. It has. Why would that make me nervous?"

He lifted his hands in a shrug and looked out the window. "What I meant before," he said, "is that I get the feeling we won't be having much of it after the baby. Sex."

Katherine turned onto the narrow country lane leading to Margaret's forested estate and tapped the panel's blue SELF DRIVE option. The road was clear and dry. Margaret and the dozen other homeowners who'd staked out private pieces of land to create their own separate, but not too isolated neighborhood had pitched in equal amounts for a solar powered snowmelt system. Katherine would have liked to have something like that to dry the roads in a circular mile surrounding the stores.

"We can have as much or as little sex as we like," she said.

"Really!"

"Not coitus, of course."

"Ah. See."

"Is it absolutely essential that there be penile penetration of my lower body?"

"Nope."

Free to not watch the road, Katherine could focus entirely on Graham. He was not similarly focused on her, but on the passing trees, and then on a vast clearing with a white-tailed rabbit running through the snow's scattered remains.

She said, "Is it that important to you?"

"Isn't that Murphy?"

"Is what—? Oh! I think so."

In what at first seemed a substantial distance from the rabbit, a shaggy gold dog bounded across the field. Within seconds he was a snout's length from the dodging, flailing, leaping rabbit, its evasive movements so sharp and erratic that the dog lost all control, his front half moving one way before his back could catch up. He toppled and rolled, displacing enough wet, melting snow to create an impressive and violent spray. One quick flip and he was off again, this time seemingly anticipating every direction the rabbit might take—jerking right when the rabbit jerked right, jerking left when the rabbit jerked left—until the rabbit flung itself into the air and directly into the leaping dog's open mouth.

"There's symbolism for you," Graham said as Murphy pranced to the tree line, rabbit limp and dangling from its jaws.

"It is that important, then," Katherine said. "To you."

"I wish it were to you."

"Were I not susceptible to pregnancy, it would be." The dog disappeared into a thick patch of evergreens marking the far edge of Margaret's property. Katherine hoped to avoid being greeted by a blood covered Murphy. "But as an apparently fertile female," she said, "what is important to you has, for me, become a decadent luxury not without lasting side-effects."

Graham turned to her with a closed-lipped smile. "I understand."

"I hope so."

"I don't blame you."

"Why on earth would you blame me?"

"We did have a good amount of pregnancy-free sex before that little slip in Austria, but I guess I completely understand why you'd never want to have sex ever, ever again."

"Sex is fine, Graham, and plenty of it, but not—"

"Not the good kind. I get it."

"Do you want a divorce?"

He laid his hand on the back of hers. "No."

Katherine turned her palm to lace their fingers. They sat that way until the car parked itself in front of Margaret's intentionally rustic wood mansion trimmed in large, colored bulbs.

Bing Crosby's "Merry Christmas" and four flickering red candles did little to mitigate the awkwardness between Katherine and Margaret. "How do you like the salad dressing?" and "What does Murphy do with the rabbits once he catches them?" were the best efforts each managed over salad before transforming themselves into politely smiling dullards. Between bites of garden greens, they nodded and made feminine noises of encouragement at the men's conversation about daily liquor store operations and the challenges of renovating timeworn structures.

To be fair, neither Katherine nor Margaret had ever had much to add to Ernie's construction stories, and Katherine hardly expected Margaret to contribute anything now. Although Margaret carried the bulk of the financial burden of Ernie's renovation projects, they were his personal philanthropic endeavor, an idea he had brought to Margaret after he received a phone call from a woman pregnant with her second unexpected child. Ernie had taken Margaret with him to see just where she hoped to add a small room to her trailer.

"I couldn't imagine one more person living in there," Margaret had said. "Who knows how many more could be on the way?"

From that point forward, Margaret's sole and deliberately chosen role, aside from showing her genuine interest, had been providing Ernie with the money he needed to build, money that rarely returned to them once the homes went to their new owners. (Ernie and Margaret had agreed they would accept whatever the recipients could give, whether all cash, some cash, traded services, or gifts. A self-published author—"He's wonderful," Margaret said—sent Margaret a new novel every six months. Ernie displayed a helmet from the final Super Bowl on a shelf in the living room. One homeowner, a knitter, had sent socks, blankets, pot holders, toilet seat covers, and, when he learned Margaret was pregnant, a little yellow hat.)

Katherine, for her part, had historically participated in, if not led, conversations about her liquor stores, but tonight she sat in obedient silence. Ordinarily, if Ernie directed a store-related question at Graham, she would interject or at least playfully remind Ernie that she was the authority on the subject. Tonight, for now, she let it pass (each time tamping down increasing surges of perfectly legitimate resentment). After all, Graham was deeply involved in the day to day running of the business and could reasonably claim some ownership.

More challenging was to pretend to not notice that Graham chose not to invite Katherine's insight when the answers to Ernie's questions were beyond Graham's knowledge or experience. She controlled her temper by listening for the bells on the cuffs of Ernie's and Margaret's Christmas shoes. Ernie's would jingle when he shifted or bounced his feet, but Margaret's seemed to express her own frustration with Graham. When faced with a question or led into a subject area that was Katherine's forte, Margaret's bells would jingle at Katherine not being consulted. "Say, how did you get the banks on your side, anyway?" Bells. "What kind of price negotiating can you do?" Bells. "You're really doing all right for yourselves, which I guess I wouldn't have expected from a liquor store. What are your margins? If you don't mind me asking." Bells, bells, bells.

When Margaret could clearly take no more, she interrupted Ernie and jabbed her finger at Katherine, but Katherine stopped her short by asking for a fresh glass of water with some ice and only smiled at Margaret's manipulated eyebrows.

Had she and Margaret been talking over the past months, all it would have taken was mouthing the word "coitus" to explain Graham's behavior and Katherine's (frankly, remarkable) tolerance. Margaret would have known about Katherine's aversion to traditional intercourse and would have guessed that she and Graham had finally had the conversation. But Katherine had shared only news clippings, so Margaret knew nothing about Katherine's life since their visit to the Eighth Street Clinic, and Katherine knew equally little about Margaret. Including why she seemed more concerned than Katherine thought necessary when Ernie mentioned vandalism at one of his work sites. It was a foreign and miserable sensation to feel that asking about it would be prying.

"Anyway, enough about my little problems. Glasses up!" Ernie raised his drink. "You're here to celebrate Christmas, but we also wanted you to help us celebrate the sale—'s'cuse me, 's'cuse me, the *acquisition*—of Mox's latest novel, *Elmore and Lenore Steal the Light*. Cheers to my brilliant and successful author wife!"

The men tapped their liquor to the women's water glasses. Katherine tried to catch Margaret's eye to congratulate her, but Margaret smiled past her.

Ernie slid back his chair with a vague announcement about waking up the bird and went to the kitchen, his shoe bells jangling a path around the breakfast bar.

"Margret," Katherine said. "Congratulations." She lifted a wide spinach leaf to her mouth. Salad dressing flicked onto her cheek. "I had no idea." She looked at her place setting, but there was no napkin. She used her hand.

Margaret indicated a missed spot of oil by touching the side of her chin. "You don't want to talk about babies."

"But this is your book," Katherine said, the ball of her palm dragging oil across her jaw.

"Oh, no," Ernie called from the kitchen. "You can't separate that," he said, wiggling a finger over the breakfast bar at Margaret's pregnancy, "from those names. She won't even find out what sex it is. Doesn't want to know either Elmore or Lenore won't make it. I told her if she has a boy, she should just kill off that one in the story, and vice-a versa. You know, so the one that doesn't make it in real life gets to live on, in a way."

"Hey. Hey." Graham leaned forward on the table, sliding his drink to sustain its ideal proximity to his mouth. "What a—I have it. Idea. Say you two have one sex, and we have the other sex. No problem! You take ours."

"Graham."

"We're giving it away, anyway."

"Graham."

"Katherine?"

"I didn't know," Margaret said.

Ernie carried in a platter loaded with an uncarved goose. He set it at the end of the table and demonstrated his expertise with a battery operated carving knife. With Graham both intoxicated and distracted by Ernie's bone sawing, Katherine murmured over the table to Margaret that it had been a last-minute decision.

"By the way," Katherine nearly whispered, "did you find any of the articles interesting?"

"They were all—"

"In particular," Katherine raised her eyebrows, "the batch including the clippings about the toy stores. And the miscarriage laws."

"I…That was so long ago. I'm not sure I…"

"What's that?" Graham said. "Which stories?"

"Did you know," Katherine said loudly, "the government has begun rationing all fruits, vitamins, spices, seasonings, and over the counter medications with the slightest potential, mythical or otherwise, to induce miscarriage? As if a woman's temptation to attempt such a thing would persist in the face of a life sentence." She looked at Margaret over the rim of her water glass.

"Sure do!" Ernie set out the carved portions on a new plate. "Moxie read about it on some writer's forum. No rationing alcohol, though. Lawmakers like it too much, I guess. I tell you what, I had a hell of a time getting parsley. Three places—all sold right out! And you can't get the full bunch, anymore, either. They quarter the suckers."

Margaret glanced at the section of table hiding Katherine's middle. "Oh, I see." During Ernie's insistence that everyone load their plates, she mouthed, "I'm so sorry."

Katherine took a bite of goose. Oil dripped down her chin, and she remembered she had no napkin. She checked Graham's place setting, and then Ernie's and Margaret's. No one had napkins. She used her hand the best she could and wiped it on the overlap of the tablecloth.

"All these laws, you know," Ernie said with a full fork hovering in front of his mouth. "They don't affect me and Mox, but you'd figure everyone else who's worried would do that fucking thing. Right? Why not?"

Katherine had opted to not think about fucking, nor to think about Graham thinking about fucking. She wedged herself out of her chair and hunted for napkins. "But fucking is so dangerous," she said lightly, her back turned. "Right, Graham?"

Margaret said after a sip of water, "I agree with Kat. It's not so easy to find someone. It isn't like they wear nametags saying 'infertile' or 'sterile.' And even if they did, how could you ever be sure?"

Chewing, Graham said, "What do you mean, it doesn't affect you? You having more?"

"No," Margaret said.

"Ah, so no 'coitus' for you, either. Poor bastards. Cheers." He slammed his glass against Ernie's.

"No coitus!" Ernie laughed and shook his head.

Katherine closed the sideboard drawer. Only placemats there. She moved to the bar.

Graham leaned into Ernie. "You mean you're keeping having sex?"

"Yeah, we're keeping having sex. You're not?"

Graham waved a hand at Katherine's abdomen. "Not once that's done."

"Graham," Katherine smiled, "please stop drinking."

"I've had two, Katie. All's well." He winked.

Katherine opened the bar's bottom cabinet. She found a short stack of cloth napkins among an ice bucket, swizzle sticks, cocktail shaker, and an assortment of corkscrews. In the top napkin's bottom right corner, an infant in a red and green striped diaper crawled along a straight-line surface, the red diaper stripe trailing behind to spell, in one case, *Graham*. Beneath his, *Ernie, Margaret,* and *Katherine*. She also saw, tucked far back, a bottle of Graham's (and Katherine's) favorite pinot noir. She pulled it out and looked at Margaret. Margaret snapped her eyes away. Katherine took out the napkins and the wine, closed the door, and brought everything to the table.

"Found it, huh?" Ernie said. "Yeah, sorry about that. I got it from one of your competitors so it'd be a surprise for Graham, but Mox didn't want to tempt you."

"Oh, damn it, Ernie," Margaret said.

Graham swallowed the last of his drink. "No drinking and no coitus make Katie a dull Jamaica girl. I know people say penetration isn't everyth—"

"Graham."

"—ing, but you don't really, *really* miss it until you can't even talk about it, anymore."

Katherine picked up Graham's glass and tipped it against her lips for the taste of a single drop. With Margaret watching, she put down the glass and uncorked the wine.

Margaret said, "You're still going to Jamaica? That's wonderful. How long did you have to postpone?"

Katherine said there had been no need to postpone. She had a C-section scheduled for bright and early at six o'clock on the thirteenth, allowing for a full week of recovery before their flight. Every obstetrics website she'd consulted, she said while pouring a glass of wine "for Graham, of course," had suggested a week was more than enough.

"I'm confused." Graham held the stem of the full pour Katherine had set in front of him. "Stop drinking or drink more?"

Katherine took the glass from him and had a small sip, but slowly, because Margaret's hand started moving toward her on the table and she wanted to see how far it would slide in what seemed to be an unconscious reflex. When Katherine set down the wine, the twitching fingers relaxed after having crept all the way to the holly-leaf centerpiece. Margaret shifted in her chair, blinked, ate a bite of goose, and wiped her mouth with the top napkin. The *Graham* baby fluttered over her hand.

"Is a C-section necessary? For your health, I mean," Margaret said.

"Nah," Graham said. "Vacation planning."

"Oh." Margaret looked at her plate. "Well, but what's a little delay? Jamaica will always be there, won't it?"

"It will, most likely," Katherine said, "but we already have the tickets, and not only are they not refundable, but the prices have gone up."

"But the stores are doing so well, Kat. You can afford a ticket that's a little more expensive."

"We can, but—"

"What about the risks?"

"In Jamaica?" Katherine pulled the *Margaret* napkin from the stack. "Or do you mean travel risks? Margaret, if you paid attention you would know that terrorism has moved to the—"

"No, I mean risks of the operation."

Katherine smoothed the napkin on her lap. "I have full confidence in the procedure."

"But do you really want to put yourself through that?"

"Clearly I must. Why are you—?"

"She has some kind of opinion and doesn't want to tell you," Graham said into his wine.

Margaret held her napkin with both hands. "It's just better for the—I just don't see why it would be so tragic to postpone your vacation."

"We always go on the first day of spring."

"But you'd be surprised how much better it is for the baby—and, and for you—to have it naturally. Why not wait, just to be on the safe side?"

Katherine winced at an inside kick to her bladder. "Because, as I explained, we already have our tickets and the plane leaves on the first day of spring."

Margaret ate a roasted potato cube. Katherine also ate a roasted potato cube. Graham watched them eat. Ernie slept in his chair. Katherine sipped Graham's wine. Margaret stopped chewing. Katherine ate another potato and then reached again for the wine, only intending to taste it on her lips.

Margaret shouted, "Will you stop that!"

Katherine jerked her hand back, and Ernie sat straight up in his chair.

"I know none of this is what you wanted," Margaret said in as measured a tone as Katherine had ever heard her use, "but if you cared at all about that baby, you would want to give it the protection of essential bacteria from the walls of—"

Katherine slammed her fork on the thick walnut table.

"—your vagina."

Graham smiled and comforted Katherine with pats on her thigh.

Ernie coughed.

In the few seconds of ensuing silence, Bing Crosby sang uninterrupted about glistening treetops, boots, and shooting pistols.

Ernie pushed away from the table and glided with uncanny grace to Margaret's side, the bells on his shoes faintly jingling. He offered his hand in an invitation to dance. When Margaret shook her head, he carried on alone, hands positioned around an invisible partner he led around the adjoining living room, bells tinkling with every step.

"All right," Margaret said. "Well, you have to know about the potential injuries the operation itself could cause the baby."

"Have I."

"Yes!"

"Now, Margaret, you can ease up on her," Graham said. "She's so risk averse I'm surprised you could get her to eat that goose. This is the first time she's even touched alco—"

"Graham." Katherine squeezed his hand. They stood.

Ernie stopped dancing.

Katherine said, "I think we should go, now." She brushed at her protruding belly, where dried spices from the potatoes had fallen and clung to her shirt. "That is, my dear friend Margaret, if I may be allowed to make one goddamned personal decision."

FIVE

In her nearly complete avoidance of the outside world to hide her nine-month pregnancy, an avoidance Graham seemed more than happy to accommodate by taking over the majority of her store duties, Katherine sat in the kitchen and watched the falling snow.

It was ten in the morning. The Oxford stores' quiet hour, the only time of day she would sneak out to make her short visits, was still four hours away.

The *Daily Fact* sat unread in front of her, the weekly insert removed and set aside. Typically it would have been in the trash, but to distract herself while waiting—four hours, one day, the final excruciating week—she would read every word of every issue, but not until the time of day when sitting and waiting became unbearable. She always saved the paper for last.

For now she would watch the snow.

It fell so predictably these days that it failed, this time, to induce the hoped-for mental escape.

At a jab to her inside, she got up from the table and stood in one spot.

Surely there was something to do for the store from home, before her visit. Being at home hardly had to mean she was entirely useless. She slid the phone toward her on the counter and dialed Oxford I.

"Please check the wine labels," she told the new clerk. "Customers turn them when they browse. They should all be face-out."

"Yes, Ms. Oxford."

"Every single one."

"Yep. Will do."

Katherine hung up. The snow continued to fall. It would be nice if there were a hard wind to blow it sideways.

Her back hurt.

It was a problem, really. The snow. A much larger problem than her own problem. Fatal in some cases.

She sat to think about it.

She and Graham, while not yet technically wealthy, were fortunate enough to find the snow only a minor nuisance, because they had invested in a truck and plow at the first forecast of heavy precipitation and lasting cold temperatures. But those without the means or the foresight to have bought their own plows had difficulty finding one for hire, the *Fact* had recently reported. Until now there had been no reason for anyone to create such a business. (Those who had made a quick business of it only targeted the wealthy, charging the maximum of what they believed the wealthy would be willing to pay. The wealthy were willing to pay a lot.)

Katherine's right leg begged to stretch. She stretched it. Next, it was the left. The right leg again, and again the left, but no matter how hard she stretched the nerves in her thighs continued to jump. She heaved herself out of her chair and paced the kitchen with her focus on the window.

Low income neighborhoods. They suffered the most, their roads channels of chest-deep snow. This was something she had seen, herself. A trench occasionally appeared where a desperate pedestrian had burrowed a path, but it inevitably ended not far from where it had begun, the exhausted soul having given up and turned back. Where there was a cleared road in an impoverished neighborhood, it was typically a throughway carved by a plow owner who needed to get to the other side, and where it led was of no use to anyone but the driver.

The snow stopped.

An inch, if that, covered the car and had barely filled in the plow tracks a breezy, smiling Graham had made when he left that morning. Brightly.

Katherine sat again. She bounced her feet to keep her legs busy and slid the *Your America* insert toward her. She opened it to a random—and as luck would have it, the newspaper's most ridiculous—page. She almost turned to something else but looked at her watch and saw that only six minutes had passed.

She read.

This month's contribution to the "Celebrity Voice" section (which she never, ever read) was a syndicated, single-page, self-flagellating missive by wealthy actress Greta McNeill, who began with an acknowledgement of the privileges of the wealthy before gradually twisting herself into a guilty (and impressively fallacious) confession:

> …You say we could clear your neighborhoods with our plows. We say we won't do it because we want you to pull yourself [*sic*] up by your bootstraps. Do you think that's true? Does it make you happy to believe it is? Well, I'm sorry, but it isn't. The truth, I'm sorry to say, is that if your roads are cleared just like ours are, how can we display or even recognize our own privilege? Privilege we worked hard for, in many cases, and that's the gist of it. If the poor

and unsophisticated can have the same luxuries we have, it can only mean we've failed.

A bright orange behemoth of a plow, one not used in decades, graced the insert's cover. The reason for that, a problem Katherine knew would receive little more than surface-level exploration in this tawdry "magazine" (really an embarrassment for an otherwise respectable publication), was less about the weather than it was about the victims of a relatively new system whose potential ramifications had not been thoroughly considered. When, six years before, the state had made the decision to eliminate road maintenance and improvement from its budget to align with the majority opinion that citizens should (and most definitely would, they were sure of it) bear the responsibility themselves, there had been a long, reliable history of dry winters. No one could have imagined the practical threat of excessive snowfall. Consequently, road access throughout the region was wildly unpredictable. Ten miles of cleared state highway ended at a wall of snow on the state line, an inconvenience first discovered by a family of three traveling sixty miles per hour until they stopped abruptly (all three died on impact). Another casualty of the impassable roadways was a Tinytown woman who died of hypothermia trying to dig her way to her job at the InSystem microchip manufacturing plant half a mile away. She had thought she was strong enough to make it to the nearest plowed stretch, one of her friends had told the *Daily Fact*.

Katherine turned the page when she finished and stared down at a vodka advertisement.

She called Oxford II and spoke with their manager, Curtis.

"Labels, yeah. Okay. I'll get right to it as soon as I can, Ms. Oxford, but with such a light snow this morning we're pretty busy. Everyone's stocking up for the next few days."

She knew Graham spent much of the day in the rear office, so she recommended Curtis ask him to check the labels.

"Uh…"

"Say what you will, Curtis, but the appearance of the store is every bit as—"

"No, no, I—It's not that, it's just that he's not here. But I'll tell him as soon as he's back. By then everyone'll probably be gone anyway, so I can probably just—"

"Back? Where did he go? Oxford I?" It seemed unlikely. Graham usually spent the second half of the day at Oxford I. Perhaps there was a problem. But she had just called Oxford I, and they would have mentioned any problems to her. She had insisted Graham tell the employees that if she were ever away from the store, it meant she had chosen to work from home, so no one should feel obliged to shield her from anything that pertained to either of the stores.

Curtis breathed for a moment into the phone, then said, "Uh, he—He said he was taking the plow out. You know. To do some clearing. But he said if you called to tell you he'd be back soon."

Katherine hung up.

It was fifteen minutes to eleven.

She moved to the living room and turned on the TV. That insufferable Dean Stacey was talking about the Greta McNeill column, saying it had already inspired widespread protests, the most observable from the "poor and unsophisticated" readers she had effectively convinced to make an enemy of the wealthy class. The wealthy, too, were rebelling against Greta McNeill's statement, he said. Some had already posted open letters online, and others were booking time "on this very show!" to reject her character assassination.

"Oh!" Dean Stacey said, pressing a finger to his ear bud. "Okay, folks, I'm hearing there's been a break-in—two? Two break-ins in Haver—Correction, two home invasions in Haverton, and—Can I just say, is this great for ratings?—and in one of the invasions, the man was—Hold on, police now reporting another home invasion in an affluent Windbury neighbor—"

Katherine turned off the TV and called Margaret. Her neighborhood was ten miles southwest of Tinytown, nowhere near Haverton or Windbury, and, really, too far from everything for anyone but the most ambitious criminal to bother, but Katherine needed to be sure. When the ringing ended at a voicemail prompt, she hung up without leaving a message and half-jogged to the car.

The snow had been just heavy enough that morning to create problems for the AV on fully untreated roads, so she selected the route to Oxford II, which Graham had plowed on his way to work, and reclined the seat a few taps to reduce the pressure on her pubic bone. If he was still gone when she arrived, she would follow his path, find the truck, and trade him. She had to get to Margaret.

The truck was at the store when she parked, a layer of snow on the window and roof. She pulled her coat around her middle before going inside.

"Ms. Oxford!" a voice said from somewhere. "My goodness, are you preg—"

"No, no, no." She sailed through the Cabernet aisle to the office.

It was empty. Graham had left his keys on the desk beside a years-old photograph of the two of them on Heidelberg Castle's windy balcony, Graham's socked foot fitting into the impression of a shoe print created, according to legend, by a knight's leap from a window to escape a fire. She took the keys without leaving a note. On her way out, she looked for Graham but saw only customers and Curtis, whose back was to her as he talked with a man in the imports section.

The snow had been falling hard for several minutes by the time she reached Forest Retreat Estates. From where she parked on the street, Katherine saw a blurry Margaret walking Murphy toward the house on her solar-warmed stone path, a thick dome of white on her head. She wedged a bundle of mail under her arm before bending to scoop up Murphy's business, and Katherine recognized a large yellow envelope. She had sent only four clippings, this time:

Missing dog found eating scraps in restaurant kitchen
InSystem stays mum on rumored revolutionary microchip project
Shuttered family planning center to open as homeless children's shelter
Military enlistments rise as families grow and job opportunities shrink

She had included the dog article because it would make Margaret happy. And that Margaret could still be happy, that no one had come to kidnap or kill her, was enough for Katherine. She slid her foot to the gas pedal, then returned it to the brake. Margaret was alive, yes, but without the news to warn her.... Katherine set the parking brake and left the engine running and the wipers thudding.

Margaret opened the front door with her hair in a towel and her feet in slippers. Murphy stood beside her. She flicked her gaze at the opening in Katherine's coat. "What's the matter? What happened?"

Katherine got only so far into her warning before Margaret waved her hand and told her not to worry. She knew plenty. Why, that morning while she was choosing a new phone bud with a store clerk, she said, someone had painted RICH BITCH in "a really pretty yellow" on her car's red hood. "I'm getting the whole thing painted the same yellow next week," she clapped. "What fun!" And news of the home invasions had sneaked through Margaret's hunt for music on her way to visit Ernie after the phone bud errand, she said as she pet Murphy's retreating head, so she already knew to look for anything unusual in her neighborhood. Her visit to Ernie had also ended up being fortuitous for him—he had needed a ride home before the snow piled up because someone had stolen his plow.

"He said she was nice about it, at least." Margaret pulled the door halfway closed behind her and wrapped her thin cardigan tight around her. "She had a gun, but she didn't use it. And she did say she was sorry. That's what Ernie said, anyway."

They could afford another plow, Margaret said. They were less expensive now.

Katherine asked where it had happened, and Margaret said it was at the Summit Street gas station. Katherine sighed through her nose. Summit Street had been in the *Fact* at least four times in the last month. The snow was high with no one to remove it, and people unable to free themselves from their homes were tired, restless, hungry, and frustrated.

"Ernie was more upset about the drones," Margaret said. "He wanted one to watch over his sites, but did you know no one sells them again?"

"Yes, Margaret."

"Well, it's silly. If someone climbs up a tree to peep in your bedroom, they don't take out your eyes." She shuffled in her slippers and looked at the sky.

Katherine looked, too. Gray flecks of fat snow dropped hard and fast and tapped soft on landing.

"You must be looking forward to Jamaica," Margaret said.

"How are you managing with all this?" Katherine wiped a flake from her eyelash.

"Isn't it magical? It can be wonderfully inspiring to be imprisoned. I've written chapters and chapters."

Murphy's head poked around the door and pushed it open. Behind Margaret, beyond the foyer and past the kitchen and through the dining room, the living room's tall, wide windows overlooking the forest reflected a wood burning fire. Katherine wished she could stay. She said, "All right, then," and started to leave.

"You're still doing it, then?" Margaret's hand rested on her curved middle.

Katherine said nothing.

Margaret stepped toward her and hugged her shoulders. "Be safe," she said. She stroked Katherine's back. She whispered, "It's almost over."

SIX

Katherine returned to the truck, but the thought of leaving Margaret's only to go home to sit again and wait again—for anything—made her want to throw herself on the ground. She needed more to do.

As she plowed away from Forest Retreat Estates and toward the liquor store—back arched, rear end at the edge of the seat, belly dipping between her parted legs—she explored what that "more" might be.

She dropped the plow for one of the infrequently traveled roads into Tinytown, and it occurred to her that anyone who lived south of that road would have a hard time getting to the store. She and Graham were wrong to have thought they were doing enough by plowing a three-block radius around each of the stores before opening. (Occasionally, Graham would take out the truck in the afternoon—not in the morning—to "clear random streets and help people out." At least, that was what he told Katherine any time he came home late, pink-cheeked and smiling, his sneaking hand grazing her belly as he passed by her to take off his coat.) It was clear to Katherine now that they should have been more strategic, even more generous, with their plowing by providing access to regulars beyond the three blocks.

Katherine stepped into the store, her stooped shoulders and manipulated coat an automatic reflex. Graham was laughing in the entry with the man offering IPA samples while Curtis smiled at the counter through orange, two-day stubble as he slammed bottle after bottle of sauvignon blanc into a paper bag for Sauvignon Blanc George. As one of the town's few plows for hire, Sauvignon Blanc George always managed to make his regular visits to one or both of the Oxford locations.

"...only kind of abortion I can get behind, is all I'm saying," Sauvignon Blanc George bellowed with a look around for shows of approval. "Though, it's too bad she had to take that baby with her. If she'd 'a' waited 'til she popped before jumping in front of that train, at least she'd 'a' done something of value with her life, know what I mean?"

"I guess kids today just don't have any common sense," Curtis said. *Slam.*

"Hey, you break it, you bought it." Sauvignon Blanc George guffawed, snorted, and again looked around. Katherine turned away before he could see her body or catch her eye. "And listen, now, fourteen is hardly a 'kid,' if you know what I mean." He bumped his pelvis against air, laughed again, paid Curtis, and scooped up his bag. "You know they've got some that age putting themselves out for fucking?" He leaned over the counter and lowered his voice to something just below a shout. "Hey, you know anything about, uh, how to get in on that? My woman's been wearing a 'closed for service' sign on her pussy since the ban."

Curtis yelled, "Hey, anyone here know any teenage girls on the fucking circuit looking for a thirty-three-year-old?" He *tsk*ed himself. "Aw, shit, sorry, George. I should've asked. Is a teenager good, or did you want something a little youn—"

Sauvignon Blanc George shielded his face with his free arm and dashed out to the parking lot.

"I don't feel right about taking his money, Ms. Oxford," Curtis said.

"The man has a drinking problem, Curtis," she said. "Would you rather someone else get paid for helping to destroy him?"

Curtis tore the plastic wrapping from a case of miniatures. "Hell, no."

With no one left in the store, Katherine called Graham and Curtis to a meeting she had planned while in the truck. Together, ideally, they would generate a list of customers that included their places of residence and take shifts clearing access to their neighborhoods.

Unfortunately, because most of their patrons had had no reason to share where they lived, the list was short.

One regular whose absence Curtis noted was Absolut Meredith, whose first visit and a demand for vodka had immediately followed a divorce and her move to an "I guess it's fine, right?" apartment. While ringing her up on a day she had only meant to check the bourbon supply, Katherine had fixated on the spidery knots in Absolut Meredith's long, red hair, and then on her tense jaw and faded red lips. There had been something about Absolut Meredith's, "Hi, how are you?" as she set down her 1.75 liter jug that had compelled Katherine to walk around the counter and pull the woman into her arms and hold her until she cried. Afterward, Katherine had rung her up and given her a lemon lollipop from Curtis's jar behind the counter. She had been a regular ever since.

Graham said, "Maybe she doesn't need the vodka, anymore."

"Oh?" Katherine said.

"You haven't been around to see it, but she smiles, now. She has a…it's disarming. A downright disarming smile, when she uses it." He smiled, himself.

"Yes, well, Graham, since Absolut Meredith is probably not our only West Tinytown customer, we should probably clear the roads from here to there, either way," Katherine said before urging the meeting "forward and more useful, please."

"'We' will clear nothing, love of my life," he said. "I'll take care of it." He rubbed the small of her back and, when she tried to argue, said he would hear no arguments. (She argued nonetheless and insisted she would have a shift every bit as long as anybody else's.)

Six-Pack Tyrone, a twenty-two-year-old professional dog trainer with his first television show and a new house in Haverton, had also not been seen in some time.

"He's right there," Graham said, and sure enough, Tyrone walked through the door, smiled at the three standing at the counter, and stopped to sample the IPA.

"The last, then, is Prospect," Katherine said, holding her coat away from herself, but closed.

Oxford I's Eight-Nips-a-Night Victoria lived six miles away in Prospect. Weather permitting, she drove a motorized bicycle into Tinytown to work in the cannabis fields. She never said more than "Hello" and "Thank you," but Katherine knew she lived in Prospect from the driver's license she had once left face-up on the counter.

Curtis said that if they were considering Prospect just for Eight-Nips-a-Night Victoria, "don't bother." Victoria had stopped visiting Oxford months ago, he said. "She's probably had the kid by now, though, now that I think about it."

"Prospect, then," Katherine said.

After the meeting, Katherine followed Graham out to the truck and kissed him goodbye, just catching the corner of his mouth before he stepped up to his seat.

"Graham."

He dropped the remote key in the empty ashtray and looked down at her. His hair had grown longer and messier. His bangs touched his eyelashes, making his eyes appear much bluer, somehow. He looked so devastatingly beautiful she was suddenly afraid, as she had never been before, of losing him. Or, she thought as she stood beside the truck, maybe a fear of losing him made him more beautiful. This was something she would have to think about, because it suddenly seemed important to know the diff—

"Something you need, love of mine?" he said.

Katherine studied his smile. He held it steady. She said, "Is that real?"

"Is what real?"

She mimicked his expression with only a little exaggeration. She let it sit on her face until he turned away and started the truck.

"Something is happening, Graham."

He scratched his neck. Without looking at her, he reached across the passenger seat to open the door. Katherine wrapped her coat against the curious eyes of an approaching customer as she walked around the front of the truck and climbed inside. Graham pulled out of the parking lot while taking her hand and bringing it to his lap. He slid it between his legs, and she let it stay there, not entirely still, until he parked at a snowy dead end on the outskirts of the cannabis farm. He helped Katherine lower and remove her pants before removing his own, and then he helped her get to her hands and knees before sliding in behind her.

"Not too deep," she said.

"I know."

He started slowly, carefully. The sensation paralyzed her. His hands slid down her back, the intimate gentleness of it weakening her elbows. His fingers slipped to her sides. She stiffened. He caressed her stomach. She stopped moving.

"Graham."

"I'm not doing anything."

She was preparing to push him off, but then one of his hands took control of a hip and the other reached around and down.

While stopped at a red light on the return trip to the store, he said, "Just so you know, I think it's beautiful."

She said nothing. A bundled-up man with a suitcase hurried across the intersection in front of them, and something flashed in the corner of her eye. A small stuffed animal had dropped from somewhere and bounced on the shoveled sidewalk. Katherine searched until she spotted a little girl wailing in an open second story window.

"Your pregnancy," Graham said, and the light turned green. "I think it's beautiful."

She shifted in her seat, but there was no way to be comfortable. "I know you do."

"What's so wrong with that? Why do you get…?" He reached over and touched her hair. "Do you feel unattractive?"

"Why on earth would I feel unattractive?"

"I don't know, Katie, that's what I'm—"

"I feel pregnant, and I look pregnant."

"And it's beautiful. That's what I'm saying."

"Yes, and my point, Graham, is that the aesthetics of pregnancy are neither inherently good nor inherently bad. How I look is a simple consequence of the condition. Do you understand?—I only ask because I genuinely want to know."

"Sure, Katie!"

Katherine slid down in the seat to unfold her pelvis. "I feel none of the things you expect me to feel," she said. "That this ends in a week is a relief. Nothing else." She pressed her lips together tight to steady them. Snow piles on the sidewalks passed in blurs of dirty brown. Katherine took deep, even breaths until she could speak. "It terrifies me that you might hate me because of it."

He looked at her. "Don't you use you and me and hate in the same sentence ever again, do you hear me?" He pulled into Oxford II's parking lot and set the brake. "Katie, do you hear me?"

Katherine slid close and tucked herself under his arm. The clean scent of his deodorant clung to his shirts even after he washed them. She pressed against him and closed her eyes.

Graham said, "I think I'm going to fuck Absolut Meredith."

She looked up at him, but his attention was on the sky. He squinted at it.

"When?"

He rubbed her arm rapidly, up and down. "Oh, not now! Not until later," he said. "After. And not because I don't love you." He smiled down at her.

Her reflexive need to fully possess him nauseated her. She said, "Punishment."

"No, damn it, Katie. Don't you know what love is?"

She asked him if he loved Absolute Meredith.

"She's infertile," he said. Matter-of-fact. That was all there was to it, he said. Nothing more. "So, see? Nothing for you to worry about."

"Does she know you plan to approach her about fucking?"

"Katie, it's—Listen, now, it's nothing. Nothing! You had your new condition that you introduced, and this is mine. I think it more than meets both of our physical needs. And it's fair. It's fair to both of us. You see, don't you?"

She did see. She liked nothing about it (although, it did relieve some pressure, which she appreciated), but it was fair, just as he said. Even so, she felt nauseated and possessive and incomprehensibly sad. She tucked herself deeper under his arm.

He reached around her shoulder and stuck a finger in her eye.

"Ow."

He laughed. "I'm sorry! Oh, Katie. Did I hurt you?" He tried again.

Her cheek tickled under the warm fingertips stroking her hair away from her face.

"You know," he said, "I can't imagine living my life without you, Katherine Daisy Oxford. But I could if I had to."

She lifted his arm off her shoulder. "I should hope so." As she slid away, she told him not to forget Prospect.

Katherine shoved through the liquor store doors and slipped past the beer sample man (Curtis had arranged the whole thing, and Katherine neither knew the man's name nor cared at this moment to learn it). She squeezed between the wine racks on the way to the office to get her keys, spotted a bottle on a low shelf with its label face down, and stopped to correct it. She bent over and bumped the bottles behind her. She tried to kneel and bumped them again. She sweated in her coat. The store was much too warm.

"Curtis!"

He rushed over.

She said, "What temperature are we running?"

"Sixty-eight."

Sixty-eight was correct. "It feels warm."

"I checked it first thing. Always do."

"Have any customers complained about the narrowness of these aisles?"

"Uh...I don't know. Maybe. You know. People complain about every-thing."

"When are you doing something about it?"

"When? They're regulation. I can't make changes every time someone complains about something. What if someone comes in and says the low shelves are too low or the high shelves are too high? What would we do with all those bottles?"

"Has anyone complained about that?"

"No. But Ms. Oxford, the aisles have been like this in both stores since they opened. You never said anything before.—Oh," he said, his gaze on the roundness pushing past the panels of her open coat. "Oh. I mean, yeah. I mean, I could—"

Katherine pushed past him. "Never mind, Curtis. Thank you."

She tried not to look like she was hurrying. She dusted a bottle at the end of the aisle with a swipe of her fingers and nudged a stack-display beer case with her hip to align it with the others. When she reached the office, she forced herself to open the door delicately and close it quietly behind her.

The lights were off in the wood paneled room, the dull sky turning it darker.

The air smelled like him.

His chair was pushed in the way it always was when he would be gone for the rest of the day.

She stood rigid in front of the desk, afraid to breathe.

Graham laughed out from the picture in the frame.

Katherine well remembered the day the Brazilian tourist had taken it for them. Before struggling up the hill (with several pauses to rest their legs), she and Graham had sampled Dampfknödel from a bakery on the Hauptstrasse and made love in their room overlooking the Marktplatz. They had been happy.

She faced the picture away.

Her lungs forced a deep breath, and her stomach moved against her shirt. With every successive inhale and exhale, the material rubbed as irritating as cotton on a sunburn.

She pinched a gathering and held it away from her skin.

She stared out the window, at the grays and the purples crashing in the clouds, and willed the scream to dissolve.

SEVEN

Katherine woke on the morning of her C-section appointment to Graham's mouth breathing inches from her nose, his lips in a carefree smile.

She used to like to know everything about the absurd stories created by his sleeping imagination. More recently, she had suspicions about what he might be pursuing in the dark freedom of his private recesses and tried not to wonder about his dreams.

With an hour, still, before her alarm would go off, she bounced out of bed and started a shower.

To reduce the risk of infection they had recommended she not shave herself, but she refused to have a stranger come at her pubic hair as if she were some overbreeding cat brought in for spaying. She guided the razor blindly, stroking wider than she normally might, and lower than usual, too, while trying not to make herself look completely ridiculous. At what felt like a nick, she whipped open the curtain and ran dripping to the mirror. She cleared a low circle in the fog and stood on her toes to lift her pelvis above the counter, then turned from side to side, looking for blood. A watery red line snaked its way down to what was left of her pubic hair. She rubbed it away, and no new blood appeared. Their curt instructions had been without an explanation of exactly how shaving could lead to infection, but she assumed cutting herself might be one way to do it.

She lowered herself on her heels. The taut roundness of her middle now completely filled the circle in the fog.

Had she just killed herself?

Not once—until now—had she seriously considered the possibility that she would die that afternoon.

She closed her eyes to shut out her image, to pretend nothing was as it was, but that only pulled her inward, her consciousness diving into the arms and legs and cord and blood scheduled for removal. Her head tingled and pricked with panic and she mentally grasped for a way out, a way back, a way to undo it all.

A dream came to mind, a nightmare she had had after learning she was pregnant.

She was pressed flat to a skyscraper's roof, the tar cool and smooth against her cheek and the palms of her hands. Her arms and legs were spread for balance, but inconceivably strong winds still inched her, bit by bit, toward the edge. When for a second they died down, she adjusted her grip, creating a pocket for a sudden gust to fill. Its brutal force lifted her and rolled her over the side, and as she plummeted through darkness, the distance to the bottom a mystery, she worked frantically through her options for survival: If she steered herself into bushes, they would break her fall. If she landed on her side, her shoulder and arm would protect her ribs and organs.

But her sleeping mind ultimately conceded to logic. Katherine would fall until she hit the ground and died.

This moment felt very much like that.

The tingling in her head worsened. She could see nothing, feel nothing but such penetrating fear of death that she believed the fear alone would kill her.

This was not what she wanted to feel on her day of freedom.

She got back in the shower, hoping a return to practical tasks would be calming, but the hot, confined, beige space only scared her more. She turned off the water, leaped out, wrapped herself in a towel, and cleared a streak across the window so she could see the living, moving world outside.

A white airplane glow floated through the dark sky.

Fresh feet of overnight snow spread smooth and gray under the half moon.

A window in the distance turned yellow with the lighting of a lamp.

She might die that afternoon, yes. More likely was that she would leave the hospital and return to the life she had been enjoying before accepting that her period was two weeks late. This day, the day she had once thought would never come, was here.

The relief hit her with such force that it took tasting the salt on her lips to know she was crying.

She started another shower, stepped in, and leaned against the cool wall.

She would pack a bottle of wine in her bag.

She would also have a tobacco cigarette as soon as it was over. Just one, from one of the doctors she had seen standing beside the ashtray every time she had visited for her ultrasounds, heartbeat checks, or any of the other costly procedures deemed critical routine care.

There had been only one cigarette in her life. In her second year of college, a classmate named Peter, whose mother, thanks to a tip, had made a fortune in land-line telephone stock after the ban on cellular and smart phones, always smoked expensive tobacco cigarettes. ("No way I'm using juice after that last contamination.") While standing outside after their American History final, he held one out to her. Katherine of course knew the chemicals were dangerous and hated the very behavior of smoking for that reason, but with every drag that enveloped her lungs, she loved it for the same reason. How effortless it was, she thought through a deliciously long exhale, for someone like her, always the good girl until twenty minutes before when she and Peter had cheated on their final, to punish herself.

She had smoked the cigarette down, inhaling so long and so deep she had gagged on the heat of the cherry flooding the filter.

Katherine listened for signs that Graham was awake, but the upstairs was quiet. Her alarm, which she had set for both of them, would go off in five minutes. She turned up the TV as she sat on the front edge of the couch cushion, her legs spread and her pelvis dipped. She broke off a bite of cranberry muffin and set the rest on the coffee table.

"...stopped allowing stores to sell the tried and true tighty-whities because of reduced sperm growth. What next?" Dean Stacey challenged viewers from his red couch. "I'll tell you! People—men *and* women—*giving* themselves chlamydia and gonorrhea. *Chlamydia! Gonorrhea!* On purpose! These are the people none of us want having kids, anyway, right, folks? May they succeed beyond their wildest dreams." He shaped his finger and thumb into a handgun and shot himself in the temple. "In other news, finally, *finally*, the government is doing something about this welfare crisis. Sources saying democrats and republicans are—hold on, now—working *together* to abolish welfare. Good, because I see no reason my tax dollars should pay for not only my kids, but yours. If you can't afford 'em, don't have 'em. And we all know how not to have kids, now, don't we boys and g—"

"What're you watching?" He yawned behind her.

"Nothing." Katherine slapped the power button.

"I thought you hated that stuff."

She twisted to face him. "Which is why I never watch it."

He swept a glance from her top to her bottom. "Already dressed and ready to go, huh? Have the car loaded, too?"

She did, but she said nothing. His wide smile and sloppy shirt and pants unnerved her. "The coffee is made," she said.

His walk to the coffee pot lacked its usual springiness. The heels of his slippers dragged.

"When this is over," she said to Graham's back as he poured his coffee and added a lot or a little bit of cream, "please tell me we can return to being who we really are."

He turned and winked at her and stirred. "Of course! I'm looking forward to it."

Katherine got up and sat at the kitchen table with the day-old *Daily Fact* she had already read that morning after finding it on her placemat. Deliveries had been sporadic because of the snow, and Katherine had been missing her daily updates. It touched her that Graham had gone out of his way the night before to bring her a copy.

"Thank you for the paper," she said. "What time did you get in last night?"

"Not too late." He sat across from her and sipped his coffee. "What's new in America yesterday?"

"Well," Katherine said and skimmed the headlines. "Let me see... A...um, a doctor imprisoned for providing...for providing illegal abortions—is there any other kind, I wonder?—'hopes to appeal her conviction citing mitigating circumstances. Harriet Beaman, forty-one, claimed in court Tuesday that her procedures were never intended to succeed. Instead, she said, she wanted to,' and this is her quote, "'assist law enforcement and reduce the burden on taxpayers by eliminating vile abortionists before they could reach the court system.'" End quote. It goes on to say they can connect her to the deaths of three women, but that there may have been more."

"And?"

"And what?"

"Will she get off?"

"Let me...Let me see. ... She has yet to appeal, as I... Her attorney...her attorney thinks she has a case, but the prosecution says vigilantism, 'even when performed with the best interests of the general population in mind, is unlawful.'"

"Good," Graham said. "What else?"

"What is this, Graham?"

"I don't know what you mean." He scratched at the dark stubble on his cheek, pulling at the skin under his eye. Katherine noticed how loose it was, how gray it looked.

She said, "Yes, you do."

He crossed his legs and sipped his coffee. "This is me trying to have a nice, normal morning with my wife."

"This is not normal."

"It'll do, Katherine." He turned toward the window. She watched him for so long that he eventually flicked a glance in her direction, making brief and clearly unintentional eye contact. Eyes on the window again, he said, "Please."

"Do you love me, Graham?"

"Painfully and forever."

She opened the newspaper to pretend to read the second page.

"Do you know," he said, "I think you've asked me to confirm I love you too many times, now. Even today, when I'll see our baby come out of your body and go home in someone else's arms, you want me to reassure you again, to tell you yes. So, yes. Yes! I love you, I love you, I love you." He sipped from his mug and slammed it on the table, all the while holding a pleasant expression. "I think I've told you enough for a lifetime by now, don't you?" He laughed a strained, good-natured laugh and flapped his hand to shake off coffee pooled between his thumb and index finger.

Katherine said, "Yes, Graham," but because he had just mentioned the hand-off to the agency, she was incapable of concentrating on almost anything else. In a matter of hours, she would walk back through the front door as Katherine. Just Katherine.

But, no, she remembered, she would in fact not come home that afternoon. She would still be in the hospital.

Graham looked at her with raised eyebrows.

"Yes?" she said.

He pointed at the paper with his eyes. She scanned the *Fact* for something she wanted to read.

Pound employees elated by recent dog fostering trend
Pennyroyal overdoses rise, straining urgent care centers
Economists predict gradual increase in poverty and crime

"'Formation of anti-vigilante group vigilante group vexes police,'" she offered.

"Ha!" he said. "Read it?"

The headline's levity was misleading. Police had arrested two women and a man, all in their twenties, after discovering two bodies in a basement apartment. The victims had been

strangled to death with black market ribbed-for-her-pleasure condoms knotted together at their ring bases and reservoir tips. The apartment's walls were papered with photographs and detailed, handwritten notes cataloging everything from home addresses and weekend habits to the daily schedules of at least sixty individuals believed to be targets of the pro-creation vigilante group calling itself "The Guardians."

Police Lt. Hazel Mapleton said photographs of two women, alleged victims of the Guardians vigilante group, were glued with contraceptive gel to the foreheads of the deceased. Names are being withheld pending notification of next of kin.

"I do recognize one of the women from the forehead photographs, yes. A science teacher. She disappeared, oh, two years ago, and we found her last Easter. The case was very tragic, very tragic," Mapleton said.

Sgt. Deirdre Bole apprehended suspects Witherell, Jacobs, and Anderson in a narrow tunnel behind a false end to one of several plowed paths police believe the alleged perpetrators created as diversions. Bole said she identified the false wall after noticing small holes in the snow formed and held in place with plastic straws. The suspects, who were found huddled at the far end of their shelter near an empty box of granola bars, have been hospitalized to treat dehydration, police said.

"Killing is hungry work," Bole said, adding, "It's kind of funny they didn't think to bring water. Everything takes practice, I guess."

Katherine looked up when she finished reading.

Graham checked his watch and rubbed his eyes. "How about another one."

"Did you not already read the p—"

"I came home, I put it down, I went to bed." He smiled, an afterthought.

She turned the page to **State to join national fuck database**, and it occurred to her that she could close the newspaper and slide it across the table for him to make his own selections. So, she did. He smiled, said thank you, and somehow opened directly to that article. She went upstairs.

Vague shadows filled the dark bedroom. Katherine pushed the curtains aside and stood at the window. She looked at her watch. They would leave in fifteen minutes to be there well before her surgery for what the doctor had said were essential preparations.

The sun, sitting just below the horizon, spread thin light over the wash of snow concealing their acres of wild grass and weeds. Their red truck with its dull metal plow sat in position to take them to the hospital.

"Graham," she called.

"Still here," he called back.

"Gas?" she yelled.

"Last night," he screamed.

A bright sliver started to crest the low, distant hills, fogging the window with gold. She squinted as the sun climbed higher, her eyes inadvertently lowering to the reflection of her abdomen, draped in black. (It had not been a symbolic choice, but a question of comfort. It was a cotton shirt, big and soft, old and worn. It was her favorite. She felt no need to defend the shirt to herself any further.)

For the first time since learning she was pregnant, Katherine pressed one hand to one side, the other hand to the other side. Her spread fingers moved as if independent of her control, exploring the massive curve, sinking into the dents, examining the foreign shape of her belly button. She rocked side to side and hummed a tune, the words working themselves out in a near whisper. "See you later, alligator..." She cradled the weight and watched clouds creep toward the sun, ignoring the sudden ringing in the kitchen and Graham's muffled voice.

When his talking went on longer than she thought it should so early in the morning, she went to the door to listen.

"...don't know, Ern. If Margaret's saying not to, I don't—"

"What is it? What is Margaret saying?" Katherine shouted.

"She's saying Ernie shouldn't ask us to drive her to the hospital," he yelled, "but Ernie says—"

"The hospital?" Katherine ran to the stairs and gripped the railing on the way down. "What for? Is she all right?"

Graham yelled, "Ernie says he thinks she could be—Oh, there you are—breech."

Katherine took the phone from Graham and told Ernie they would of course be there. "Why do you think the baby is br—"

"They said wait and see," Ernie said, "that it might turn, but she's really hurting and we don't know, and—Look, I know you have your own appointment, but I have no truck, and she wasn't due for a week, anyway, and you'd think hospitals would've found some way to get a team of plows..."

Katherine jerked her chin at the front door. Graham plucked his key chain from the bowl in the entry and started the truck, then put on his coat.

"I'm sorry, Kat," Margaret hollered in the background. "This is your big day, and I'm ruining everything!"

Ernie said to Katherine, "She didn't want to call you. We took the car and hoped for the best, but we kept hitting snow. The ambulance we called forty-five minutes ago is probably doing the same thing and getting stuck every which way."

Katherine dragged the phone cord to the coat tree and worked her arms into her sleeves while juggling the hand set. "Please tell Margaret I appreciate that she remembers my big day, but that we have plenty of time. The truck is already warming up."

What Ernie had said about "every which way" was proving to be true along the way to Forest Retreat Estates. Graham could leave the plow raised for three blocks before having to lower it for three more. Up for two, down for five. Up for one, down for a half, up again for three, and down again. Katherine watched the clock and was satisfied they would make it on time for her appointment. If she were late at all it would only be for the preparatory steps. They had probably exaggerated how much time was needed.

"Uh, oh." Graham hit the brakes.

Katherine lurched against her seatbelt. Just ahead, at the breakaway from a tight curve, a cluster of vehicles had accordioned themselves against a front car facing the wrong way, its rear end embedded in a snow barrier where whoever had thus far cleared the road had abruptly decided to stop and turn around. (Another citizen street clearer would presumably have been responsible for the connecting section, but people slept in, or they fought with their plowing partners, or they ran out of gas, or they simply forgot.) No bodies lay in the road. She and Graham searched the cars for anyone injured or dead, but each of the mangled cars was empty. They returned to the truck.

They were half a mile from Forest Lane, and evergreens lined either side of the road against a shoulder too narrow for the truck.

"Go back," Katherine said. "Take the field around the woods."

"We don't know what's under the snow out there or how far out of the way these woods'll take us."

Katherine got out and went around to the driver's side, scooted Graham into the passenger seat, and climbed behind the wheel. The reflection in the rearview mirror took her only as far as the bend.

With Graham positioned at a point in the curve that allowed him to watch for approaching traffic while remaining visible to her, Katherine lowered the plow and aimed the truck at the cars that had the highest probability of being moved out of the way.

EIGHT

Katherine, Margaret, Graham, and Ernie arrived at American Healthcare fifteen minutes late for Katherine's procedure (she had more than missed the two hour preparatory window). The critical fifteen minutes had been used at the scene of the pileup trying to placate a driver of one of the abandoned cars, a woman who had returned with a tow truck at the same time Katherine was passing back through the clearing she had made by all but destroying three vehicles. Upon seeing the plow, the woman had jumped out of the moving tow's passenger seat and planted herself in front of Katherine's truck until Ernie leaped out, charged her, and tossed her into the snow. This alarmed the tow truck driver, who backed down the road as fast as he could with Katherine following close behind, their trucks nearly nose to nose.

Upon entering the hospital, Ernie grabbed a wheelchair, plopped Margaret into it, and, screaming, "Breech! Breech!" raced her past reception and through the double doors reading EMERGENCY.

Katherine and Graham went directly to the elevator. Between the ground floor and the second floor, Katherine was so worried about Margaret that she held Graham's hand. He released himself when they reached the sign-in station on the second floor, where Katherine pleaded with the man behind the counter to find Doctor Martin. Surely the doctor would understand why they had been late and could find time for Katherine in the schedule. It would hardly do, she said cheerfully, to have no baby to relinquish to the agent from the Happy Baby Agency, would it? Could Katherine not possibly put on the gown and wait in a room for however long it took Doctor Martin to be available?

Katherine could not wait in a room, the man said. The doctor was quite busy and had, in fact, just been called away to perform an emergency C-section, which would back up her other appointments "with patients who were on time."

As luck (or misfortune—undoubtedly both) would have it, the stress of not achieving her long awaited autonomy was seemingly too much to add to Katherine's anxiety over Margaret. At least, that was what she would credit with breaking her water as she stood in front of the reception nurse.

Shaking what she could of the amniotic fluid off her feet, she said, "Epidural, please." Katherine had read plenty about childbirth in preparation for an unplanned delivery. She tried not to be upset that it was happening. There was nothing she could do to change it. She could numb herself, and that was all.

Graham looked down at Katherine's feet, and then up at her. His eyes bulged and a manic grin followed. Katherine sighed.

"Ms. Oxford, I'm sorry, but like I said, Doctor Martin won't be able to perform your C-section today. And she rarely gives an epidural for a scheduled C-section, anyway. She likes the spinal."

"Her water broke!" Graham yelped. "She's having it! She's having it!"

"Epidural, please."

Katherine and Margaret delivered their daughters two hours and two floors apart, they would later learn.

Because she had thought she was hearing Margaret's birthing moans, and not her post-operative grief over an unwanted C-section, Katherine had listened throughout her own delivery (greatly relieved that Margaret was alive) to share in Margaret's moment in some small way.

Listening had also effectively distracted her from hearing things having to do with her own experience. For the rest of it, the epidural had prevented her from feeling any more than she had to, and closing her eyes had saved her from seeing. She would never know Graham's reaction to whatever it was he had witnessed at his end, whether before, during, or after. Katherine's only conscious involvement had been to push when told. When it was over, she had kept her eyes closed (ignoring as well as she could the activity and loud chatter among hospital staff and Graham) until Doctor Martin's replacement had taken the baby out of the room at Katherine's instruction. The last she had heard from Graham was the sound of his hard tapping heels following close behind the doctor.

Katherine's hands rested at her sides to avoid her still-round abdomen. In each of her fantasies, she had had the baby, yawned and stretched as it was carried away by a smiling go-between, hopped up to put on her pre-pregnancy pants, and marched out of the hospital under sunshine, her hair bouncing on her shoulders. She had not counted on being exhausted and in bed, a room so dry her nostrils burned, or the obduracy of her body's physical memory.

Stretch marks, she had read about and prepared for. But this—This, she had not looked into. This was disappointing.

She tried to sleep.

At gentle pressure on her arm, she awoke to Graham and a stranger with dark, spiked hair and unusually large eyes standing beside the bed.

"This is Thelma," Graham monotoned. "From Happy Baby."

Thelma extended a hand.

Katherine shook it and said, "Pleasure!" Graham winced behind his polite smile. Katherine fixed her blanket and pushed her hair away from her face. "The baby is available. Graham can show you the way."

Thelma blinked and said, "Um." She adjusted a clipboard pressed flat to her pelvis.

Katherine looked at Graham. He shrugged.

Thelma looked down at her clipboard and then at Katherine. "You did, um, initial the clause explaining the agency's right to revise or terminate the agreement."

Katherine's throat spontaneously burned with vomit. She leaned over the side of the bed opposite of where Graham and Thelma stood and splattered it on the linoleum. She hovered there in case there was more to come, but that seemed to have taken care of it. She wiped her mouth with a tissue from the box on her nightstand.

"I'm sorry, Ms. Oxford. I would come back later, but I can't leave without these forms signed."

"Terminated is terminated," Katherine said. "Either way, my future is—"

"Oh, no, this isn't a termination. It's a revision." Thelma laughed.

Graham looked at Thelma, and he laughed.

Thelma looked at Katherine, and then at Graham, and she quieted herself into a nervous smile. "Um, I don't think there should be a problem." She handed the clipboard and a pen to Katherine. "See, it's just a simple last little thing to make sure this is what you really want."

"Oh, I see. You want to protect me from my thoroughly considered and personal decision. How thoughtful."

"Katie, she's just doing her job."

"Yes." Katherine read the form, which was not a form but a single sentence followed by signature and date lines on an otherwise blank page:

I hereby permanently surrender any and all custody of my child(ren) to the Happy Baby Agency for the purpose of re-placement with an adoptive family.

"What confuses me," Katherine said, "is that we already signed something like this."

"Yes, Ms. Oxford. But they said sometimes people change their minds right about now." Thelma looked over her shoulder at the hospital room door, where Katherine saw a figure waiting behind the window. Thelma waved her hand, and the notary pushed through the door with a yellow-swaddled baby in his arms.

"What is that?" Katherine said.

The notary carried the baby to the bed and plopped it on Katherine's chest before backing away to stand against the wall. Without looking at it, Katherine slid the baby to the space between her breasts and the leftover lump. She positioned her arms into bumpers to prevent it from rolling off her body and dropping to the floor. It was soft and warm against her, and the approximate weight of a house cat, she mused, remembering the stray female cat her college roommate had brought home. Chopin.

Graham, his face suddenly shining and red and his eyes wet and bright, leaned over and put his mouth to Katherine's ear. "It's a girl" was a whispered shriek that made her ear canal itch.

"Well, you are absolutely right that there should be no problem," Katherine said to Thelma. She propped the clipboard on the baby's side and signed her name and scribbled the date. She handed the form to Graham, who held the board loosely with his eyes on the baby.

"Graham."

He laid the clipboard on the bed and, in an automatic, fluid glide of his arms, lifted the baby off Katherine. He rested the head against his bicep for support.

Katherine bounced her knee under the blanket to slide the clipboard toward Thelma. "The form is signed—by me, Katherine Oxford, the person who gave birth—and the original forms are signed, as well, so you may feel free to take it away, now."

"She's a her, Katie," Graham said. "A widdle baby her-she baby, yes you are."

Thelma apologized profusely and said the signatures of both biological parents were required at the time of transfer. "This is, um, the new standard procedure now that there's kind of an overload," she said. "We want to give everybody one last chance to keep their babies."

"But I do not want to keep the baby," Katherine said. "I already signed a full, notarized stack of papers saying I do not want to keep the baby. Graham, please sign the form—again—so the notary and this nice young woman can get on with their day. No doubt they have plenty of babies to collect."

"We actually do." Thelma exhaled a laugh of nervous relief. "Luckily, they hired a lot more people. I was having the hardest time finding a job until the Hap—"

"Graham."

Graham took his eyes off the baby long enough to look at Katherine.

"Sign the form, please," she said.

Graham closed his arms more snugly around the yellow blanket.

Katherine said, "Will you please excuse us?"

"Of course." Thelma nudged the notary away from the wall. "We'll be right outside."

When they were alone, Katherine said, "Please, Graham."

Graham looked at Katherine, and then at the pale head nested in his elbow.

Katherine slid gingerly off the bed (she would have to remember to buzz somebody about the mess on the other side). She had already passed her bathroom test, but her legs wavered, still weak from the pain killer. Using the side rails for support, she dropped into a clumsy kneel. A tiny rock or bit of dirt dug into her left kneecap, but she ignored it and joined her hands in so tight a prayer fist that the stone of her wedding ring pierced her pinkie. Graham looked down at her over the balled up newborn pressed to his chest.

"I am begging you," Katherine said.

"Oh, come on, Katie. It'll be fun!" he bounced the baby. "Let's just do it!"

She unclasped her hands. With a palm planted on the floor for support, she sat on the cold linoleum.

"Well? What do you think?" he said. The skin under his chin gathered happily at his neck as he peered down at her.

"Do you care what I think?" she said.

"What do you mean?—What happened to your hand?"

The ring had broken her skin. She had blood on her pinkie. She wiped it on one of the bunnies printed on her infantile hospital gown. "Please answer me, Graham. Does what I think actually make a difference? Do you truly care?"

"Of course I care."

"In that case, please allow me more than fifteen seconds to reconsider my entire future."

Graham touched his nose to the baby's and said, "Okie dokie, boogie bokey." He whispered, "Boogie bokey. Who's a cookie? Who's a little baby cookie boogie?"

Katherine tried to be positive, to visualize only good things. She activated fuzzy, glowing images created by the likes of romantic novels and family movies. A baby sparkling with unlikely dewiness. A squealing toddler crashing through a leaf pile. Soft curls backlit by late afternoon sunlight. She imagined the joy of witnessing a first crawl, a first step, a first "pee in the potty," as she would likely call it.

But then she inevitably visualized the struggles of potty training. Of pees in the pants and poo on the walls. Of exhaustion, marital strain, parent teacher meetings, car seats, and diaper bags.

None of it bothered her very much, she discovered with some surprise. Each item by itself was manageable, and altogether the list of to-dos struck her as nothing more than a byproduct of having a child. She was repelled not by the work, and not even by the child. It was parenthood. She had no more desire to be a parent than to be a podiatrist.

Still, for Graham, she tried again not only to see what he saw, but to embrace his vision, to repress her automatic and overwhelming instinct to recoil from the mental image of them as a picket fence Family smiling under glass. She allowed herself to envision the development of uninhibited, wholly vulnerable affection for the baby in Graham's arms.

Her aversion grew, manifesting physically as a tickling, sickening weight pulling at her chest from behind her ribs. She also felt inexplicably, crushingly tired. Bored. Unenthused and hopeless about a predetermined (and irreversible) future.

She knew that if she allowed herself to love that baby, she would be consumed. Inextricably bound to a disagreeable life.

Graham's feet rolled to their sides one at a time as he rocked the baby. "It's not her entire future she's reconsidering, is it? No, it isn't. No, it isn't! She'll still have the stores, and she'll still have me, and we'll have the house and all the stuff in it. Why, you're the only little chan—"

"No." Katherine shook her head. She shook it and shook it.

Graham's feet stopped rocking.

"Please," she said to his shoes. "Please sign. Is there anything so wrong with our life as it is?"

"But Katie, there's no reason anything has to change!" He sat on the bed and made mouth noises at the baby.

She pressed her hands together again. "What do I have to s—"

He tapped the toe of his shoe at her, just once. "I don't want to raise my voice in front of the baby," he said. "Don't beg me. It's kooky. And it's making me see you in a way I don't like seeing you."

"But you already signed it once. It was a legal contract, Graham. It was notarized."

He smiled. "Do I need a lawyer?"

She dropped her head between her knees and screamed into the pastel bunnies.

He stroked her neck and rested his hand on her shoulder. "I really hope you'll stay."

She could leave, she knew, but the only thing more devastating to her than a life with a child in it would be a life without him. She moaned into her knees, "Why must bad things happen to good people?" before being overtaken by spontaneous, spasmodic sobs. Graham petted her thigh with the toe of his shoe.

The curtain over the window was drawn, and—but for the unfortunate orderly tasked with mopping up her vomit—Katherine was alone. The wine sat unopened in her bag on the floor. The nurse named Barry had recommended breastfeeding, so Katherine had consented to do it, but, "No alcohol just yet, Ms. Oxf—please leave that there for now," Barry had insisted more than once while struggling to help Katherine give the baby, Millicent, a nipple.

That they would name the baby for Katherine's paternal many times great-grandmother had been Katherine's idea, as had a new condition of their marriage.

"If you truly want to keep her," she had told Graham, "that means wanting—not accepting, Graham, but wanting—the bulk of the bur…the responsibility. Yes? Graham?"

He'd bounced the bundle in his arms. "Sure! Of course!"

That there would be no fucking had been his idea.

"You didn't say it, but I know you didn't like it," he'd said. "I think it's an even trade, don't you?"

At the time she had not thought that, no, nor did she think it now, but, "Yes," she had agreed. Had he not brought it up, she would have. She could only suffer so much.

"Someone's knocking, ma'am," the orderly said from the floor.

Margaret's nose and eyes filled the bottom half of the door's small glass pane. Katherine waved her in, and Margaret battled wheelchair wheels against the door while holding her baby steady on her lap. The orderly stood and offered to help, but Margaret waved him off and worked her way in. Katherine smiled at the baby Margaret displayed with an uneven lift as she rolled toward the bed.

"Name?" Katherine said.

Margaret covered her nose with the sleeve of her patterned gown. Her eyes were bright and red, the skin around them dark. "Lenore," she said behind her hand.

The orderly mumbled a shy, "Congratulations to you both," and left the room with his rags and bucket.

Her nose still covered, Margaret parked her chair at Katherine's knees. Her gown's print was teddy bears and rainbows.

Margaret gestured to her chair. "C-section. You?"

"Oh, Margaret."

"I'm okay." She laughed. "Well, I am now. I decided I'm happy she has an interesting birth story, and I can't wait to tell her."

When Katherine said her delivery was natural, Margaret frowned and then cried into her sleeve. It was her fault, she said, that Katherine had missed her appointment—"Margaret, you idiot," Katherine said—and all because she and Ernie always paid too little attention to the world around them. Had he not used that gas station on that street...

"But," Margaret said, sniffing and stroking her baby's dark brown hair, "you saved her life. She would have died, they said. If not for you."

"And you named her Lenore instead of Katherine?"

Margaret laughed again. She uncovered her nose and gave the air a tentative sniff before lowering her hand and looking around the room. "Is yours already...Is it...It's not here, so I assume...?"

Katherine straightened the blanket over her midsection. "Graham has her."

"Her?"

Katherine closed her eyes, then furiously wiped them and looked away. "Yes."

Margaret nudged Katherine's leg. "What's the matter?" After a moment, she said, "Oh, Kat. Is he leaving you?"

Katherine covered her face with her hands and wailed, "No!"

NINE

Police typically parked half a block, or so, from popular drop-off points. The unmarked patrol cars were the first thing Katherine had learned to look for when driving around with the baby tucked to rigid safety standards in her car seat. Until recently, she had of course not known what an unmarked police car looked like. On television, they were dark Ford sedans with tinted windows and painted black grilles. She now knew, from frequent runs around town since the last snow had melted, that they could be anything from a ten-year-old manual-drive Mercedes to a rumbling Mustang 6sT-AV. The only somewhat obvious tell, she had learned online, was a narrow LED strip behind the grille, which took some maneuvering to spot. Harder to search for (also learned online) was the pinhead reflection of a camera lens in the rear license plate's dark, coiled snake graphic. Over time she had noticed on her own that the wheels on the older cars they used were often a bit too shiny, too modern.

Katherine pulled into the parking lot across the street from the Department of Social Services, an unlit cigarette between her fingers. She set the parking brake and was reaching for the door handle when she saw a man in a hooded jersey creeping away from the building's entrance, his head bobbing over manicured bushes lining the sidewalk. Just then, a car she had hardly noticed screeched into motion, zipping away from the curb and skidding to a diagonal stop in front of the man before he could cross the street. He dropped to his knees, clasped his hands behind his head, and released such a guttural, sorrowful cry that he might have been dying.

The police cuffed the man and dragged him toward their light blue sedan, one of them knocking him off his feet with a sucker punch while the other officer looked back across the street. They bent to pick him up, and the cap of the officer who had punched him fell off as she swept his wallet off the ground. Thick blond hair spilled to her shoulders. She opened the wallet, took a moment reading what was inside, and closed it. The officers said something to each other, and when the male partner broke off to head toward the government building, the female officer picked up her cap and looked around—at her partner, at the sidewalks, at the windows of surrounding houses.

Katherine started to slide down in her seat, but remembered what Margaret had taught her and froze. The officer threw another quick look at her partner's back, then tripped the man with a deft strike to his bare ankle. When he was flat on the ground, she kicked him between the legs. He screamed so loud Katherine heard it through her closed window. The officer dropped on top of him, then, and pressed her chest to his back while tucking a knee between his thighs. She seemed to say something into his ear as she stuffed his wallet into the back pocket of his shorts, and when she finished, he flattened his cheek to the road and lay limp. Using his body as support for her knees and the balls of her hands, the officer stood, kicked the shining metal toe of her boot into the man's side, and casually opened the car's back door and waited.

Her partner returned with a child Katherine could only tell was old enough to walk. Dark hair fell to the collar of a t-shirt worn with blue jeans and brown shoes. The officer was having a hard time keeping the small hand in his, grasping for it and smiling down every time the child yanked it away, until he finally surrendered and scooped up the toddler, who pressed away with elbows locked and palms flat against the officer's shoulders.

When both officers were busy securing the child inside the car, Katherine lowered her window one click.

"...hell else was I supposed to do?" The man on the ground lifted his head. "I'm not a bad man. I am not a bad man!"

The male officer popped his head over the roof. "Quiet."

"She said she couldn't get pregnant! But guess what? She got goddamn pregnant, and then she left with the kid and came back a year later to goddamn drop him on me. Why don't you go find her and arrest her?—Wait, serious, now. Can you do that? Can you find her?" He struggled for balance when the male officer yanked at his elbows to pick him up off the street. "Well, can you, or what? You're police, aren't you?—Why won't you answer me?"

The officer tucked the man's head and shoved him into the back seat. Katherine could no longer see him, but she could hear him.

"What would you've done if you were me, Officer...?" His head emerged from the car as he struggled to read the male officer's nametag. "Davis? Officer Davis? Do you know how many seventy-hour weeks I put in to make partner? It was all I ever wanted. I had—"

"Your little boy could have starved to death," the female officer said. "He could have been raped. Tortured some other way. Murdered. Abandonment is a Class A misdemeanor, you know that? So, you see, Hurlbut, it doesn't matter what you wanted. Thanks to the good citizens actually looking out for the welfare of this nation's children, what you'll get is the next full year of your life in prison for—"

"Up to a year, Sal," Officer Davis said. "Most only get a month or two, tops."

"Up to a year in prison, Hurlbut, for leaving this boy on the street. Do you—"

"Might not go to prison at all, Sal. Could be probation, but maybe house arrest with groceries delivered."

"Well, there you have it, Hurlbut. You might or might not go to prison for subjecting your child to who knows what torment, but I tell you what you will most definitely have, and that's a very dark tic mark on your record. Do you think you made the right choice, Hurlbut?"

Hurlbut screeched, "Choice?" And then he laughed. He laughed and he laughed. He laughed so hard and so loud Katherine smiled unconsciously. Sal silenced him with a slam of the door. Katherine remained perfectly still with her unlit cigarette until they disappeared.

Her drives continued over the next several weeks. (She had little else to do, having decided to seclude herself during the breastfeeding period.) When the most viable local spots were catalogued along with whether she noticed a law enforcement presence, she expanded her surveillance to towns ten, twenty, and thirty miles away, often spending much of every day in the car with her quiet passenger. So quiet, in fact, that Katherine habitually watched the back seat in the rearview mirror, waiting long stretches at a time for a foot or a hand to move. If after what seemed too long she saw no sign of life, Katherine would reach behind her into the car seat and tug at the baby's sleeve until she got a kick or a gurgle.

When not analyzing covered entries and public parks—when driving on the interstate, for example, or through neighborhoods she would never even in fantasy consider—Katherine busied her mind building stories.

The first was a kidnapping, but she rejected it as flawed. Not only was she not yet wealthy enough to be an attractive ransom target, but almost anyone who desperately wanted a child could adopt. The last she had read, agencies nationwide had lowered the age requirement yet again, this time from eighteen to the individual state's age of sexual consent, where any such gap existed, "to eliminate undue age discrimination by providing equal parenting opportunities to those deemed by the state to be legally competent to reproduce." Agencies had also stopped requiring references and home visits. For the rare applicant who was turned away for having a violent criminal record, children—whether huddled in doorways or wandering the edges of the cannabis fields—were reliably in stock.

The next story, one she kept returning to, was the honest mistake: She had accidentally left the carrier in a store. But the ending, no matter how many times she revised the details leading to it, made her anxious. How, precisely, would a distraught mother behave the moment her husband breezed in from nowhere and, in a characteristic display of his impulsive and fleeting interest, ask, "Where's Millie Willie?" The scope of possible reactions and imagining herself attempting to perform any one of them with conviction could haunt her for miles at a time.

More often than not she skipped past that part. Instead, she imagined the future, after Graham had accepted her explanation and they had moved on. As it was, Graham only saw the baby in the morning before work for a fast kiss and a nuzzle, if he had the time. When she needed a diaper change, a bath, or a response to her cries, he found other things to do. Were the baby not there anymore, Katherine was confident, he would recover.

Then again, he would also undoubtedly end their agreement. She did still believe it was technically fair to allow for fucking in their marriage, but more time to think had convinced her it would be hard for her to accept with any grace unless she, too, were doing it, and she had no desire to do it.

But these were, obviously, just innocent thoughts she entertained while driving around hour after hour. At home, where she and Graham and the baby lived, her imagination was less inspired. After a day out in the car, Katherine would typically put the baby on the rug in the middle of the living room and make dinner or read, thinking nothing at all.

Now and then, however, she did catch herself showing involuntary interest in the baby. Once, while standing in the doorway and watching her under her mobile, Katherine wondered about her choices—why this toy over that toy?—and about what made her coo to herself. It took a few minutes of thinking about it to realize what she was doing, and when she did, she put an immediate stop to it by calling each of the stores to find Graham and ask him when he would be home. (As it happened, he had already left, according to both store managers.)

Another time, her evening glass of wine poured and chili steam sneaking out of crock pot, she smiled at the baby's stubborn attempts to roll over. The smile paired with unanticipated eye contact, and Katherine flew to the kitchen cabinet for her Marlboros, which she kept behind the flour. (Because Graham wanted Katherine to do nothing that could reduce the time they had together, she hid her smoking. They had agreed any behavior damaging to their health had to be done in unity or not at all, and he refused to smoke.) She brought her cigarette outside to her spot by the window, where she could occasionally look in on the baby in case she managed to find something small to put in her mouth.

Millicent did eventually find something small to put in her mouth.

It was a morning of breezes and open windows, of high, sliding clouds. Millicent played on the living room floor with a soggy stuffed cow, "A gift from Lenny," Margaret's card had read. Katherine planned to take her on a local drive after Graham left for work, all four windows rolled down. They would pass by some of the regular buildings and then explore a wealthy neighborhood or two.

While Graham dressed upstairs, Katherine peeled the tissue from her cranberry muffin and assured herself, as she tended to do in the moments when she felt less frantic, that parenthood could be a workable obstacle. As she sometimes did on days like this, she considered doing something else with her time, but the drives had become a necessary habit. Without them, even on a good day, the tension would be unbearable. Without them, there might not be any good days.

She was pulling a cranberry from her muffin to eat it separately when Graham skipped down the stairs, dropped on all fours, and crawled to the baby. He lifted her over his head, kissed her belly, and nuzzled her neck. "Love you love you lots and lots, little lady tater tot."

Katherine said, "She has a checkup Friday."

"And she'll pass with flying colors. Won't you, silly Millie?" He set her on the floor.

"Perhaps you could take her to this one."

Graham looked at his watch and wrinkled his nose. "Uh...I don't— What time?"

"What time are you available?"

"Well, I...It depends. On whether there's a customer issue, or an inventory emergency, or... Come on, Katie. You know." He sighed and dropped his shoulders, but corrected himself with a smile. "Why don't you tell me when I need to be available?"

"Four."

"Oh. Oh, no, no, no. Four?"

"What do you have at four?"

"It's nothing. Just a thing, a meeting, but I can get out of it if I need to. If there's no other way. I'd have to reschedule it, but—"

"Since when are there meetings at four?"

"It's impromptu."

"Yet, you know about it three days in advance."

"It was an impromptu idea at the time, I mean."

"Graham, you wanted this child. You have yet to spend a full day with her."

"With Millie? With my silly willie Millie?" Graham picked her up and rocked her with shallow bounces.

"Yes. You have yet to spend a full day with your silly willie Millie."

"But she's been with you. I sort of assumed you'd ask me to stay home with her when you wanted me to."

Katherine squished the cranberry between her thumb and finger. "As her father, Graham, when you spend time with her is your decision to make. And because I am not your mother as well as hers, I refuse to tell you when you should be with your d—"

"All right. All right!" Graham laid the baby in a sunbeam and went to Katherine, arms spread wide. He wrapped them around her and held her tight. "It's been an adjustment. I'm a dad, now. A dad!" He released her and held her arms at the elbows. "That's…It's a lot of responsibility."

"Is it."

"Sure! And I know it's been an adjustment for you, too, having to go to all the appointments while I take care of the stores, and… But Katie, everything'll be fine. You start pumping soon, right?" He sailed to the counter to fill his travel mug. "So you won't even have to be there to breastfeed her regularly, anymore. You can hire a babysitter or a nanny, or something, and we can both get back to a normal life. People hire help all the time."

"You can hire a babysitter or a nanny."

"What's that?"

"You, Graham. You can hire somebody. Or—and I believe I mean this sincerely—did I misunderstand our agreement?"

"No. Nope, you're right again!" Graham screwed the cap onto his mug and winked and smiled. He stood where he was, waiting, she knew, for her to smile back. "So, okay, then," he said. "I guess I'll see you lovelies later." He kissed Katherine on the cheek, bent to the floor to kiss the back of the baby's head, and headed for the door.

Katherine said, "You may want to let the employees know today about Friday so they have time to make other plans, if they choose."

Graham stopped with his back to her and a hand on the doorknob. "You bet!" He turned to look at her, again with a disingenuous smile, and she wondered when they had disconnected. "But careful, though," he said. "That almost sounded like mothering." He kissed the air and stepped out. When the door closed behind him, it was with such softness and control Katherine wondered whether he would ever come back.

She stood where Graham had left her, her unseeing eyes on the door. It took a glint of something on the floor, something quick, something bright, to awaken her. As soon as she directed her attention to where the flash had been, she saw the baby lift something to her mouth and pop it in.

Before it disappeared completely, Katherine thought she saw copper.

A penny. Millicent had eaten a penny.

Katherine dove across the room, swept Millicent up with one hand, flipped her face-down on her forearm, and held her chest while issuing a hard slap to her back. The penny dropped out and landed heads-up on the carpet.

Katherine's eyes and face exploded in heat and sobs. She was cold, trembling, zinging, sick. She laid Millicent on the floor, then pocketed the penny and stumbled into the kitchen. Over her choking gasps she heard the baby's own frantic shrieks.

TEN

The safest place to donate a baby, Katherine had learned from her diligent surveillance, was not an adoption agency. It was also not the new Eighth Street Children's Shelter, a hospital, the fire station, or the police station. Each was too obvious, each had been used prolifically, and each was too closely guarded. Daycares were also unfeasible. On a curiosity visit to a nearby daycare facility, Katherine had learned that while they received no police monitoring, they had begun using live-feed interior cameras and expensive government-quality scanners with the ability to identify every professionally counterfeited form of identification from birth certificates to passports. "You'd have to be an idiot to try to leave your kid here," the young man behind the desk had said, his unsmiling eyes accusing Katherine. For parents who opted not to officially register a child before making a daycare deposit, high-resolution exterior cameras recorded all activity within a block of the building.

The surveillance was effective, but not perfect. Children who were capable of it were sometimes made to walk from outside of a two-block perimeter, the *Fact* reported. The details of one story had been so disturbing Katherine was unable to put them out of her mind days later.

> …"Mommy said go to the yellow door," five-year-old Clementine Piper told police when asked how she arrived at Sunshine Days Daycare. A child psychologist supervised the hour of questioning that led police to the home address of Henrietta Piper, 20, who according to Clementine had threatened to "rip up" the family hamster if Clementine revealed her last name or where she lived.
>
> Upon their arrival at the household with Clementine in tow, police saw Ms. Piper emerge from the home and tear apart the live hamster with her bare hands. She then hurled its bloody pieces at her daughter, police said…

Small neighborhoods with single family homes were the safest, most practical possibility. There were too many of them for law enforcement to watch.

The baby was silent in the back seat. Katherine reached back to tap her arm while turning left onto a dark Windbury street. At a snort, Katherine let her be. She watched the signs for Morncrest Drive, an unusually wide and beautified residential road she had discovered weeks before. The mature trees, privacy fences, manicured lawns, stone fountain, speed bumps, and neighborhood watch signs made it an ideal place to raise a child.

She turned onto Morncrest and switched off her lights, immediately snapping them back on when she realized how conspicuous that was. She crept past the lit houses and pretended to sing along with music. When the light of a street lamp fell on her through the windshield, she would appear to anyone watching to be casual. She remembered to smile.

Once past the fountain, a blue-ish, six-foot cube in the center of a grass island, Katherine drove a few more yards before parking at the curb. She touched the power button and watched for neighborhood watchers. When no front doors opened and no shotgun-toting silhouettes appeared on the sidewalk, she pressed the button to release the door latch. It opened with what sounded to her like a booming *thuk*. She waited again until she felt safe to get out.

A peek inside the rear window confirmed the baby was still asleep. Her arms were crossed over her middle and a crease divided her eyebrows. Katherine saw that she had not pulled off the note pinned to the waist of her purple pants, the top half of the message tucked snugly under the hem of a yellow t-shirt: *I never knew you...*

The baby opened her eyes, and Katherine ducked below the window. She backed away from the car and stood against a tree at the edge of someone's yard.

Coarse wig fibers tickled her neck. She scratched until her skin burned. She pulled her cigarettes from her pocket and lit one, inhaling until the heat and the flavor of it gagged her. Drool spilled down her chin and inside her v-neck. She swiped her hand across her chin and scrubbed her shirt between her breasts, dried her eyes, took another deep drag, and considered the lit windows.

The original (theoretical) plan had been to leave the baby on a doorstep where people were clearly home. Whether to ring the doorbell had initially been the only sticking point. (Not to ring, she had decided. Ringing was too risky.) But now, standing here among these many fine-enough homes, Katherine was no longer sure it was within her purview to choose the baby's home. Again she was faced with the hypocrisy of presuming to make parental decisions for a child she was choosing not to parent.

She scratched her scalp under the hot wig and noticed the glow from the fountain.

A beautiful setting, and plenty of directed spotlights. Mature tree branches formed a tangled arc over the island, which meant she would have shade during the day.

But of course she would be gone by then. People would soon be leading their dogs out for walks, and someone would snatch her up long before sunrise.

Katherine scraped her cigarette on the sidewalk and tucked the butt in her pocket. She stretched with her arms high, feigning a yawn and neck twists in checks of the street and sidewalks. No one seemed to be out. She double-checked the integrity of the muddied rear license plate on her way to open the back door.

"Oh, no," she said, reaching inside. "Do you have a poo? Do you have a little poopie-poo?" She peered over the top of the car. The street was deserted.

The "thing," for which there was no perfectly appropriate word, took ten seconds. She counted unconsciously: One to three: Unbuckle the car seat. Four and five: remove the baby. Six to eight: Run to the fountain, place carrier in corner floodlight. Nine and ten: Return to car.

She lit a cigarette before pulling away from the curb and watched the speedometer through stinging eyes and blurred vision. Five miles per hour felt at once exceedingly fast and impossibly slow. Halfway to the end of Morncrest, she saw a man walking toward the fountain with a stroller and a black and white dog. She puckered her lips in an air kiss and winked. The man responded with a confused smile and a hesitant wave. Katherine watched him in the rearview mirror after she passed, but she was too close to the end of the road to see what he did when he reached the fountain.

Surely a man out on a walk with a child and a dog was a man who would not leave a baby alone at night.

Katherine stopped at the stop sign at the end of Morncrest. A broadly smiling couple pushing a twin stroller rounded the corner. Both parents noticed her, and their smiles impossibly widened. They fussed with their children as they passed, bending over to touch their cheeks, smooth their hair, poke their chests. In her rearview mirror, as she pulled onto the main road, Katherine saw the woman sneak a glance over her shoulder.

She took off her wig and put it on the back seat, ignoring the dark openness of the unoccupied space. She powered on the music to Benny Goodman's "Get Happy." She turned it up.

Through ten songs and twenty-three miles, she incrementally raised the volume. If a distressing thought or feeling broke through the barrier of sound, she sang along, making up words if the lyrics were unfamiliar. At a notoriously long red light, she took the last drag of her fifth cigarette and stuffed it into the flower of squeezed filters filling the ashtray. The light was still red when she lit the next one.

"I stopped the cart in the freezer aisle," she whispered. "We needed peas." She had read that for a lie to be persuasive, it was important to include minor, but not too many, details. "But then I also wanted a pie crust. It was only three freezers down, so I walked away. When I turned around, she was gone."

There are unwanted children filling up shelters and adoption agencies all over the country, he would say. Why would anyone steal one in a grocery store?

"Convenience," she said to the empty car.

Katherine opened the window and reached out her hand. It was cooler, but the forecast had predicted it would get no lower than seventy degrees. She would be comfortable enough until someone claimed her.

The man with the black and white dog had probably already taken her home.

But what if he had walked right past her?

What if his dog had smelled Millicent, turned wild, and attacked her?

What if other hungry, nocturnal, animals found her? Rats? Bats? Raccoons? Cats?

Katherine crushed out her cigarette, opened all the windows, and stared up at the red light. Two cars waited across the intersection, but no one was behind her. Rather than draw attention to herself with a brazen maneuver, she reversed onto the shoulder, used her turn signal, and made a U-turn.

She tried to maintain her speed limit on the long, dark stretch but unconsciously pressed harder on the gas at each vivid image of Millicent's carrier cradling nothing but her shredded and bloody yellow t-shirt. When she turned onto Morncrest twenty minutes later, she became so distracted she drifted right and bumped the curb. She stopped the car.

The street was, for the time of night, swarming. Singles with strollers. Couples with toddlers. Most were accompanied by dogs, even the few couples without children Katherine saw walking in her direction. If not for the avoidance of eye contact they all seemed to make with equal commitment as they passed each other on the narrow sidewalks, Katherine would have thought they were going to a block party, or a private concert in someone's a garage. But there was no air of festivity, no urgency or excitement. Every single person on the sidewalk was exceedingly, identically casual.

That oddness aside, the numbers comforted her. She doubted, now, that there was any reason to worry the baby had been or would be attacked by a dog, or by any other animal, for that matter. She had probably already been taken in, and that was all Katherine needed—to see that she and her carrier were gone. She pulled away from the curb.

The distant light of the fountain came into view as a blue dusting on the tree branches bending over it. The closer she got to it, the wider the birth the late night strollers seemed to give the fountain until—at once, it seemed—the sidewalks cleared. No one ahead of her, no one behind. A little father ahead, a motion light caught the white sneakers of someone stealing around the back of a house, but everyone else was magically gone.

Katherine unconsciously released pressure from the gas pedal when she drove close enough to see the fountain's base. It had changed, somehow, had more texture and shadows, or—

Children. She stopped, put the car in park. Toddlers. Babies laid like flowers at a memorial in the light at the stone base. Where she had left one baby, there were four...five...six...a cluster propped against Millicent's carrier, and then against one another, one baby used as support for the next. And there were older ones, too, anywhere between five and eight years old (she had no idea about children's ages), sitting among the babies.

Katherine got out of the car and headed for Millicent without closing the door. She took a quick survey of the children surrounding the carrier and was relieved that most wore cool clothing—t-shirts or thin cotton onesies, open-toed shoes or no shoes at all. They were also calm, quiet.

Obvious when she got closer was that not all of them were bathed, and their clothes, in many cases, were dirty. Millicent was by far the most promising-looking baby there. Katherine was frankly baffled that no one had taken her. But there really were so many of them. Too many. An intimidating choice for anyone, which meant they would all likely stay where they were until the police came to take them to a shelter.

Shelter life was not what Katherine had envisioned for Millicent.

She pulled at the carrier handle, and the babies stacked against it shifted.

"You can't take that." A boy, a young teenager, maybe, stepped out from behind the fountain. He sucked on a narrow cylinder and blew a cloud of blue smoke. It hovered briefly, hypnotically, in folding, swirling clouds, and then steadily descended, molded over small, bald heads, slithered into t-shirt wrinkles, curled into tiny, dark nostrils. "They're all gonna fall down, can't you see? You can take the baby if you want it, but leave that seat there."

Katherine needed to be clearheaded to drive, so she flapped the smoke away from her face as she let go of the handle. She rearranged the babies around the carrier and lifted out a glassy-eyed Millicent.

"You want an older kid, too?" The teenager tucked his hair behind his ears, uncovering a bruise high on his left cheek. His yellowed t-shirt was starched. He shrugged a narrow shoulder at Katherine. "Thirteen's not so bad, you know. It just means I know how to do stuff."

"No, thank you," Katherine said. "I only—Just one child, please." She realized with some amusement that she sounded like she was making a purchase.

The boy apparently had the same thought.

"That'll be fifty dollars, then."

"Pardon me?"

"Babies are fifty. Toddlers are…uh…I don't know, twenty-five, and teenagers like me, we're only ten. Ten dollars. And I can do more than clean, or some shit like that. I'm good at solving problems, and, uh…and I also have organizational skills."

"I have no use for any of that. But, thank you." She looked around. People were emerging from the darkness, watching her. A trio—a woman with a stroller and a dog—jogged down the sidewalk from the far end of the street.

"So, you don't want an older kid," said the boy, who seemed unfazed by what was happening around them. "I get it. Whyn't you take two babies, then, instead of just one? I'll give 'em both for seventy-five."

"No." Katherine held Millicent to her as if she were feeding. It was the only time she had ever held her, the only way she knew how. She stepped gingerly to the street.

"Fifty dollars for that one," he said. "But if you want this one over here, I'll give it to you for five." The boy picked up a baby of Millicent's approximate age and cradled it comfortably in one arm.

"I really only want this one."

"What makes that baby so special? This one's just as nice, and a lot cheaper."

She laid Millicent on the driver's seat and reached past her to get inside the glove box.

"Hey, hey, you don't need to—take him for free. You don't have to pay me at all. Just don't shoot—"

Katherine stepped out of the car with a short stack of tens and twenties flat on her palm. She brought them as close to the boy as she could without stepping on any hands or feet. He reached out and took the cash. He counted it slowly, the baby bobbing in his arms with the movement.

"This is a hundred," he said.

"Yes."

"That baby, it's yours, right?"

"No."

"That's why you want it so bad. You left it and changed your mind, right?"

"No. I simply like this one."

"Yeah? I bet you'll like this one, too, if you don't want me to run to one of these houses and call the police."

Katherine looked out at the houses. Motion lights flicked on and off as people continued to come out of the bushes and the dark spaces between garages. The woman jogging with the dog and stroller had stopped on the sidewalk half a block away and was tying the baby's shoe. There was no way to know for certain that all of these people were here for the same reason as Katherine, but she had a good feeling they were. They would be allies, were she to call out the boy as a threat. But threatened people were unpredictable. They could deal with him civilly, or they could do it violently. He was just a boy.

Katherine insisted that she had left no one at the fountain. She said he could call the police if he wanted to, but that when they arrived she would tell them she had been so appalled by the recent spate of baby-selling she had taken it upon herself to perform a citizen sting operation.

"As evidence," she said, "I will point to that baby in my car and the money you have in your hand. Do you know what the penalty is for selling children?"

"No."

Katherine had no idea, either. She would have said the punishment was a year in prison, as it was for abandonment, but that hardly seemed an impressive threat to a boy like this.

"Labor camp," she said.

When he rolled his eyes, Katherine explained what conditions were like for prisoners at the isolated prison. Meal worms for meals, sewer water to drink, weeks at a time of pitch-black darkness—

The jogger approached on the sidewalk, stopped for a moment to watch Katherine and the boy, and continued past them. When they were alone again, Katherine added that there were beatings, torture, and rape at this labor camp. And that no one, to anyone's knowledge, had ever left.

"Ever," she said.

The boy tucked the bills into the diaper of the baby in his arms and then held the baby out to Katherine. "See, I'm paying *you*. I'm not selling babies, I swear. Me and him got dumped here just like everyone else. Please take him. If you don't, I don't know what'll happen to him." He leaped over the tiny bodies to the street and pushed the baby against Katherine's chest, holding it there when she didn't reach up to take it. "Please, lady. I can tell you're not crazy. He'll be safe with you."

Katherine backed into the car and slid Millicent to the passenger side. She gently pushed the boy and the baby distant enough to close the door and instructed him through the open window to call the police and tell them where he lived. He laughed at her and took the baby and Katherine's hundred dollars to his original spot beside the wall. When she asked if she could drive them somewhere, the boy ignored her.

"Why are you staying here? Can you not at least use the money to stay indoors tonight with your brother?" she said.

The boy shrugged at her. "And then do what?"

Katherine watched in her rearview mirror as the boy set his brother in Millicent's carrier. The jogging woman returned to the fountain, and a second teenager appeared from behind the wall. The two teens thrust their middle fingers at the woman scooting her stroller into place. She ran off with a return finger flashed over her shoulder, the dog trotting at her side.

PART TWO

ELEVEN

For as many mornings as she was young enough for toys, Millie played in the kitchen corner while her mother made breakfast. When she was allowed to sit at the table, it was to eat her oatmeal and berries and listen as her mother read stories from the newspaper. Her smooth fingernail would underline the words as she sounded them out.

"...argued against repealing the Citizen Amendment. 'This is not a states' rights issue, dagnabbit. If we as human beings, as citizens of this earth, accept that 'right to life' means every person, born or unborn, has the right to life, how can we, by all that is just and holy, condone the future denial of said right to life in this or that backward state? I say hogwash,' state representative Lester Hightower said..."

"...strongly opposed the proposed trial-basis return of welfare benefits. Frelinger cited recent findings by the American Employment Initiative that job seekers 'not highly selective' about their employment options will find work within one to three months of becoming unemployed. 'Someone is always hiring,' Frelinger said. 'Whether they want you to wash dishes, clean toilets, enter data, or pour their coffee doesn't matter. What matters is, will they pay you? If the answer is yes, there's a job. So take it, you entitled, lazy [expletive]. And if you know you can't afford to have a kid, how about this? Keep your d— behind your zipper where it belongs!' A chorus of hisses and loud, unintelligible muttering silenced Frelinger..."

Story time was the only one-on-one time Millie had with her mother. Sometimes she tried to play with her in the kitchen after the stories were done. Once, she crawled under the table where her mother sat looking out the window. She had her arms almost all the way around the baggy bottoms of her mother's loose, dark pants when the chair slid back and the ankles were gone. She followed the feet to the counter and went for her ankles again. Again they slipped away, this time going all the way through the living room and out the front door. Her mother looked in from the other side of the square window, her face glowing orange and then hiding behind fog. When she came back inside, wind and burnt perfume rubbed into her clothes and long, yellow hair, Millie said, "Play," and held out her favorite thing, a blue bus with yellow stripes on the sides.

"Later, Millicent," her mother said, but Millie understood "no."

"Play," Millie said again, this time holding up a black racer with a red top.

Her mother took the car, dropped it in the box, and brought Millie to the table for a story.

"A Haverton woman disappeared Tuesday after taking the family car in for detailing, her partner, Jonathan Flores, said. Flores said he last saw Joan Spellman, 26, at breakfast Tuesday morning. 'She said the car was dirty and she needed to take it in. I never saw her again,' Flores said. Sources close to Spellman who wished to remain anonymous said they believed the disappearance was intentional. 'She wanted out,' one source said. Said another source, 'She's been waiting for this for weeks. I think it can just take some time, you know, to get the nerve.'...."

Millie didn't know why her mother was crying, and she didn't know enough words to know what was being read to her.

But she learned fast. Millie was reading like a ten-year-old on her fourth birthday. She could also print forty-two words that had more than one syllable. But the most important thing she learned was that reading and writing were the only ways to get her mother's good attention, so she practiced all the time. Every night after she went to bed, she did spelling quizzes on her tablet under the blanket. In the car on the way to Lenny's house most weekday mornings, she mouthed the words in books her mother kept in the back seat pockets. She also read at Lenny's house during nap hour (Lenny always slept), and when everyone (except her Aunt Margaret) went to one of Lenny's dad's sites, she read the words printed on drywall and on tools. The workers also left magazines in the outdoor bathroom that she was allowed to take outside to read in the fresh air, as long as she stayed away from work areas.

Millie taught herself three new words a day, but she only told her mother one every day and saved the big ones for when she needed them. A word like "remarkable" or "distinguished" could get a "Very good," a "Well done," or sometimes, a smile—right before her mother ran outside to smoke her cigarette. (Millie went up to her bedroom whenever that happened, now, even if her dad was home. She wanted to stay in the living room with him, but he didn't pay any attention to her when her mother was out there. All he did was jump off the couch and walk back and forth and back and forth in front of the window. Sometimes he'd bang it with his fist.)

Her dad's attention was easier to get than her mother's. He gave it to her whenever he wanted. He came down in the morning halfway through the reading-aloud sessions and listened while making his coffee, saying,

"Ah!" and "Really!" as she pushed through stories she only half understood, when she understood them at all. When it was his turn every other day to drive her to Lenny's house, he tossed her over his shoulder and tickled her all the way down the path to the truck. On really nice weekends, if she wasn't staying at Lenny's house because her parents were on one of their vacations, her dad took her out to play in the weeds. Sometimes he brought her way out to the edge of their property and pointed into the distance at the wild meadow land they would own "any day, now, Millie girl, and when you're all grown up, you can have your very own house out there so we never have to be too far apart."

He stopped making that promise when Millie was six.

It was the third day of straight rain, and the whole time she watched her dad pack his suitcase he talked about the sunny skies in Nevada. Millie followed him and his suitcase downstairs when he was done, and after rolling his bag to the door he picked her up and brought her to the front window. He told her to think over vacation weekend about what color her house on the other side of the meadow would be.

"Please stop feeding her that fantasy." Her mother sat in the living room with her newspaper. Her suitcase was a shiny square against the wall. "Outside of what we put away for her education, we spend nearly everything we make. Yet, you insist on promising her a small fortune."

"So, we'll save," he said.

Her mother turned and rested an elbow on the back of the couch. "No more vacations?"

"We'll find another way."

"No new car, then?"

He laughed.

"Millicent," her mother said, "you may not understand any of this, but I think hearing it earlier is better than hearing it later. Are you ready to listen?"

"Ya."

"Yes."

"Yesss."

"We are not the kind of people who believe in spoiling a child. Do you agree, Graham?"

"Yesss." He winked at Millie. She snorted.

"Thank you, Graham. Millie, if you grow up believing everything will be taken care of for you, you will have little incentive to work hard to take care of yourself. Do you understand?"

Millie looked at her dad. He wrinkled his eyebrows.

Her mother said, "The money we have is money I...we...earned after years of struggle and personal effort that taught us about our perseverance and resilience. For that reason alone it is highly rewarding and something neither of us takes for granted. We insist that you have that same experience, that you mold your own value. Do you understand?"

"We never talked about this," Graham said.

"Do you disagree?"

"Well, I don't agree. I know that. She's our daughter, Katie."

"All right. When you tell me what you want to give up—vacations, the new car, the property you want to buy, or the riding lawn mower to mow our many new acres—we can discuss how much to put into savings for her unearned, and therefore unappreciated, future of leisure."

Millie's dad threw his hands in the air and shrugged with a goofy smile. "Sorry, shrimp. Your mom makes too much sense for me."

"Do you understand any of this, Millicent?"

Millie shook her head.

"Well, someday you will. And you," she said, "will be very grateful. Right, Graham?"

"Sure! What fun is money if it doesn't hurt to spend? Just think, Millie. One day, when you have a good job and you're making lots of money and your mom and I are forced off the property to die in an old folks' home, you can buy it from us and live here just like you always have. Isn't that nifty?"

"Can we please save death for another time?"

"Speaking of death, silly Millie, when's the last time you fed that parakeet?"

Millie couldn't remember, so she went to check on Annabelle.

He was green and yellow, her favorite color combination. She had loved him since her dad had given him to her after one of their long vacations. She'd named him after fun, happy Annabelle, who worked at Lenny's dad's houses and hugged her hello whenever they went to work with him. Lenny had Murphy, big and licking and soft, but Millie thought Annabelle was almost as good. Because he couldn't show feelings the way dogs did, though, he needed help, sometimes. Millie would hold him in both hands with his whole body covered except for his rough, tickling feet, and when he started flapping around against her fingers, she'd spread her hands just enough for him to try to push out his face to see her. "See, Annabelle? It's me! Don't worry, I'm here," she would say.

Millie stuck her finger in the seed bucket and swirled it around. She screamed, "He has food!" and ran back down to the living room.

Her dad was at the front door. Her mother was nowhere.

"She's in the car," her dad said. "You ready?"

"I don't want you to go."

He smiled and picked up her backpack. "What's all this about? We're just going away like we always do, silly Millie."

"I want to go."

"You want to go with us on our vacation?"

"Ya. Yes."

"'Yes'! Very good. We'll tell her in the car. Do you have everything?"

Millie looked around at everything. "No."

"What are you missing?"

She shrugged.

"Are you sure you don't know what you're missing?"

She shrugged again.

Her dad looked at his watch, then clapped his hands and smiled brightly. "Great. Let's get going!" He picked her up and carried her to the door.

The smell of him made her cry.

"You know what?" he said. "Someday you'll be eighteen, and you can go on exciting vacations of your own. Would you like that?"

"No."

When they got to Lenny's house, Millie held onto her dad's sleeve. He was smiling when he took her hand off his shirt and pushed her toward Lenny's dad.

"She forgot Annabelle, again," he said. "The spare's in the mailbox."

Her uncle Ernie laughed. "One of these times maybe you could bring the bird, yourself."

"C'mon, Ern," her dad said. "How's she supposed to learn self-sufficiency?"

"Ah," her uncle Ernie said.

Her dad patted the top of her head. Millie turned at the sensation of his hand leaving her scalp, but he was already jogging to the car when she reached out for a hug. Her mother pulled away after he jumped in, and he didn't look back or wave out the window.

But when they came back, Millie had some new thing to play with, just like she did every time her parents showed up at Lenny's door to take her home.

TWELVE

From the day she was born, Lenny had a friend in Murphy, who was a pillow, a blanket, and a playmate. He liked to roll the ball, so they did that a lot, but he also liked hide and seek. Lenny could make him look for hours and hours. She had three floors and all the rooms to hide in (minus her mamma's office, where Lenny wasn't allowed to play until after four), so when Murphy finally found her he'd be so tired and happy he'd bark and pant and then fall on his side and just lie there.

Lenny and her poppy also played intercom hide-and-seek, sometimes, but only after breakfast was done. Her mamma would kiss her on the mouth and hug her and then go upstairs to work, and her poppy would say, "Ready? Go!" After counting to twenty-three, he would yell out crazy places he was looking for her—under the rug, in the sink, on top of the door—to try to make her give herself away by laughing. But only until her mamma would open her office door and sing, "That's enough," because she could hear "every delightful word you loves of my life are screaming through the intercom."

The intercom game was mostly a rainy-day activity. On nice days, her poppy would start the morning after breakfast with internet time, helping Lenny look up anything she was interested in (animals, but not kangaroos, which scared her, and all the bugs with wings, but not carpenter ants, because they were gross). The research started with pictures of caterpillars when she was three. As she got older, they started reading basic facts, and a little later she learned about things like characteristics and habitats. When internet time was over, if he didn't have to go to a site and if Millie wasn't coming over, they walked through the woods around their house and looked for what her poppy said were "local specimens."

For a long time, a year at least, Lenny liked to just pick up the bugs (if they were on the ground and if they didn't jump or fly away), look at them, and put them back down. But she started liking certain ones so much that she wanted to bring them inside, so her poppy helped her research what she should have to take care of a cricket, a grasshopper, a praying mantis, or—if she could ever find one—a giant black ichneumon.

Her first bug was a grasshopper that lived in a shoe box with grass she kept wet with a misty spray bottle. She only had him for a week, but she cried for three days, anyway, after she found him crinkled up and headless in Murphy's downstairs bed.

"I'm sure it was quick and painless," her mamma said. "That's the best way it could have happened for…?"

"I didn't name him."

"Oh, but he should have a name! What do you want to name him?"

Lenny said, "Beauregard?"

After burying Beauregard, they all drove to the pet store for a real bug terrarium Lenny could use for almost anything that wasn't an arachnid.

She knew her parents didn't want an arachnid in the house, but Lenny couldn't resist the bright, colorful beauty of an orange orb weaver that sat in its web outside the front door, up high between the roof and the rain gutter. One night, while her mamma was on a call in her office and her poppy was in the kitchen making dinner, Lenny carried the footstool and a broom outside. She tried to use the soft bristles at the corners to knock the spider to the "veranda," but the broom stuck to the web and took the spider. She shook it, and then she tapped it over and over again on the ground until the spider bounced off and made for the stairs. Lenny dropped the broom and dove, catching it right before it could sneak over the edge.

Its legs tickled her palm as she tip-toed past the kitchen and up the stairs to the hallway outside her mamma's office, where she could watch it race gracefully across the shiny wood floor. She was thinking about what to add to the terrarium for the spider, who she'd named Aranea, when her mamma opened her office door, saw Aranea spidering toward her, and smashed her four times with her thick binder.

"We all have our unique endings," her mamma said before the funeral. The whole family, including Murphy, stood in the shade while Lenny dug a hole with a plastic shovel under the dried, orange pine needles at the edge of the woods. "I'm sorry I took her away from you, sweetie. But after a week or two inside, when you finally released her again, she could have been plucked out of her web by a sparrow and swallowed alive. I promise she didn't feel any pain today."

"What your mom's saying is that she did that little spider a favor by flattening her in the hallway," her poppy said.

Lenny didn't want to laugh, but she accidentally did. A round glob of snot shot out of her nose onto Aranea's black velvet jewelry box sitting in the hole.

Her mamma picked up a maple leaf for Lenny's nose and said her poppy was right. Even better than the quick way it happened, she said, was that Aranea got to have a far more interesting death story than any of her spider friends. "And when it's the last thing you'll ever do, it may as well be interesting."

Aranea would have been the first to live in the terrarium, but instead it was Orthop, a bright green katydid Lenny found weeks later. ("No more spiders," her mamma made her promise.) When Millie came over with Annabelle that Saturday for one of her weekends, Lenny dragged her through the foyer and straight to her room. She pointed into the glass. "That's Orthop."

"Oh," Millie said. "Want to play hide and seek?"

Lenny didn't. Playing hide and seek with Millie meant running all over the house and up and down the stairs to find her, every single time. Millie only liked to be found. But Lenny never said no, because whenever she opened the right door, pulled the right curtain, or looked under the right bed, Millie squealed and slapped her hands over her eyes. It made her so happy.

Lenny said, "Sure."

When it was Lenny's sixth turn in a row as Seeker, she stopped in her bedroom for a quick peek at Orthop, who was nibbling on his antenna at the highest point on a curved branch Lenny had put in the terrarium after learning katydids didn't like being on the ground. Annabelle clicked and fluttered as Lenny passed the bird cage. She opened the top of the glass case and curled her fingers under Orthop to pull him out, smiling at the sticky feeling of his feet on her skin. She grabbed a lettuce leaf from inside his house and held it in front of his mouth.

"I can spell eucalyptus."

Lenny jerked her hand and Orthop went fluttering. Annabelle hopped sideways on his perch. Millie stood in the doorway, her hands in her front pockets. Murphy shoved by her and lay on the floor.

"What's a eucalyptus?" Lenny's voice perked Murphy's ears. He got up to walk toward her.

"Some kind of tree," Millie said, springing to hold Murphy back. She held his collar with one hand and patted the top of his head with the other.

"Oh." Lenny looked at the leaf still in her hand. "This is from the ground." She picked up Orthop from the bed, set him in his case with the lettuce, and closed the top.

"But I can spell it. It's e-u-c-a-l-y-p-t-u-s."

"Do you want to see him eat?"

"I can also spell audience. A-u-d-i-e-n-c-e. And last week I read a book that's almost three hundred pages."

Lenny saw how proud Millie was, so she said, "Wow!" Murphy looked at her, his ears flat, his head bobbing under Millie's hand. "Let's go see if we can find another katydid so Orthop can have a friend. Want to?"

Millie stopped petting Murphy, but didn't let go. "I want to keep playing."

"But we already played six times today."

"We didn't finish. You wanted to play with your bug, instead."

Lenny's mamma always told her that an honest person telling small lies for the right reasons was "performing one of very few truly selfless acts of kindness." She thought she should maybe lie and say she didn't like playing with the bug more than she liked playing with Millie, but she couldn't do it.

"Don't you like playing with Annabelle?" she said.

Millie shrugged. "I guess."

Lenny walked over to Annabelle's cage and stuck her finger inside, under the bird's belly, nudging gently until he climbed on her finger. Millie let go of Murphy and stomped over to the cage. The bird jumped to its perch. Lenny yanked out her hand and Millie slammed the door closed.

"I'll go hide," Millie said. "Count to fifty and come find me!"

But Lenny didn't have to find Millie again, because her poppy called them both to the foyer and put them in the truck with Murphy.

"Today you'll learn the exciting job of placing a lumber order," he said.

All the way to the store, Millie squeezed Murphy to her, holding him back whenever he moved closer to Lenny. The drive was slow and long because of weekend traffic, and Lenny felt bad that it meant Murphy would have to spend that much more time locked in Millie's arms. He looked at Lenny so sadly that she turned to the window.

Most people didn't have trucks like Lenny's poppy. They were too expensive. Most had old vans or small cars, and a lot of the small cars were so stuffed with kids the only place left for anyone who could fit was in the sunny spot under the back window. Her poppy had to keep slowing down because cars and vans were swerving into other people's lanes as arm shadows slapped at backseats from between front seats. Making everyone go even slower was the gray van a few cars up that kept pulling over—but not far enough for people to get by—and stopping to let a dirty, sunburned lady in a bright yellow vest jump out to grab older kids sitting alone on the sidewalk or in front of store doorways. A lot of them got right in, but one boy ran. The lady chased him to the door of a pawn shop, and the kid pulled and pulled, but the door wouldn't open. The lady dragged him across the sidewalk to the van and shoved him in.

"Why didn't he want to go?" Lenny said.

Her poppy didn't answer.

"Poppy, why—"

"He wasn't looking for a job, pumpkin."

Millie's parents' car was already in the driveway when they got back from the store. Millie got out of the truck as soon as it stopped and ran toward the house. She stopped at the bottom of the stairs when her mom came out the front door holding Annabelle's cage.

"Hi, Aunt Katie!" Lenny said after getting out with Murphy. She held his collar because he could get happy when people were over.

"Hello, Mother," Millie said.

Millie's mom carried the cage down the stairs, and Millie jumped and waved when her dad came through the doorway. "Hi, Da—!"

Murphy yanked out of Lenny's fingers and ran straight for Millie's dad, knocking hard against one of Millie's mom's legs. She dangled all her balance on one foot and swung the cage in the air. Murphy zoomed up the stairs and slammed his paws on Millie's dad's thing, and Millie's dad jumped back with his butt out and laughed something about "more action than it got all weekend" just as Millie's mom fell over. The cage went high up in the air, then smashed on their gravel driveway with a *clang*. The wire door popped open. Millie's mom was like Aranea going for the cage, but she was too late to grab Annabelle, who flapped away in a yellow-green streak over the roof of the house.

Millie's mom hooked her fingers in the cage and threw it away from her, then picked up a handful of gravel and flung it at the ground. Lenny's poppy yelled at the house, "Hey, Mox? Mox!" Millie's dad ruffled Murphy's ears on the veranda and said, "What happened, boy?"

Lenny's mamma came out and ran down the stairs while Millie's mom stuck a cigarette in her mouth.

"Where's Annabelle going to go, Poppy?" Lenny said.

He stood next to her and put his arm on her shoulder. "Annabelle's going to die, sweetheart," he said in a way that made it sound like a secret.

"But, happy." Lenny's mamma smiled at Lenny through a cloud of Millie's mom's cigarette smoke.

"That's right," Lenny's poppy said with a quick squeeze. "So don't be too sad, now, Millie, all right?" he told the sky. "Your bird's just gone off to do what birds do."

Lenny didn't see Millie, and she hadn't heard her say anything, so she took a fast look around. She wasn't on the veranda with Murphy and her uncle Graham, and she wasn't with her mom and Lenny's mamma. Lenny peeked over her shoulder, and there she was, standing alone near her parents' fancy car, the empty, mashed up cage by her feet.

Lenny asked her parents in the kitchen that night if they could please keep Murphy away from Millie, especially now that Annabelle was gone. The only way Lenny could ever make Millie let go of Murphy was by playing with Annabelle.

"She's mean to him," she said.

"She's just a little needy," her poppy said. He opened the refrigerator and pulled out meat wrapped in brown paper and set it on the island.

"What he means," her mamma said, "is that Millie wants love. She likes the kisses Murphy gives you, and she just wants some, too."

"But he doesn't want to," Lenny said.

"Dog sense," her poppy said.

Her mamma smacked her poppy on the arm and said, "When school starts next month, Murphy will get a nice, long break."

"Why does she have to be over all the time, anyway?"

Lenny's parents looked at each other, and then her poppy leaned in front of her on the other side of the island, his short sleeves showing all of his tattoos. While he talked, she poked out her finger to pet the small, inky footprint near his wrist. That one was hers.

"It's a long story, pumpkin, for another time," her poppy said. "Right now you just need to remember two things any time she gets…the way she is. One, it's not her fault.—Nope, don't—Close that little question hole. Another time, I said. Two…Are you listening?"

Lenny nodded.

"Two, Murphy's kisses make her happy, and as her friend, you want her to feel happy whenever she can as long as it doesn't hurt anyone else. Has she hurt Murphy?"

"No."

"Don't worry about the dog, then. If he doesn't like something, he'll let her know."

When Millie came over again two days later, and every day for the rest of their summer vacation until they started second grade, Lenny put Millie and Murphy together on purpose, a few times going away from Murphy before Millie had a chance to pull at him. Sometimes, if Millie's face was shoved up to Murphy's nose long enough, he'd lick her, and she would squeak and wipe her mouth.

When Millie left at the end of every day, Lenny found Murphy and whispered apologies into his big, floppy ear and fed him three of his favorite cookies.

THIRTEEN

School was full of stories, so Millie took notes on just about everything but the upper-grade pregnant girls. The one pregnant girl she'd written about—an eighth grader who'd walked on the wrong side of the rope and tripped over someone's back—was the first and last pregnant girl story her mother had wanted to see.

"Nearly anyone can, and probably will, get pregnant once they reach a certain age, Millicent. That is not an interesting story." Yes, her mother had said, that the girl had obviously been tripped was somewhat interesting, but, she'd wanted to know, what happened next? "Do you know why they have the rope, Millicent?" Millie didn't. "To give pregnant girls their own section of the corridor, which minimizes their risk of 'falling,' which thereby minimizes the risk of the pregnant girls' parents suing the school board."

Millie didn't care about any of that. What did stick in her head, though, was what her mother had said next about what an interesting story was. An interesting story, she'd said, was about a person who wasn't like other people and who wasn't doing what other people were doing, unless it was a lot of people doing the same thing for the first time and for a new reason.

"An interesting story, Millicent, provides the reader with new information."

Finding stories her mother didn't know was easy. A lot of her classmates (and she, when she had to on a Tuesday or a Thursday) sat on the hard orange carpet or crowded against the wall when all the desks were taken, so there was always someone right next to her to listen to. Even though she didn't really join the groups the remainders made, there was so little space left in any of the classrooms that Millie could sit close enough to them without being noticed. She took her notes in secret, pretending she was writing school material while jammed up around a monitor during research hour, or as the teacher yelled lectures over them from the front of the room. After school, while on the bus to her own house or in the truck on the way to Lenny's, she read over and over her notes so that as soon as she got to a computer she was ready to sit alone with the door closed and put it all into Times New Roman for the reading.

The nightly readings for her mother—and her dad, when he was home—followed a required reading of at least one *Daily Fact* article. When it was finally time for her own stuff, Millie had one copy for herself and one copy for her mother so she could see the text Millie was reading aloud.

Millie stood in the living room and read her stories night after night, year after year, and her mother never went a single night without offering "constructive criticism."

> Wilma Mezrich, grade four, said her parent's made her 14-year-old brother, who's name is Leonard Mezrich, quit school and lie about his age to work overnight at InSystem...

"Watch your apostrophes to avoid creating possessives out of plurals, Millicent," her mother said. "And before bed tonight, please research the difference between 'who's' with an apostrophe and w-h-o-s-e. As a fourth grader, you should already know this. And, Millicent," her mother said, lighting a cigarette with her back to her, "this is an intriguing story."

> Erma Banks grade four, saying her uncle said her 21-year-old cousin died of a secret operation. Erma, she whispered to her very best friend, who's name is Chastity Yarbrough, that it must be "some kind of spy thing"...

"Have you been watching television news?" her mother said. "Your grammar is suddenly atrocious."

"'Some kind of spy thing,'" her dad laughed. "That's why I love kids, Katie. See?"

Her mother said, "Never underestimate the value of a properly placed comma, and please straighten out your 'who's' versus your 'whose.' Do you know what an abortion is, Millicent?"

> Shirley Knight, grade five, ~~told~~ confessed to Lenny Mabary during art hour that she was the one who poured a coffee poop stain onto Mr. Snapper's yellow swivel chair because it was the only way she could see the school guidance counselor because he was always too busy...

Her mother blew smoke to the side and tapped her ashes. "A nice use of 'confessed,' but your sentence is too long. Is fifth grade when you learn conjunctions?"

"Yes." Millie wished her dad could have heard her use of the word 'confessed.' She asked where he was.

"Wherever he says he is, Millicent."

> Gerald Beaman, grade five said his 11th grade sister stole the
> family car and disappeared last week. He said his sister left a weird
> note in their mom's makeup bag about a "dirty little thing named
> Mary down by the river"...

"What the hell is wrong with people?" Her dad flung out his hands and
accidentally knocked his beer off the coffee table. Instead of cleaning it up,
he went outside and slammed the door. Millie heard his car start up and
roar down the driveway.

"You missed a comma," her mother said. She moved the table away
from the wet spot. "Do you know what incestuous rape is, Millicent?"

> Floyd Lowe, grade five, brought a bag of fruit candy for lunch
> again and tried to trade it like he always does for someone's
> sandwich or apple, but no one wanted to trade with him anymore.
> Floyd got in trouble for taking all the milks and drinking them in
> the project corner during research...

"You still have milk provided in fifth grade? I wonder whether
Margaret had something to do with that."

Millie hoped her mother wouldn't ask her to make that a story, because
she didn't care why they got milk.

"Continue," her mother said.

> Chuck Hill, grade five, told Mr. Snapper he got the cut on his
> mouth because he lives in an old house with wood floors that pop
> up and whack him on his face and trip him at the top of the stairs...

"If what you mean to write is that the floors are attacking this Chuck
Hill, you could be clearer. And Chuck Hill did not tell Mr. Snapper about
the cut because he lives in an old house, as could be inferred from your
wording. Nor does Chuck Hill have the cut because he lives in an old
house. He has the cut because (ostensibly) wood planks in the old house
pop up and hit him in the face."

> Louise Berg, grade six, said her new baby sister was kid-
> napped by aliens...

Her mother lit a cigarette even though one was already burning in the ashtray. "Can you think of a better word than 'kidnapped'?"

"Abducted? I was gonna use—"

"Do you mean you were going to?"

"I was *going* to use abducted, but everyone says 'abducted by aliens.' Anyway, I don't think she was abducted," Millie said. "No one does."

"Yes, well. One never knows."

"Everyone thinks she was dropped. She must have been really ugly or stupid, or something, because Louise's parents kept Louise, so why not—"

"Move on, please, Millicent."

> Frank Andrews, grade six, said doctors killed his sister, whose in grade nine, because they wanted her to have a living baby. Andrews said, "Since she was older than the baby, that's why they let her die, instead"...

"You are in sixth grade. I refuse to draw your attention once more to 'who's' versus 'whose.' And the appropriate phrase would be 'a live birth.'"

> Bernie Merritt, grade six, told Geraldine Tanner, grade six, that his mother went to life in prison—

"Received a sentence of life in prison," her mother said.

> —after she had her dead baby because doctors found aspirins in her blood. He said his mom gets bad headaches just like he does but no one believed her...

And so on.

If while Millie was reading her mother unintentionally smiled and then ran to the kitchen for a cigarette, Millie knew that particular story was one of her better ones and saved the printed copy in a special file labeled "Mom." (She folded an index card over the label in case her mother went into her closet for something. She never did). As rare as the smiles were, Millie had, in a way, grown used to them. But the last week—the *final* week—of seventh grade, Millie managed to write something that made her mother do something completely diff...something *queer*.

The story was about Wilma's brother, Leonard, who still showed up after school a few times a week before going in for his shifts at InSystem. Usually he just wanted to hang out with kids his own age, but the last time he came he'd bragged about having information on some "secret project." Leonard said he got to hear a lot more of what was being said around the plant now that he was on the floor ("I'm one of the people putting the initial component on the line, so the whole thing starts with me, pretty much," he said a few times). Just the day before, he said, he'd heard someone walking through the plant tell someone else that the chip they'd been manufacturing was for people. "Like, to go inside them."

"One guy said something 'fail-safe' this or something 'fail-safe' that, so it's probably for escaped prisoners, or something," he said.

Millie wasn't even finished reading, yet, when her mother said, "A *scoop*," and came around the table, her arms raised toward Millie the way her dad's would be when he was about to hug her. But Millie had no idea what her mother could have been doing, so, without thinking, she stepped away.

Her mother whipped her hands behind her back and kept them there until she got to the kitchen and reached up to her cabinet. Looking at the flame as she lit her cigarette in front of the refrigerator, she said so low Millie almost didn't hear her, "Well done."

That summer between grades seven and eight was the first time Millie wanted to write during vacation. Her mother's reaction to Wilma's brother's story had buzzed her with a frantic need to produce more, present more, make her mother smoke her brains out. But there wasn't much to write about if she couldn't use—*utilize*—the kids at school.

For a few days she followed her mother around the house to try to write about her, but her mother never did anything but eat cranberry muffins and smoke in the morning, go to work, and come home to smoke and drink wine. (She wouldn't want a story about herself, anyway. It wouldn't be new information.) And when her mother brought her to Lenny's house and stayed to hang out—*socialize*—with Lenny's mom, Millie couldn't get anything interesting out of them, either. The adults either stayed in her aunt Margaret's office, whose door was too thick to listen through, or they went for a drive and left Millie and Lenny at home with her uncle Ernie, who'd make them pick tomatoes from the patch out back.

Murphy died that June, but everyone knew it was coming, so that wasn't a story, either.

The only one left was her dad.

FOURTEEN

Lenny stayed as far away from Millie as she could in elementary school.

At first it was because Millie always had to beat everyone to the classroom so she could sit in a desk up front. It was hard to write on the floor or against the wall, so most kids would fight for almost any kind of table top, but no one except Millie wanted the front row desks. She ran in every day and threw her backpack at a chair to get a spot before someone else could, and even though no one really wanted to sit there, everyone still hated her seat saving.

One day in second grade, someone Millie really bugged got to class before Millie did and threw their own backpack so that it landed on the floor right in front of her as she came whizzing into the room. Millie tripped over it and flew through the air with her arms and legs straight out, then landed on her face at the same time as her lunch box hit the floor. It bounced open next to Mr. Unger's desk, and a green apple, carrot sticks, yogurt, and a wrapped sandwich fell out. Lenny saw it all happen from where she was standing in the back of the room and thought she should do something. She just didn't know what. Millie was already on the floor, so she couldn't really stop it from happening.

A boy named Floyd went for Millie's sandwich, but he jerked the other way when Millie moved her arms.

"Crap, she's not dead," one kid said.

Lenny whispered to Floyd, "I can share my lunch with you, if you want."

Floyd looked at her and went to the other side of the room.

Millie got up. The only mark on her face was a little red rug spot on her chin. She started picking up her food.

Another kid said, "Someone shoulda dropped her on the side of the road when she was a baby."

Millie didn't seem to hear any of it as she grabbed at her carrots.

Lenny said, "Stop being so m—"

Mr. Unger lumbered into the room in his mustard yellow jersey and baggy tan pants, and Lenny immediately took a seat. She was the only one who did, but that was the way it was in Mr. Unger's class. If there was anyone everyone liked less than they liked Millie, it was Mr. Unger, and even Mr. Unger didn't like Millie. He stepped over her apple on the way to his desk and used the toe of his ratty flat shoe to roll it away from him. "Come on," he whined. "Get this cleaned up. Everyone sit down. Come on, now, sit down."

No one sat. They just whispered and giggled while Millie crawled after her apple. Lenny didn't say anything to them this time, but she did go to Principal Well after school to tell on Mr. Unger.

"Thank you, Margaret Mabary's daughter," Ms. Well said, but Mr. Unger was still there in the morning.

By fifth grade, Lenny was still staying away from Millie, but she tried not to be around pretty much everyone else, too. *Elmore and Lenore Steal the Light* was on its third printing, and her mamma—her *mom*, her *mom*—was famous again. Everyone already knew Lenny's family had money, but her mom's book reminded them, and they didn't like it very much. No matter how small Lenny tried to make herself by staying quiet in class (and keeping away from people like Millie), they still noticed her and came for her. Twice she had her backpack stolen. Some of the boys stared at her and pretended to gag when she passed them in the hallways. Others ignored her in that way that made sure she knew they were ignoring her.

To make up for her family's money, Lenny stopped sitting in desks on Mondays and Wednesdays, even though it was her turn in the rotation. There were kids in her class who probably didn't have anything at all to sit on at home. Some of them only got to be in school in the first place because Lenny's mom paid enough money to make up for the parents in town who didn't have any. (A lot of those kids didn't like Lenny for that, too. "Thanks to Loser Lenny's mom, not only do we have to go to school, but we have a school to go to.")

She didn't mind not sitting at her desk. It was more fun to be by the table in the project corner, where there was always something to look at when the teacher was boring. One girl, Wilma Jenkins, had cut up cereal boxes to make a model of her house for a "Role of Money" activity in social studies. Miniature cutouts of her mom and dad stood in an office with a calendar on the wall, and tiny little stacks of green paper flowed out of a cash box on big brown desk. Her brother slept on a toothpick bed in a small corner room with the curtains closed. Cardboard Wilma stood in front of the house wearing really short shorts and the brightest red lipstick Lenny had ever seen. She had an arm up that seemed to be waving at a blue plastic car parked on a gray tile road. Lenny's favorite part was the kitchen, because it had a little dog in it standing by a food bowl behind the safety gate.

Another project she liked was one by a boy named Gerald Beaman. He hardly said anything in class, so everyone was surprised when they saw his current events painting that was supposed to "demonstrate how current events relate to personal life." Gerald painted a game of living room hide-and-seek in deep reds and yellows. It was so good everyone could tell it was Gerald sitting on the couch and his sister hiding behind it, and that the man coming down the stairs was his dad. (They all knew what his dad looked like because he picked Gerald up from school every day.) Gerald got an F on the project because he didn't have an article to go with it, but he said to Mr. Snapper, "So if some stupid writer isn't writing about it, it's not happening? I don't care if it's on the internet or not, it's a goddamn current event." Everyone gasped, and Mr. Snapper raised the grade to a D+.

The project corner was also safe from Millie. Most kids sat against the wall or near the computers, so that was where Millie sat now. Lenny could see everything from the project corner, including Millie. If it looked like Millie might come back to talk to her about something, Lenny found a reason to go up front to ask the teacher a question. That hardly ever happened, though, because Millie was usually too busy crawling around with her notebook and tilting her ear at people. She'd always look at the teacher while she wrote with that one ear tilted like she was taking lecture notes, but Lenny had seen Millie's notes in the car on the way home after school and knew she was writing about their classmates and not the class subject. Millie never showed Lenny her notes on purpose or talked about any of the kids, and none of the things Lenny saw in Millie's notebook got around school, but it bothered her, anyway.

"So what if she tilts her ear?" Her popp—Her *dad* used a spoon to take vegetables out of a heating sauce.

"Oh, sweetie, you're much too concerned with what Millie does." Her mom fed Murphy one of the scooped out carrots. "You just have to let people be who they are."

"If the people she's listening to don't like it," her dad said, "they'll let her know."

Lenny didn't want her family to be a part of Millie's notes any more than she wanted to be in them, herself, so when Millie was over after school, Lenny watched the office door where Millie did her typing. If she finished and came out of the room while Lenny's parents were talking, Lenny took her out to the tomatoes or ran ahead to her parents to stop their conversation. She didn't want Millie to know about how someone had stabbed her mom's tires while she was in the pet food store, or that people kept trying to destroy her dad's houses. Those were what her dad called "private family matters."

She got so used to saving her parents' private matters from Millie's nosy pen that soon she was hiding around corners or at the top of the stairs to listen to them even when Millie wasn't over. A lot of times she'd hear her dad helping her mom with problems in her stories. Other times it was boring publishing contract stuff, or boring house building stuff, and sometimes they put on the music and Lenny peeped in on them dancing.

One night, though, Lenny heard through the end of Glenn Miller's "Pennsylvania 6-5000" that someone had vandalized her dad's new Grant Street house by spray painting a stick figure dangling over a biting tiger.

"It was a great tiger," he said. "I ought to take a picture and show it to Bev. The tattoo could go right here."

Her mom laughed, but Lenny didn't think it was funny, at all, and stomped through the open door.

Her dad got up from the couch. "What's up, Pup?"

She ran to him and threw her arms around his waist. "Why does everybody hate us?"

"Because we're so damn wonderful," he said. He tucked his feet under hers and swirled her around to "The Woodpecker Song."

Her mom said, "They don't hate us, sweetheart. How can they? They don't even know us."

"What do you mean 'us,' anyway?" Lenny's dad tapped her head to make her look up at him. "I thought your mom and I were special. You're telling me they hate you, too? Who? Who could hate you?"

"Everyone in the fifth grade hates me. Almost as much as they hate Millie, but Millie's a brat, and I don't do anything."

"Oh, Lenny, that's no way to talk about your friend," her mom said.

"But it's true. Nobody likes her because she's weird. And she's not my friend. She's—"

"Lenore Katherine Mabary," her mother said with a hand guiding Lenny to sit with her on the couch. Her dad sat at her mom's swivel chair behind the desk and turned down the music.

"All right," her mom said. "Let's say, for the sake of argument, that Millie is weird."

"Millie is weird."

"Ernie."

"Well, Mox."

"You're ten, now," she said, "which means you're old enough to keep a secret. Right?"

Lenny nodded.

All the way through her mom's lecture, which felt like it took half an hour, her dad swiveled and rolled around in the desk chair to the faint music coming from the ceiling. Any time Lenny looked over to see what he was doing, he pointed at her mom and mouthed, "Pay attention." A few minutes later the music would send him into a full spin and he'd hold his arms out like a ballerina, distracting her all over again. When she was paying attention, though (and she mostly was), Lenny learned things about Millie she never knew—that Millie almost wasn't Millie because she almost wasn't born, and that once Millie was born, her mom tried to give her to different parents.

"Like who?" Lenny said.

"I don't know."

"Anyone," her dad said.

"Aunt Kat and Uncle Graham were going to *drop* Millie?" Lenny said.

"Aunt Kat did drop Millie, sweetie," her mom said. "But she went back for her."

Lenny said, "Why?"

"Ernie," her mom snapped, "don't you dare say any—"

"I wasn't going to say a word." But he did ask Lenny how she knew about drops.

"I don't know," she shrugged. "Everyone knows."

Everyone did know, but no one talked about drops unless they happened to people outside of school. If someone in school was a shelter drop or an adopted drop or had a dropped brother or sister, it was one of the things no one teased about. It was like if a kid came to class with burn marks or something broken. Everyone knew what it was, but even the meanest kids went by the rule that it was something you didn't ask about no matter how fake the stories sounded.

"Millie doesn't know what happened," her mom said. "And she never will, Lenore. But it's possible that on some level she senses it. Or that she senses something, at least."

"What you call weird, we adults call damaged," her dad said.

They made Lenny promise with both hands on her heart to never tell Millie what she knew, and then they reminded her (again) that it was all thanks to Millie's mom that Lenny was alive (because of "so, so much snow," and Lenny's "nonconformist entrance into the world," and on and on…). The very least they could do as a family, her mom said, was to always be kind—"and loyal, Lenore"—to her aunt Kat's daughter in return.

"There are reasons people are the way they are," her mom said. "That goes for every one of your classmates you say is rude to you. Get to know them, and you'll see."

Lenny did what her mom said. She started small, by taking back her desk rights on the days she fell on the rotation. After that, she practiced looking people in the eye. By sixth grade, she could smile at some of them. The first one to smile back was Louise Berg, so when Louise said her sister was abducted by aliens and everyone else got quiet, Lenny felt strong enough to be kind. She told Louise that so many people talked about alien abductions it must mean they happened more than anyone thought, and she asked if Louise had seen any bright lights. (Millie tilted her ear at them and wrote in her notebook.)

By seventh grade, instead of listening to conversations in secret the way Millie did, Lenny chose spots on the floor right next to the kids who scared her the most. All she said to start was, "Hi, how are you," but her interest caught one boy so off guard that a sputtering sob flew out of him before he could catch it. He called Lenny a stupid taint-berry and bolted out of the room.

A lot of her other classmates said things like, "Fine, freak," or, "What do you care," but she learned that year after slowly getting them to talk that almost half of her classmates really were fine, and the rest didn't want to know why she cared. They were just glad she did.

When summer vacation between seventh and eighth came, she left school for the first time feeling good about coming back the next year.

FIFTEEN

The more she thought about it that summer, the more Millie knew her dad would make a perfect story. When he wasn't at home, he was at work, he said. By itself, that wasn't something her mother would call interesting, but Millie didn't know exactly what he did there, so it would be new information to her. And since her mother had said "I don't know" more than once when Millie had asked what was taking so long for him to come home, there was new information to give her mother, too.

She decided to collect her notes in secret the way she did at school. Her dad probably would have let her follow him around if she asked, but she noticed at school that when people caught her watching or listening they stopped doing what they were doing, or they did what they were doing in a different way. Millie wanted to see her dad—*observe* her dad—just being himself.

Her chance came one late June night after dinner when he ran upstairs for his shoes.

"Can you believe I forgot to set the alarm again?" he said, huffing out of sight.

Millie slipped outside while her mother stared up the stairway. She climbed into the trunk of his car and double-checked her pockets for her reporter's notebook and favorite ballpoint. She had everything.

The car bounced when her dad hopped in, and her elbow banged the back seat when he zipped into reverse. The ride was sweaty and bumpy and long, and her notes were sloppy and smudged, but the story she got was one she believed her mother would like.

Appreciate.

Millie wrote the majority of the piece the next day on her uncle Ernie's computer while he and Lenny were out…*gawking*…at the tomato patch and her aunt Margaret was writing in her own office. She finished and printed the story at home that night on her bedroom computer, excited that both her parents were home to hear it. And she knew for a fact her dad would be staying home, because a reporter from the *Daily Fact* was coming at seven to interview her mother about her fourth store. He was so excited he'd closed the new store early.

Millie grabbed the article when the print finished and went downstairs to get the *Daily Fact* reading out of the way. The shortest story she could find was a brief about a 25-year-old activist named Frankie Justice…

> …arrested today outside of the *This Morning* studios. Justice leaped over the barriers during the meet-the-audience portion of the program's outdoor segment and pushed aside host Delia Buckworth before demanding into the camera that lawmakers increase the penalty for "dropping," or abandoning, children. Members of the studio's security team promptly seized Justice and confirmed Buckworth was unharmed. Justice has been a familiar face to law enforcement since his first known forced press conference, incidentally outside the same studio, when as a fifteen-year-old he pleaded with authorities to find his two-and-a-half-year-old brother. Justice claimed, and to this day maintains, that sex traffickers seized his brother from his arms while the two waited in line for kettle corn at the Windbury farmers market.

Her mother absently reached out to take back the paper when Millie finished, and Mille picked up her own typed, formatted, and printed article. She read quickly, because it was almost seven:

"Newchester resident Graham Harrison, forty-one, is a good Samaritan in disguise. By—"

"Slow down, Millicent." Her mother smiled, but at him. "A good Samaritan, Graham?"

"Yes," Millie said. "A good Samaritan in disguise. By day, the Oxford Spirits co-owner—"

"President," her mother corrected.

"I'm really more of a CEO," her dad winked.

"President," her mother repeated. "If you like, COO. Always check your facts, Millicent."

"Yes, Mother. By day, the Oxford Spirits COO juggles many jobs— ugh! *tasks*—such as watching the front counter and listening to customer complaints. His job doesn't end there, though. I mean, *however.* When the work day is done, Mr. Harrison—"

"Do you know, Millicent, I think you should avoid honorifics."

"When the work day is done," Millie said, "Harrison gets into his car to make deliveries to customers who can't leave home. One night after eating his dinner, Harrison drove ten miles—I guessed because I really don't know and I didn't want to ask because I wanted to surprise you—and then got out of his car with a bottle of…vodka, Dad? It looked like that one bottle, but it was hard to get out of the trunk in time to see for sure. You were already going up the walk."

Her dad cleared his throat and nodded. Her mother took her hand off her dad's knee.

"A bottle of vodka. When he came out of the building—"

"Emerged."

"Huh?"

Her mother spoke louder. "Emerged. You can replace three words with two if you use 'emerged from' rather than 'came out of.'"

"Oh. Oh!" Millie ran to the kitchen for a pen and raced back into the living room, dropping to her knees at the coffee table to make the note on her page. She stood again. "When he emerged from the building about thirty minutes later, Harrison didn't have the bottle, anymore, and he looked messy and wrinkled, leading this reporter to…decide?"

"Conclude," her mother whispered.

"To conclude that after making the delivery he helped someone do work around the house."

Millie looked over for approval at the precise moment the vomit sprayed out of her mother's mouth. It splattered on the coffee table, covering Millie's pen and the *Daily Fact*. Her dad jumped off the couch.

"I'll get a towel," he said. "Millie, get your mother—"

"Get me nothing, Millicent. Thank you."

"I can help," Millie said.

Her mother wiped her chin with her sleeve. She used her free hand to hold onto the couch.

Millie dropped her article on the floor and ran to the kitchen, calling over her shoulder, "I'll get you a warm washcloth and a cranberry muffin! Okay? Don't go anywhere, okay?" She found a clean dish rag in the drawer by the stove and ran it under warm water. There were no muffins left in the bread box, so she pulled out a slice of marbled rye. She hurried with it and the warm dish rag to the living room, but her mother was already gone. There was only her dad, gagging and turning away from the table he swept and scooped at with Millie's favorite orange beach towel.

Millie rushed past him, jumped over her article, and went upstairs to her parents' bedroom. The door was closed.

She tapped on the center wood panel. She tapped again. "Mother?" She held her breath, closed her eyes, and rested her hand on the cool glass doorknob until it warmed in her palm and the bread flattened between her fingers and the dish rag hanging over her wrist turned cold. She puffed her cheeks with air, held onto it, and released it in a slow stream as she turned the handle. It caught abruptly after a fraction of a twist. Locked.

"Mother?"

The bed creaked.

"I have some bread and a dish r—and a...and a washcloth. I can warm it up again."

"No, thank you, Millicent."

"Are you sick?"

After a moment, she said, "Something like that."

"I'm sorry." Millie molded the dish rag to her forehead. It was cold and damp and felt good. "Is it because of my story?"

"Millicent, please put on something nice for when the reporter comes. I want you to sit downstairs with us and listen carefully to her questions. Do you ever speak to the subjects of your stories? Do you ever ask them direct questions?"

"No."

"You should be doing that by now."

"Okay." Millie's stomach rolled at the words before she pushed them out: "I love you, Mother."

The only reply was the sound of the bed creaking again. Millie imagined her mother turning away from the sound of her voice.

Lenny's mom would have told Lenny to come in.

On her way down the stairs, Millie saw her dad lying on the couch with an arm folded over his eyes. The coffee table was clean and bare. She returned the bread to the bread box and draped the rag over the kitchen faucet to dry, then went out to the living room and lay on top of her warm dad with her head on his chest.

"Bad timing, Millie girl. I was just about to get up."

Millie lifted her head to look at him. His eyes were still hidden under his arm. She said, "Does she love me?"

"Sure she does! Does who love you?"

"Mother."

"Oh! Well, she's your mother, isn't she?"

"Did you like my story?"

He peeked at her from under his elbow. "Highly impactful." He smiled. "But you know your mother is a much better judge of that kind of thing. Now, roll on off, silly Millie. I need to wait for the doorbell."

"Millicent," her mother's voice said from the top of the stairs. "Clothes, please."

Millie ran up the stairs. She chose something black and white and was pulling on her pants when the doorbell rang. She hurried back down to find her mother and the reporter sitting on one couch, her dad on the other. Lemon wedges floated in the water glass each woman held in her lap. Millie sat next to her dad and smiled at the reporter, who smiled back.

"Nellie, this is Millicent. Millicent, Nellie."

Nellie was twenty-three, at Millie's best guess. She wore black and white, too, and sat with a straight back. Millie straightened her own back. Nellie had long hair that she tucked behind her ears. Millie unconsciously tucked her own frizzy hair behind her ears. The reporter's name was Nellie. Millie's name was Millie. Nellie and Millie.

"Okay to begin?" Nellie said.

"One moment, please. Millicent, where's your notebook?"

When Millie returned from her bedroom, flushed from all the stairs and gripping her notebook and ballpoint, the interview began. After talking about how Millie's mother got into the liquor business ("With trepidation, initially, but counting on humanity's reliable affection for mind altering substances in times of difficulty. The overturn was all but decided when I rented my first storefront, you see.") and Millie's dad's role at the store ("In flux."), the reporter looked at her notebook and said, "What can you tell me about your security system?"

"What would you like to know?"

"Your fourth store is located in a...well, a troubled neighborhood, and—"

"Every neighborhood is troubled."

Nellie tilted her head. "How so?"

Millie tilted her own head and mouthed, "How so?"

Her mother said, "Are you wealthy, Nellie?"

Nellie said she was probably middle-middle-class.

Millie whispered to her dad, "What's middle-middle-class?" and he shushed her with his elbow.

"And are you fertile?" her mother asked Nellie.

"No."

"You sound relieved."

"Oh, yes," Nellie said.

"But you could easily afford a child."

"Easily enough."

"Then you understand why every neighborhood is troubled. In its own way."

The reporter wrote something. "How do you deal with drops?"

Millie's mother glanced in Millie's direction without making eye contact.

"Cameras," her mother said. "Signs. Bright lights. As it turns out, probably a complete waste of money for the new store."

"Because of chipping."

"Yes." Her mother did look at Millie, then, and told Nellie that "a twelve-year-old-child" had actually come across the information first, that Millie had "scooped" the *Daily Fact*.

Nellie smiled at Millie. "We aren't even sure whether or when it will actually be implemented."

"No?"

"No one's saying. I'll put it that way. Though I don't see the harm in it, personally. I think it makes sense to have their basic information on them at all times in case they find themselves lost or otherwise…mislocated."

"Lovely. In any case, had I had more foresight, I could have avoided spending quite so much money. Why install drop surveillance when the drops are apparently going to be walking names and addresses?"

"They say chipping could save thousands of children. What do you think about that?"

"Save them from what, exactly?"

"The shelters."

"The expensive shelters, I think you mean. Expensive for the government to build and maintain."

Nellie nodded while drinking her water. She wiped her mouth, and said, "Very."

"And those children will now be returned to the same parents who released them."

Nellie kept her pen over her paper. Millie thought Nellie's pen looked too fat. Millie preferred narrow pens.

"Is there something more you would like me to say?" Millie's mother said.

"Oh, I'm—Was that it, then? You're pro-chipping because it can save businesses money on their security systems?—I'm sorry, I'm supposed to get something. My editor. You're a figure."

Millie's mother rubbed her glass, then plucked the lemon wedge from her water and hurled it at Millie's dad. It stuck to his neck. He peeled it off and set it on his knee. Millie smacked her hands to her mouth and snorted through her fingers.

"All right," Millie's mother said. "How about this. By the time my daughter is old enough to have your job, the consequences of chipping will still be feeding the *Daily Fact*, and in ways neither you nor I can foresee."

Nellie finished writing almost as soon as Millie's mother stopped talking. She closed her notebook. "Thank you, Ms. Oxford."

Millie's dad got up to help her mother walk Nellie to the door, but something her mother did must have changed his mind, because he sat right down again.

SIXTEEN

Lenny waited until the end of the day, when almost everyone else was out catching buses, to strap on the extra backpack she'd packed that morning and go looking for Floyd. She'd saved him for last because he wasn't mean like the others. He could look mean, sometimes—his small face was pointy and pale, his wide lips frowny—but he was polite and never tried to get in trouble with teachers.

When she found him, his long, skinny body was bent halfway in the trash can next to the second floor elevator.

He kept digging even when she stood next to him. "Hold this."

He gave her an unopened coconut yogurt that wouldn't fit in his stuffed pockets, dug around some more, then took back the yogurt and headed to the stairs.

"Wait," she said, but he didn't.

Short sleeves draped loosely around his arms, which were narrow everywhere but at his jutting elbows. Lenny imagined his poor bones clacking around inside his skin, where there didn't seem to be anything to soften the spaces in between.

She went down the stairs after him while pulling the sandwich container from her bag. She opened it and used the flat top to fan the smell at him. A student volunteer coming up the roped side of the stairs plucked a crude poster from the wall, a pen sketch of a rat…doing it…with a girl on her back and a bunch of little rats making a trail around her. She added it to the stack in her arms. "Yuck, onions," she said and wrinkled her face, but Floyd stopped on the third to last stair and stuck his nose in the air and closed his eyes.

They sat on the worn couch in the main floor lobby. Floyd grabbed the only sandwich with onions and ate it without talking. He'd asked Lenny for it right away, but all the way to the lobby she'd held the container out of reach, switching hands every time he bounced around her from one side to the other. She would have given it to him right away if she hadn't thought he would take it and run off.

Floyd started on a second sandwich. Lenny watched patiently, happy he wasn't shoving them into his mouth whole. He wiped his face with his wrist when he finished and said, "So, what do you want?"

Lenny's mom had told her once that she should try giving something of herself before asking for trust, so she said, "My dog died." It had been months, but it was something. She shared what little there was of the whole story: The vet had said the cancer would probably kill Murphy by the end of summer, so everyone at home had let him eat and do whatever he wanted until he left his life one night in June. They'd buried him in Lenny's bug cemetery.

Floyd said, "What'd you tell me that for?"

"In case you thought my life was perfect."

"What makes you think I think your life is so perfect?"

Lenny didn't know, really. She'd just always thought everyone thought her life was perfect. And it kind of was, but her dad told her she shouldn't ever say that out loud.

"Maybe because I never get in trouble." She picked up the top to seal the sandwich container, but Floyd put his hand in the way. "Though," she said, "you never get in trouble, either."

Floyd dropped his jaw and zoinked his eyes, making Lenny laugh. He got in trouble all the time, he said, but no one ever saw it because it only happened at home.

"My mom kicks me a lot," he said. "Somehow I'm always in the spot she wants." And if he did something like spill water, his dad would bop him on the head and say they should have dropped him like they did his sister back before the laws changed. "Only reason they didn't is the laws *did* change. My mom's afraid of prison more than anything."

His parents yelled at each other, too, and sometimes it wasn't about Floyd. One thought the other was lazy, or someone got a phone call they couldn't explain in a way the other liked, or someone lost the remote control. Other times, though, most times, it was about Floyd. How he wouldn't be there if Mr. Stumpy Dick didn't always have to stick it somewhere, how if his mom wasn't such a coward they probably could have dropped him at a soccer game and gotten away with it, how it was his fault they had to spend money on him.

"'Thirteen-year-old boys ain't cheap,'" he said in woman-voice. "Last year they said the same thing about twelve-year-old boys, so."

"Then why do you always bring a candy lunch?" she said. "I think an apple or some other fruit costs less than a bag of gummies."

"My dad has nectarines." Floyd picked up another sandwich and took a big bite out of a corner. Mouth full, he said, "But he gets mad even if my mom takes any. One time, she bought two extras just for her, but he kicked her in the stomach, anyway, when he caught her eating one. Thing was, she still had this huge bite in her mouth that got popped out when he kicked her. Flew all the way across the kitchen and pinged him dead on the forehead." Floyd smiled around soggy bread clinging to his teeth. "Didn't end up too good for her, but it was funny for a second." He swallowed the bite, took a deep breath, and stuffed another sandwich corner in his mouth.

"You don't have to eat them all right now," Lenny said. "You can take the rest home."

"Can't."

"Why?"

"Might find 'em."

"So hide them."

"Nah. They're always digging in my room."

"What about outside?"

He stared up at the ceiling, chewing. He nodded. "Yeah. Maybe."

When he finished that sandwich, Floyd said he'd better get home.

Lenny offered to go with him to find a good hiding spot. "I could carry them," she said. "To be safe."

Floyd said didn't she have to go home, or something, but Lenny had already talked to her mom about her plans, so she didn't even need to make a phone call. (And because it was Friday, Millie had taken her own bus home to see her dad before he and Aunt Kat dropped her at Lenny's for the weekend. She didn't tell Floyd that. She didn't want to talk about Millie.)

Floyd said she could walk home with him, if she wanted, but that it was four miles. Lenny led him instead to a nearby streetcar stop and bought both tickets, at first laughing when Floyd said they were going to Haverton.

Lenny and Floyd peeked over a short brick wall outside an open iron gate. His house, two stories of pretty gold wood and tall, arched windows, was almost as big as Lenny's. A stone veranda led to the kind of doors she had only ever seen on churches, and a silver car sparkled in front of the three-car garage set back from the house.

Floyd tugged her sleeve. They made a crouched run for it up the driveway and hid behind the car.

"He jerks off to it," Floyd said, tapping the paint. "No joke. One night I saw him doing it right where you're squatting. Splooged right there."

Lenny snatched her hand off the bumper.

Floyd gave the sign to go and led Lenny to a wide, sculpted hedge decorating the opposite side of the driveway. They huddled behind it, the only thing between them and the wall at the far edge of the property a flat lawn of bright green grass. Floyd clawed into the faded soil at the base of the hedge, squinting through the branches every now and then. Lenny pulled her bag's zipper tab to get the container ready, but Floyd grabbed her wrist.

He held a dirt-caked finger to his lips and pointed with a tip of his head.

Lenny looked through the branches. A tall, lean man in pressed slacks and a black t-shirt bounced down the wide staircase to the car. He got in and backed it out to the street. Floyd didn't let Lenny move or speak until the rumbling of the motor faded.

"Sometimes he comes and gets me when I'm walking," Floyd said.

"That's kind of nice, isn't it?"

He picked up the backpack and held it out to her. "He'll go all the way to the school and look around a little if he doesn't see me, so he'll be gone at least fifteen minutes. Maybe we can find a spot inside. This'd be hard for me at night."

Except for the small white angels Floyd said were suction-cupped year-round to each window, Floyd's living room wasn't much different from Lenny's. Two pillowy couches faced a wide stone projection wall, and a remote control disc sat in the middle of a square coffee table. Dried moisture rings made a flowery cluster on a section closest to the couch. (That was different. Lenny's mom and dad always used coasters.)

Floyd asked for the sandwiches and jammed the container under the couch, then showed Lenny the kitchen. It had a lot of iron and wood, and shiny white counters. Stained glass lights dropped over the island. Like hers at home, the refrigerator had five compartments, but unlike hers it had a stainless steel combination lock built in above the handle.

Lenny noticed, then, that short wire cables painted to match the cabinets wrapped around most of the knobs, their looped ends joined in the middle by combination padlocks also painted to match.

Floyd flipped one of the locks with his dirty finger. He wiped the dirt away with spit. "Food's theirs," he said. "If I want to eat, I have to wait and see who loses the game I call 'Who's feeding Floyd?'"

The loser usually ended up throwing a bag of something at his face or his dick, he said. But it wasn't always candy. It could be a package of dried apricots or a bag of plain potato chips.

Lenny asked what was in the unlocked cabinets.

"Dishes," he said. "But they don't lock the dishwasher, either, so sometimes I'll get to lick the plates after they go to bed. If they didn't already start it, or."

"Really?"

Floyd blushed so hard his eyes turned red. "No, dumb a—" He jerked his head and held up a finger. "Sh," he said and listened, his ear tilted a lot like Millie's. He stretched out his neck and squinted. "He's coming. We have about a minute."

"I don't hear anything."

He wrapped her arm in his long fingers and took her out of the kitchen. "Yeah, well, I do."

"But maybe it'll be better if company is here."

He ran her to the foyer. "Nobody ever comes over. Too many cables to undo. A real pain." He pushed her out the door and told her to hide behind the hedge until his dad was inside.

"If friends can't come here, can you go to their house? You can come over any time," she said.

"How'll I get there? What, you'll pay my way? Forget it." He nudged her down the shallow stone stairs. "Who really gives a shit about anyone, anyway? Thanks for the damn sandwiches."

SEVENTEEN

"Childbirth is an inevitability," said the smiling old woman standing in front of the projection wall. Behind her, babies gliding left to right in a giant slideshow cried in high chairs, ate beige pudding, slept, and performed other ordinary baby activities.

Millie didn't write that down. It wouldn't interest her mother. All she'd recorded so far was the old woman's name (Ms. Oster) and that this was the first Wednesday assembly the school board said grades eight and up had to attend every week to "reduce reproductive behavioral tendencies." Millie felt lucky to be in grade eight. Had the assemblies started last year, she might not have been granted access and would have had no idea what was happening.

She listened into the darkness for something to note, then looked around the auditorium. Almost a thousand eyes, hardly visible in the light bouncing off the wall, watched Ms. Oster. Millie could see smiles and funny looks on the faces of the kids closest to her, but even though they were sharing shoulder bumps and eye rolls, no one was talking. (Millie wanted someone to roll her eyes at, so she looked for Lenny. She'd tried to stay behind her when they filed in so they could sit together, but Millie guessed the crowd had pushed her to another part of the room.)

At some low laughter, Millie watched the projection. Images of things like condoms, saran wrap, and herbs and spices (all labeled—ginger, cinnamon, pennyroyal, parsley, black cohosh) appeared on the wall and faded away, each one taking the place of the one before it.

"Any effort," the Ms. Oster said, "to thwart this inevitability while greedily enjoying the benefits of the reproductive act is worse than irresponsible. It is the immature strategy of a coward and a cheat."

The projection cut off and the room went dark. The auditorium said, "Ooooh."

"Much worse," boomed Ms. Oster's disembodied voice, "is the attempt to deny any unborn, any hopeful soul, the opportunity to enjoy what you enjoy. Who are you to say, 'You are not worthy!'?" A candle wick flamed next to Ms. Oster on the left side of the wall. She had switched places in the dark. Gold lines and curves on the right came into focus a little bit at a time until everyone could tell it was two naked people humping. "Children," Ms.

Oster said, "we do not condone people your age engaging in the terrible, sensual, very bad"—the man slid away from the woman's face to put his head between her legs—"enormously physically gratifying experience you see behi—You! In the front! Get your hand out of there! Teacher, separate those two girls immediately!" The projection turned off. Ms. Oster roared, "Turn it back on!" When the wall came to life again, Mr. Snapper was dragging a girl over people's knees and feet. Ms. Oster stood with her back to the auditorium and watched the golden couple for many minutes. It wasn't until the man took his face away from the woman's vagina that she spun back to the students and then crossed the stage to the flame. "Self-control," Ms. Oster said. "Unless you are a mindless, flea-riddled animal, you possess it. To say you have no self-control is to identify as a grunting, instinct-driven primate." The man on the screen behind her arched his back and stretched his neck and jammed himself hard inside the grabbing, writhing lady underneath him. A girl in the auditorium gasped and moaned.

Millie squirmed and looked away from the projection for something to take notes on while the old woman kept talking. She refused to be interested in sex, whose outcome, her mother had repeatedly told her, was always "the prosaic condition of pregnancy followed by the birth and care of just one of half a million other unremarkable children being birthed around the world every single day."

"But if you do insist that you have no self-control," Ms. Oster said with a finger in the air, "if you are a fertile person and still you behave like a dirty animal, know that you are in effect making a conscious decision to invite a precious being into your life."

"My sister didn't invite hers," yelled someone in the back. "Her manager did. She said he trapped her in his office for six hours."

"Yeah," said someone up front. "My aunt drugged my uncle to get one. Twice."

A voice in the roped-off corner not far from Millie yelled, "I'm dropping mine as soon as I get it out of me!" The girls around her shushed her. Millie thought she heard Ms. Oster mumble, "We'll see."

"I love you, baby!" called a boy from the other side of the room.

"I love you!" the pregnant girl called back.

Millie stood up to try to get a look at the girl, but it was too dark to see details. If what she'd said was true, and if Millie could figure out who she was and watch her and follow her, it could be her first drop story. All she could see in the pregnancy pit, however, was a muted cluster of long hair and loose shirts.

"Even so…Excuse me, children, even so," the old woman said, and it sounded like she was pushing her microphone bead between her lips, "We do not punish the child for the parents' transgressions. *Do we.*"

Angry voices in the auditorium rose up so loud that Ms. Oster's voice disappeared. No one seemed absorbed, anymore, by the humping couple, who looked like they were having seizures. The lady had her legs around the man's behind and dug her fingers deep into his back, and the man squeezed the bed sheet in his fists. Both of their faces looked ugly.

That was another reason Millie doubted she would ever have sex.

Ms. Oster walked off the stage, and everyone stopped screaming at her. The lights came up. Millie pushed past people standing and stretching, using her elbows if she had to, so she could get to the pit.

She was too late. The last two pregnant girls were already leaving through their special door.

On the way out to the buses, Millie heard people wondering out loud about what the next Wednesday assembly might be, but it ended up being the same subject every week, month after month, their teachers taking turns hosting because Ms. Oster hadn't wanted to come back. After the first few weeks, unless it was time for the humping couple, no one paid much attention to the presentation. They used the time to talk or fool around under the bleachers. (Millie didn't write about the bleachers. The one time she tiptoed over there, someone kicked her ankle bone.)

The good—*fortuitous*—thing about each assembly resembling one giant recess was that Millie was able, throughout eighth grade and into ninth, to gather all the notes and quotes she could hope for in the room of a thousand stories.

> …"They said once I turn sixteen they can put me in the database for safety, but I guess I don't mind the illegal ones that come pick me up now," Wilma Mezrich, grade eight, said to a boy who's name is unknown. "There's one that gives me red velvet cupcakes if I wear pigtails. I guess he's my favorite if I have to pick one. My least favorite is the one that doesn't believe I can't get pregnant, but I guess he pays the most. My mom keeps saying I'll get used to the way he does it."

Millie's mother covered her eyes and shook her head. After a while, she told Millie she could go to bed, but before Millie got to her room her mother called up the stairs, "Your 'who's,' Millicent. At thirteen years old, you should know the difference."

Wilma Mezrich's brother, Leonard Mezrich, attended the assembly before his shift at InSystem again this past Wednesday just as he has every Wednesday since the end of last school year. This time he sat beside Marion Whittaker, who is in grade nine but who everyone says hasn't gotten her period. He yelled into her ear that he could tell her a "pretty big secret" about InSystem if she would go with him to the bleachers. She said she would go if he told her the secret first, so Mezrich told Whittaker that everything at InSystem was "crazy" while they wrapped up for an operation that would go out in a press release in a few weeks. "You watch. You'll be standing in line by the end of the month to get a shot into your arm or your supremely gorgeous ass, or wherever," Mezrich said.

Millie's mother lit a cigarette right there in the living room. "The on-going information about InSystem is simply wonderful," she said. "Did you interview this Mezrich boy?"

"No."

"Have you interviewed anyone about anything?"

"No."

"Why not, Millicent?"

Millie didn't want to tell her. She didn't want to know, herself, that no one wanted to talk to her.

But that wasn't the reason. Millie decided who she did and did not want to talk to, and the truth was that she got much better information by listening from the side than she'd ever get from people lying to her face.

"Of course," her mother went on, saving Millie from having to say anything, "as a practice, what seems about to happen is as unfathomable and unethical as it is unavoidable and, sadly, seemingly necessary, but this is a fine story, Millicent."

Millie had never known her mother to talk to her dad about stories he'd missed, but after he came home that night she listened at the stairs and heard them talking about it in the kitchen.

"If they do this," her mother said, "who knows what conditions the children will return to, or what lives some undoubtedly perfectly well-intentioned mothe—parents will be forced to lead?"

"I'm sure it's nothing, Katherine. He's probably just a kid saying whatever he has to say to have sex."

A thick, white cloud crept into the living room from the kitchen. "How nice it must be to have the freedom to be so absolutely cavalier. *Graham*. Speaking of, how is she?"

A window slid up. "Ah! Fresh air, for a change.—Look, if you think it's a real story, why not send it to the *Fact* for her? I'm sure there's enough there for them to look into it. She has first and last names and everything. Our silly Millie is a pretty good reporter, huh?"

The wind pushed a jerking flower of smoke out of the kitchen light. "Her stories are on printer paper without as much as a header. She also obviously still has no personal interactions with her subjects. No one at the *Fact* would take her seriously. Besides," Millie's mother said as Millie slid away from the railing, "the *Fact* will apparently receive a press release in a matter of weeks."

Millie closed the door to her bedroom and stood at the window. She looked way past their acres of weeds bending under the moon.

At school the next day, she skipped lunch to meet with Ms. Well.

"You expect me to trust the children at this school to write something intended for distribution?" Ms. Well's narrow, penciled-on eyebrows rose over her big, black sunglasses. Little slivers of light striped her windows through the blinds. "I'm sure you haven't considered the financials," she said. "Paper and toner and potential litigation."

Millie shook her head.

"Once upon a time we were a peaceful little school, Katherine Oxford's daughter." She smiled. "I bet you thought I didn't know who you were."

"I don't know. No. I'm nobody."

"K through eight. But fifteen years ago, we had to take on four new grades and thirty new teachers. That's minus the seventeen we had to lay off, now. There's financials for you. We also took on six hundred extra students. It would have been seven hundred, but we had to expel over one hundred in the first month. The first month, Katherine Oxford's daughter, and we've expelled at least ten a month ever since. Do you know why?" She flipped out her hand, palm up, and pushed down a finger. "Kids hacking into the fuck database during research hour." She pushed down the next finger. "Kids handing out party balloons and calling them condoms." Another finger, and then another, until she started over from her thumb: "Kids selling black market Plan B, kids doing you-know-what under the bleachers during Wednesday assembly, kids terrorizing pregnant kids, kids taking part in some fool note chain about how to have sexual relations without getting pregnant—all of which but one, by the way, are correct, but how much do you want to bet, Katherine Oxford's daughter, that seventy percent of those pregnant girls had sex that one wrong way?" She waited, then sighed. "Come on, now, how much?"

"Five dollars?"

In a picture on her shelf, Ms. Well in her sunglasses smiled and hugged a girl a few years older than Millie.

"Little girl, we already have far too much to worry about without having to worry about some ninth-grade student starting up some student-written school newspaper." Ms. Well took off her sunglasses and held them in front of her on the desk. Millie couldn't think of anyone who had been allowed to see her eyes before. They were brown. Ms. Well said, "I'm sorry, Millicent."

Millie skipped lunch again the next week to try again. The paper wouldn't count for any kind of credits, she offered. Ms. Well said, "I'm sorry, Millicent." The following week, Millie promised to never write about a teacher. "I truly am sorry, Millicent," Ms. Well said.

The next week, on the Friday before their three-day winter break, Millie tried one last time. She said she would be the only writer, which would *minimize* risk. She would also pay for everything herself—the paper, the printing, and any staples, if needed. (She'd been saving what her mother and dad paid her for doing things like ironing their clothes, dusting their bedrooms—two, now, ever since Millie's dad moved into his office—and washing their cars.) But also, she read from her notes, "As I am now in the ninth grade, it is the school administration's obligation to encourage me to take on new challenges and responsibilities."

Ms. Well never turned away from her monitor, not even when she said, "All right, Millicent."

She had only one requirement, and that was that Millie not write about the chipping rumor.

"We don't want anyone getting excited. Obviously no one in white coats will be here late next week to insert tiny computer chips into your necks," she said. "But what I just said is off the record, you understand?"

By the time school began again on Tuesday, Millie was ready to be the sole writer, senior editor, and publisher of the *Students' Weekly*.

EIGHTEEN

It was hard to find anyone (anyone but Millie, who Lenny knew without having to see her was probably, as always, somewhere right behind her) in the Group A crowd. On stage, where the lines were supposed to start, adults in light purple medical blazers were setting up a row of green chairs that had their own attached side tables. Some of the pregnants had already gotten into their safe section, but the rest of the kids ignored both the chipping stations and the teachers' orders to "choose any one of the markers in front of the stage and fall in single file, please."

Lenny gave up looking for Floyd and tried to find William and Jacob. It helped that they were always together, and it also helped that they were tall, because except for the elementary school kids running around, the auditorium was as crowded and wild as it was for Wednesday assembly. (Or what she remembered of how the assembly was before she'd started skipping it to meet with the Collectors.)

If it weren't for Floyd, who liked helping the abandoned just as much as she did, Lenny never would have thought of Jacob and William for the Collectors.

"They work out and everything," Floyd had said one day after a wriggling little girl named Agnes tried to fight them off. "But also, they eat food. Not that powder and pill stuff, or. They're strong for real. One in each van could help with the tough ones."

Lenny stood on her toes and finally saw William and Jacob eating apples near the water table all the way on the other side of the room. She politely shoved through her classmates, stood on her toes again, thought she lost them, found them standing in the same spot when someone moved, and pushed through again. William and Jacob were upperclassmen, and because she would never miss a Wednesday Collectors' meeting, Lenny didn't know when she'd see them again if she didn't get them now. She had to talk to them before everyone was told for the real last time to get in line.

She got to the red ropes of the pregnant line and almost ducked a shortcut underneath, but any non-pregnant seen entering the pregnant zone would be suspended. (A few of the girls who weren't pregnant anymore had gathered there, but they were carrying babies who would be in the basement nursery any other day but today. The rule was that any parent carrying a baby also had to stand in the zone.) Most of the girls had their heads down, but one bounced her baby fast as she searched the auditorium.

Lenny guessed she was looking for an eleventh grader named Orville. He was the only boy in school with hair that matched the thick orange tuft on the baby's head.

"I think I saw him over by the bleachers," Lenny said. She pointed.

"Huh?"

"If you're looking for Orville, I think he's over there." She pointed again in the general direction.

"Right. Thanks."

The girl never looked at her. She just bounced and bounced, slowly backing through the pregnant line.

When Lenny made it past the ropes, Millie's voice filled her ear. "Did she appear nervous to you?"

Lenny jumped.

"She did to me," Millie said. "Do you think she plans to drop it? Is it possible she can? I wonder if—*whether*—there's a way out of here for people like her." She looked around the auditorium.

"I don't know," Lenny said, not thinking about it either way because William and Jacob were moving.

She pressed forward with Millie behind her until she was standing in front of the boys, her nose at their chests. Lenny looked up at them and invited them to a quiet corner, then told them about the Collectors and why she needed them to volunteer.

She stepped a little closer and stood on her toes to say, "But you can't tell anyone, okay?" She knew Millie had heard it all, but she also knew Millie wasn't a gossip. The most she would do is write her notes and put them wherever she put the rest of them.

"We're not agreeing to anything, but suppose we did," Jacob said. "Why can't we tell anyone?"

Lenny looked over her shoulder at the rest of the pregnants stuffing themselves between the ropes. The one who'd been looking for Orville was gone.

"We just think it's better if they don't know they have someone to go to, if you know what I mean," Lenny said.

Jacob nodded. "Yeah. Well, I guess it sounds—"

William said, "Nah. No, thanks. C'mon, Jake."

He pulled Jacob to leave, but they got stuck in line in front of Lenny and Millie when an announcement ordered everyone to line up "immediately, right where you are, unless you are pregnant or accompanying a child and are not in your designated area, in which case, please move right now to your designated area or face expulsion. Voices down while waiting, please. Once again, if you are eighteen or older and your class is Group A, you are excused from this procedure and are to report to the cafeteria for silent study."

A new voice, soft and soothing, took over.

"Chipping is not a violation," he said from the recessed speakers. "Chipping is for your protection. For sixteen years, children of all ages, children just like you, have been abandoned on street corners, drowned in our state river, transported cross-country and left to starve, or sold to sex traffickers and made to suffer unconscionable indignities and imaginative ab—er, unimaginable abuse. Let not one more young citizen be left behind." The sound of multiple swallows, and then a soft thud and a throat-clearing. "Removing an implanted chip is a federal offense punishable by up to ten years in prison. Chipping is not a violation. Chipping is for your protection. For sixteen years..."

The line moved forward, but Lenny was tugged back. She felt Millie's chin on her shoulder blade.

"I could have told you they would say no," Millie said. "I can help."

William and Jacob had only one interest, Millie said. They wanted to fly for the military. What she'd learned from the *Daily Fact*, and what she thought William and Jacob may not know, was that all military branches were nearing "peak saturation levels" and had "become highly selective." People like Jacob and William, who wanted to join after graduation, needed "unique altruistic extracurriculars."

Millie said, "If you let me ride with you and write about your drops, I'll secure their services for you."

"Why do you want to write about the dr—the abandoned children?"

"What difference does it make? Do you want them or don't you?"

Lenny and Millie caught up with the line, and with William and Jacob. They were close enough to the stage to see all seven stations.

Sylvia, whose mom was in prison for throwing Sylvia's infant brother against a wall and into a coma, didn't blink at the needle going into the base of the right side of her neck. (That didn't mean the injection didn't hurt. Sylvia had come to school with a broken nose and a dislocated shoulder, so a shot probably felt like nothing.) Lenny stood on her toes to see how a regular kid like Herman did. He squinted through and after the shot, but he seemed surprised when the purple jacket tapped him to get him out of the chair.

Only three people were in line ahead of William and Jacob.

Lenny touched Jacob's back. "The ones already on the street won't have ID chips to get them home," she told him. "You'd be doing a good deed.—Um," she looked at Millie, "unique altruism."

William shook the back of his head at them. "You talk like drops are some kind of charity case, or something."

"They are," Millie said.

William spun on her.

"Oh!" Millie sort of smiled. "How old were you?"

"How old was I what?"

Millie sighed. "Fine. Well, all I mean is that, yes, the military will classify it as charity work, but a completely new and different kind of charity work, which is precisely what you need if you hope to be accepted."

Jacob was looking down at Lenny in a way that made her neck warm. Floyd was the only one who had ever done that. She switched her attention to Millie, who was now shining her light blue eyes at Jacob. Millie moved even closer to him, wedging herself right between him and Lenny.

"Listen, William," Millie said while smiling and blinking at Jacob. "And Jake." Jacob lowered his eyebrows. "It isn't merely your strength that has value. You have so much more to offer. If you've ever felt neglected or abandoned," she looked at William, then, "for even one second, you can relate to these children in a way no one else can."

She went on to talk about the benefits of William's and Jacob's "superior wisdom as upperclassmen" and, granted, their "impressive physical strength," all of which, she said like a breathless, romance-scene actress, "are a perfect fit for this conveniently timed invitation to participate in a legitimately unique volunteer opportunity that will have any military branch clamoring for you."

"Why do you talk like that, freak?" William said.

Millie didn't move, but her body got somehow smaller. Lenny thought she might cry. Instead, she stiffened her back and got at least an inch taller.

"There's nothing wrong with the way I speak," Millie said, "but if you want me to dumb it down for you, dro—William, Duh. Duh duh, duh—"

Lenny said with a hand on Millie's arm, "You don't have to like the way Millie talks to agree with her. She's probably right."

"Yes," Millie said. "Yes. And! I'll write a story about both of you for the school newspaper, and it'll be so extraordinary the *Daily Fact* will definitely publish it. Won't that look much better in your submission packet?"

"No!" Lenny said. She didn't even know there was a school paper. "You can't *write* about it write about it. What school newspaper? It was just supposed to be for your note collection."

"Then, no," William said. "If it's not in the paper, I don't want to do it."

Jacob said if William wasn't doing it, he guessed he wasn't doing it, either.

Millie whispered in Lenny's ear, "I promise to write them any way you ask me to."

Lenny asked Millie why she didn't just go outside and interview someone. There were kids all over the street she could talk to. Millie said she'd tried, but that the kids would either run, turn away and ignore her, or scream. Lenny believed her. She knew enough about the abandoned to know they probably did do all those things, and that it wasn't Millie's fault. They didn't trust anyone, Lenny and the rest of the team included. They would usually get in the van, eventually, but they hardly ever talked. Millie couldn't even visit a shelter to interview to the kids there, or Lenny would have told her to do that, instead. Shelters only let in people with an appointment to adopt.

It was William's turn for the stage. Lenny poked him before he could leave. She said, "It can go in the paper, okay?"

William shrugged and said, "Yeah, okay, whatever," as he walked away.

Jacob was called next, and then it was just the two of them. Lenny told Millie she'd let her ride along, but only if she got to read every single word of Millie's notes before they became a story. She'd get to read the story, too, before Millie even thought about publishing it anywhere.

"Yes, yes! I agree to those terms," Millie said, shaking both of Lenny's hands. She let go, smiling, and stared off into nothing with a look on her face until it was her turn to go on stage.

Lenny watched the needle go into Millie's neck. She didn't flinch at all.

NINETEEN

Millie used to make a special effort to listen to every word of her parents' arguments, but she was too excited about her own life that morning to go upstairs to eavesdrop. (That, and her mother had learned to open the door at unpredictable intervals in case Millie was listening on the stairs or lying on the floor with her ear to the gap.) She had caught the gist of it before they closed the door, anyway: money. Millie's dad had spent her college fund, so she would have to pay her own way. If she went at all. But that was still three years away, and she didn't care enough one way or the other to spend any time thinking about it.

Scratching her neck where she'd received her chip the day before, she unfolded the newspaper. Her introductory ride-along with the Collectors—and the story she'd write that would convince her mother she certainly was *Daily Fact* material—would all happen that afternoon if someone still hadn't beaten her to the first in-depth drop story. She skimmed the front page, as she had for months, for the one that would kill her idea:

> **Newborns respond favorably to identification implants**
> …Lakeland expressed his satisfaction with the process thus far, noting that side effects have been limited to minor rashes and scabbing.
>
> "Like many of you I had my doubts about this measure, but I think it's safe to say we all—most of us, that is—agree that anything we can do to see fewer instances of cruelty to children, even if it causes a rash or two, is worth doing. Let's hope the so-called adults of this nation make the necessary changes to prevent further action," Lakeland said.
>
> Pressed to elaborate on what further action might be taken, Lakeland suggested that such a focus indicated "questionable priorities"…

The door opened upstairs. It would be time to leave, soon. Millie hurriedly flipped to page two, and a headline she ordinarily would have passed over caught her attention: **Military raises enlistment age to 21**. She skipped to the part she knew would probably affect her personally, assuming William and Jacob or their parents read the *Daily Fact*. (It was, after all, the only newspaper in the state. "Our sole source of objective, reliable information," her mother had lectured many times. "Before the *Daily Fact* restored the abandoned press on Progress Drive, there were so many citizen journalists flinging their contributions at 'reputable' online publications that no one knew who was an actual journalist and who was a so-called self-taught blogger permitted by editors—'editors'—to fill the internet with unsourced, utterly biased commentary. If not for the boycott and the demand for at least one professional press willing to return to paper (even at the expense of such a thing) in order to leave no possible avenue for the publication of unvetted material, who knows to what level our ignorance, and our intentionally and maliciously stoked anger, would have climbed?" Etcetera.)

> ...approved the Department of Defense order that those enlisting or seeking a commission must be age 21 or older, a move that has been in quiet negotiations for two years. Under pressure from the public, Congress will also consider encouraging states whose age of majority is 18 to raise it to 21 to match federal drinking, smoking, and enlistment ages.
>
> "It's about time," Gwyneth Masters, 20, said of the proposed change. "I'd rather they just lowered everything else to 18 even if the military sticks with 21, but at least they're finally making some sense."
>
> Asked whether she had concerns that a reconsideration of the age of majority would affect the minimum voting age, Masters laughed and said, "You mean people still bother?"...

"Ready to go?" Her dad walked stiffly down the stairs with her mother behind him.

Millie picked up her school bag. She assumed William and Jacob watched the "base bait" news her mother had always said would uncoil her brain, and programs like that weren't likely to give time to such an uncontroversial story. She could only hope and wait and see.

Millie was sitting inside the gym's hockey goal, far away from Lenny and the others, when Jacob arrived at the end of the school day to meet the Collectors for the first time. He held a half-eaten eggroll in his fist, and his eyes looked heavy.

He approached the Collectors in their corner of the gym and announced loudly that William wouldn't be coming. The group's four members looked up at him, all but Lenny returning their attention to the school pride poster they pretended to paint. (Technically, they were painting it, Millie knew, but only to appear school-spirited and uninteresting. Lenny had explained that they repainted it at every meeting.)

"I mean, what's the point?" Jacob bit from his eggroll.

Lenny stood. Millie flipped open her notes and stared down at them as if she'd heard nothing. She'd already decided during second period that if Jacob and William did back out, which she now hoped they would so she wouldn't have to write about them, she could easily convince Lenny to keep their deal. After all, Millie couldn't control what Jacob and William did now. Millie had done her part. Lenny owed her.

Millie peeked away from her notebook when she heard Lenny's paint brush drop to the poster.

"But you said—"

"Yeah. Yeah, Lenny, I know what we said, and we meant it, but that was when we thought we'd be enlisting in a few months. Say there is some little story on us. What difference will that make when we're twenty-one? And who's to say there's even a story to write? No one's going to drop a chipped kid."

"But they're not all chipped!" she said. "What about people who have their babies at home? What about the ones who were abandoned before the chip—"

"Sorry." He offered Lenny a loose, eggroll salute before crossing the gym to the exit with a "Good luck. And I mean that, too, gorgeous...girl. Gorgeous girl..."

Millie waited inside the goalie's net through the closing of the metal door and through everyone getting up and dropping their brushes, afraid (even though she'd prepared an impenetrable rebuttal) Lenny would say she wasn't welcome, anymore.

Lenny didn't address her until they all started walking out. "Coming?" she said.

Millie rode with Lenny's rotating team for three long years in the clunky, burgundy van with windows tinted so dark the sky from inside was always gray. She might have left after two or three months, but her drop stories were so popular at school (they liked the ones about kids with neck gouges the most) that students would track her down in classes they didn't share with her, or corner her in the bathroom (ten times over three years), so they could read about the latest child found in...well, wherever they found them.

Each drop's situation was unique, even if at their foundations the stories were all basically the same. They'd found a child sitting with a picture book on a mall loading dock, a baby screaming in a car seat on the interstate shoulder, and a toddler sleeping on old bags of garbage behind a shuttered drug store. They had picked up a ten-year-old girl clutching an empty superhero lunch box outside a barber shop, an eight-year-old boy wearing a flowered sunhat in the middle of an abandoned strip mall parking lot, and outside a Drink-and-a-Donut, a twelve-year-old girl—her southern accent so thick it was gibberish—anchored in place by a rock-filled backpack secured to her chest with three bike locks. (They could have used William and Jacob for that one. It had taken Lenny, Floyd, and a temporary Collector named Carlotta fifteen minutes to lift her and then wrestle her into the van. Millie, an objective journalist, could obviously not participate.) In each of the cases, no matter how varied the details, the story always began, *Child dropped...* (And almost all of the drops smelled like one disgusting thing or another, but Lenny said she would stop allowing Millie to tag along if she ever included that detail "in one single sentence of one single article.")

However repetitive the stories may have been to Millie, reader response, faculty included, convinced her that when she finally wrote the right story about the right drop at the right time, the *Daily Fact* would publish her. So she kept writing, and she submitted each and every one.

The *Fact* had rejected her first unsolicited story—which was also her first drop story—at the end of her freshman year. *We don't accept freelance work. –Ed.* She'd continued submitting one story a week, just the same, up through her junior year, fantasizing with each submission about her mother seeing her byline in the morning newspaper. In most of the daydreams, her mother would smile and get out of her chair to caress Millie's hair and hug her head to her chest. In real life, she would probably just keep a steady string of cigarettes lit. Millie had decided long ago that she would accept that.

To speed things up during her senior year, Millie had been submitting a story every three days (excluding weekends), and she'd received not a word from the *Fact* until now, five minutes before breakfast on the morning of the last day of school.

Upon seeing **Daily Fact** in her inbox, Millie slapped her palms flat to her desk and touched nothing. Until she opened it, it could be an acceptance.

Rather than click to view, she found the last piece she'd sent them and read through it once more while pretending to be a *Daily Fact* editor reading it for the first time.

When the Collectors meet the Protectors
WINDBURY—A volunteer drop collection group calling itself the Collectors encountered a vigilante group calling itself the Protectors Wednesday. As the Collectors' van approached the Main Street VFW, the Collectors' driver, Floyd, 17, saw a man leaving a little girl on a bench outside the military veterans' building. Seven individuals wearing knit face masks with "Protector" stitched into their foreheads jumped out of the bushes and attacked the man several feet away, prompting Floyd to stop the van at the VFW. The Collectors exited to ask the child whether the person being beaten was her father, and the girl, who did not provide her name, said he was. The Collectors, along with this reporter, waited with the child while the Protectors kicked and punched the man curled up on the ground. They said such things as, "What kind of person leaves a little girl alone in the world," and, "Someone could be doing this to your kid right now, you a--hole sick sh-- bastard." At a break in the beating when the little girl screamed for her dad, the dad jumped up and ran, but the Protectors caught him and dragged him away. The Collectors and this reporter waited for an hour for the dad or the Protectors to return, but no one did. The Collectors and this reporter safely transported the girl to the Nelson Street Shelter, where in seven days pending no family pickup she will be available for adoption.

It read quite well, she thought. Well enough for her to feel positive about their response. She straightened her back, took a deep breath, and opened the email.

Thanks for your interest. –Ed. P.S. 1. Keep yourself out of it. 2. Don't bury the lede. 3. Identify the story. Your proposed headline, "When the Collectors Meet the Protectors," is misleading, and it isn't really the story, here. 4. Shorter sentences. 5. Don't give up. Try again, sometime. Not tomorrow. Wait until you have something good. Good=even more compelling than this potentially compelling story.

The editor had mentioned nothing about the drop stories, specifically. Did they want something different? Even her mother, who had been interested in them for the longest time, had stopped seeming engaged when Millie read them aloud. "I have no idea how I feel about these 'drop' stories, Millicent, other than supremely conflicted," her mother had said through her smoke after Millie's last presentation. Millie had stopped showing up to read after that. A week had now passed since her first absence from the living room, and her mother hadn't seemed to notice. (Millie wished her dad, who said he liked everything she wrote, were home to hear her stories, but he was there less and less frequently. She concluded that it was because her mother was locking him out at night by changing the codes on the doors. Though, Millie had never heard him trying to get past them.)

That the *Fact* hadn't told her not to send more drop stories had to mean they enjoyed them, she decided. She would just have to improve them.

She would begin with the story she'd write that afternoon about their final run of the school year.

Floyd pulled into the parking lot of the Eighth Street Shelter so they could deposit a few toddlers and the older girl they'd picked up near the animal hospital.

Millie didn't bother taking notes on the toddlers. They were no different from any of the other toddlers they'd found. And she couldn't take notes on the older girl, because the only exceptional thing about her was her odor. Even with the windows open, everyone was finding reasons to hold their hands over their noses and mouths until they could get out at the shelter.

Millie was the first to escape into the fresh air. She breathed and stretched and noticed there was no one outside to greet them. For every other deposit, no matter the shelter, the van had been met by a worker who'd take the drops straight away and whisk them into the building. She hoped no greeter meant they could go inside. She would finally get to see how the drops lived. After all this time, she had never seen the quarters. There had been one series about shelters in the *Daily Fact*, but they had been the government shelters, described by the investigative reporter as "unsanitary" and "deplorable." This was a privately funded shelter—the Collectors would only make deposits at vetted, privately funded shelters—and the media had yet to gain access to a private shelter.

"Everyone grab someone," Floyd said.

Nearly everyone did: two babies for Lenny, a baby and a toddler for a new volunteer named Pearl, and two toddlers for Floyd. The smelly girl was left behind.

"Millie," Floyd said.

Millie stepped back. "Objective observer."

"Last day," Floyd said. "Learn something new." He released one of his own toddlers to grab the girl's hand and thrust it into Millie's. Millie held onto the cold, tiny hand with her thumb and the tip of her index finger.

"Locked," said Lenny, who'd reached the doors first. Millie let go of the girl and ran to the entrance. A set of interior doors was closed, as well. The backs of two heads blocked the narrow windows to the inside. Lenny banged and Floyd tapped with his long fingers until one of the shelter workers opened the interior door and backed toward them with a palm held out behind her until she touched the glass. She turned around and, eyes closed, held up a piece of paper.

The chipping rush has overwhelmed our shelter. We are sorry we cannot help you. Please continue to the closest hospital, fire station, or police station.

The woman turned away from them and went inside and closed the door, again blocking the narrow window with the back of her head.

When the Collectors' van reached the police station, they waited in line for twenty horrifyingly smelly minutes behind child-filled vans similar to their own before finally being instructed to unload.

"More?" Floyd said as they pulled away. "We'll just have to bring 'em here."

"Maybe it's better than the street," Lenny said.

"Depends, I guess," Floyd said. "So? Yeah? No?"

After a minute, Lenny said, "Yes."

For their final collection, Floyd drove the narrow lanes behind the upscale Tinytown shops. Lenny was the front-seat lookout, and Millie sat in back with Pearl on the stacked dog mats they used as chairs or, when necessary, mattresses for the drops. It was Pearl's introductory ride-along to determine whether she thought she'd want to volunteer next year. As a former drop, herself, she said, she thought it was very wrong that they would or could listen to "Shake, Rattle and Roll" while scouring the area for abandoned children and repeatedly asked Floyd to turn off the music.

"You act like it's some joke," she wailed.

"You get used to—" Floyd touched Lenny's arm. "Look there. Might be something."

"Great eye!" Lenny said, and Floyd smiled stupidly at her.

Millie touched his shoulder over the back of his seat. "You're so observant." She took her hand away after he blushed at the rearview mirror.

"Here? Something here?" Pearl looked out the window at the bright buildings and clean sidewalks.

"Oh, yes. They're everywhere!" Millie smiled.

TWENTY

The woman poked her head around the corner of a store with *Fashion Able: Accessorize* painted over its loading dock entrance. She wore a light, pretty scarf in a knot around her neck. Lenny thought she had to have seen the van, but then she stepped out into the alley with a boy she'd been hiding between the stores. He was three, maybe. A cowboy hat too big for his head shaded him to his chest. The woman dragged him into a parking area behind Big Beautiful Bagels, then stopped and spun around, swinging the boy off his feet. She stared straight at the van and screamed, "Who's is in there?"

Lenny looked at Floyd, who poked out the tip of his tongue and made rings with his finger at the side of his head.

The woman marched toward them. The toes of the boy's green shoes dragged behind him and his head hung to the side. His hat fell off. Pearl gasped even though they'd already seen a few like him that day.

"What do you want?" the woman shouted. "What do you have in there? A child? Help! Help, someone! They're abandoning"—she pushed the boy to the ground—"a defenseless child!"

She ran away down the tidy alley, stomping the little boy's hat under her narrow red heel. It stuck to her shoe and went with her.

Floyd started the engine. "When I stop, grab the kid fast."

He screeched the brakes beside the boy and Lenny jumped out to pick him up. He was limp and heavy and still bleeding. The gouge in his neck looked a little deeper than the others they'd seen. She called to Pearl and got help loading him onto the mats.

Floyd said, "She took the path," and was off again before they had the door closed.

They couldn't drive on the flower-lined walkway connecting the shopping area to an upscale neighborhood, but Lenny could keep an eye on the woman through the trees while they took the vehicle access road.

"Stop," Lenny said once they'd driven inside the heavily manicured subdivision. The woman had broken a heel somewhere and limped around a corner property tucked inside a tall privacy fence. The hat was gone.

Floyd pulled over short of the end of the road. "What kind of idiot drops a kid so close to home?" He turned off the van. "Probably shouldn't give him back. She's too dumb to raise him."

Lenny opened her door. "Maybe leaving him so close meant she didn't really want to. Maybe it was a bad day." She jumped out of the van, ran on her toes so her shoes wouldn't stomp, and crouched behind the corner fence. The woman hobbled up a short, wide driveway to a grand front entrance cluttered with pots of yellow pansies.

"I don't think the *Fact* has ever published a story about a returned drop."

Lenny turned at the voice and hit her nose hard against Millie's forehead.

Millie rubbed her head and nodded at the house. "She went inside."

Lenny and Millie hurried back to the van.

"The one with the yellow pansies," Lenny said, climbing in. Millie stayed outside and wrote in her notebook.

Pearl thrust herself between the front seats. "What are you going to do?"

"Give him back," Floyd said. When Lenny started to move, he said, "Give it a minute."

"But…what about the shelters?" Pearl said. "The police?"

"Police'll arrest the lady and drop the kid in the government shelter."

"Well," Pearl said, "I don't know. I mean, I'm glad no one returned me."

"Oh, yes, but you live in a private shelter," Millie said on the sidewalk. "So wh—?"

Millie popped her head inside Lenny's open window. "Government shelters release them to anyone willing to take them, and that age is very popular on the dark fuck database."

Lenny didn't like to think about the dark fuck database. If she did think about it, she wouldn't have any idea what to do with the kids they couldn't get into private shelters. So, instead of thinking about it, she looked at a tree and traced the length of a branch from tip to trunk. There were terrible things happening all over the world that she couldn't control, and her thinking about them wouldn't change a thing. It would only make her unhappy.

"But he's so young," Pearl said.

Lenny heard shuffling and looked over her shoulder. Pearl was sitting on the floor next to the boy. He hadn't moved since they'd laid him down. She asked Pearl to check him.

Pearl wet her finger and stuck it under his nose and said, "Just sleeping, I guess."

"Can't be too young for the dark fuck database," Floyd said. "Only thing they don't want is someone that wants it back."

Pearl shuddered. "I hate sex."

"How do you know all of this?" Lenny said.

Floyd said, "I read."

"And don't you see how unhappy you are, sometimes?"

Millie left Lenny's window to stand in front of the open sliding door, her pen over her notebook. She said, "You've had it, then, Pearl? Intercourse, I mean."

Pearl stroked the little boy's shiny green shoe.

"Oh! OH!" Millie flapped her notebook at Pearl. "Did someone coerce you into having it?"

"Coerce me?"

"Well, 'rape,' as still defined in dictionaries, but I should use the new terminology I'm sure the AP will adopt per a pending revision to the legal definition meant to reduce the burden on the courts." After a few seconds of silence, she said, "One-sided heterosexual abstinence?" She sighed at Pearl. "Marital and cohabitational accusations?"

"What?"

"Let's go now," Floyd said. "Doubt she's still watching the windows, so she won't see us come up."

"Us" wasn't really "us." Floyd wasn't strong enough to lift a three-year-old. Lenny had been feeding him for the last three years, but he hadn't gained much weight, muscle, or color. He'd once tried using a sledge-hammer at one of her dad's sites, and then a regular hammer, but her dad had finally found other things for him to do in return for houses Floyd could live in while they were being renovated. Lenny's dad said Floyd had "amazing spatial awareness" and "a real knack for motivating workers," so now he helped with floor plan design and crew supervision.

Floyd reached back from his seat and pulled at the boy's foot. "Hey," he said. "Kid."

The boy opened his eyes.

Lenny set the boy on the mat exclaiming WELCOME! and saw "Chester" markered on his shirt tag before she rang the doorbell. She and Millie raced down the stairs and ducked behind a car parked on the street. Lenny couldn't see anything, but she heard the door open and the woman hiss, "Damn that van to hell." The door slammed.

Lenny peeked up through the car windows and saw that the boy was gone. "Let's go," she said. She started toward the van, but Millie headed for the house in a crouching jog.

"What are you doing?" Lenny tried to whisper.

Millie showed Lenny her notebook over her shoulder and kept going. Lenny followed her across the driveway to the big front window.

They saw it all.

It started in the living room, on the floor. Then it moved to the foyer.

Lenny wanted to run away, but she couldn't. She couldn't do anything. She was afraid to even close her eyes.

Millie wrote furiously beside her.

At the end, when there was no question it was over, Lenny kept looking in, transfixed, until the woman saw them. She sneered and lunged for the front door.

"Go," Millie said, but Lenny still couldn't move. Millie pulled her with a strength Lenny didn't know she had all the way to the van and shoved her in. Lenny fell and rolled and was on her back trying to catch her breath when she saw the woman's wild face in the open door for a single terrifying second before Floyd peeled away from the curb.

"What the hell happened?" he said.

Before Millie could answer, Lenny asked Floyd to please take them to the police station.

Lenny stayed curled up on the van floor for the return trip to the school. She and Millie had made the report alone, so they—well, and the police— were the only ones who knew what had happened. Whenever Pearl or Floyd asked about the drop, Lenny would give Millie a look that warned her to keep quiet about the boy. *Chester.* The mailbox at the end of the driveway had read WALTON. Chester Walton.

She rubbed her cheek on the soft dog mat and tried to convince herself that what had happened to Chester wasn't her fault. She couldn't have known. "You weren't the one who did those things to that poor boy," her mom would say. "You can't control the actions of others." But her mom had also said, once upon a time, "Things don't happen for a reason, but there is a reason things happen."

They were the reason this thing had happened.

Millie typed on her tablet while turning pages in her notes.

"No details," Lenny said.

Without looking up, Millie said, "The details are the story."

"But what happened in there," Lenny said.

"Yes? What? What? Did I miss something?"

"Not everyone's like you," Lenny said. "Most people would never want to see what we saw, and I just don't think you should force it into their heads."

Still typing, Millie argued that the details were the only thing about another dead toddler that would make the story "resonate with the public" and that Lenny shouldn't be so sensitive. "Abuse is a simple fact of life just like drops are."

Lenny thought about what her mom had said about her aunt Kat and the snow. She reminded herself of it all the time. But she was sure her mom would agree with her about this.

"If you write what happened in there," Lenny said, "I'll tell Ms. Well that everything you've ever written about our team was a lie. And she'll believe me." Ms. Well would believe her, too, because her work with the Collectors had earned her a reputation among the school faculty (they understood the identities of the volunteers had to be kept a secret from the student body). If Lenny went to Ms. Well, not only would Millie's reputation as a writer be destroyed around school, but it would also ruin any future she might have with the *Daily Fact*.

"But I do thank you for saving me," she said as Millie turned off her tablet. "I promise I'll make it up to you one day."

TWENTY ONE

Without the details, Millie's story about the abused boy took a single day to reach the Associated Press. She had worked harder on it than she had ever worked on anything, even calling the spokesperson for the Windbury police department to gather what she needed from the police report. Her rough draft had taken half an hour to write and three and a half hours to edit before it was ready to submit to the *Fact*. The return email from the town's section editor had arrived within fifteen minutes: *Get a quote from Ms. Walton's attorney (Jeannie Wilson, 860-555-9825) and a hospital update on the boy before 8 a.m. and we'll run it today.*

Her story had published almost as she'd written it and within three days began appearing in the majority of online publications, whether they were somewhat or not remotely reputable. Some reproduced the article in full and others in part, but none omitted a certain selection of paragraphs from the text, frequently using a line or two for the callout box:

> ...The details of the abuse suffered by two-and-a-half-year-old Chester in the family living room are too graphic to document anywhere but in a medical examiner's report...
>
> ...Delilah Walton was not available for comment. However, according to a police report filed Friday Walton said she had repeatedly told authorities upon discovering she was pregnant that she should not have a baby due to a documented history of mental illness. She told the arresting officers that she had at one time pleaded with the governor to grant her what she called in the report a "pre-offense pardon" that would allow her to terminate the pregnancy without persecution. According to the police report, Ms. Walton shouted at the police, "Do you know what the governor said? 'No exceptions.' She said it was her 'civic and humanitarian duty to protect that unborn.'"...
>
> ...Defense attorney Jeannie Wilson, speaking on behalf of Walton, said she is optimistic about the sentencing hearing. "Six months, maybe eight. A year at worst. It wasn't first-degree homicide, after all. Manslaughter, if anything, and as you know this state has a one-year maximum on child torture. I'm confident Delilah will be out in no time to get the mental health care she

desperately needs," Wilson said. Walton will be arraigned Monday
at 8:30 a.m....

In addition to going viral online, Millie's story quickly became a big-
network television news sensation with Chester Walton as the leading topic
on each of the twenty-four-hour news channels. It was a Saturday that the
story took over the television, and while her mother hadn't accidentally
smiled at or touched Millie again, she did bring her to Lenny's house to
watch the news on Lenny's mom's newer, bigger projection viewer. Because
Lenny's dad was out working—with Floyd, as usual—on one of his houses,
it was just the four of them in the spacious, smoke-free attic office watching
commentators debating everything from abortion laws to why Chester
Walton's mother was pregnant in the first place.

"Because you cannot regulate sexual behavior, you simpleton," Millie's
mother said to the projection of the rosy cheeked blond man.

When Millie and her mother arrived home that night, her dad bounced
off the couch as they entered and stood beside his largest suitcase. Her
mother stormed past her and lit a cigarette from the pack in her pocket.
Millie wondered how long he had been there. She wished they all could
have watched the coverage together before he left again.

He opened his arms and Millie stepped into his hug. Behind him, her
mother evaporated a cigarette in the kitchen.

"I sure am proud of you, silly willie Millie," he said. "Better enjoy it
while it lasts! This kind of passing fascination never does." He snapped out
his bag's handle and turned to look at Millie's mother. She floated smoke in
front of her shining eyes.

"How long will you be gone this time?" Millie said.

He gave her shoulders a squeeze. "It's not how long you're gone, it's
where you go and what you do when you get there!" He messed up the hair
on the top of her head, sailed to the door with his suitcase rolling behind
him, and was gone.

Chester Walton's death was not a passing fascination. As it turned out, the
details Millie had omitted from the story only fueled people's imaginations,
elevating her story into a national conversation and Chester Walton into a
national symbol. Because each person's imagined worst case scenario was
different, Chester Walton had, in the mind of the public, suffered every
manner of abuse possible. Of those interviewed for on-the-spot reactions
to what they believed Chester Walton's mother had done to him, however,
none managed to imagine anything worse than what had actually happened.

(Because her mother always had the television on, now, so they could watch the ongoing reaction to Millie's work, Millie made sure to never miss the guesses sad-faced people offered for the "On the Street" segment. When once she started to tell her mother just how wrong they were, her mother said, "Millicent, you are never to tell me what happened inside that house.")

Millie applied for a full-time reporter position with the *Daily Fact* following graduation from high school. They immediately hired her for the next position to become available, which the email read was *to be determined.* In the meantime, she lived with, and did household chores for, her mother, who held firm in her demand that Millie earn her own way whether she was waiting for a job or attending college (a useless…*endeavor*, since the only reason to go would be to improve her odds of being hired by the *Daily Fact*). They spoke little when they were home at the same time. Instead, they watched hours a day of base-bait debate over "what should be done," the suited figures in Congress fighting battle after battle in pursuit of a solution.

The Wednesday of Millie's fourth week waiting for word from the *Fact*, her mother stayed home so the two of them could follow the latest lunchtime development. Whatever was to happen, her mother told her over her breakfast muffin and cigarette, promised to be "momentous."

Millie wondered whether her dad had been watching the news lately. Or, at least, whether he'd been watching the one time they'd mentioned her specific article and her name along with it. But, no. He would have called. "Congratulations, silly willie Millie! You're a star!" she was sure he'd have said.

Her mother gouged a chunk out of her muffin and held it over the newspaper as she read.

Without allowing herself time to hesitate, because hesitating would scare her into the same place she'd retreated to every other time she never asked, Millie said, "Did he love me?"

Her mother's hand stopped just before it was about to feed her mouth the muffin, then quickly slipped it in.

"Never mind." Millie stirred her soggy Grape-Nuts, then grabbed her bowl and slid back her chair. "I need more nuts for all my m—"

"It had nothing to do with you."

Her mother looked at her, directly into her eyes. Millie was so unprepared for the intimacy of such contact—she could count on less than one hand how many times it had happened—that she had to contemplate her cereal to fight the hollow, shaking feeling.

"Do you hear me, Millicent?"

"Yes, Mother."

By lunchtime, the morning's conversation was understood to be over, the matter settled. As they ate sandwiches on the couch while watching the people in charge, their projected faces grim, Millie only glanced once or twice at the shelf, where the foil-wrapped chocolate alligator her dad had brought her from a New Orleans vacation poked its head out from behind a red vase. She also watched her mother's smoking to see if it got faster or more intense. It did, but not remarkably. Half a cigarette faster, if that. Millie tried not to be nervous about what that might mean. Was she saving up to say something? What would that feel like? What would Millie do if her mother told her she was proud of her? How would they celebrate? They'd never done anything fun together.

Millie watched the projection.

"We must fix it," said a congressmember named Anita Bennington. "We've ignored the abandoned for years, turning away while building shelter after shelter. But we cannot ignore this."

"I say we overturn the overturn," said a congressmember named Abe Lakeland.

"Outrageous!" said a congressmember named Theodore Belinski.

A long moment of silence followed. Theodore looked around.

Anita sighed. "And what *is* it that's outrageous, Theodore?"

"What is…? Right! Ah, why, the very idea of overturning the overturn is outright outrag—"

"Thank you. But, Theodore, didn't you support the federal overturn to save the unborns?"

"Correct!"

"I don't need to tell you that an alarming percentage of your unborns were born to detrimentally apathetic, monumentally selfish, unwittingly but undeniably dangerous, or simply terrible people," she said. "Surely you must know Chester Walton is not the only abuse case of his magnitude."

"Ah, but we don't even know the magnitude!"

"He's dead, Theodore."

"Yes, Anita, yes, he's dead, but we don't know the magnitude of the abuse, itself. He very well could have been hit on the head and accidentally fallen into something hard."

Anita dropped her shoulders. "Isn't there someone else I could do this with? Mirabelle?"

"Mirabelle's not on unt—" Abe cleared his throat and ruffled his notes around. "That is, Mirabelle's not in….not in until some other time.

Mirabelle—I mean, Theodore—is here now, and his position is clear, I think."

"His position is clear," Anita said, "but he has no idea how to argue it. I tell you, Abe, I just wish we'd chosen someone a little more capable of delivering a cogent and persuasive rebuttal."

Theodore sneered at her. "When they finally activate that demon fail-safe, the only good thing that'll come of it is that you'll be too goddamn old to—"

She whispered, "Theodore!"

He covered his mouth. The hushed room looked at him and at one another before all faces turned down, away from the cameras mounted in the high chamber corners, each congressmember suddenly focused on a spot on a tie, a hair on a sleeve, a crumb on a lap.

Abe coughed. "Listen here." He fingered through the loose papers in his hand and selected a page to move to the top. "One-year-old girl in Oklahoma with bruises on her head from being punched with a closed fist." He looked up for effect. "Traumatic brain injury." Eyes back on his notes, he said, "This infant here in Utah starved to death after fourteen hours of being deprived of food."

Theodore rolled his eyes. "Who knows how many times an hour a baby has to eat? I'm sure it was an innocent mistake. Why wasn't the mother home feeding the baby?"

Abe read his notes. "She appears to have been at work. The baby was in the care of his father."

"Well!"

"And this child here in Virginia," Abe went on. "Four years old and paralyzed. Her mother backed over her with the car."

"Another innocent mistake!"

"And then she did it again."

"Could happen to anyone."

Abe waited with his notes. He blinked at Theodore.

"Right! Well, I'm sorry, Abe, but you haven't convinced me to vote in favor of overturning the overturn. That's a small number, right there, and we can't very well sacrifice the lives of the unborn for the lives of the born."

Abe gave a flick of his eyebrows before going on to read case after documented case from his notes: a six-week-old with bone and skull fractures; a one-year-old whose mother had starved him because she didn't want him to get fat; a six-year-old thrown off a bridge by his father; a four-year-old whose mother kept him chained outside in a dog pen; a—

"Enough! All of those children—Hold on. The one with the skull fractures. Alive?"

"Oh, yes. Technically."

"And bridge boy?"

"Brain dead."

"But alive!"

"Yes."

"Good enough. Thank you, Abe. All of those children are alive, as are the children whose cases aren't even bad enough to qualify for that folder you're holding, there. That is the point, isn't it, Anita? Without the overturn, all of these precious children would never have been born, and then where would they be?"

"Where is anyone who hasn't been born?"

"Who knows? But these children are here and able to suffer their unique torments thanks to me. When we save one unborn, Anita, we save all unborns, whether they're wanted or unwanted, loved or beaten silly. Why, you would have those children believe they should never have been born, and that's no kind of thing to say to a child."

"No, Theodore, I would suggest that their parents should never have reproduced."

"What's the difference?"

"All of it." Anita addressed the room. "You are clearly not prepared to change your position on the overturn. Correct, Theodore?"

"No, ma'am. Yes. Yes, that's correct."

"Noted. Now, I should mention for those motivated more by numbers than by emotional appeals that the lifetime estimate of healthcare costs, lost worker productivity, criminal justice expenditures, etcetera, caused by parents who create abused and neglected children is upward of two hundred billion dollars. And that's for just one year of confirmed abuse cases. What legislation do you propose that will address the fifteen infants and children dying daily of abuse and neglect, correct the one-point-five million unique cases of abuse in the last reported year, and reverse the nation's lost productivity by ensuring children grow up abuse-free?"

"Legislation?"

"Well, Theo, do you think we should impose harsher penalties?"

"Hogwash! We have too much to do already without worrying about changing sentencing laws willy nilly. Besides, what use is it? The ones who're dead will continue to be dead, and the ones who survive are too young to vote, which makes them of little use to us."

"But they'll vote someday."

"Fine. When they can, let them change the laws." Theodore strode off projection and returned with a large poster board. He flipped it to reveal a sonogram image of a fetus curled up in a womb. "I will never agree to revert to a time when we would allow the termination of this embodiment of human potential."

"You do know, don't you, Theo," Abe said as he straightened his notes and slipped them in a folder, "that before your embodiment of potential becomes just another one of us it's going to be one of those kids you don't care to change the laws for."

Theo looked at Abe, and then at Anita. He shrugged. "Was that supposed to be part of—"

"Sh!" Anita stalked off and returned with her own poster board. When she flipped it around, the image that faced the chamber elicited gasps and covered eyes.

Millie's mother looked away from the projection.

Millie leaned in to study it. Still not as bad as Chester.

"What the hell, woman!" Theodore gagged. "Obviously…obviously some kind of solution is…is…" He stumbled off projection with his hands pressed to his mouth.

Anita and Abe gathered their things and the chamber cleared.

Over the next several weeks, as Millie continued to wait for a hire date, Congress publicly addressed the millions of emails they'd received in response to their debate. Some citizens continued to advocate for a revocation of the overturn, but most pleaded for hormonal birth control.

"'I know it's bad,'" read Anita from one email, "'and I know they say it causes abortion, but that isn't one-hundred-percent proven, is it? Can't we consider making it legal again just to try it out for a little bit? What's one or two little hormones, anyhow?'"

The majority, however, expressed anxiety about the trustworthiness of their own population. How did they know people would take their birth control? What if they didn't? Could they implement some kind of government-sanctioned vigilante monitoring system, complete with rules and a tiered system of punishments increasing from light (*ration card suspension and shunning!* wrote a citizen named Betty Cox) to harsh (*exile, solitary confinement, surprise assaults with some kind of metal tool,* suggested emailer F.J.)?

Still weeks later, and still with no word from the *Fact*, Millie and her mother watched as Congress met for what they announced would be the final conversation on the matter.

"The people are right to question themselves," Theodore said, once again positioned in the front of the room. He stood with his back to Anita, and to the photograph she'd propped on an easel for public viewing. "I've given it some thought, and—"

"I agree!" Anita slammed her fist into her palm. "We must implement licensing!"

The word "licensing" was repeated by nearly everyone in the chamber and reverberated under the high ceiling in clashing tones of disbelief and wonder. One woman in the back looked genuinely surprised.

"Wait, wait!" shouted a front-row congressmember named Mirabelle Brown. "What would that do to our economy?"

Anita fluttered her fingers. "We've been outsourcing for tens of decades. Who's going to suffer when we reduce the number of people in our own country we're denying work?"

"I'm sure I don't know," Mirabelle said.

Abe stood to speak. "Look at it this way. Just give me one second, please." He took a deep breath and read from a notecard he pulled from the inside pocket of his suit jacket. "If we reduce the number of children, we reduce the prison population—that bores everyone here, I know, but it does interest the fringe groups—and we shrink the homeless population. We cut unemployment. Further..." He squinted at the card. "Further, children born to willing, prepared parents will have a better opportunity to experience a safe, loving, and supportive environment that will instill in them the confidence to start a company or a factory, or in some other way be a job creator." He returned the card to his jacket. "I agree with Anita that licensing might be the next, perhaps the only, logical step in healing our nation, as much as I must officially disagree with it for its potential to go horribly awry."

A small voice from the back of the room offered, "What if there aren't enough qualified...reproducers? What about the perpetuation of the human race?"

Abe whispered to Anita, and she shrugged. He said to the chamber, "Is this, uh, is this a serious question?"

"Yes."

Abe thought a moment. "To what end?"

"What?"

"To what end? Perpetuate the human race why?"

"Because."

Another voice from a sitting member shouted, "You can't stop people from having children! What kind of monster are you to try to strip us of our basic human right?" The woman stood and stomped to the front of the room. "I will not allow any person, any law, any government body to deny someone a child due to some missing arbitrary qualifier—"

"OH, EDWINA, THE VICTIMIZATION!" boomed a voice somewhere in the middle row. A thick barrel of a man rolled his wheelchair to the front of the room and parked beside Edwina. "You with the weeping heart weeping only for you and *your* rights, *your* rights, *your* rights! Heaven forbid we trample on your personal rights. May I say, Edwina, this is a miraculous one-eighty on your part. Weren't you one of the first to set flame to individual rights when you didn't agree with those rights?"

"I was, Mick. I most certainly was, but that was a right that didn't... well...it wasn't...it was to protect the *children*, you s—"

"Well, hallelujah! Individual rights matter again. Certain rights of certain individuals, anyway." He muttered, "And you wonder why you're kept out of the loop," then raised his voice when she started to sputter. "All right, Edwina, all right. But individual rights at whose expense?"

She looked down at him, and then out at the chamber. "The...the taxpayers'?"

"No, Edwina. Or, yes, but we don't really care about them, either, do we? The expense—the worst of it, that is—is paid by children like Chester Walton. And by this child." Mick picked up Anita's poster board and flashed it at her, and then at the room. Eyes snapped to aversion. "But why concern yourself with them when you have your personal, individual, precious procreation 'right' to protect?"

The political conversation ended there, but it went on in the *Daily Fact*. Millie waited in the living room every morning while her mother read in the kitchen, and when her mother finished without saying anything about any of it to Millie, Millie took the paper to her room where she couldn't smell the smoke or hear her mother's watery cough.

The licensing conversation had infiltrated coffee houses where reporters, as they reported it, observed young people nodding at each other about it in universal agreement. According to one writer who had stood for two hours with a protest group on Tinytown's Main Street, the pro-creation activists saw a victory in the survival of the overturn, but they couldn't help feeling defeated by any measure that would in any way say "no" to creation. The overworked and traumatized shelter volunteers said they refused to get their hopes up. Historically oppressed demographics bristled in their letters to the editor. Heterosexual men and women who had abstained from romantic coitus for years expressed a sudden and inexplicable desire to have children. The designers of the dark fuck database, and others involved in child sex trafficking, reportedly began exploring their options in some of the other high-birth rate countries "just in case," said one anonymous source.

Editorial writers took the predictable pro and con stances, the con insisting, *The fantasy of eugenics is once again rearing its devil head*, and the pro assuring, *If this child-saving measure comes to pass, no doubt all consideration will be given to fairness and equality*. The suspicious wondered, *Just how long has this been in the works? Dare I say the American public has been manipulated?* and, *Exactly how does the government intend to enforce the consistent use of hormonal birth control?*

Millie's first day at the *Fact*—which began with a second of mild disappointment when she learned Nellie had long since moved on—was the same day her new employer ran a story that answered the question of consistent hormone use. The hormone, the White House Press Secretary announced in a brief press release, was already in the microchips the government had been implanting into children and newborns over the last four and a half years. Activation was scheduled for "soon."

Millie's first assignment, to run the following day, was to interview InSystem public relations specialist Juanita Escallon.

"This is the first interview InSystem has granted us," said her dark haired, bright eyed, smiling editor, Hugh. "I left some of my own questions for her on your desk, but feel free to add your own if she'll let you get that far. Don't do a feature. Simple Q&A with a short intro."

Millie's interview with Juanita Escallon, who agreed to answer only four questions, published the next day just as Hugh had promised.

InSystem's Juanita Escallon: Daily Fact Q&A

InSystem public relations specialist Juanita Escallon agreed to speak with the *Daily Fact* as part of the company's media campaign to quell fears about the birth control hormone currently active in chips implanted into every known biological female in the country. As Ms. Escallon had only enough time to answer four questions, the *Daily Fact* selected those it believed would address the public's most pressing concerns.

Daily Fact: Isn't eight years old a little young for activation?

Juanita Escallon: No. And I consider it a grave tragedy that we know that for a fact.

DF: How do you know when to stop releasing the hormone? Who gives the order, and when?

JE: The Parent Licensing Board notifies us with an approval of a client or clients, and we deactivate the hormone release within twelve hours of receipt.

DF: How do you respond to people's objections to being forcibly sterilized?

JE: Are there really so many objections? I have seen quite the opposite. They embrace this solution to overcrowding and child mistreatment—not to mention personal financial distress—as if we had injected each of them with a vaccine for cancer.

DF: But there are those who believe the mandated hormone treatment is an infringement of their right to privacy and bodily integrity.

JE: Oh, if they want children, they can have them easily enough. Do you want to know the worst that will happen with the hormone in place? Women who enjoy sexual intercourse with men can expect to want to have sex again. (*Laughs.*)

DF: This leads to my next question: why sterilize women and not men?

JE: You understand these were not my decisions and that I speak only for the company manufacturing the chips and carrying out the orders of the licensing bureau, yes? With that said, I can tell you that this is a very expensive undertaking being paid for entirely by the government—and so, by the people. This is why we have the rudimentary subdermal microchip versus a retinal implant. To further reduce costs, I can only assume it made sense to sterilize just one sex, and of course it had to be the woman. One man with a malfunctioning hormone could impregnate countless women in a single week, whereas one woman with a malfunctioning hormone...You see?

DF: Can women expect the hormone to cause any physiological side effects?

JE: That's one extra question, but you may have it. To answer, yes, certainly. I expect many women will experience vaginal fulfillment. Oh, don't look so frustrated, young lady. The hormone is completely safe, and side effects are both minimal and unlikely. I think we should look on the bright side, don't you? Do you know half of the crimes in this country have been caused by sexual frustration? I believe it's true. You wait. You'll see.

In addition to small and scattered protests decrying the injustice of being forcibly sterilized ("Technically it isn't sterilization, and I wish people would stop using that irresponsible word," Congressmember Abe Lakeland told the *Daily Fact*), the Main Street protest signs Millie drove past on the way to her new apartment reflected what she was seeing in the articles written by her new colleagues: no one knew exactly what they were protesting, beyond the broader idea of licensing. Some expressed a fear that they wouldn't qualify (even those who didn't want children at least wanted to qualify). Others, Millie's mother among them, wondered why such a solution hadn't been proposed a long time ago.

Licensing measures moved forward in spite of minority opposition. The announcement that hormonal birth control had been activated came three weeks into Millie's new job—and approximately three minutes before she invited Hugh on their first date. The same day, print newspapers and any online sources accepted as official media published an identical six-inch brief introducing a new system of corrections referred to only as "Exile."

> STATE—The state in conjunction with support from anonymous donors completed construction Wednesday on property referred to only as "Exile." Governor Harryette Michaels said the facility, built at an undisclosed location and described by Michaels as "the state's best answer to an overcrowded prison system," will differ from a traditional prison in minor ways whose details Michaels declined to outline.
>
> The governor said state officials initiated Exile facility planning three years ago and that it did not seem necessary at the time to inform or consult the public.
>
> "It's just another prison, in essence. The end," Michaels said.
>
> In anticipation of public concern and protest, Michaels stressed that exile as a method of corrections and the Exile facility itself are "perfectly legal and utterly necessary."
>
> In an encrypted and anonymous email sent Tuesday to media outlets, an individual claiming to be the facility's overseer characterized Exile's system of punishment as "effective" and the overseer's duties as "principled."
>
> The facility is expected to house only those convicted of such child welfare felonies as kidnapping, abuse, neglect, and/or abandonment, Michaels said. Exile will receive its first inmates as early as Friday.

Also published that day, in each publication's version of a special section, was the complete list of provisional parent licensing guidelines:

Guidelines per Executive Order 25538—Parent Licensing
1. Licensing requirements apply to any citizen seeking to be a primary biological and/or adoptive parent.

2.   Primary Applicants may not be denied a license based on race, sex, gender, sexual preference, marital status, or political affiliation.
3.   Primary Applicants must be between the ages of eighteen (18) and thirty (30).
4.   Primary Applicants must have a verified Family Care Plan (FCP). A Family Care Plan is defined as one or more licensed individuals who will assume the guardianship of any Primary Applicant's offspring in the event of the Primary Applicant's absence due to death or other causes.
   a.   FCPs may extend to family, friends, and all other parties invested in the welfare of the child.
   b.   Applicants for secondary guardianship licenses under the FCP must be between the ages of eighteen (18) and sixty-five (65).
   c.   FCP volunteers signing as physical guardians must be licensed as secondary guardians.
   d.   Primary Applicants and FCP secondary guardians must:
      i.   pass a cognitive evaluation.
      ii.   pass a six-month in-home dog care evaluation.
      iii. prove a sole or combined income matching or exceeding the minimum cost of raising a child as determined by each year's calculated projections.
   e.   FCP volunteers wishing to contribute solely by financial means (FCP(f)) need not be licensed, but finances must be verified.
5.   License is valid for the lifetime of the child(ren) born of a sanctioned pregnancy. Each additional pregnancy requires an additional license.
6.   Hormone regulation resumes upon the reported birth of the sanctioned child(ren).
7.   Any unlicensed individual or individuals convicted of willful chip manipulation or hacking, directly or indirectly, for the purposes of damaging the hormone component in order to bypass birth control and conceive a pregnancy will incur a $5,178 fine and lose licensing privileges in perpetuity.
   a.   Should pregnancy occur as a result of willful chip manipulation or hacking, the individual or individuals responsible will be sentenced to an indefinite period in Exile.
   b.   Unlicensed pregnancies conceived as a result of willful chip manipulation or hacking will be carried to term, at which time the child will become the ward of an

       adoptive family or, in lieu of an available family, the
       state.

8.   Licensed parents convicted of abuse, neglect, or abandonment of a
      sanctioned child will be exiled.

        a.   The abused, neglected, or abandoned child will become
           the ward of a licensed adoptive family or, in lieu of an
           available family, the state.

9.   Licensed or unlicensed individuals convicted of willful termination
      of a pregnancy face lifetime imprisonment.

10. Licensed or unlicensed individuals convicted of inadvertently
      terminating a pregnancy by means of negligence will face
      manslaughter charges and ten years confinement in a state prison.

PART THREE

Sheetrock and yellow paint covered the interior brick walls Lenny and Floyd had panted and sweated against twelve years before. It was a hot summer day during their senior year when Floyd had finally escaped his parents' house and run home with Lenny. He'd had been so sure his dad would find him on the street that they'd climbed through one of the mill's broken windows and hidden for two hours among gritty brick dust and spiderless webs. Half an hour in, Lenny and Floyd had kissed for the first time.

She smiled at the memory and squeezed his spindly hand.

The silk mill had been vacant for as long as Lenny could remember before it became one of eight hundred licensing evaluation centers across the country. (She knew there were eight hundred because Millie, while bugging Lenny to promise that she'd give her a referral, had told her there were eight hundred. "If this one refuses me, there are seven-hundred-ninety-nine more to choose from," she'd said.)

Decorating the sheetrock and yellow paint, a crowd of life-sized cutouts of happy children danced along the baseboards, balanced on the mounted coat hooks, and peeked over door frames. The rest of the wall space, minus the projection wall, displayed images of licensed carriers. Some were singles, and some were in pairs with one or both in the couple pregnant. All of the carriers had shining cheeks. Their hands held bulging bellies, and each posed in front of a nature scene—a wildflower meadow, a springtime forest, a rippled lake. There was also a hazy white light that glowed behind them, but it was so subtle Lenny didn't notice it until looking away. She stared at it now, trying to see it straight on, but she was having a hard time making it out.

Floyd tapped the folder on her lap. "Why don't we apply, too? For in case."

"In case of what?"

He shrugged. He said almost under his breath, "Maybe the basement people are giving the wrong idea about things, or. It could be good. Never know."

Lenny searched the waiting room for the restroom sign. "Goofy-bear, we're here for Millie, so don't get all silly." She whispered, "Please, please don't talk about the basement in public." She got up and asked Floyd to watch her folder.

"You aren't leaving, are you?" Millie jumped out of her seat on the other side of the waiting room and dropped her briefcase on Hugh's lap. Hugh moved it to her empty chair.

From inside her stall, Lenny heard Millie sighing and fiddling with things at the sinks. She flushed the toilet and opened the door.

"If the general reference doesn't work," Millie said, "will you please reconsider applying?"

Lenny ran water over her hands. "Aren't there seven-hundred-ninety-nine mo—"

"Obviously they all share the same information in a central database. Not everything I say actually means something.—Lenny," she said and moved between Lenny and the exit, "one licensed reference can nullify as many as two failed sections, depending on what they are. If I fail to provide appropriate answers on the emotional evaluation, for example." Millie tilted her head, reminding Lenny of the way she used to be in school. "Doesn't Floyd want one?"

"He does," Lenny said.

"Then you could also be a carrier."

"He wants to adopt."

"Adopt." Millie's chin tucked into her neck and her mouth turned down. "Is he incapable?"

"I don't think so."

The truth was, Lenny didn't know. She hadn't come up with a painless way to ask him to find out. Any talk about children gave him hope that she'd changed her mind, but she was so sure of what she didn't want that she called the toll-free Microchip Monitoring Center on a weekly basis to confirm her hormone was active. She knew too well that chips failed, sometimes. Her shelter had taken in more than a few unregistered, un-chipped infants, most with apology notes stuffed in a pocket or a sock. (Her shelter had then brought them in for chipping, as the law required, and then transferred them to a new shelter with neonatal professionals on the volunteer staff, all of it funded for the most part by a small portion of Lenny's inheritance.)

Millie said, "So what if he wants to adopt? You could still impregnate."

"Impregnate!" Lenny laughed. "Why?"

"Because. It isn't enough to be licensed, what do you th—What do you…do you suppose would happen? Every applicant seeking a reference would persuade every person they know to apply, and that would overwhelm the system. Carrier references are the only references of true value to the board."

"You said licensed."

"Correct. Licensed. I naturally assumed 'and carrying' was understood."

"But I don't want to be a carrier."

"Yes, Lenny, you've said that, but couldn't you do it for me? What about the benefits?"

Do It for Your Country's Continued Positive Growth, urged the pamphlets Lenny threw away at least once a week. The carrier on the cover was a silhouette wearing a sun halo. Inside, a bulleted list praised the integrity and patriotism of licensed parents.

- *A licensed parent is a proven paragon of moral superiority.*
- *Empathy, gentleness, patience, and kindness are the hallmarks of any licensed parent.*
- *The license to parent is a high honor reserved for the country's select few who exhibit excellence of character.*
- *In a world of uncertainty, a licensed parent's contribution is a certain step toward global harmony...*

Lenny had somehow been added to the Parent Licensing Bureau's mailing list, a recruitment effort everyone knew was narrowly targeted. Some of the shelter staff Lenny worked with had been getting them, too, and a few had been convinced to go through the evaluation process. Lenny stuffed all the pamphlets she found tucked in her door to the bottom of the trash can where Floyd would never see them. (She'd never told Millie about them, either, because she knew the bureau hadn't sent Millie any pamphlets. Millie would have told her if they had.)

Millie went on: "You do know that you wouldn't have to carry beyond the referral process. I've made contacts through interviews, if short-term pregnancy is your preference. The board's only requirement is a positive pregnancy test. However," she said quietly, "you should know they urine test all references in-house. No faking."

Before Lenny could respond, Millie sidled close enough to whisper in her ear. Lenny instinctively pulled back, expecting nicotine breath, but Millie must have held off that morning for the interview. She smelled like mint.

Millie murmured against her ear, "If you're opposed to early eviction and elect to carry to term, we both know you of all people can make a successful drop."

Because Lenny refused to impregnate, she didn't see the point in telling Millie a drop could only be a guaranteed success if the government didn't know about the pregnancy. They didn't surveil families, but they did have records of positive pregnancy tests and live births.

Millie pushed on: Not only would Lenny not be caught and therefore not exiled, but Exile couldn't possibly be as terrible as everyone believed it was. That it was worse than prison was an unsubstantiated rumor, Millie said. Its true conditions were known only to Exile workers and residents.

"I do know it can't be any worse than what Chester Walton's mother would have done to us had she caught us," Millie said.

Lenny couldn't remember Millie having brought up that day once in the twelve years since it had happened, and she hated the sudden, sickening suspicion that she might have been holding onto it, waiting for a moment like this.

She remembered, then, that that was the same day she'd promised Millie she would owe her for censoring her Chester Walton story.

"Is this about the Chester article?" she said. "Because I never said it explicitly, but I thought I paid you back for that with the house Floyd and I—"

"No! No, no."

"Is it—Is it about Chester's mom? Do I owe you for that?"

"Oh, Lenny! Do you think you owe me for that?"

Lenny assumed the best and hugged her, and Millie stiffened the way she always did. Lenny let her go, smiled, and said, "Good luck today."

When they returned to the waiting room, Lenny took her seat next to Floyd, who looked past her at Millie. Millie smiled at him as she tucked herself into her chair.

Lenny said to Floyd, "Are you two colluding?"

"What? No, we're not canoodling. What do you think?"

She bumped his shoulder with hers. "I said 'colluding.'"

"Anyone'd be a fool to collude with her." He kissed her cheek. "Here."

Lenny took the zippered folder of tax documents (her mother's included, in case the board needed them) and laid it on her lap.

"The combination is your dad's birthday," her mother had said over shrimp cocktail in the dining room the night before she'd killed herself. She'd bought the neatly packaged shrimp precooked, pre-peeled, and deveined. (Lenny's dad would have demanded fresh shrimp, had he been there, but he'd been gone five years, and her mom had always liked the circle of pink shrimp from the grocery store cooler.) The Isley Brothers played around them.

"Tell me what you're going to do," her mom said.

Lenny pushed a shrimp through the cocktail sauce. "Take the winter painting—the one with the white house, not the one with the horse—off the wall and open the safe."

"Tell me what you're going to do tomorrow."

Lenny took a bite and wiped the cloth napkin against her lips. "Leave at the same time I do every day, come home at the same time I always do, and don't look for you."

"And."

"And make sure the basement room gets finished."

"Promise me all of it."

Lenny's parents had taught her to take promises seriously, so she never promised anything unless she meant it. She thought back to the day her mom had told her she was ready to die—"I've decided it's my turn, sweet daughter"—and truly believed she hadn't imagined her mom's genuine happiness when she'd told her she was not, and had never been, depressed, but was simply ready. Lenny also remembered that when her aunt Kat was dying, her mom had said it was beautiful that people could decide how or when they would leave.

"Your aunt Kat has known for years what smoking is doing to her," she said. "Every filter she bites down on with those bloody teeth is a tiny step toward saying goodbye." The only tragic deaths, her mom had said, were the ones the living fought against. "Like those poor, belittled girls you knew in high school. I don't care what the legal word for it is. They were murdered by judgment every bit as much as your dad was murdered by a gun." She'd sighed. "My poor Ernie-bear. Those last moments must have been so devastating."

"He didn't go in a boring way, at least, right?" Lenny said.

Her mom had laughed. "Right. But he'd never want to leave without saying goodbye, you know that."

Her mom was still waiting, taking tiny bites of shrimp and bopping her head to the music. Lenny wanted to run to the basement and hide forever in the construction dust, never promise a word, but that would only delay things. "It's a simple matter of time," her mom had said after Murphy died. "The greatest mystery—to me, anyway—is who goes first? Will it be your dad? Will it be me? Will it be you?" She'd lunged at Lenny to tickle her, and they'd all laughed over the fresh pile of Murphy dirt.

Lenny wiped her eyes with her sleeve and promised everything she was supposed to promise. "I'll miss you."

"I know. But sweetheart, you're happy and grown and in love, so I know you'll be just fine. And besides, you would miss me whether I died by choice tomorrow or against my will ten years from now." She picked up a shrimp and moved it like a puppet. In a deep shrimp voice, she said, "You have to allow people be every bit as true to who they are as you should always be to yourself."

"Oxford."

The whiny, nasal voice pulled Lenny from the dining room, but she could still smell the spicy cocktail sauce.

"Millicent Oxford."

TWENTY THREE

The bureau counselors sitting before Millie wore matching lilac suits. Baby rattles decorated their green ties. A soft yellow ceiling lamp shined a cone of light over their shared desk and two brushed nickel name plates. One read WILLARD. The other, MAXINE.

"We don't expect perfection," Maxine said.

"I'm afraid I don't know what you do expect," Millie said. "With all due respect, of course."

Willard said, "It's a simple question, Ms. Oxford. This is an enormous responsibility with any number of potential outcomes. Not all of them are...pleasant. You might have regrets, later down the road."

"Yes, regrets," Maxine nodded.

"Some people report feeling depressed," Willard said. "Some experience anxiety. Drinking. Not as much now as there was before, thanks to licensing, but uncertainty is a tricky little demon, isn't it, and it just loves to hide behind denial. Are you in denial, Ms. Oxford?"

"No."

"Do you drink?"

"No." But she did very much crave a drink, and a cigarette, too.

"You might start. Do you smoke?"

"No."

"There are also medical risks to the carrier pre-childbirth," Maxine said. "Ectopic pregnancy. Placental abruption. Gestational diabetes."

"Despite all your best efforts—and I'm sure you'd put forth your best efforts—your child could be born with special needs," Willard said. "The demands on you could be...demanding, and for all the years of your life. Yet, here you sit." He looked at a tablet on the desk. "What's more, you're involving others, asking them to commit their time and energy to this future child. What we want to know—again, Ms. Oxford—is why." He leaned back in his chair. "Some tragedy in your childhood, maybe."

"Tragedy?"

Maxine squinted. "Abuse?"

Millie sad, "No."

Willard said, "Alcoholism."

"No, sir."

"Was it your father?"

"Was what my father?"

Willard gestured at Millie's crotch with a wave of his finger.

"I understand these questions may seem offensive," Maxine said. "Non sequitur: It's been two years since the death of your mother, and you've been on the wait list since that time. It strikes me that your initial request for an evaluation might have been influenced by grief, which is transitory, or by an oath you made to your dying or dead mother who, as you know, won't be here to witness whether you have a child. Does either reason sound legitimate to you?"

Millie wasn't sure whether Maxine meant legitimate as a reason or legitimate as a guess. She thought of her mother lying in bed with a dwindling roll of paper towels in her arm to catch the red phlegm, and the only thing she had said about parenting since Millie was young: "It may have been unfair of me to shape your perspective of childbearing, but it was necessary. It comforts me to know that if you do have a child some day, it will be your conscious intent and not what many so ludicrously reduce to a biological imperative. In rational, thinking human beings, if you can imagine." She took a shallow breath, and then another. She looked at Millie—straight at her, for the first time since Millie was a teenager sitting at the kitchen table—and Millie waited, steeling herself for something she suspected her mother must have been saving for when she was close to death. A sentence that would explain the last twenty-seven years. Just one, because her mother had never offered more than one sentence at a time (unless lecturing about the media), and Millie hardly expected dying to change her completely. Knowing that did nothing to stop the rush of hope that her mother would tell her she was proud of the writing she'd done and that she'd always loved her "quite a bit."

The short, unbidden fantasy made Millie's face so hot her cheeks itched.

Her mother said, "—Or an immature impulse, as it was for your father. Have you heard from your father?"

Millie had handed her mother a new paper towel sheet for her bleeding cigarette mouth and said no.

She hadn't heard from him then, and she hadn't since.

Maxine said, "Ms. Oxford."

"We can give her a minute," Willard said.

Millie said she didn't require a minute, but thanked him for his consideration. She admitted to being confused by their hesitation to approve her on the spot for an evaluation. Her mother had been a prominent figure, and her letter of request for an evaluation had named her late aunt Margaret and uncle Ernie, two of the state's leading philanthropists, as part-time guardians throughout her childhood. She explained that her good friend Lenore Mabary, daughter of the state's leading philanthropists, not only devoted herself to "the abandoned" but had also recently built Millie a small house on the Mabary property, which was tangible evidence of the support Millie could expect to receive as a carrier.

"Yes, Ms. Oxford," Maxine said. "But everyone in your letter, excepting the young Ms. Mabary, whose support, I understand, will be solely financial, is dead. Your child will have only you. We kn—"

"And...what's his name?" Willard consulted the tablet. "Hugh."

"We know," Maxine continued, "what the people around you have done, Ms. Oxford, but what have you done?"

Millie's hands and feet turned cold. She wanted to scream that she had been a writer for the *Daily Fact* since she was eighteen, thank you—and without having attended college or any formal writing classes!—, but the only person who had ever cared about the newspaper was her mother. Millie blamed her mother, now, for having made her believe writing for the *Fact* was an achievement unattainable for most, one that made Millie unique, deserving of respect and reverence (words her mother had never uttered, but that Millie had naturally inferred). Strangers who made eye contact with her on the street had done so, she'd once assumed, because they'd read something she'd written. The only reason they never spoke to her, she'd of course believed, was that she intimidated them.

It had taken Millie until three and a half weeks after the funeral, when her mother was no longer confined to a bed and asking Millie to read to her, to recognize what little to average value the general public assigned newspaper writers. Everyday readers rarely, if ever, noticed bylines. The man who claimed to love her, a writer himself before he became an editor, took her writing for granted. Lenny, who more than anyone else should have delighted in her dearest friend's talents and accomplishments, would merely smile politely and say, "Not yet, but I will," any time Millie asked whether she'd read her latest story.

To Willard and Maxine (and the rest of them), Millie had done nothing of value. As herself she was, therefore, nothing of value. Not interesting enough as a person to have captured her mother's attention, and not lovable enough to have retained the affection of the one man who was (ostensibly) biologically predisposed to love her. She wasn't warm, she was objectively unattractive, and she wasn't funny (although Lenny did sometimes laugh at her). She was intelligent, but Willard and Maxine hadn't indicated intelligence mattered, nor had the world at large. "What have you achieved," or as Millie understood it, "What makes you worthwhile," was not a question ever, ever directed at someone like Lenny, who was openly affectionate, extraordinarily wealthy, and observably beautiful. Had Willard and Maxine, or any stranger, noticed upon encountering Millie for the first time that she was carrying, they also wouldn't have been inclined to direct such a question at her. The bulge beneath her shirt would have told them everything they needed to know. *This person*, it would tell them, *is to be admired and adored.*

Millie remembered she was supposed be formulating an answer to their question. Because she couldn't think of a single logical reason to want or have a child, she told Maxine and Willard what she'd once heard Lenny's mom say: It was a feeling. A very strong feeling. Something "deep in her belly." She'd simply always known she wanted to be a parent.

"Oh, you want to be a *parent*," Maxine clapped. "Why didn't you say so?"

"Your application says biological only," Willard said.

"I'm sure she didn't know she could check both boxes if she wanted to, Willard. Did you know that, Ms. Oxford?"

Millie did know that. She shook her head no.

Maxine's face lifted in an exaggerated grin. "Wonderful! Then you are open to adoption?"

Millie had prepared for this question. She'd researched body language and what others looked for when trying to determine whether something was a lie. She would not hold eye contact for too long, one of two major tells, and she wouldn't fidget or touch her face while speaking.

"I considered it quite seriously." Millie scratched her nose, froze, then scratched it again and asked for a tissue. "We both—Hugh and I—did." She blew air into the soft cloth, bore it as convincingly as she could into a nostril, and then crumpled it in her fist. "But after months and months of painful conversations, we came to the conclusion—the *excruciating* conclusion—that it would be irresponsible of us to not parent biologically." Earnest eye contact with Willard, then Maxine. "We would, of course, prefer to give a loving home to a parentless child who's spent years sleeping on a dirty cot, but it would be…as I said, irresponsible. May I explain?"

Willard and Maxine sighed and leaned back in their chairs.

The explanation, as Millie explained it, was that she and Hugh felt it was their civic duty to inject proven intelligence and decency into the gene pool. Hugh had been raised by his biological parent and was an upstanding newspaper editor with an innate tendency toward fairness. She was an award-winning reporter (she'd twice earned Reporter of the Month, and the entire staff—including Millie—had received notification via intraoffice email) whose daily mission was to inform the public and hold people accountable. Although she and Hugh had agreed in the midst of one of their emotional discussions that some of the shelter children were probably good people, there was no way to be certain, she said. Had they not been born to parents who could so easily discard them?

"A dro—A destitute product of the birth explosion murdered Ernie Aronne, as you know," Millie said. She sniffed for effect, having never mastered producing a tear. "Or Uncle Ernie, as I called him. According to the police report, the woman shot him right in the face for simply sitting in the passenger seat of his wife's sports car." She waited for a reaction. There was none. She swallowed. "My own mother was so upset by the degrading state of the world that she smoked herself to death, which in turn destroyed my father." She had no knowledge that he'd heard of her death. "He left the country," Millie assumed, "and has never been seen again. Without his influence, the businesses my mother spent her entire life building have failed."

"Oxford Spirits," Maxine said.

Willard said, "Ah, yes. Eyesores. Addict dens."

Yes, Millie said, yes. But she and Hugh could aid in the gradual correction of society by adding their own healing offspring to the existing disease.

Maxine absently tapped a finger on the desk. Willard's eyes were closed.

"That was my conclusion," Millie said.

Willard opened his eyes and scratched inside his ear. He and Maxine made notes on their tablets. Willard tapped his screen and the tablet slid out a piece of paper he pushed across the desk. It was a standard evaluation agreement form with unchecked boxes beside BIOLOGICAL and ADOPTIVE.

"You're a go for evaluation," Willard said. "Before we schedule you, we'd like to ask you one more time to consider adoption. All you'd have to do is check both of those boxes, there. Just the adoption box would be fine, too. You never know, you could get one of the teenagers and it'd be gone in a few years. Short commitment."

"The box you check has no bearing on the outcome of the evaluation, of course," Maxine said. "We simply need to know in advance so that if you pass we can be expeditious in forwarding accurate information to the chip command unit."

Millie had no intention of downgrading to adoption. Adopting meant never impregnating, which meant never being seen while impregnated.

"As I said," Millie lowered her head in apology, "I would love to adopt a precious, needy child, but—"

"Yes, we're sure you would." Maxine reached for the form and put a check inside the box beside BIOLOGICAL, initialed it, and then had Willard and Millie initial it. (Millie clenched her teeth and forced the smile out of her mind, because she was supposed to be sad, so sad that her commitment to a better world prevented her from adopting.)

Maxine duplicated the form in the desk copier and handed one to Millie while filing the original in a drawer. Willard instructed Millie to keep her copy in a safe place. She would need it with her when she returned for her evaluation.

Maxine pressed a button. "Donald, send in Ms. Lenore Mayberry, please."

"Mabary," Millie said.

"Correction, Donald. Ms. Lenore MAYbahry."

Millie asked why the referral slip couldn't simply be emailed, which seemed more efficient.

"Doesn't even have a child, yet, and already she wants us to babysit for her." Maxine gave two bats of her eyelashes.

TWENTY FOUR

Lenny looked around the room while the licensing people studied her documents. Big windows framed green trees. The walls were mauve. A perfectly straight line of framed photographs circled the room, four on each wall. All of the faces behind the glass were parents with children or carriers in the late stages, and all of them had straight, white teeth.

Millie sat next to her with her hands in a tight knot on her lap.

"I don't see any paperwork reflecting rent payments," Willard said.

Lenny explained that Millie and Hugh had only recently moved in and that she and Floyd were giving them time to get settled. The first three months had been rent free, and their first payment wasn't due for two weeks.

Lenny didn't want them to pay at all, but Hugh insisted even though they didn't ask for the house. Lenny had heard something on the radio about peak levels of violent crime in Prospect, where Millie and Hugh were sharing an efficiency apartment, and she'd tasked Floyd with getting it built as fast as he could. Within six months, and with the help of the entire crew he'd taken over from Lenny's dad, Floyd had cleared a wide path through the trees, cleared even more trees for a lot for the home, and built the small, simple, but sturdy two-story Dutch colonial one hundred yards from Lenny's back door. It was far enough away for their respective privacy, but—unless Millie veered off the crude driveway or rough field to wade through the trees—close enough so that Lenny would always see Millie coming. (This was just a fact. It wasn't the reason she'd asked Floyd to build the house—or to build it in that spot. Lenny could have offered to help pay for an apartment in a nicer neighborhood miles away, but nicer didn't usually mean safer unless it was a remote neighborhood like Forest Retreat Estates. Building Millie a house on her own property was the first thing Lenny had been able to do that had felt like a meaningful return favor. It was a bonus that Lenny could sit in the living room with Deborah, or whoever might live in the basement in the future, without worrying Millie would suddenly appear in the big back window, the cigarette she'd taken the long way around the house to finish smoking burning between her fingers.)

"And will this Floyd Lowe be in any way involved in the life of Ms. Oxford's child?" the one behind the MAXINE name plate said.

"I don't think so," Lenny said. "But he likes children, so he might play with it. Is that fine?"

"That's fine," Willard winked.

"Most of your wealth, Ms. Mabary, appears to be a sizeable inheritance," Maxine said.

"And she insists on driving an old, rusty van," Millie said. "She could have bought at least ten brand new AV vans with what Aunt Margaret left her."

Maxine looked up. "You raise an interesting question, Ms. Oxford. As you characterized the relationship in your letter of application, you were all but blood related to this family. Why did the woman you call your aunt not leave you some of her fortune?"

Millie opened her mouth, but said nothing. She turned to Lenny.

A lifetime of what Lenny knew must have been unimaginable loneliness and rejection changed Millie's features for a flicker of a second. In that shortest of moments, the Millie Lenny had known since birth was hardly recognizable. Lenny had seen the forced frowns Millie used when she wanted something, but this was different. It was as if she couldn't pull together the strength she needed to lift her lips into a flat line. Her face was usually ruddy, but now her cheeks and nose filled with deep pink, and her shoulders, her back, and even her forehead seemed to sag. The bursting energy Lenny had always seen in Millie's eyes was, in that flash of unguarded emotion, replaced by such lifelessness that her irises dulled.

She had a strong urge to smooth Millie's hair (but didn't) and was suddenly prepared to do or say anything (short of applying for a license, herself) to help. For once, it had nothing to do with what she owed her aunt Kat or Millie.

Lenny cleared her throat. She had only ever told kind, little lies, usually by answering "Yes" or "No," depending on what the person wanted to hear. And she'd kept a secret, like anyone else, but that wasn't lying. It was loyalty to the secret. Intentionally putting together a string of words and pretending they were facts, though, was something she'd never done, and it made her throat swell. She silently asked her dad for his understanding (and knew he would have given it to her).

"Daddy was a miser, see." Lenny's index finger twitched. She clasped her hands. "He wanted all the family money to stay in the family. But Mamma, she wanted to change her will to include Millie after Daddy died." Peripherally, Lenny saw that Millie was looking ahead at Willard and Maxine. "But then," Lenny said, "she up and died, too, before she ever got the chance. She sure did love Millie, though. Like she was her own kin. She'd 'a' wanted her to have this money."

Lenny held her breath. She was almost positive Millie knew enough to play along if Maxine or Willard asked any questions. Millie, of course, knew Lenny's mom could easily have changed her will before she died. She was the only other person who knew the truth about the suicide.

When the house cleared out after the memorial service, Millie had stayed behind. (At the time, the basement was still in the process of becoming the panic room Lenny's mom had wanted her to build, so there'd been nothing to hide from Millie and no reason to be nervous about her hanging around.) Lenny had hoped Millie would be a comfort, but Millie was too interested in the what, where, how, and why of Lenny's mom's death to be anything but her exhausting self by pinging Lenny with questions: "What could Aunt Margaret possibly have been doing out there in the woods during her writing hours?" "I wrote a story about heart failure, so I know nearly everything there is to know about it. I don't accept that that's how she died." "What if someone killed her? They killed Uncle Ernie because of money, so why wouldn't they have done the same to Aunt Margaret?" "It's all highly suspect. I can't comprehend why you wouldn't want an investigation or an autopsy. Both!"

Lenny's mom wouldn't have wanted Millie to know about the suicide. "People will get the wrong impression if they know," her mom had said, but Millie wasn't "people," and it was hard for Lenny to keep things from her. Millie was cunning, and she knew Lenny.

At first it was fun to watch her pacing the kitchen with a glass of wine, her eyes flitting around the room as she scraped around inside her head for answers, but Lenny was too sad to find humor in anything for very long and too tired to be evasive. She told the truth.

Millie swirled the wine in her glass and stared off into the living room, nodding. "Hm!" she finally said. "I wonder if there are others like her out there. Of a similar sentiment regarding death, that is. And still alive, obviously. It could be a story, don't you think? 'You only die once, and for some, it's an opportunity to do it right'? I may pitch it. They'll most likely change the headline, because they always do…" She trailed off when Lenny started crying right in front of her.

Lenny didn't know what she expected, or even what she wanted, from Millie. Condolences, at least.

Millie put her weight on one foot, then the other, and fiddled with her wine glass. "Oh." She rubbed the narrow stem with her thumb. "I suppose it wouldn't be a relief for you, would it? You must feel very privileged to be sad."

Millie had never written the story. (Not because of Lenny, but because, she'd said, it wasn't easy to find happy people willing to talk about death planning. The stigma was "too oppressive.")

Lenny returned her attention to Willard and Maxine at the flick of something bright. Maxine was holding her tablet with its lit screen facing out.

"I don't see your name listed here as a secondary guardian," Maxine said. "You'll commit to carrying the financial burden, but not to providing physical support?"

"Yes, ma'am. I don't want to be a guardian, no."

"Too bad. You'd be a shoo-in," Willard said with a *tsk*, and Millie tensed so fully that Lenny saw it happen.

Maxine laid the tablet on the desk. "And how would you characterize Ms. Oxford's potential as a parent?"

Millie looked quickly at Lenny, her unnaturally light blue eyes holding eye contact just long enough for Lenny to feel the pressure.

She tried to imagine Millie being attentive to someone (or something) else's needs. Instead, she saw Millie grabbing twice as many dog treats as Lenny so Murphy would sit by her, and then pushing Murphy away when she lost interest. Millie taking notes while abandoned children answered questions for a story, and then walking away from them—some in mid-sentence, some crying—when she had what she needed. Millie writing the Chester Walton story in her head throughout the…event. Millie at twenty hustling to the food table at a shelter Christmas party to beat a little boy named Jimmy to the last sugar cookie. ("Oh!" she'd said, pink crystals packed into the corners of her mouth. "I didn't know anyone else wanted it.") Millie on one of their rare double dates using questions to interrupt private looks between Lenny and Floyd, laughing charmingly at the men when she had their attention, and punishing Hugh with flattering comments directed at Floyd if Hugh happened to talk one-on-one with Lenny.

Maybe none of that meant she would be a bad parent. Lenny thought there must be all kinds of people who didn't care about anyone but their own children. That Millie had tried to pressure Lenny into getting pregnant for a referral, and that she had only ever mentioned carrying, but not parenting, didn't have to mean she'd be anything but a wonderful mother to her own child.

Anything was possible.

Anything but Millie making it all the way through the evaluation process, Lenny reminded herself with a relieved sigh that Willard responded to by sticking a finger in his ear. Lenny doubted Millie would even get as far as the dog. (Hoped, for the dog's sake.)

Maxine tapped a fingernail on the table and raised her eyebrows at Lenny.

Lenny said, "I reckon she'll be the best mamma imaginable to any little baby, ma'am."

TWENTY FIVE

No one but a person of measurable value would ever have reason to be in so elegant a space as Lenny's bedroom. Millie had always admired it. Even when it was still her aunt Margaret's writing office, dressed down with a plain couch and cluttered desk, there was no hiding its extravagantly high ceilings, grand wood beams, or tall, wide windows overlooking the forest— and now the pity house Floyd had built in a clearing. ("Floyd's team can build a house in their sleep. And we already own the property, so you'll only have to pay a portion of the taxes," Lenny had said. Millie had of course accepted, because even with their combined full-time incomes from the medium-sized paper, she and Hugh still only made enough to rent an apartment in a questionable neighborhood).

Had the Mabary mansion been left to her, Millie would have made the office her bedroom just as Lenny had. However, she'd have installed a more comfortable bed. Millie didn't know why, with her excessive wealth, Lenny would bother with anything less than memory foam. There were times when Millie would raise her pelvis to Floyd's mouth, and the rough pillow-top material would grate her elbows through the sheets. It wasn't painful, necessarily, but it was a distraction.

Millie tapped Floyd's head. "Come up," she said, and he did, caging her shoulders between his arms as he moved on top of her.

"Do you love me?" Millie said.

"I love Lenny," he breathed against her forehead.

"Yes, Floyd. Everybody loves Lenny. But do you love me, too?"

"Sure," he said. "Yeah. Oh… Oh, oh, what're you…oh, yeah. Oh yeah oh yeah oh yeah!"

Millie wanted a cigarette when they finished, but Floyd always made her surrender the pack when she walked in the door. Lenny didn't allow smoking inside, and Floyd said he didn't trust her to not sneak one. In lieu of smoking she picked at her fingernails, which annoyed Floyd. He slapped a hand on top of hers and said, "Quit it."

"Nothing I did would bother you if you truly loved me."

"Lenny bothers me all the time."

Millie rolled to face him and didn't pull up the sheets to cover her breasts. "How so?"

Floyd shrugged. "I don't know."

"Come on."

"I don't know."

"Tell me."

Floyd adjusted his feet under the blanket. He sighed and tucked a hand behind his head. "I mean, okay. You know Bertram."

"The black one?"

"That's Pike. Bertram is the—"

"The calico."

"The black and white one. Anyway, she feeds him with a spoon, sometimes."

"Soup?"

"Cat soup?"

"Well, Floyd, I don't know."

"Naw, what do you think? It's the regular shit from the can."

Millie adjusted her arm and the slant of her back to draw more attention to her breasts, which were substantially smaller and therefore much classier than Lenny's. "That is annoying."

"Yeah, well, it's just the cat has a hard time with the food, sometimes. It's too soft, or."

"You don't have to defend her."

"I feel like I do."

"What else?"

Floyd pressed his head deeper into his pillow. "I don't want to say any more."

Millie stroked his hair. "Floyd, you've been exiting my body for the last five minutes. How could you possibly do any of this if Lenny were completely faultless?"

"Fault's not the word." Floyd pulled up the sheet to cover Millie's chest.

She pulled it back down. "Goodness. I had no idea you found me so offensive."

"Not offensive."

"Please tell me just one more thing." There had to be more that could make Lenny difficult to love. Millie pulled up the sheet again. "Better?" She gave him empathetic eyes. "I'm not asking for me, but for you. Who else can you talk to about the woman only you and I know so well? I'm here for you, Floyd."

Floyd picked up the clock from the bedside table, looked at the time, then set it back down and flopped onto his back. He blew at the stringy hair

on his forehead. After a minute he told Millie about a time he'd come home
after fourteen hours of finishing a house. He said he and Lenny hadn't seen
each other in two days, they were so busy all the time, and he'd been excited
to see the light on when he pulled into the driveway.

"She's usually sleeping, or too busy for me, you know, so I thought I'd
get a chance to hug her, or kiss, or…and we'd, you know, sit and talk,
something."

He knew the sound of his truck carried into the house, so he'd
expected to find her waiting in the foyer. Instead, not even the dogs were
there, and no one came at his keys falling on the hallway table. He followed
the light to the living room and found Lenny sitting on the couch with
De—

He stopped.

"Who? Who was she on the couch with?"

"Uh, De—dead…dead asleep cats," he said finally, and, "She didn't
even get up, 'cause she had…she had all three on her lap, not to mention
the dogs on both sides. I just guess I sort of hoped she'd interrupt—
whatever—to come, you know, out, but all she did was say hi from the
couch. I mean, she smiled, and it was a really nice—Look, she didn't mean
anyth—"

"Obviously the animals are more important to her than you are," Millie
said. "I would never treat you that way." She stroked Floyd's earlobe,
stopping when she heard something at the closed bedroom door. "Sh."

"Cat. He scratches."

"Why don't you get rid of them?"

"The cats?"

"And the dogs."

"Serious?"

"They're animals, Floyd. Simply explain that they're having a negative
impact on your relationship. Bring them to her shelter, and she'll have
plenty of opportunities to spend time with them. Or leave the back door
open. Animals can take care of themselves."

Floyd climbed out of bed. "Time to get up." He put on his pants.
"Anyway. You don't get it."

"I don't get what?"

"It's not like that all the time. Or, I don't know, maybe it is, or—like
you said—what am I doing with you?" He picked up her shirt and tossed it
on the bed. "C'mon. I have somewhere to be."

"That isn't exactly what I said, Floyd." She had hoped an orgasm would
relax her before the evaluation, but Floyd was being obnoxious, and now

her shirt was covered in cat from having been on the floor. She picked off the hairs one at a time. "If you had a child together, the animals would come second," she said. "You know how Lenny is with children."

"She said she doesn't want one."

"And you believe her? Floyd, everyone wants to be a carrier. People who say they don't are simply being nonconformist. Secretly, they want the license and the status."

"And the kid."

"Oh. Yes. Well, obviously I assumed that went without saying." Millie turned over her shirt to pluck the hairs from the back. "Are you capable?"

"Yep. Doesn't matter. She won't get licensed, so."

"When did you last have sex?"

"Not your business. Put your shirt on."

"If she accidentally got pregnant," Millie said, checking her sleeves for fur, "if her hormone failed, for example, or had been paused for some unknown reason—no system is perfect—and you happened to have intercourse with her—today, for example—and she ended up impregnated, she would feel compelled to apply for a license." Millie put on her bra. "Most likely."

"What, you hacked her? Paid someone, or?"

"I know it's something you want. She told me. I also know she loves you and wants you to be happy. What would make you happy, Floyd? I'm not saying she has been hacked and I'm not saying she hasn't, but one way to be sure she hasn't is to advise her to call the monitors. You could do that instead, advise her to call the monitors, if you chose."

Floyd stood at the end of the bed, his pale chest a sick white in the gray light from the window. His large, flat nipples were the color of ash. He said, "They'll probably flunk you straight out if you're late."

"It takes ten minutes to get there," Millie said, but he was right. It wouldn't do to cut the timing close. She slid her arms through her shirt sleeves. Buttoning the buttons, she said, "They use authentic, twenty-three carat gold foil on the decorative license." She pulled her hair away from her face and secured it in a band. She knew about the foil, she said, because several years ago the *Fact* had received a sample certificate from the licensing bureau's publicity department for a story Millie had been writing. "I already have the perfect frame for it, and I've selected the best wall space in the living room. It's where Hugh's father's painting is now. You've seen it. The certificate is going to look absolutely beautiful there."

Millie stepped into the licensing center at ten minutes to nine. Hugh was already there, his bright blue tie a beacon guiding her to the far side of the crowded waiting room. Millie signed in at the reception window and stepped through applicants (and clearly at least some secondary guardian applicants) whose ages Millie estimated to range from as young as eighteen to as old as sixty. They leaned into one another, touched hands to legs, and laughed and joked. One in a tight group of five held out a plastic container of dark and light nuts that hand after hand reached in for. Millie noticed that their clothes were stained at the cuffs and collars, and in some cases were torn. ("We aren't concerned with the financial status of licensed individuals beyond their ability to provide nutritious meals, medical care, state-approved education, and weather-appropriate clothing to a child or children," licensing bureau spokesperson Bernard Marshall had said in a televised interview shortly after licensing guidelines were released to the public.) Millie's clothes were inexpensive, but they were at least intact and stain-free. Obviously the person in that group who was seeking the primary license needed an entire family to contribute financially as well as physically.

Millie straightened her back as she approached Hugh, who looked up, saw her, and immediately smiled. But then, with each swing of her arms, his smile faded a little bit more until it disappeared and his eyes returned to his reader.

Millie sat beside him. "Have you seen our competition?"

He said, "We aren't competing."

"Don't be silly."

"Their success doesn't mean our failure, or vice versa. We can all pass. We can all get licenses."

The happy family laughed over their container of nuts. Millie leaned into Hugh. "It's as if they brought every person they know." She was convinced the evaluators would look upon her more favorably if she had more people with her, but upon further consideration, she wasn't sure. Did more FCP volunteers indicate a stronger network, or a weaker applicant? It was impossible to know. "Well, it won't work, no matter how many reinforcements they bring to manipulate the system," she said. "Did you see their clothes? All together they can't even afford detergent."

"I'll bet our free house they have more money combined than we do."

"We have Lenny."

Hugh turned off his reader and folded his hands over it. "Maybe you're right. Maybe it is some underhanded plot to improve their chances. You probably should be worried. They have five people, and you only have one.

Maybe the licensing board'll give a lot of long, hard thought to that when comparing you to them."

"Hugh!"

"You have one person," he said again. "But one person who loves you completely. One, Millie."

"Why would you say something like that, and more than once?"

"I think I'm hoping one day you'll hear me."

"What about Lenny? She loves me. Floyd does, as well. By the way, did I ever tell you he used to rummage through the school trash cans? It's no wonder Lenny has no interest in applying for a license. They have the money, certainly, but someone who eats garbage hardly deserves to—"

Hugh slammed his reader into an empty chair. He grabbed Millie by both arms and forced her to face him. He held his nose so close to hers that the breath from it warmed her upper lip.

"You do not deserve a child," he said quietly. "Do you hear me? No one 'deserves' a child. A child isn't a cookie or a gold star. You don't 'earn' one."

"Don't be absurd, Hugh. Of course I des—"

"Somewhere inside you is the person you were before your parents got to you. Somewhere in there," he poked her chest hard, "is a tender, painfully sensitive human being. If she weren't in there, Katherine and Graham could never have done the damage they did. I wouldn't have liked you from the start—back when you let me see it, back when we used to wrestle and your favorite thing was me putting you over my shoulder—and I wouldn't like you in spite of yourself, now. It doesn't have to be irreparable, Mil. You can be that person again. But when you are, if you ever are—and I really hope you someday are, because I miss that girl—you still won't 'deserve' a child. The difference will be that you'll understand that, and that's the thing that'll bring you closer to being the kind of person a child would be even a little bit lucky to call 'Mom.'"

Millie yanked her arms free and rubbed them. She willed him to touch her gently, to pull her close and hold her head to his chest.

Instead, he sat there, his hands hanging uselessly over the arm rests.

She said, "Why, Hugh, how audacious of you to presume to have the requisite intellectual and emotional high ground to make that assessment."

Hugh's mouth turned down. He picked up his reader and turned it on.

For the next four minutes, Millie thought about what Hugh said. She was well aware that he may as well have just threatened to leave if she continued to be the person she was, but it was nothing she hadn't been prepared for since the first time he'd smiled so beautifully at her. His eventual disappearance was inevitable, but she'd become a natural at rejecting the effects of rejection.

"Hugh.—Hugh!"

"Yes, Millie."

"You're absolutely right."

She was nervous about the evaluation, she said. Could he blame her for being unpleasant under such stress?

She said, "Please give me another chance."

Without looking at her, he slid a hand under her chin to cup her jaw and cheek, guided her head closer to his, and kissed her temple.

It was the loveliest thing she had ever felt.

She turned away and looked at the ceiling, the lights.

He couldn't have meant it. If he did, it hardly mattered. It would never last.

Millie only hoped he would stay until they'd completed the evaluation. After that, if he left while she was pregnant, she was confident she could persuade Lenny to sign on as a secondary guardian. How could she resist someone who was already carrying?

They sat in silence for thirty more seconds. When Donald, the plump-lipped receptionist Millie remembered from her first visit, slowly made his way to the center of the waiting room and with a ridiculous pretense of authority said, "Proceed," the room as a whole got up and walked single-file through the door marked EVALUATION.

TWENTY SIX

Something wet and warm fell on Lenny's lip. Without thinking, she licked it. Salty. She ran her fingers over Floyd's face in the dark. She whispered, "Are you crying?"

"Crying? What, no. What do you think?"

She wrapped her arms around him (but not so tight his knees or elbows would scrape against the hard floor) and guided him deeper. She covered his mouth and giggled "Sh!" when he moaned. With the light off in the shelter's lounge—originally the clinic's reception office—it was impossible to see in, but it wasn't sound-proof. The "interim parents," as the residents called the staff ("interims" for short), knew what a locked door and dark room meant. They kept their distance, but the residents could sometimes get a little too close.

Harry Belafonte's "Day-O," Boris's favorite song, played on a loop. It was Boris's eighteenth birthday, and according to state and privately funded shelter guidelines, donor assistance to a resident ended on the resident's eighteenth birthday or the resident's adoption day, whichever came first. (Much of the funding at private shelters was distributed by shelter staff, but some donors tracked the progress of the residents and adjusted their donations according to who left and who stayed. Somehow, they chose favorites. Since resident profiles didn't include pictures, Lenny assumed they decided by name, age, or sex. Biological sex preference used to make Lenny nervous, but licensing had, thankfully, limited access to the children by sex traffickers, pedophiles, and the occasional non-sex slave shopper.)

Floyd was lasting longer than usual. Lenny had heard "Day-O" three times, now, and she was missing more of Boris's send-off than she'd counted on missing when Floyd had locked the door. Ordinarily, she'd have turned him down on a day like today. Send-offs were also naming days, an important rite of passage, but she got dizzy over sex with him and it had been too long. They'd been so busy.

She grabbed each of his cool, soft butt cheeks and pulled him against her. Over his shoulder she saw two or three young heads pass by the window. An interim named Harry urged them away and, even though all the staff members were technically equals, said, "Sorry, Ms. Mabary." Years ago she'd have wanted to yell back, "Please just call me Lenny," but they all knew (through no fault of Lenny's) that her money kept the shelter running and their paychecks regular. After enough time being treated like their superior—which meant none of them wanted to be friends with her, either—she'd let it go and had learned not to bristle at the "Ms."

A set of eyes peered in with small hands cupped to the mirrored side of the window. Lenny buried her face in Floyd's neck, which smelled like a familiar coconut and lemon scent, and said "I love you" to help him along. He wouldn't want to miss Boris's event, either. Boris had always been his favorite.

Someone pounded the glass. "Miss Lenny! Miss Lenny!"

Floyd grunted and moved faster.

"Boris is…"

Floyd reached under her and pulled her where he wanted her, his confident assertiveness and other things filling her head with blood and such loud rushing air sounds that she almost didn't hear the little girl say over Floyd's expertly quiet orgasm, "…rubbing cake all over everything in his Independence Bag!"

"I'm really sorry," Floyd said as Lenny cleaned up. He'd only pushed his pants down to his knees, so he was already dressed. He stood with his back to the vending machine and watched her until she was put together.

"What in the world would you be sorry for?" She crossed the room to kiss him on the cheek. "We only missed a little bit. He still has the naming and his speech, and he just delayed it all, anyway." She kissed him again, near his ear, this time, and breathed him in. "You smell like Millie's shampoo."

"Oh, yeah," Floyd said. "That's just 'cause we screwed this morning."

Lenny was used to Floyd saying things to make her insecure—*People stop loving, you know, People leave, People mess up*—but he'd never pretended to confess to something. She took a step back, and Floyd laughed.

"I'm kidding, what do you think?" He pulled her to him and said into her hair, "She was going off to her eval and caught me in the truck. Said her shower drain was clogged, so I snaked it and got so much dredge and hair shit all over me I took a shower right then."

He let go of her and smiled. His back and shoulders curled inward, closing his body around his chest. Fine, dirty-blond hair feathered across his wide forehead, the split ends framing large brown eyes that didn't take the smile from his lips. They never had. Now and then, when he stopped trying to, Floyd could break her heart.

And she could have lived with his trying—for years, forever—if what he'd said about Millie didn't feel like an escalation. How far would he go in the future to prove to himself that she loved him? It wasn't only herself she was thinking of. Floyd had always been free, in her mind, to do what he wanted, to be himself, but now it felt like he wanted her to be responsible for his behavior. To tell him "no." It would be selfish of her to play that role, and it wouldn't be fair to him.

"If you and Millie did something," she said, "if that's what you want, you can tell me."

"What?" He dug in his back pocket for his credit card and waved it at the vending machine's payment window. "What's that mean?" He pressed B-8 and a sugary, strawberry-like snack bar dropped from the top row.

"I mean I want you to be happy. If you don't want to be with me, if you want to be with her or anybody else, I understand. It's okay."

He tore open the wrapper and jammed half the bar in his mouth. "Goddamn, Lenny. If you cared about me at all, don't you think if something like that made me happy it could make you a little more unhappy?" He looked at her for a long time and then stuffed the rest of the strawberry sugar stick in his mouth. He chewed and swallowed. "You wouldn't be so quick to let me go if I could get you pregnant, I bet."

"What?"

"Huh?"

"What do you mean? Why?"

"I don't know. I mean—Because it'd be a baby, or."

She smoothed his hair across his tissue skin. "But you aren't mine to let go, Floyd. You can always do what feels true to you."

"And if true to me means it hurts you?"

She said the only thing that mattered was intent, and Floyd turned around to buy another sweet bar.

Lenny had heard that when her mom was young and there were condoms, people would secretly poke holes in the tips to let the sperm through. She'd thought more than once that in a moment of emotional weakness, and against his own sense of right and wrong, Floyd might consider tricking her into pregnancy if it were easier to do.

Then again, that it was hard didn't mean it was impossible.

She counted back to when she'd last called InSystem's monitoring line.

Friday. Six days.

Lenny wished they would implement the hormone interruption alert system politicians were debating. She wasn't the only one who wanted it. The Main Street protesters had rallied around the idea, too, with one sign so big it had taken three people to hold it: WHAT GOOD IS A SECURITY SYSTEM WITHOUT AN ALARM?

According to a recent article Millie had written about "malicious hacking," that kind of upgrade wouldn't happen for a long time. It was the only one of Millie's stories Lenny had saved. After cutting it out of the paper, she'd laid it on top of her underwear so she would see it every morning as a daily reminder to stay vigilant about calling.

> ..."Most often the people pay hackers to disable the hormone, but unfortunately we have also seen hacking into this profile or that profile by thrill-seeking hooligans," InSystem public relations specialist Juanita Escallon said. She added, "As you can imagine, this has created many unexpected pregnancies. Ha ha, surprise! But this is no joking matter, is it? You must know we do take this seriously."
>
> Citing budget constraints, the government has repeatedly denied InSystem's request for $185 million in government funding to offset the cost of 24-hour chip monitoring software or, alternatively, three thousand new employees to fill positions in monitoring stations around the country.
>
> "There simply aren't enough errors, or what have you, in the chipping program to warrant that kind of spending. Our current system of punishment is more than enough to dissuade the majority of people from having an unsanctioned child or fiddling with strangers' hormones," White House Press Secretary Sylvia Nangaard said. Escallon said InSystem has contacted citizen hackers with the hope of luring them into legitimate, albeit low-paid, monitoring work, but to no avail.
>
> "They draw faces in reply, silly faces, and write rude messages," Escallon said. She went on to say that while she suspects the hacker reaction is due in part to the proposed wages, she also believes they take issue with InSystem's chip monitoring job description. Paid hackers would be required to identify and then pinpoint the location of outside hacker activity, in effect "ratting out" fellow hackers or underground hacking organizations. Escallon would not divulge for the record the hackers with whom she had made contact...

Lenny didn't know whether Floyd could afford to hire a hacker. Since he'd taken over her dad's renovation business, they hadn't really talked about their separate finances.

What mattered more as he reached back to unlock the door, his nervous tooth showing over a strawberry stained lip and his left hand stroking the seam of his pants, was that she believed he might use his sperm against her. If it were an impulse, an act of spontaneous desperation, she could forgive it, but his casual threat to sabotage her made impregnating her sound too much like a plan he'd given more than passing thought.

She slapped him.

Floyd yelped, "Hell!" and rubbed his face, looking not at Lenny's eyes.

Boris pushed through the conference room door elbows first, his cleaned and re-packed duffel bag appearing to have been plopped in his arms by the interim who'd had to scrape off the cake. (Residents were usually responsible for their own messes, but interims were lenient on release days.)

"It's time, Miss Lenny, Mister Floyd." Boris let the bag fall and caught it by its canvas handles. "You're coming, right?"

"You bet," Floyd said.

Lenny said nothing to Floyd as she passed by him to help gather and quiet the residents.

"Hi, everyone. Or—Wait a minute. Hello? Hello?" Boris lowered his mouth to the microphone clip on his t-shirt collar. "Or, I guess, bye, everyone. Anyway, it's been fifteen great years…"

One of the girls squeaked a sob. Lenny searched until she found Minnie looking up at Boris with wide, wet eyes, her shiny nose bubbling mucus. Minnie was one of many residents who'd been drawn to big, clumsy, intentionally irresponsible (passive aggressive attention-seeking behavior), cuddly Boris. All of the residents stared from their chairs or from the floor, wherever and however they chose to sit, at the long-haired boy standing in front of them. No matter how uninspired the original portion of his going-away speech—"I'll miss cookie Fridays and field trips to the star place" ("Observatory," helped an interim named Linus)—the children were riveted and devastated, remembering to wipe their eyes and noses only when the lights dimmed to start the naming portion of the speech.

Boris stuck out his chest and held his hands behind his back. Rubber chair feet groaned on linoleum and sneaker soles chirped as every child in the room stood. Interims left their places against the walls to stand with the residents and signaled the holding of hands by reaching out for the person closest to them. Everyone was so practiced it took less than a minute for the forty-two residents (excluding Boris, who had made forty-three) and seven interims to link a single chain.

Floyd watched from the door to the lounge. He looked at Lenny with the pasty face she had adored since middle school, the face that had been part of every one of her days for seventeen years. She'd never known anyone more devoted than Floyd, no one (besides her parents) who was more concerned about her happiness.

She would apologize later. For now she smiled at him. His face lit and he smiled back.

"Now?" Boris said.

"Yes, Boris. Now," an interim named Celeste called out.

Boris took a deep breath and closed his eyes. "Before many of us in this room were born, there lived a hero named Chester Walton..."

Even when the residents were adopted and chose to take the last name of one or both of their adoptive parents, they gave the same core address. It had been repeated so many times—at ceremonies, as part of a memorization game, and sometimes as a peer-to-peer orientation ritual—that the children knew it by heart. Most added a new, creative detail here or there, but what the interims had started to call the Legend of Chester Walton hadn't otherwise changed much over the years.

"Chester Walton began as a drop, just like me." Boris paused here, as they all did, and dramatically added, "Just like you. Left on the sidewalk in the rain"—a new, and incorrect, detail—"until a well-meaning do-gooder came upon him and brought him home." Pause. "To the enemy."

Lenny glanced at Floyd. Floyd pursed his lips in a silent whistle and looked at the ceiling.

Boris went on, describing Chester's mother as transforming into a monster with sharp teeth and wild, purple eyes in the moments just before the attack. He said, as they all did, that he would never make guesses about the details left out of the written record because they were sacred, meant to be known only to Chester Walton.

Lenny had heard all of them speculate about the attack into the late hours. Chester had "valiantly" and "silently" suffered anything from full-body burning by branding iron to being impaled by a family heirloom harpoon. (Both untrue.)

"...The identity of the confused Samaritan will forever be a mystery," Boris said, "but we can thank that person for giving the world Chester Walton, who fought and died bravely"—not true, but only because he was much too young and small—"so that each and every one of us, and the children of the future, could live in peace."

"Chester Walton!" the children shouted in their strongest, most powerful voices.

Boris raised a fist to the sky, and the children and the interims held their joined hands over their heads.

"My name," Boris declared, "is Boris Walton."

"Hello, Boris Walton!" the residents shouted. "Goodbye, Boris Walton!"

As soon as Boris left his post to join the crying residents, Lenny ran to a private office to make a call to InSystem's monitoring department.

TWENTY SEVEN

"We're caught in a trap," Elvis sang into the orientation room. Before that, it had been "Build Me up Buttercup." Before that, Millie couldn't recall. They had been waiting since five minutes prior to the scheduled start time, and now an additional fifteen minutes. Short clips of parents performing parental duties played soundlessly on the projection wall: a couple helped a child with homework; a parent cleaned vomit from a little girl's nightgown; a parent brushed a little boy's hair; a parent wept over a short gray casket.

Seventeen people (Millie had counted) fidgeted in their metal folding chairs arranged in a U in front of the projection wall. The remaining three walls repeated the lobby's motif of attractive, flushed-cheeked parents and carriers.

"Come *on*," someone to her right groaned. "Do we have to sit here all day?"

A soft click sounded in the back of the room, followed by, "Ms. Ludlow."

Everyone turned. A woman Millie had never seen stood in the open doorway. She wore a stiff, pastel-print shirt and center-creased purple pants.

"Ms. Ludlow," she said, "you are excused. Come with me, please."

Ms. Ludlow's eyes and mouth opened wide. "No," she said. "No. Please. I didn't mean anything by it!"

The woman continued to hold the door until Ms. Ludlow removed herself from her chair and, sobbing, stumbled out of the room. When the door closed behind the two women, the music stopped and the room went black for a moment before the floor's projection lights cast a new image on the wall. A filthy, skeletal man sat at a metal table in an impossibly bright room. He faced them directly from across the table.

The camera at his end was positioned so that the orientation class could see both above and beneath the table. The man's clothes were sizes too small for him, his colorfully soiled shirt pulling at the shoulder seams and stretching taught over the hollow between his jutting ribs. Millie could make out the entirety of his crushed and misshapen genitals through the thin fabric of his pants. It was a wonder he'd been able to walk into the room.

Hugh squirmed in his chair next to Millie.

She whispered, "Exile!"

Hugh muttered, "How could they let two reporters in here?"

Millie whispered, "Exile."

He leaned sideways to say into her ear, "Anonymous source?"

They could claim to have an anonymous source, but she expected the bureau treated each class to a unique experience to make it easier to track leaks. Since exile had begun, the *Daily Fact* hadn't received a single piece of credible information about the inner workings of the facility, and no one from the press had ever been allowed a visit.

The man slid down in his chair, as if to try to relax. His pants pulled even tighter at his testicles, which Millie wouldn't have thought possible. Hugh and another male in the room protested with throat noises. The man raised his eyebrows and nodded.

"I think he can see us," Hugh whispered to Millie. "Did you see—Holy cow." He covered his nose. The entire room did. "What is that?"

A malodorous fog filled the previously stale air with every possible (unpleasant) body odor, plus a touch of vomit and something unnatural, oddly chemical.

"Jesus!" one applicant shrieked.

The man looked steadily out at them.

The woman who'd dismissed Ms. Ludlow appeared beside the projection. She clasped her hands at her waist and pointed her chin. "I am May Cheney, proctor of each of the four stages of your evaluation."

Low murmurs ending in question marks skipped across the room.

"Yes. Outside rumors limit the evaluation to two portions: a nebulous multiple choice test and a six-month dog trial. This is by design. As you can imagine—Edgar?" May Cheney looked at something on the far wall over the applicants' heads. "Cut the atmosphere feed, please." The odor dissipated and the applicants freed their noses. "As I was saying," May Cheney went on, "licensing should be, and is, a critical process meticulously constructed to ensure we can identify, to the best of our ability, the most qualified guardians. Knowing in advance what will be evaluated would too easily tempt applicants to devise cheating systems. While it may serve them in the end by guaranteeing them a license, it would do a grave disservice to their children. And we are here, above all, to safeguard the needs and best interests of the children."

Millie had nothing to write with and nothing to write on, but this was something she realized only by reflex. She no longer cared about scoops and bylines. Now that she thought about it, she wasn't sure she'd ever enjoyed writing beyond the ultimately ineffective role it had played in her relationship with her mother. She deleted all of her mental notes.

"…first is a combination physical fitness test and broad spectrum psychological analysis. Hands down, please. To answer your unasked questions, we have no intention of denying parenthood to any applicants with mild or treatable psychological conditions, nor do we expect you to have endured months of strenuous training to meet an unrealistic physical standard. The purpose of the psychological portion is, primarily, to rule out violent tendencies. The physical portion ensures you don't have a fatal or chronic illness that will lead to undue stress or emotional devastation for your offspring. Knowingly burdening young children with future caretaker responsibilities or the loss of a parent is not what we at the licensing bureau consider loving behavior." May Cheney glanced at the projection on the wall when the man's chair moved under his shifting. He stilled himself, and she returned her attention to the applicants. "May I continue, or are there additional questions about the first stage of the evaluation?"

No hands went up.

The second stage, May Cheney said, measured the applicants' decision-making acumen, and the third, an applicant's capacity for empathy.

"Self-explanatory?" She waited, swinging her chin right and then left. When no one spoke, she continued. "You must pass each of the first three stages with an eighty-five percent or higher to qualify for the final stage, which as you are already aware is dog fostering. Your scores for the first three portions will be available by the end of the day. Yes, Mr. Green."

A man sitting to the far right lowered his hand. "Are there other animals we could foster besides dogs? In case we had a bad experience with a dog?"

"You sit surrounded by fifteen fellow applicants, all of them presumeable strangers. Do you mean to tell me you've never had a 'bad experience' with a human being, Mr. Green?"

The dog conversation was irrelevant to Millie, who wasn't afraid of dogs. She wanted to move on to the next portion. She could already imagine the looks of awe and admiration directed at her carrying body.

"Ms. Oxford."

Millie jerked. The rough feet of her light metal chair scraped the floor.

"Thank you. One more such show of disregard for the process and you will be dismissed, your application privileges suspended for one year. Oh, my, but you're twenty-nine. Is that correct?"

"Yes. I understand. I'm sor—"

"The man you see in the projected image to my right is Eugene," May Cheney boomed over Millie. Millie closed her mouth. "His surname has been revoked. He can hear and see you. Please say hello."

"Hello," all sixteen applicants said.

Eugene raised a knotted finger in greeting. Scabbed blood crusted his fingertip. Dark eyebrows (surprisingly neat) pressed down, narrowing green irises floating in red and framed by matted hair.

May Cheney turned to Eugene. "Say hello."

He took a long, slow breath and let it out while massaging his throat with a clawed thumb and index finger. "Hello" pushed through blistered, barely open lips. Several applicants made sympathetic noises. His was not a voice as much as it was a primitive, earthy sound that made Millie think of a dry log scraping concrete.

Apparently satisfied, May Cheney launched into Eugene's history "because, as you may have observed, it would take far too long for him to manage it, himself."

They were viewing Eugene as he sat in Exile, she revealed for those who hadn't already guessed. Exile was not, as many imagined, a real-life Chateau d'If. There were crude, cinderblock cells, true, and the food—when they were permitted to eat—was slop, mush, and tiny animal parts (sometimes cooked, other times not) only the kitchen staff could identify. But it was not a faraway, isolated tower perched on a high cliff pounded daily by thrashing ocean waves. Instead, it was an impossibly vast system of subterranean tunnels and enclaves flooded day and night with the blinding glow of thousands of LED tubes.

Eugene, she said, had been an Exile prisoner for six years, having been apprehended four days after abandoning his daughter, Hester. ("Left," he croaked with a slap of his hand on the table, which prompted May Cheney to shush him with a splitting *clap!clap!* and to explain to the room that parents of the abandoned rarely used the word "abandoned," themselves—it was too self-incriminating, morally speaking.) When Hester was three, the applicants learned, a disgruntled, out-of-work day trader with an armed black-market drone had shot Hester's mother—Eugene's partner of thirteen years—along with four others in various and arbitrary locations. Eugene had dropped Hester two weeks later ("Overwhelmed by the responsibility, yes, distraught over the loss of his partner, certainly, but that is no excuse," May Cheney stressed). It had taken him two years in Exile to see the wrong he'd committed, and another four to try to escape.

"Prior to his incarceration, Eugene was a martial arts instructor. I'm positive he thought he had every reason to believe he could overtake the guards." May Cheney smiled widely, then controlled herself. "The room you see is what Eugene will call home for the foreseeable future. The table does not belong to him, but was given to him for this visit with you." May

Cheney passed her eyes over each and every one of them. "Doubtless you believe this facility has nothing to do with you. Am I correct?"

Shoulders shrugged and heads nodded.

May Cheney reminded them of the infractions that earn a sentence of exile. Only two were new to the applicants: willful manipulation of one's personal hormone—regardless of whether pregnancy is achieved ("Starts next week," Hugh whispered to Millie. "Leo's writing it."), and breaking the licensing bureau's non-disclosure agreement.

Because the applicants were committed enough to parenthood to undergo the licensing procedure, May Cheney said, she didn't expect to learn in the future that any of them had tried to terminate their own pregnancy or separate from a sanctioned child. But it could be harder, she said, to keep quiet about the evaluation procedure and the secrets of Exile.

"I suspect that you see Eugene sitting in his cell, and you think, 'That doesn't seem so bad. I could survive.'" May Cheney looked like she wanted to smile again. She spun on a heel and snapped at her invisible contact behind the rear wall. Eugene disappeared. "I will say only this before we move into stage one of the evaluation, and I trust it will suffice: You cannot possibly appreciate the true horror of Exile without having been exiled, yourself. You would be wise to carry on from this day forward in a manner that will ensure you never are."

TWENTY EIGHT

Every rationed item Lenny had hoarded over time covered the basement suite's coffee table: five bottles of vitamin C capsules, seven bottles of ibuprofen and aspirin (four of one, three of the other), one bunch of fresh parsley, eight containers of the dried variety, and six containers of powdered cinnamon.

"Your call is important to us…" the recorded voice said again. She'd been on hold twenty minutes and was starting to think she should call the shelter to let them know she'd be late getting back from lunch.

She'd left after Boris's naming speech without telling anyone—including Floyd, who'd been standing in a corner with Boris—when the monitoring center had reported her hormone status as "inactive."

But first, before hanging up and running out, she'd pleaded to be transferred to the control department for reactivation.

"How long has it been inactive?" Lenny asked the control department person as brightly as she could in the shelter's small, locked office.

"Just a day," the man said. "Do you have any reason to think you might be pregnant?"

"Pregnant?"

"We can't reactivate if you might be pregnant. As far as we know, the hormone doesn't terminate a forming citizen, but we can't risk—"

"Oh, darlin'." Laugh, laugh, laugh. "Pregnant? My stars."

"Have you had sexual intercourse in the last twenty-four hours?"

"Sexual intercourse? Um…good gracious, no. It's been a coon's age."

"Hold, please." He left her listening to The Beach Boys' "Don't Worry Baby" and came back to the line full of apologies.

"I'm so sorry, Ms. Mabary, I shouldn't have…Your profile is… Obviously I meant no disrespect. We'll reactive right away, ma'am, and please disregard any emails that say otherwise."

The emails, sent automatically upon reactivation request, he explained, assigned a mandatory pregnancy test for five days from the date of contact with the monitoring center. The hormone reactivated only after confirmation of a negative pregnancy test.

For her, he had said, they would of course bypass that step, and "please have a super nice day, Ms. Mabary, ma'am, and again, I'm really sorry."

Lenny separated the capsules she would need and hid the rest in a secret compartment under the bed her boarders used. Her reputation meant she was probably safe from being included in one of the bureau's surprise house-to-house searches, but the attacks on her parents had proved no one was completely safe from anything. She double-checked that the locking mechanism was still working for when Gabriella arrived. The gouge Deborah, her last boarder, had carved into the side panel with the bathroom scissors during a panic attack—"I thought they were coming to exile me, Ms. Mabary!"—looked like a knot in the wood after Lenny's sanding and staining.

The hold music paused, then re-started.

She tried to relax. Her period had ended two weeks before she and Floyd had had sex, so there was only a small chance (very small, since Floyd was unhealthy in so many ways) of fertilization.

She unwrapped the fresh parsley and peeled off five sprigs while waiting for what should have been a simple answer to a simple question. To the music of Aretha Franklin's "Natural Woman," Lenny took off her pants and underwear and stuffed the sprigs, stems down, into her vagina until the curled leaves touched her cervix.

"Hormone status is inactive, Ms. Mabary."

"Pardon me?" She pulled up her underwear. Protruding stems poked at the cotton.

"It's in queue, ma'am. Sometimes it takes a little whi—"

The basement speakers filled the suite with doorbell chimes.

"Thank you." Lenny tapped her earpiece and waited. The bell chimed again and was followed by rapid knocking. She swallowed a vitamin C capsule without water and ran upstairs.

The man and woman standing on the veranda wore matching lilac suits and yellow ties. Each held a zipped yellow folder with USPLB printed on the cover.

The woman waved at Lenny through the peep hole. "Is anyone home?" she said. "We saw—Your van is parked right out front."

"Good van. Shows she's humble," the man said to his partner.

The woman looked up at the house, raised an eyebrow at him, and pressed the bell. "It'll only take a moment."

Lenny stretched her pants at the crotch seam, took a deep breath, and opened the door.

Everyone smiled.

"May we come in?" the man said as he swept past Lenny.

The woman followed and headed straight for a painting hanging on a foyer wall. "What delightful children," she said. "Are they special to you?"

"No, they're—"

The woman stepped closer. "My, such beautiful walls. Is this fir?" She reached out to touch the wood.

Lenny watched the woman's fingers trace the grain and glide over the seam. "Cedar!" she pipped. "Iced tea?" Her stomach bounced. She didn't have any iced tea. She'd never had iced tea. "Silly me. I'm plumb out! Filtered water?"

Lenny led the woman into the kitchen where her partner was already waiting and poured glasses of water. They introduced themselves as Edna and Xavier as they took stools at the island. Edna said unnecessarily that they worked for the United States Parent Licensing Bureau.

Xavier looked at the ceiling. "How many bedrooms?"

Four, Lenny said.

Xavier smiled. "That's nice. One for you, and the others for…?"

Guests, Lenny said. She tried not to squirm against the parsley while mentally searching each of the upstairs bedrooms for anything incriminating. She had no idea how invasive their searches might be and had visions of needles and blood draws and body cavity—

"Finished basement?"

No, Lenny said. No. Just a very small storage area that had to be accessed from the outside. (There was such a space. Floyd had purposely designed it that way.)

"We're making you uncomfortable. Xavier, we're making Ms. Mabary uncomfortable. Ms. Mabary, we're aware that your chip experienced an interruption in the release of its hormone." Edna pushed her long hair over her shoulder. "Yesterday?"

Yes, Lenny said.

"And today you called to reactivate," Xavier said.

Yes, Lenny said.

Xavier sipped his water. "It hasn't been reactivated."

No, Lenny said. Not yet.

"Oh! Oh!" Edna unzipped her folder. "That's just wonderful. We have time, yet." She pulled out a glossy lilac booklet. "Ms. Mabary, we are so pleased to be granted this brief window of opportunity." She licked her finger and flipped through the pages.

"Ms. Mabary." Xavier laced his fingers together and leaned toward her and smiled. "How much consideration have you given to becoming a member of one of the most revered communities in American society?"

Edna slid the open booklet toward Lenny with her finger tapping a section of text. "You are what we consider a premier," she said.

Lenny read the short passage.

> *A premier recruit is a citizen of established and verified selflessness. A citizen whose attentiveness to and interest in children indicates an innate nurturing tendency. A citizen whose finances and maintenance of a personal residence are evidence of an ability to more than adequately provide a child with a safe, permanent shelter. A citizen whose lifestyle and day to day actions demonstrate a willingness to sacrifice.*

"You're recruiters?" Lenny said. The sprigs tickled as she relaxed.

"You all right?" Xavier said.

Lenny smiled. "Yes, thank you."

"Premier recruits receive very special privileges," Edna said.

"Insignificant extras," Xavier said. "The true privilege is to be counted among the honored ranks of this nation's licensed parents. All Edna meant was that we try to make it less of a…well, less of a hassle for people like yourself. That's why we let you sidestep the evaluation pr—"

"People like myself?"

Edna waved Lenny closer and held out her hand. Lenny gave one of her own over the island, and Edna patted it. Her nails matched the purple of her suit.

"Ms. Mabary," she said. "Premier recruits are people who, should I say, haven't exactly gone out of their way to show an interest in obtaining a license."

"Oh, I see!" Lenny said. "I haven't, no, but that's because I don't want children."

"Yes…" Xavier said.

"And believe me, Ms. Mabary, the last people—well, not necessarily the last people, but perhaps the second-to-last people—the bureau wants having children are people who think they don't want them. However, you might be surprised to learn how many change their minds as soon as they learn they won't have to sit through an unnecessary—for them, that is— evaluation. Even people who are sure they won't fail are awfully afraid they will, and that alone can turn someone away from not only pursuing a child, but from thinking they want one."

"I've never really thought about it," Lenny said.

"It's a natural insecurity." Edna squeezed Lenny's fingers.

"No, I mean I haven't thought about the evaluation process at all." She shrugged and smiled.

"Nor need you!" Xavier chimed. "As I mentioned, premier recruits who show promise that they're willing to make a sacrifice to adopt or have a biological child—"

"But I don't want a child. Any child."

"Well, there you go! If you wanted one, what would the sacrifice be? What we're talking about here is civic duty. Ms. Mabary, your reputation is unassailable." Xavier gave her an A-OK sign. "They sent us as soon as they received word from you of your inactive status."

"But I don't have a plan," Lenny said, "so, even if I wanted—"

"No problem!" Edna said.

Premier recruits, Xavier explained, didn't have to worry about arranging their own Family Care Plans because the bureau provided them.

"You may choose your guardian from among the bureau's surrogate pool, if you want to go to all the trouble, but the bureau does an exceptional job of matching surrogates with premier recruits," he said.

Lenny made a show of looking at her watch. "Oh, my. I'm fixin' to be late for something! I up and lost track of the time." She slid her hand out of Edna's and closed the booklet. "May I?" She grabbed both of their glasses and poured their water in the sink.

"I can appreciate your hesitation, Ms. Mabary," Xavier said. "Choosing pare—"

"Thank you ever so much for thinking of me." Lenny led Edna and Xavier, their folders under their arms, to the foyer.

"Ms. Mabary," Edna said, "I don't think you understand what an honor it is to—"

"Thank you so much," Lenny said, opening the front door.

Xavier exited first with the tip of an invisible hat, and Edna followed, tossing the USPLB materials inside before Lenny could close the door, "In case you change your mind," she called.

When their car was gone, Lenny stuffed the folder to the bottom of the trash can and hurried down to the basement for another dose of vitamin C before calling the monitoring department.

"Hormone status is inactive," the representative said. "Your command is in queue."

TWENTY NINE

After having been excused early from stage three of testing for her disqualifying scores on the empathy and decision-making assessments, Millie had persuaded May Cheney to arrange an emergency meeting. Twenty minutes later, she was sitting on a metal folding chair in a small, blue room. A panel of five members of the licensing center's Board of Approvals, Willard and Maxine among them, appraised Millie from behind a long wood table.

"I'm a trained journalist." Millie thought it only logical to use on the board what had persuaded May Cheney. "Of course a wounded child would eventually affect me deeply, but my first instinct is to determine how best to describe the wound and the conditions surrounding the event. What your analysts perceived as apathy was, in truth, ingrained professional distance."

"It's an exceptional skill, indeed," Maxine said to the rest of the panel.

"But how, then, can we know whether she has nurturing tendencies?" a different board member said.

"You checked the 'unemployed' box on your sign-in form," Willard said. "You don't work for the paper anymore?"

"As of last week, no. I wanted to devote myself entirely to this process. But," Millie added quickly, "habits don't break immediately."

"Yeah. Okay." Willard scratched his ear. "I guess we'll just have to give her the dog."

"We don't have to do anything of the kind," Maxine said. "We reject applicants every day. Would it be fair to the animal to subject it to a test?"

Another member hissed, "This is Katherine Oxford's daughter."

Maxine pursed her lips at Millie. "Yes," she conceded. "A true boon to our community in her time. However, she and her businesses are dead."

Another board member sighed. "Millicent *M.* Oxford."

Shrugs and frowns.

"She broke the Chester Walton story."

"Oh," Willard said. "Oh! How did we not know that?"

"Fascinating," Maxine said.

Millie, too, often forgot that it had been her story about Chester Walton that had served as the impetus for the creation of the Parent Licensing Bureau. Perhaps because it had failed to benefit her personally.

She presented them with what she hoped passed as a nurturing smile.

"I can never have children because of you, Ms. Oxford," said a woman sitting in the far right chair. "I was six months into trying to impregnate when the law passed, and I was disqualified. The rest of the board may find it easy to overlook your 'professional indifference,' but I'll want more before I agree to send you home with our blessing to create and influence a brand new life."

"Such sanctimony from a woman willing to risk orphaning or severely disfiguring a baby in her selfish pursuit to reproduce," Maxine said.

"The risks were minimal, and you know it, Max—"

"I see, Lois. When it's the to-be child who will suffer the lifelong consequences, 'minimal' risk to a non-consenting individual is more than acceptable, is that it? If you so desperately wanted children, why did I not see you in line to adopt when biological was taken off the table?"

"Climb a razor rope, Maxine." Lois leaned over the table to address the members. "My position stands. I demand more."

"I agree," Maxine said.

Willard said, "Conference," and the board members slid their chairs into a tight circle, lowered their heads into a huddle, and murmured. After several moments, they began nodding. Someone said, "Yes, brilliant."

When they returned their chairs to their places at the table, Willard announced that the board would overlook Millie's abysmal scores if she would agree to reveal the details of the assault on Chester Walton.

"We're curious, like anyone else," he said. "And since we're all members of the licensing board, who but we should get to know what put us here? Agree?"

Millie studied their faces.

But for Maxine's, they were unreadable.

Maxine wasn't merely expectant, as the others seemed to be, but waited with an unnerving air of satisfaction.

Lois said, "Ms. Oxford?"

"We're asking her to unveil the greatest mystery in recent popular culture history, Lois. Let's allow her a minute," Maxine said.

"All right, then."

Millie considered possible reasons for the board's offer. The first was that they did indeed intend to trade poor score forgiveness for information. Second, they planned to evaluate Millie's emotional response to the memory. Third, they were assessing her character.

Millie usually tried to avoid comparing herself to Lenny or using Lenny's sensibilities as a guide, but this particular case required her to be prudent. She had no doubt Lenny would qualify for a license, and so she

had to ask herself, even if it went against her most evolved instincts, what
Lenny would do.

She had no doubt that Lenny would want to "protect" the board from
such "brutal" imagery. However, they didn't strike Millie as average members of the profoundly sensitive public.

Millie said, "When we arrived—"

It wasn't Maxine's hopeful straightening in her chair that gave Millie
pause, but the sudden and absolute knowledge that if Lenny were sitting
beside Millie at this moment, she would whisper in her ear, "How do you
think the board would feel about someone using a child's tragedy for
personal gain (again)?"

Her throat pulsing and a cigarette craving curling her fingers—what if
Lenny had it wrong?—, Millie said she was very sorry, but that it would be
unconscionable and inhumane to burden them with the dreadful account of
Chester Walton's demise.

Maxine deflated in her chair, but the board voted unanimously to
advance Millie to the final stage of the evaluation. Pending verification of
Hugh's licensing status, of course.

The next day, Millie and Hugh stayed out in the yard while teams from
USPLB CANID TRANSPORT and USPLB TECHNOLOGIES installed
surveillance inside (and did whatever was necessary to prepare the home for
the evaluation dog). Millie smoked in a spot of dry grass that positioned one
of the licensing bureau's black vans between her and the house. From there,
she could also see Lenny's driveway.

Floyd's pickup truck had been parked there for half an hour.

Behind Millie, Hugh taunted the evaluation dog's snout with the end of
a knotted rope. "Take it, girl! You wanna take it? Bubbles! Take it! Take the
rope!"

Floyd finally appeared, his weak arms circling a box he carried to the
truck bed.

Millie almost called to him. Hugh was obsessed with the "cattle dog
and pointer cross," the bureau's canid team had for some reason informed
them, and it hadn't noticed her once outside of the time she'd held out the
treat Hugh had given her. ("Dogs almost always need people to give them
treats, first," he'd said between slaps of the dog's tongue on his mouth.)
Flirting with Floyd would get Hugh's attention.

But Hugh was aggressively impatient with her, lately. She didn't think it
was a coincidence that his suitcase, once out of the way in the back of the
closet, was now the first thing she saw when she opened the folding door

every morning, and correcting his inattentiveness couldn't take precedence over achieving carrier status.

However. She was more than curious to know whether Floyd had taken advantage of Lenny's temporary vulnerability. Not only had Millie had to use off-the-record information from a *Daily Fact* interview with Juanita Escallon to find the small team of hackers, but in exchange for their service, they expected Millie or another reporter to investigate a rival hacking organization. Millie had risked her standing as a trusted member of the press (all for Floyd, if only incidentally), and she wanted something valuable in return.

"By the way," Millie twisted to face Hugh, who was jumping around with the dog, "please tell Zelda she might want to take a look at the top floor of the collections building on First Avenue. I believe the hackers call themselves 'Gut Checkers.'"

"By the way of what?" Hugh pulled the rope. The dog pulled back.

"Of my thoughts."

"Where'd you get it?"

"I can't tell you that."

She turned back to check on Floyd. He finished arranging things in the back of the truck and looked up at the second floor of the Mabary house with his hands on his hips. Millie put out her cigarette on the hard dirt and watched as a tall, sturdy figure, each shoulder supporting a large box, joined Floyd at the back of the truck. When the two boxes were loaded, Floyd and the guest returned to the house. Six trips (and no hint of noticing Millie) later, they climbed in and set off, Millie assumed, to deliver the items to a shelter, whether Lenny's own or one of her favorites.

"Good to go," a voice said.

Hugh jumped up and reached for Millie's hand. She stood and concealed her cigarette butt with her sandal.

The tech team's instructions were brief: "The cameras are all visible. Don't move them," said one whose red hair clashed with the purple of the team's uniforms. "There's no camera in the bathroom, but there's a mic on the corner shelf. Hope you don't mind, we had to dust there. Anyway, don't get the mic wet. Any destruction of licensing bureau surveillance property will be considered intentional sabotage. They'll fine you the inflated cost of the damaged items, send us to collect the stuff and Bubbles, and both of you lose your approval ratings. Always assume the cameras are recording. Always assume the mics are on. Secret: They are. Good luck."

Millie knew reaching the dog stage of the evaluation should have elated her—she was so close to the end—but six months seemed like a tiresomely long time to take care of a strange animal to prove she could commit to a child (it was an even longer time to have to sneak cigarettes outside).

An animal was also not comparable to a child, which made the dog trial a nonsensical exercise. Their assigned animal, in particular, had clearly been trained to defy the humans being evaluated. It was nothing like Murphy, a fluffy, quiet dog that had sat when told and had otherwise occupied itself. This dog, when not following, leaning against, or licking Hugh, sat its first night in their home some distance from Millie's feet, its eyes averted. At one point it decided to stand on all fours in the middle of the already cramped living room and stare at the front door.

Millie asked what it was doing.

Hugh said, "Just call her 'her,' will you? She's a girl. 'Her' or 'Bubbles.'"

"I think she needs to piddle," Hugh said from his desk on the third evening as Bubbles watched the door. (Millie had been ignoring her since that morning. Twice before breakfast she'd crouched with her arms out to receive affection only to have Bubbles look at her sideways, slink past her, and launch into a tongue-flapping gallop at Hugh's, "C'mere, Bubbles! Who's a pretty Bubbles?")

Millie understood, of course, that if Bubbles had to urinate, she should let her out. However, Bubbles had so consistently—and so pointedly!—dismissed her that she had no desire to put down the newspaper, get up, open the door, wait for her to finish, and let her back inside when the only gratitude Bubbles would express would be to run straight to Hugh.

"She could be watching a squirrel," Millie said and went on reading the *Fact*. Samuel Buford had taken over her beat when she'd resigned, and his story about weekend protesters demanding that the IVF ban be lifted was nearly as accomplished as something she'd have written. (That he'd neglected to secure a comment from a protester that addressed the number of children presently available for adoption gratified her more than it annoyed her. She'd have closed that hole.)

Hugh pushed back his chair so hard that it toppled on the tile and scared Bubbles's feet out from under her. He coddled her, cursed himself aloud for doing so, and guided her outside.

"See?" he argued at Millie as he watched the dog from the window. "Piddling."

Millie didn't know why any dog should require so much effort. She didn't remember Lenny having to go out of her way for Murphy.

"Try bonding exercises," Hugh said after a bite of a peanut-buttered English muffin at the beginning of day six.

It was a Monday, and he was leaving for work again. Millie was suddenly ready to return to the *Fact*. Days in a row, the only company she'd had was a judgmental animal. She was impatient with being at home and exhausted by the dog's unknown and decidedly unknowable demands.

"I have no idea what bonding exercises are," she said.

Hugh shrugged while rubbing muffin dust from his fingers into the sink. "Play fetch with her. Teach her something."

"I've tried. She's neither playful nor capable of learning. This dog is unnatural, and the bureau gave it to me on purpose. They want me to fail, Hugh. If I fail the dog trial, that failure reinforces the unjust scores I received on the flawed sections of the evaluation, thereby obviating the need to revise the whole system."

Hugh slid the peanut butter jar off the counter and turned away to screw on the top before putting it in the cabinet. He picked up his briefcase from the kitchen chair and kissed Millie's forehead, touched her waist. "You just have to relax," he said. He bent to pet the dog, who sniffed around at his hand and licked his fingers. "They can sense your feelings, you know. The more you sit around thinking she doesn't like you, the more she senses how uncomfortable she makes you. It's not you she doesn't like. It's all the negativity and insecurity."

"I don't sit around thinking this dog doesn't like me. I hardly think about her at all."

"Well, then." He stood. "Maybe it is you."

More than once after Hugh left that day, Bubbles inched closer to Millie, even throwing her paws up on Millie's ribs at one point, nearly knocking her down. Millie laughed and sat down for all the licking and pawing Bubbles had given Hugh, but the dog jerked its snout away from Millie's hands and dodged to her side. When Millie reached out for the dog again—"It's all right! Come *here*! I only want to pet you!"—it jumped away and sat at a distance, eyes looking to the left and right of Millie, alternating eyebrows lifting and lowering.

Millie screamed, "Well, I don't like you, either, you stupid animal!"

The dog's feet slipped and scraped in a scamper to the far side of the living room, and Millie instantly came so close to crying that her eyes burned. How terrible a person was she that even a dog couldn't love her? She willed herself cold and resisted the impulse to lunge for the dog, pull it to her chest, and squeeze it until it kicked. Instead, she stomped to the corner where they kept the starter toy basket the bureau had provided. She dug around until she found a ball and threw it so hard into the kitchen that it bounced off the wall and zinged back at her, slamming her ear before she could dodge it. Ear burning, she dove to get it from where it had rolled under the couch and hurled it into the kitchen again.

"FETCH IT, YOU ASSHOLE!"

In Millie's imagination, Bubbles ran after the ball, carried it proudly back to her, dropped it at her feet, and waited for the next toss just as every family dog did in the movies. Their evaluation animal only huddled near the end of the couch with its ears straight back and its head tucked low.

"FETCH IT!" she screamed again.

The dog lowered its head even more and looked away. Millie went to it and wrenched it to standing. She pressed both hands to the dog's solid hind quarters and shoved it toward the kitchen, its toes squeaking on faux oak laminate.

"Stop that immediately, Ms. Oxford," a voice said from the walls, the ceiling, the corners.

The dog escaped to its crate. Millie looked for a camera and found a small lens on the shelf between her New Orleans chocolate alligator and one of Hugh's writing awards. She stood in front of it.

"If the board would assign me a better dog," she said, "I'm positive—"

"Thank you, Ms. Oxford."

"You're…I'm sorry, what do you mean?"

"That will be all."

"And what do you mean by that, please?"

"This concludes your trial."

"But your dog doesn't like me!"

"You would like another opportunity."

"Yes. Please."

"All right, Ms. Oxford. How much time did you invest in researching and then actively trying to accommodate the dog's needs? How much exercise does Bubbles require, for ex—"

Millie screamed at the ceiling, "IT'S A DOG!"

"No, Ms. Oxford. It was an evaluation."

When Hugh came home that night, he asked why Millie was smoking in the house and why Bubbles wasn't there to greet him.

"They assigned us a defective animal, Hugh, but they'll let me try again," she lied.

Hugh nodded, went to the refrigerator, opened a beer, and brought the bottle upstairs to the bedroom.

Millie followed him. She watched him pack.

"I told myself I'd stay until you didn't need me for this, anymore." Hugh scooped rolled socks from his drawer and arranged them in a flat layer in the bottom of his large suitcase. "At first I thought I really got through to you. 'She'll try,' I thought. 'She'll change.' You didn't, not even for a day, and I was this close to leaving when then they gave us the dog. I thought, 'Well, I can't leave her alone with that dog.' I told myself I'd stay until Bubbles was gone. For a minute I even thought the dog'd help, somehow. Maybe she'd bring something out of you I couldn't. But then the second day came, and the third. So, this morning I told myself, 'If I get home tonight and that dog still couldn't like her after I smeared goddamn peanut butter on her shirt, this thing is done.'" He tossed in a stack of neatly folded t-shirts.

THIRTY

From the far side of her bedroom, far enough away so there was no chance of Millie seeing her through the window, Lenny watched Millie watching the house from her small yard. Hugh popped out from behind one of the black vans in their driveway to waggle a rope, and a gray dog with black spots and big, pointy ears flew at him and grabbed it, pulling Hugh back behind the vans.

Floyd said, "Hey, uh."

He stood in the bathroom door with a small box in his arms, the green top of his shampoo bottle poking out from under his gray towel.

"You know," he said, "maybe I could leave the stuff here. For later, or. Boris can sit alone for an hour, can't he? I can still visit."

Lenny had talked about Boris off and on for years between Floyd's visits to the shelter. "Love that kid," Floyd would say, and Lenny would say, "Oh, he's loveable, but…"

Floyd had told Lenny he didn't remember exactly how the whole thing happened. "He saw me after the naming, and next thing, we were talking. He's eighteen, so not like a real kid, but there's no evaluation, so…"

She could imagine how the conversation might have gone during the few minutes she'd been on the phone with the monitoring center. "Mr. Floyd," Boris would have said, knowing he'd be an easy target without Lenny around. "Could I come live with you and Ms. Lenny? I'll do anything. Clean the house, walk the dogs, iron Ms. Lenny's napkins…" Before his next heartbeat, Floyd would have said, "What, yeah? Sure!"

Lenny wished she'd had a chance to warn Floyd before he decided. Boris Walton was the kind of boy—man, he was a man, now, according to law—who would need to be cooked for, cleaned up after, and reminded to shower. And because his abandonment at three years old in the plush aisle of a toy store had left him with a crippling fear of being alone, he demanded constant companionship. (At the shelter during naptime, the interims' treasured break time, if Boris happened to be awake when the rest of the residents were asleep, he'd barge into to the lounge for their attention. He'd done it so regularly they'd started locking the door and eating their mid-morning snacks in the dark.)

Boris could only be alone if he were truly alone, and with no one close by to worry about him. Lenny doubted he'd survive that way for very long, but his life was his own to manage. Or, it would have been, had Floyd not said yes to managing it for him.

"If you want to take care of him," she'd said, "you can't do it here." It hadn't been an ultimatum. She'd never expected him to have to make a choice. He'd said yes to Boris, and she knew he'd stand by his commitment even if it meant moving out.

Lenny loved that about him.

She pressed the top on his shampoo bottle so that it clicked closed. "I'll visit you, instead," she said. "Do you think you'll buy a house? Rent an apartment?"

He shrugged. "Probably crash in the renos for a while. They stay pretty cool. Don't cost anything. Saves time in the morning, getting to work, or." He smiled and shifted the box in his arms. "Anyway, I could build my own house."

"Right." She laughed.

"I could put it out there." He pointed his chin at the window. Lenny looked outside and saw Millie smoking a cigarette with her head tucked between her knees.

"If you put Boris anywhere near this property, I'll put a shock collar on him and install one of those electric fences."

"Worth it," he said.

Lenny checked her watch. In two minutes it would have been an hour since her last vitamin, and she wanted to take each one exactly on the hour. Whether being off by one or two minutes would ruin its effectiveness, she didn't know. She didn't know whether taking everything exactly as instructed would work, either. After a full day of taking vitamins, some cinnamon, what was left of the dried parsley, and some ginger she'd forgotten she'd bought for a recipe, there'd been no bleeding and no cramping. That could have been a sign of something or a sign of nothing. She didn't feel pregnant, or what she imagined pregnant would feel like, and that there'd been no cramping could have meant nothing more than that there was no work for the vitamins to do. Her period might still come on schedule in six days.

But she also had to accept the worst-case possibility that she was already pregnant, or would be soon (that his sperm could live for days like stubborn squatters inside her body seemed like the worst kind of invasion, a strange thing to feel about someone she loved). If that were true, the vitamins and everything else had to work faster. If she miscarried too late, if there were complications, if they found her unconscious and took her to the hospital...

"Worry doesn't change a thing," her dad had taught her when Murphy was sick. "What will be will be. That's the only way anything's ever been."

Lenny had to accept that she wouldn't know anything until her period came on schedule or it didn't.

"What's wrong?" Floyd said. "You sick?"

He was looking down. Lenny relaxed her hand, which she hadn't realized was clutching her shirt at her abdomen. It hurt to uncurl her fingers.

"Why don't you take that box out?" she said. "I'll make sure Boris isn't getting into anything downstairs."

Floyd stepped closer. He kissed her over the box the way he kissed her when he wanted more. "In a minute?" he said. "Boris'll be fine. He's got a list."

Lenny patted his arm. She'd have no sex of any kind until she knew she was pregnant or until her hormone was reactivated, but she didn't know how to say that to Floyd. He was the one person she hadn't told even a compassionate lie. Surely omitting information didn't count if it meant saving him from being frustrated or unhappy.

She said, "Oh, you!" and giggled her way out of the bedroom.

After taking her vitamin and making sure the door to the basement was still locked, she found Boris standing in the middle of the living room with the fingers of one hand hooked into Floyd's slippers and his other hand clutching the list.

"I forget what's next," he said.

Floyd said he'd planned to take with him only what he'd brought to Lenny's, but she insisted he pack up some dishes, pots, pans, and any doubled-up utensils taking space in the drawers.

Boris found his way to the kitchen after Floyd had gone outside with a small box and while Lenny was making a list to prepare the basement for Gabriella.

"Thank you for everything, Ms. Lenny." Boris hugged her with big, tender arms and thanked her, too, for not talking "Mr. Floyd" out of it. Bertram rubbed at his ankles, and he bent down to pet him. "I don't know if I'd make it on my own."

"Oh, Boris, probably not," she said. "But that's okay. Not everyone can." She patted his back. "He's just as lucky to have you."

In six days, the basement suite was ready with clean linens in the bathroom closet and snack food in the cabinets. (Lenny would do the real grocery shopping once she knew what Gabriella wanted or needed.) An hour before Gabriella was due, Lenny took a vitamin, inserted the fresh parsley finally allowed by her ration card, and stood at the breakfast bar where she could watch for Millie without being seen.

Arrival days always made her nervous. Outside of the trusted channel Lenny had cultivated, the only person who knew about Lenny's basement boarders was Floyd.

"They catch you, I couldn't live knowing you were in Exile, so I'm dying too," he'd said after finishing construction on the suite. "Together, right?" They'd shaken on it.

Now that Floyd had Boris, she assumed—hoped—he would let her go alone, if it came to that. She hoped it wouldn't come to that. But if it did, and if Floyd did stay behind, at least there would be someone to take care of the animals.

The sun went down. An interior downstairs light across the field allowed Lenny to see Millie smoking at her dining room table, a glass of wine in her free hand. Lenny heard a car pass her kitchen window, and soon Hugh's headlights shined on his and Millie's front porch. Millie crushed out her cigarette and stood. She flattened down her hair before pushing it behind her ears, then faced the door with her hands on her hips. Hugh entered, but didn't go to her. (Floyd had always come to Lenny.)

Millie's powerful stance crumpled after Hugh had been inside for just a few seconds. She waved her arms, excited, as he passed her to get to the kitchen, and then she followed him to the dark staircase. The upstairs bedroom light flicked on and Hugh marched to the closet. Millie looked small watching him from the doorway.

Lenny waited for the dog to show up in the bedroom, but it didn't. Her dogs followed her everywhere—up and down the stairs and from this room to that room. They kept her company now, Andy sleeping in front of the refrigerator and Jenny half in the foyer and half in the kitchen with her chin between her paws. She looked for the dog crate she'd seen earlier that week, tucked against the wall near the kitchen. The space was empty. She squinted, watching the shadows for any non-human movement at all, but the house was too far away. She got her parents' old camera from its case in the coat closet and focused the zoom lens on the lit windows. There were no dog toys on the floor, no food dishes in the kitchen.

Lenny clapped, forgetting the camera. The strap yanked hard at her neck when it fell. She kept clapping, almost crazily, even though she'd known—she'd *known*—Millie would never pass. She tossed off the camera and crouched to pet her dogs.

Whoever Millie's baby might have been was safe. "Safe!" she said aloud. Jenny moved to stuff a snout between Lenny's thighs (the parsley, probably), but knocks at the front door stopped her before Lenny could shoo her away.

Onetwo. Three. Four...Five.

Gabriella.

"Upstairs," Lenny whispered to the dogs. They went.

"I don't know quite what to think of this," Gabriella said about the painting in the foyer. She let go of her suitcase handle and crossed her arms under her breasts. Her starched white shirt wrinkled stiffly. A long wave of dark hair fell into her open collar.

Lenny's boarders didn't usually pay much attention to the little girl and boy. If they weren't familiar with the fairytale, which most weren't, it was just a painting of two children eating from the side of a candy and gingerbread house. Lenny had bought it for the suite's entry point because the abandoned brother and sister have a happy ending.

"Am I the evil step-mother?" Gabriella said.

"The step-mother?" It hadn't ever crossed Lenny's mind that someone who did know the story would identify with the step-mother. She massaged a dull ache creeping into her lower back and said no, of course not. Gabriella was the woodcutter.

"But the woodcutter is poor. He has an excuse. What's my excuse? My *explanation?*"

"Oh, you can't take fairy tales literally," Lenny said. She pressed her thighs together to scratch a parsley itch. "We all have our own versions of impossible situations. But if you're having a change of—"

"No," Gabriella said. She touched a finger to Gretel's cheek.

Lenny invited Gabriella to stand closer to the painting, then asked for her hand and guided it to a section of wall to the left of the frame. They pushed it together. A panel separated at the seams where the ends of the short wood boards met. At a soft click, the door opened outward on a spring to a narrow downward staircase. Soundproofing panels lined the walls to the bottom.

Lenny recited the rules of living in the suite—when and when not to go upstairs, where to find the circuit breaker, that phone calls could only be made from the basement's untraceable phone line—while Gabriella put away her clothes. Afterward, Gabriella changed into a long red robe and tucked herself into the corner of the loveseat. Her collar, stretched to one side, revealed an indented, shiny scar the size of a dime.

"You've seen it once before," Gabriella said, touching it. "I don't expect you to remember. There were others, and they were much younger."

Because most abandonds were afraid to give even their first names, Lenny usually remembered them when they did. Lenny said "Gabriella" didn't sound familiar, and Gabriella confirmed she was one of the many who hadn't identified herself.

"But then, I wasn't Gabriella when you found me," she said. "I was Rose…Well, I think Rose is enough."

Gabriella tucked her feet under her robe and began telling Lenny when and how she'd been found, but Lenny's back pain distracted her from listening. Was it her back, or was it her abdomen? Both? Wishful thinking, probably.

"…nine years old when your van came," Gabriella said, "and deathly hungover from the first and only birthday party my parents ever held for me…"

…parents had filled her with glass after glass of peach schnapps and orange juice …(Was *that* a cramp?)…no memory even now of having gone to bed that night…scared awake on a strange sidewalk in a strange town by a small, barking dog, "an ugly little schnauzer, I remember," she laughed (Lenny instinctively clenched, a reaction to dampness—or perceived dampness, because it was probably nothing, and it was so hard to say with the parsley stems)…

"Oh, quiet me down. I'm boring you," Gabriella said.

"No, not at all."

"The tales you must have heard over the years. I shouldn't bore you with another."

Lenny encouraged her to go on. The truth was, she wanted to hear about Gabriella's life as an abandoned. She'd never knowingly come across one of her old collections in their adult years, and she was thrilled to see that one seemed to have turned out so well. She ignored the soreness and listened.

Gabriella stroked her scar and said Lenny must have been just a teenager when she and her friends had found her across the street from the Tinytown animal hospital, though at the time they'd all seemed very adult to Gabriella. They'd brought her and some younger children to a shelter that wouldn't let them in. Gabriella remembered that part vividly, she said, because she'd felt incredibly lucky at the time to have been delivered by chance to a different shelter where she was adopted almost immediately.

"I never thought this woman would choose me over all the little babies," she said. "They tried to give her a teenager, and then a younger teenager, but no, she said, she wanted a nine-year-old girl and only a nine-year-old girl. I was the only nine-year-old girl."

Young Rose was worried when the woman told her matter-of-factly, over the popping motor of her dirty bike, that she was a replacement for Esther, a daughter who'd died of cancer just after her ninth birthday. But when the woman asked Rose what she wanted to be called, Rose thought everything would be wonderful, after all. Someone who didn't plan to care about her surely would never have cared enough to ask, she reasoned.

Gabriella, Rose had said without hesitating. *Gabriella*. It was the name of a movie star.

"Gabriella Fernandez." Gabriella said. "Always a character of deep love and great strength. Do you know, she never went without a flower—on her wrist, in her hair...anywhere a woman might wear a flower. It was the first thing I would look for the moment she arrived on the screen."

Gabriella's vision was romantic. Her future wasn't. Because Esther's cancer treatments had put her mother deep into debt, Gabriella was forced to work two jobs—one as a forged infertile on the dark fuck database, the other as a cannabis farmhand alongside her adoptive mother. There were apologies before the bedside light went out, and there were promises that it would be "just a little while longer," but for three years she sweated in the fields. For three years she shut her eyes to heavy, hairy chests and anesthetized herself by becoming Gabriella Fernandez on a beach, Gabriella Fernandez on a balcony, Gabriella Fernandez on a rainforest riverboat being overtaken by jungle snakes.

She was allowed to quit both jobs only when, at twelve, she was assigned to marry the farm's owner.

"Ah, but!" Gabriella pushed up her sleeves and fanned herself. "Eight short years later, thanks to my husband's advanced age and timely death, I now own everyth—Doggie!" She slipped her knees out of her robe and patted the cushion. Jenny jumped on the sofa and licked her face.

Andy came down next, followed by one of the cats.

Floyd was the only other person with the entry code to the house, and he'd never show up unannounced unless he was alone, but Lenny still didn't like that she'd left the door open. It was impossible to be too careful.

"Do you have oxygen cleaner?"

Lenny looked over her shoulder at Gabriella.

Gabriella pointed with her eyebrows, and Lenny touched a finger to the center seam of her pants.

"To be so fortunate!" Gabriella fought off a paw swiping at her face. "I finally sleep with a man for pleasure after a lifetime of not impregnating, and this," she jabbed a thumb at her pregnancy, "is what happens to someone like me." She rubbed Jenny's face with both hands, flapping the dog's ears up and down. "Please do let the animals stay while you clean up?"

THIRTY ONE

The house across the street, unimaginatively called Hack House Five, was a white Cape Cod stained green with mold, the exposed facade a twenty-foot journey from sidewalk to stoop. Millie had been instructed not to sneak around to the back, however tempting it might be. She was to walk straight to the front door and ring the bell. "Trust us," the woman had said. "No one knows how to find us unless we want them to."

She looked back at the car, the only memen...remem...*thing* her mother had left her, sitting alone in the cemetery parking lot. The house seemed so far away. There was still time to leave and to approve the hack by phone as she had for Lenny.

No. The sole reason she was here was that she'd already determined that hacking by telephone only worked for an outwardly targeted manipulation. Had Lenny reported activity on her chip and Millie were discovered— unlikely, because police rarely wasted time tracking down pranksters, and even if they did take the time, to find Millie they'd have had to previously placed a trace on the hackers' line that would miraculously lead them to the gas station telephone she'd used—the punishment would be nominal. The remote possibility of a traced line and the direct connection to her own hormone, however, wasn't remote enough considering the not-so-nominal punishment for self-hacking.

Millie stood straight, extending her spine and the back of her neck until she felt tall. She reminded herself that what she was doing was one of the more impressively illegal things a person could do. "Noble." That was what they called carriers. She didn't require a license to be noble, to be self-sacrificing. Why, she was actively courting her own exile.

Had Floyd impregnated Lenny (and Millie knew from what she'd found in Lenny's trash that he hadn't), Millie would have been standing here just the same. She'd learned a few days prior to discovering Lenny's blood that no one—not even a licensed, carrying Lenny—could have offered a recommendation so persuasive the board would have overlooked Millie's final evaluation results. (She'd called, just to be certain. "Sorry. No more than two failed sections may be expunged regardless of recommendation.")

Sweat pulled Millie's t-shirt against her stomach as she waited in the fine dirt of the shoulder for cars to pass. She was uneasy in spite of the fact that AV occupants were too distracted by reading, sleeping, watching their dashboard monitors, or talking to pay much attention to the road, never mind to the woman standing at the edge of it.

To calm her anxiety, she concentrated on a row of miniature pumpkins propped on top of the Hack House door frame. They were uncarved despite the impending holiday. Millie didn't like the mess of carving, herself, so she never bought seasonal pumpkins. Hugh had bought them, once they'd started living together, but he'd also been the one to carve them. He'd not been an accomplished carver. Millie could rarely tell what his sculpted shapes were until he told h—

The road cleared. Millie sprinted across, slowing at the sidewalk and strolling as casually as she could to the front door. She knocked five times, as instructed.

"Who's there, please?" said a male voice on the other side.

"Millicent Oxford."

"Pass phrase?"

"It's…It's a great day for a granola bar, said the rabbit to the thief."

The door opened.

In the partially finished basement beneath the convincing "home" level—couches, plants, Oriental rugs, and rotating holoframes filled with family images—a team of five hackers sat at private stations separated by folding screens. There were no introductions. The man who'd led Millie to the basement had also not given his name before returning upstairs.

"Move your hair," a girl of sixteen or seventeen said before applying a scanning wand to Millie's neck. It issued a rapid series of beeps. "Wait over there," she said, pointing to a plush, red chair in the corner. Millie did as she was told and watched the girl's fingers flick over her keypad.

"Before you advance beyond a critical point," Millie said, "I'd like to make sure you're aware this has to appear as if the command originated from an outside source."

"You failed empathy, decision-making, and the dog?" the girl said.

"Not officially."

"It says here, 'Fail.' It's in your official file."

"Yes. 'Officially,' I did fail empathy and decision-making. However, the dog was defective, and that should be reflected somewhere in the notes.— But, as I was saying, please, this must look like a prank hack. There can be no evidence of a scan. I'd like you to tell me you understand. Please. For my own peace of mind."

"Nuh-uh. It says right here you failed two stages...that was on September seventh...and then you failed the dog trial on September fourteenth." She raised her eyebrows at Millie. "I can't believe they still gave you the dog. Did you hurt it?"

Millie said no, she didn't hurt the dog, and the girl said that was good, because too many people used to hurt the dogs.

"'Used to' when?" Millie had never heard about any of this at the *Fact*, which bothered her only because this obnoxious girl did know about it. "Which dogs?"

Typing and watching her monitor, the girl explained in halved, distracted sentences that the bureau had placed surveillance equipment in a random sampling of applicants' homes during the early dog trials. The objective, she said (in her vexing teenage vernacular), had been to evaluate their trial animals and make any necessary adjustments to training methods or breed selection. When they discovered the level of abuse being inflicted on some of the dogs, Tyrone the Dog Trainer had personally removed each animal from the applicants' residences (including personal pets, but this had of course required the approval of state animal control services). All dog trials were suspended until one hundred percent in-home surveillance was implemented.

"One guy loved his dog," the girl said, leaning in to examine something on her screen. "You know. Loved his dog? It was this really pretty greyhound."

"Too pretty in the right way," said the back of the chair at the desk neighboring the girl's.

"Yeah. Or the wrong way, Henry. Don't be disgusting. And this lady—remember that lady, Henry? Her dog was Jasper?—She was so bugged out about not wanting to hurt Jasper's feelings. Or neglect him, or whatever. She was on him day and night, constantly hugging him, feeding him, petting him. Touching him all the time. He couldn't hide under the bed without...Why is that there?" She pressed a key. "Yeah, poor dog couldn't even hide under the bed without her following him under there. He finally nipped her on the face and she had a nervous breakdown. Anyway, that's why the bureau got all camera-happy." The girl swiped at her monitor and tapped on her keypad. "So, what do you want a kid for, anyway?" She spun in her chair to face Millie, accidentally knocking over the flimsy divider.

Henry, a long, narrow twenty-something with dyed white hair, groaned "Aiyanaaaah" and caught it before it fell on top of him.

Aiyana swung her feet, touching the toes of her bright orange shoes one at a time to the chair rail. "So?" She twirled her hair. "I mean, if you want me to help you…"

Millie hadn't expected to be tested by an impertinent hacker, but she did need her. "Being a carrier," she said brightly, "is one of the more exceptional things a person can do in a lifetime."

"Huh." Aiyana blew at her hair. "I bet there're a lot more carriers than hackers."

"Hm," Millie said. "Yes. Perhaps. But there's more to consider than numbers. How many actually pursue hacking versus those who aspire to be carriers? How difficult is the barrier to entry for each? My point," Millie said, "is that any—any *one* can learn clever computer tricks. Not just anyone can be a carrier."

"I guess that's true." Aiyana shook the offending strand of straight black hair out of her eyes. "Lots of people can't even pass the first part of their eval."

Millie crossed her limbs tighter. The girl relaxed in her chair, her arms open and hanging over the sides. She smiled at Millie.

Millie said, "How much longer, please?"

Aiyana rolled her eyes, sighed, and spun back to her screen. "The hormone's blocked, so you can impregnate in the next five minutes, if you want. All I have to do is check this little box right here in the bureau's system saying you were approved. You know. In case the wrong person sees you and gets curious?"

"I can't even begin to imagine why you would think anyone would look at me and question my—"

"Ugh, never mind." The girl held her finger just short of the screen, waving it tauntingly where Millie assumed the checkmark was supposed to go. Aiyana turned slowly and peered at Millie through her long hair. She frowned at her, then jabbed the screen. "Done!" she said with a wide smile.

It took the car thirty minutes to drive Millie from Hack House Five to Hugh's new apartment. She hadn't visited before, but she knew he lived among many single *Daily Fact* reporters in red-brick efficiency complex built early in the twentieth century. A quaint, rustic courtyard offered a pleasant enough view to the thirteen apartments fortunate enough to face it, but the others looked over a sloped parking lot and garbage bins on one side, and on the other, a vacant lot crowded with struggling saplings and arching, tangled vines. (A toddler had been found there the previous fall, sitting under the vines and wrapped in an adult's lightweight jacket. Were the drop rate what it used to be, Millie suspected the lot's shade and seclusion would make it the newest prime location.)

She didn't know what direction Hugh's windows faced. She knew only that he was in 3B, which she assumed was the third floor. And she was in possession of the precise number not because he'd wanted her to have it, but because he'd forgotten one of his work bags in the coat closet the day he'd moved out.

Millie found it the following weekend in the midst of a complete rearrangement of everything in the house combined with a thorough search for any reminders of his rejection. She called him at work.

"Can't I just come by and get it?" he said.

"I prefer not to see you."

"Drop it at the paper, then. I'm out half the time, anyway."

"Your address, please, Hugh. I have bread toasting."

Cynical newsroom laughter floated in the background. He said, "I miss you."

It was the voice of his first "I love you," of his warm (but unnecessary) murmurs at her mother's funeral. She rubbed the contracted, sensitive flesh on her arms.

"—Hello? You there?"

"You miss me?" She looked at the briefcase they'd shopped for together and that he'd used every day for three years before retiring it to the office closet. When his small desk drawer at work filled up with story and interview notes, he would gather them and store them in the closet briefcase until he needed them for something or could safely throw them away. "Why?"

"I don't know." He laughed.

Millie used a fingernail to gouge a long scrape into the leather.

"That's not what I meant," he said. "Come on. Mill? Hey, if you were the one who wanted to see me, I'd let you. It's how you treat someone you care about."

She said, "I imagine it is."

The line had stayed quiet with both of them listening until Hugh hung up, and when Millie called back for his address, he'd given it to her. She'd mailed the bag the following day.

Hugh's parking lot was full, which the car had determined before reaching it. It found a legal spot on the side of the road and eased to a stop. Millie scanned the resident spaces until she found Hugh's car, then pressed the button to lock all of her doors manually before turning off the power and waiting for someone to happen by.

She hadn't expected it to take longer than a minute or two, but after fifteen minutes she was getting warm and had to turn on the engine for air conditioning. Five minutes later a woman exited the building, and Millie poked the OFF button. She banged at her windows and screamed, "Help!" until the woman came close enough to hear Millie ask her to please tell the man from 3B to come outside, that it was an emergency.

Hugh rushed out in a red tie knotted at the neck of a gray business shirt hanging just to the fly of his boxer shorts. His feet were bare. "What are you doing here?" he shouted at the window. "What are you doing in there?"

Millie showed him the towel she'd brought—a towel he could easily have left behind, since it looked like all of the other towels they'd shared—and yelled, slowly and with exaggerated enunciation, "The controls aren't working."

"Did it charge?"

She rolled her eyes.

He instructed her to try to open the door. She pretended to pull the lever. He mimed turning on the car. She leaned just far enough to hide her actions and pretended to press the button. She wiped her forehead and fanned her neck, then used the towel to dry her face.

"I don't have the other key," he yelled. "I left it at the house, in the bowl. Are you okay in there? Pretty hot today, isn't it?—Wait, okay? Wait here. I'll go call the fire department or a locksmith, or something. I'll be right back." He turned to go.

Millie honked the horn. She pointed at the hood and pulled the lever under the steering wheel.

He yelled, "I only know basic…I don't know—"

Millie pointed again, and he lifted the hood. It really was hot. She wished she'd have thought to lower a window a crack.

"Try turning it on," he shouted.

Millie faked the motion.

He peered over the hood and she shook her head. He disappeared again and a moment later held up a hand. She pressed the button and the car started. Hugh ran beaming to her door, bouncing penis poking out of his fly.

Millie lowered her window, reached out, and pushed him inside his shorts.

"Hey!" He jumped back. "What th—"

"It's so hot," she said. "Do you have water? I'll trade your towel for a glass with ice."

Apartment 3B was a dark, second-floor single bedroom overlooking the lot of cluttered vegetation. Hugh's six framed Reporter of the Month awards made an arc on the wall behind his desk, where he'd arranged a micro-camera on a wire tripod. A blue sheet he'd draped over a rolling clothes rack created a backdrop behind the chair.

"Interesting," Millie said, taking off her shirt.

"Why shouldn't I? So I can stay loyal to the *Fact* and enjoy this hole until I retire?"

"Channel?"

"Does it matter?"

Millie couldn't help noticing that even though her shirt was off, his boxer shorts weren't stretched around an erection.

Hugh said, "Do you want to know how well I know you?"

"Is that important right now?"

"You're hacked. Right?"

"Don't be silly."

"What's your plan? Where're you going to hide? They almost always find out eventually, Millie. You know that."

She said, "I always enjoyed having sex with you."

"That's not true."

"Hugh!" She pouted her bottom lip. It felt dry, so she licked it.

He slapped his hands to his eyes. "God, Millie. You're—"

She stepped closer. "Yes?"

"I didn't make editor at twenty-two by being an idiot. Do you really think I didn't notice that the only time you wanted sex—after the first three months, anyway—was when you wanted something else?"

"I liked the way you would get on your knees to unfasten my pants," she said. "The way you kissed me when you helped me out of them."

Hugh's boxer shorts started to misshape, and Millie tried not to smile. He stepped toward her, reaching down to adjust himself as he walked. He was fully ready, now. She wished pregnancy didn't take so long to show, that she could leave after they finished and immediately flaunt her condition on the street.

Hugh came close enough to tap against her hip bone. He breathed into her ear, "I'm not capable."

"Of course you are," she purred in the voice she knew he liked. "They're a simple clip and zipper. Have you hurt yourself?"

"Millie." He stepped back and raised his eyebrows at her abdomen, then mimed a bulge by curling his arms to create an arc over his belly. "I'm not capable."

She let go of her bra clasp before she could unhook it. "Since when?"

"Since inguinal hernia surgery at fourteen."

Millie put on her shirt. "But you participated in the evaluation."

"I figured it was a phase." He picked up a pair of folded pants from somewhere behind the couch. "I thought you'd grow out of it."

"And if I didn't? If I had passed my evaluation and we'd continued living together, would you have told me then?"

"So you could find someone else to do it?" He laughed and jammed a foot into a pant leg. "Hell, no. But I did think I might have to stay, if you'd passed. At least until you didn't want a kid, anymore. I'd have kept it going—we'd 'try' and 'try'—until you either changed your mind or I couldn't take it, anymore." He pulled up the other pant leg. "Millie, you— and I mean this, seriously—you have qualities. You're smart, you can be funny as hell, you're ambitious, and you're determined. That's all damn sexy, and I'm sure some part of me'll always crave some part of you. But you're also selfish. Inconsiderate. You're so insecure you're borderline narcissistic. And that'd be fine, you know, for anyone who wants to be with you, because it'd be a choice, a consensual...you know, agreement." He sucked in his stomach and buttoned his buttons. "But you can't subject some poor, innocent kid to all that. To you."

Millie went to the door. "Thank you for not waiting until after intercourse to tell me."

"Don't think I didn't think about it. It's what you would have done, isn't it?"

She stepped out and closed the door behind her. It was noon on a Saturday. Floyd would be having lunch at the Broad Street deli until twelve-thirty, and if she left now, she'd arrive before he left.

THIRTY TWO

Lenny had only come over because she'd seen his truck and had thought there must be another problem with the house.

It should have been easy to know what to think. Or say. There must have been something to say. A word. But she thought and said nothing, felt nothing as she watched the backs of Floyd's pale thighs flex as well as they could with each thrust into Millie.

Lenny had heard other women moan during sex (movies, television), but never Millie. A soft, girlish, and restrained "Eh!" pushed out of her every time Floyd's body slapped against hers, even as she cracked her knuckles one-handed, that arm lying otherwise limply at her side until Floyd finished the way he always did, with a euphoric "Oh, yeah!" and a collapse. Millie used both hands to clutch his butt cheeks and held him close, her hips raised.

"Was it an impulse, at least?" Lenny said.

Floyd sprang out of Millie and stood beside the bed with his shining penis standing high. "Oh, God, Len." He reached for a pair of striped underwear draped over the bed post. "Oh, God, yeah, what else? What do you think?"

Millie curled into a ball on her back, covering her chest with her knees but flashing the rest at Lenny before pulling the sheet over herself.

Lenny left the bedroom while Floyd was still struggling to slide his foot through the correct pant leg. She was almost across the field when he screamed her name from Millie's front porch. By the time she'd run inside, locked the door, and made her way to the upstairs window to watch for him, he'd only closed half the distance between the two houses. She could tell from the droop of his torso and the swing of his head that he was having a hard time. To run after sex would be overkill for Floyd's system. Lenny watched from the bedroom until Floyd crumpled, heaving, a few yards shy of the back door.

It hurt her to see him lying there, so she went downstairs to the kitchen and kept her back to the window as she made two sandwiches. She ate lunch with Gabriella in the basement suite, the only part of the house without windows. When she went back upstairs to look for Floyd, he was gone.

"It wasn't anything," he said in a phone call two days later.

Lenny said she understood, because although she was sad, she did. "Be happy, Floyd. You're a beautiful person, no matter what."

"Goddamn, Lenny." He took a breath like he had more to say, but he only sighed it out and kept her on the line, waiting. He sniffed, and in a guttural cry said, "Friends one day?"

"Oh, Floyd, of course. One day."

Millie's call came the day after Floyd's. "I apologize for…for what you must have thought when you discovered us in that position."

"Oh," Lenny said.

"All right?"

"I have to go, Millie."

"May I come ov—"

Lenny hung up. She'd been ready to understand Millie, too, but she could only extend herself so far.

After two weeks, Millie called again. Lenny heard the phone ringing as she opened the front door, her arms filled with groceries for Gabriella. She ran to the kitchen for her earpiece.

"I can appreciate your anger," Millie said as soon as their lines connected.

Lenny waited for her to say something closer to an apology. When she didn't, Lenny hung up.

For a week after that, whenever she came home from the store, the shelter, or a walk with Jenny and Andy, the phone rang the second she stepped inside. She activated the identification announcement and stopped answering until she heard who was calling.

"You can't go upstairs during the day, anymore," Lenny warned Gabriella in the basement after the tenth perfectly timed call. "I don't know how closely she's watching the house."

"I almost wish I could meet her," Gabriella said. "She sounds fascin— Do you hear something?"

Lenny ran to the bottom of the stairs and looked up to see that she'd accidentally left the secret door open again. She crawled halfway to the main floor and stopped, listened, but didn't hear anything out of the ordinary. She went the rest of the way to make sure the front door was locked, looked through the peephole, and caught the wispy ends of Millie's blond hair disappearing around the corner.

Lenny bolted into the kitchen and got there just in time to see Millie's eyes and forehead zip past the window. Lenny ran to the living room and watched from the shadows as Millie tore across the field to her little house.

She swatted at an overgrown arm of blue morning glories as she hopped onto her porch.

Millie had probably never once pruned the vine that (now) climbed the downspout and reached inside the rain gutter. Lenny thought, as Millie slipped inside and closed the door, that she and Floyd should have known better than to give Millie something she would have to take care of.

The calls kept coming. Lenny stored her earpiece in a drawer in the kitchen, silenced the ring tone, and, to make the house look empty so Millie wouldn't come back around, started spending evenings and her off days in the basement suite.

Two months into Gabriella's stay, Lenny was fingering through the Margaret Mabary books on the den shelf while mentally lecturing herself (again) about how irresponsible she was being.

She'd made it a rule to keep her boarders at a distance. They could be caught any time after leaving her basement (it hadn't happened, yet, but there was always that chance), and the less she knew about them, the less tempted she would feel to risk her own safety trying to help or save them. She had one job: to keep the current boarder hidden until the delivery so she could make sure the baby (or babies—Thomas had had surprise twins) got a safe and untraceable drop in a trusted shelter's jurisdiction. Once the transfer was made, Lenny and the boarder parted ways, and Lenny went on with her life until another unwilling carrier found her.

But hiding from Millie had forced her to get to know Gabriella, and Lenny liked her so much she went down to the basement even when there was no reason to hide. Gabriella had introduced Lenny to the spiritual enrichment, and fun, of having long talks over coffee. And she never treated Lenny like anything but an equal—one she was interested in knowing. She was also fancy without pretension, a quality Lenny's mom had had, and she laughed at her own personal tragedies—"Any feeling we give to a moment after it's past and gone is a lie. Don't you agree? The mediocre becomes magical, the unpleasant we turn into torture," she said. This, too, reminded Lenny of her mom.

Lenny decided she was willing to deal with any anxiety or sadness that might someday punish her for being Gabriella's friend.

She found the first-edition book she was looking for and brought it down to the basement.

Gabriella took it from her with uncertain, but open, hands and wide eyes.

"I grew up on her!" Gabriella said after fanning and smelling the pages. She hugged the book to her chest. "My first Mabary book was at the farm, one of Esther's collection. I read every one of them until there were no more left to read. How did you know my favorite, my very, very favorite," she kissed the hardcover copy in her hands, "was *Elmore and Lenore Steal the Light*? Ah! I wouldn't have had the courage to do half of what I had to do without it. If two mere children could defeat a scary, criminal government, then I could bear…Well, it's as you said. Everyone has their own impossible situation," she laughed.

They watched movies at night, the house kept locked and dark, the door at the top of the stairs (usually) secured. Gabriella liked many of the same movies Lenny did, stories of women traveling to exotic corners of the world. Why they traveled didn't matter. The movies were vicarious journeys.

"What happiness money buys," Gabriella said when the projection of Marla Helmsworth stepped onto a windy balcony overlooking the Tyrrhenian Sea. "There are people who would kill us for our advantage, even if they had no plans to make any more use of it than we do. But I sometimes think having the option must be enough." She ate popcorn from her cupped palm. "I wonder if we might be insulting them by not enjoying our wealth. For them, we should go to Italy. Anzio!"

As much money as Lenny and Gabriella had, both also had their reasons for having never taken a single vacation to a single exotic location. Lenny played along, anyway. It was more fun to imagine traveling with Gabriella than it would be to travel. She couldn't relax with the animals in someone else's care, and she didn't like being away from the shelter for more than three days at a time. And Gabriella couldn't fly. Her adoptive mother hadn't replaced her chip, and Gabriella had decided she was better off without it. "I don't like the thought of it," she'd once said with a dramatic shiver. "Those strange chemicals running through my blood."

Over the next few weeks, Lenny developed a habit of checking the call log before going downstairs (seeing Millie's name had become strangely comforting), but she forgot all about Millie in the basement, where she and Gabriella made and changed fantasy plans for overseas vacations in between movie viewings, book discussions, and lunches. As Gabriella's growing pregnancy pulled her tops into new grooves, she would absently rub and stroke her middle while speculating on the beauty of springtime in Punta Arenas, the magic of Neckarsteinach in the fall. At night when Lenny took the narrow staircase to bed (never before the sun set on her west-facing bedroom window), she'd hear the jerks of sound and silence as

Gabriella flipped channels for another movie to take her somewhere out of her reach.

Lenny's avoidance of Millie had become such a mindless routine that she sometimes forgot she was crawling up the stairs while she was crawling. During the day, she regularly exercised the dogs inside instead of taking them out, giving them treats ten straight minutes of "upstairs" and "downstairs" commands. When Jenny and Andy did have to go out, Lenny took them only if she knew where Millie was (or wasn't), sometimes posting Gabriella in a living room corner as a lookout. And every night, while creeping through the main floor on the way upstairs, Lenny squinted to see past each of the windows and into the dark. Sometimes Millie was there, her light hair a disembodied moonlit puff floating in the field. Usually she wasn't. Lenny never heard her trying to open the front door again.

"What could happen if you talk to her?" Gabriella said one morning over coffee in her suite. Her bump was big enough to support her mug.

Lenny said, "I don't know," and realized she really didn't. Millie wasn't a physical threat, or anything like that. There was no reason to be afraid of her. She imagined it: the bell, opening the door, Millie's calculating, light blue eyes.

In her daydream, Lenny slammed the door before Millie could open her mouth. She was sneaking around to avoid a woman she'd known since they were born, she suddenly understood, because Millie would never take responsibility. It was so frustrating that just thinking about it deflated and exhausted her.

"Nothing would happen," she answered Gabriella.

The next afternoon, in the upstairs bedroom, Lenny stopped short with the warm bundle of sheets she'd brought up from the laundry room when she saw on the call log that there'd been nothing from Millie since the night before. It was almost dinnertime. Millie's routine ever since Lenny had started hiding in the basement had been one morning call and one in the early evening. At least.

Across the field, Millie's vine-strangled house dropped a shadow on the empty driveway. That Millie's car was gone was the only reason Lenny had felt safe near her windows that day, but now she had to try not to see the shattered windshield, the body in the street, Millie's hair flat with blood.

She was relieved—and then annoyed—to see Millie's distant figure in miniature leave her house without closing the front door and start across the field in a sprint. Her fuzzy hair, backlit by the sun, flickered around her head like white fire. The second Lenny noticed she was standing in the same beam of light, she forced herself not to move. A trick her mom had taught her, but one Lenny, always the seeker in games of hide and seek with Millie, had never been able to use.

Millie waved up at Lenny as she got closer to the house. Lenny pretended not to see her and didn't breathe or blink—just in case—until Millie finally disappeared from view. Free to move again, Lenny picked up the fitted sheet from the floor and flapped it across the mattress. She pulled it around the corners, ignored the doorbell when it rang, and stuffed a pillow into a case while keeping an eye outside.

Millie reappeared in the field, stomping across dead grass with a trail of white smoke following her fingers. She faced the house and pressed her thumb to an imaginary control panel.

Lenny sighed, tossed the pillow at the headboard, and opened the window.

"I understand why you might avoid me," Millie yelled up to the second floor. "I feel—I feel terrible about…about…" She looked around, took a drag from her cigarette, and blew the smoke over her head. "About what you witnessed."

Lenny put her mouth to the screen. "That's your apology?"

"No."

Lenny walked away from the window. After a few seconds, she went back to make sure Millie was heading home, but she didn't see her where she expected to see her. She pressed herself to the screen to get a view straight down. Millie cut around the corner to take the path to the front.

Well, Lenny thought, she could ring the doorbell all day long, but—

She searched for the memory that would reassure her she'd locked the door the moment she came home.

She'd meant to. She always locked it, every day, every time. But today she'd had the groceries, and the sheets had been sitting wet in the washing machine for an hour, and then something else had distracted her…

"Hello?" Millie called from downstairs.

Lenny had thought, once, that it might be a good idea to install a door at the bottom of the basement stairs. Extra protection for the day someone entered without permission while the secret door was wide open.

"Up here, Millie," Lenny yelled down to the foyer, hoping her voice was loud enough to reach Gabriella. "I'm coming down."

She skipped every other step with her hand wrapped around the railing, but by the time she could see the foyer, she could also see that Millie wasn't there.

THIRTY THREE

A deep sofa and an oversized chair fit comfortably in the underground living room the approximate square footage of Millie's house. Lenny stood in front of a wardrobe Millie knew had been open when she'd first entered. It held an assortment of slippers, a wide selection of colorful shirts, silk nightgowns on hangers, and a dark red robe on a door hook.

"This used to be the gift wrapping room," Millie said. She went into the kitchen and ran her fingers along the length of the short counter. She opened a lower cabinet to saucepans, deep pots, and three unique sizes and styles of colander. "I used to hide in the original cabinets with Uncle Ernie's wrapping paper and his bins of bows and ribbons." She closed the door. "Some of them were embroidered with your name, do you remember? Lenore Mabary, Lenny Mabary, Lenny. I'm sure you must still have them, somewhere. In a special frame?" She looked at the wardrobe.

Lenny stepped back, almost pressing herself to its doors.

Millie said, "I needed to find some way to occupy my time while you were looking for me."

"You hid so well you were hard to find."

Millie remembered waiting, and waiting, and then finally creeping up the stairs to the main level only to hear clattering in the kitchen, Lenny and her dad talking and laughing together. She remembered seeing that green bug on Lenny's finger after having been folded up in the dryer for eighteen minutes. "I'M A CARRIER, NOW. WHAT DO YOU THINK ABOUT THAT?" she wanted to scream, but it wasn't the time. However, it might be the time much sooner than it would have been now that it was obvious Lenny was desperate to hide some woman in her basement.

Millie whispered, "Is she in the bathroom?"

"Is who in the bathroom?"

The toe of a blue shoe was visible beneath the oversized chair. Millie made a point of kicking it before sitting down.

"Millie, don't—Why don't we go upstairs?" Lenny said. "Do you want a glass of wine?"

"No."

"I'd like one. Come on. We'll go upstairs, and—"

"Why? Who is she?"

"She's no one, Millie. Just someone who needs a safe place and some privacy. Let's let her have it. All right?"

The only reason a woman might need a safe place and privacy, Millie figured, was abuse. Millie couldn't use abuse. For it to work, she'd have to manipulate Lenny into revealing the abuser's name and contact information, and that could take weeks. She needed a place to hide now.

Millie covered her eyes and forced pressure to her head. She tried to think of something that would make her cry, but it had been a long time since tears. The redness in her face would have to suffice.

Millie blubbered, "You're the only person I've ever truly trusted. I can hardly expect you to understand the significance of that. How could you?"

Her face once again in her hands, Millie accused Lenny of having had the advantage of a childhood with "insufferably present" parents, a solid support group in her Collector friends, and teenage love from Floyd, whose "simpering, spineless obsession" with Lenny had persisted year after y—

"That's why?" Lenny said. "You wanted to break his loyalty to me?" She stepped away from the wardrobe to sit on the sofa.

Millie scrubbed at her eyes and peered through the burning dryness. "Don't be ridiculous." She made a show of standing up to retrieve a tissue and blew her nose in the middle of the room. She sat again, sniffed loudly, and leaned forward on the chair with her hands clasped tight together in an earnest, supplicating gesture.

Lenny watched her, waiting.

Millie asked herself what Lenny would say at a moment like this.

It would have to be something that sounded true.

Millie picked at her finger (it wasn't yet time for a cigarette) and, feeling inexplicably bilious, explained that all she had wanted was to experience what it might be like to be Lenny, "if only for a minute or two."

Lenny rested her chin in her hand and raised one dark eyebrow.

It was clear Lenny needed more, so, "I'm sorry," Millie said around the sick feeling.

Lenny leaned forward and grazed Millie's tangled fingers with her soft hand. "Thank you."

That was finished, then.

The queasy feeling vanished.

Now all Millie had to do was allow the passage of exactly five seconds of silence. If she spoke too soon, she would seem eager, and Lenny would construe the apology as a ploy. If she waited too long, she would seem too calculated, and the result would be the same.

After two seconds, she lit a cigarette. By the time she exhaled, five seconds had passed.

"I'm a carrier." Millie was aware of the great expanse of the smile on her face, but she had no control over it. Lenny was the first person to hear the words. Someone finally knew. "Me, Lenny!"

Many more seconds went by.

Lenny said, "Hugh's?"

"Mine," Millie said.

"I mean—"

"If you mean to ask whether Hugh will be involved, the answer is no."

Hugh, Millie said, had moved to be on camera at a small Wisconsin station.

"Oh," Lenny said. "I see. You're not here to apologize, at all. You need me to replace him as your FCP. I already told you, Millie, I'm not—"

Millie said no, no, that was not the case at all. She explained the bureau's analytics error and her resultant—and unjust!—dismissal from an evaluation process whose sole function, she suspected, was to burden people with the ever-present fear that they might someday have their licenses revoked. She extolled the generosity of strangers who didn't believe that whether someone had a child should be determined by anything other than their whim or wish to have one.

"Those generous strangers, the kind people who allowed me this," she rubbed her belly, "operated out of a house the police raided last month."

All were arrested, Millie said, their data confiscated. She didn't know when or whether they would discover her information, but caution dictated she could not live at the address the bureau had on file. Because Lenny was her best and lifelong friend, she could think of no safer—nor more welcoming—place to hide.

"I'm asking not because I want to..." Millie had allowed her cigarette to burn low. She brought it to the sink, wet it, and lit another. "But because I have to. I would induce a miscarriage myself and have you help me dispose of it, if—"

"Of course!" Lenny said. "Please. Let me help you do that."

"I *would* have asked, I said, but I'm sure it will only take a month, possibly two, for the police to access my data, search my house, and move on. You'll be free of me after that. In any case, it should take the same amount of time for this pregnancy to show, which means there's no point in engaging with the public until then. It's just as well that I hide myself here."

The bathroom door opened. A tall, silky woman looked out with a face that made Millie think of childhood.

"Please put out your cigarette," the woman said. "The smoke is coming through the door."

Millie recommended she turn on the fan.

"Please," the woman said. "Out of concern for your own fetus, if not for mine."

"This is out of concern for my fetus." Millie puzzled through the possible reasons another carrier would be hiding in Lenny's basement. "A low birth weight will mitigate the strain of labor." She put her cigarette between her lips.

Lenny swatted it out of her mouth and stomped it where it landed on the carpet.

Millie attempted a guess and asked the woman when her hacker was arrested.

"I have no hacker."

"That must be a relief."

It was an abuse situation, after all.

Millie devised a more immediate way to use the woman's vulnerability to her advantage: she would offer something that would indebt Lenny to her. Millie told them she would do her best to keep the woman's presence a secret from whoever her abuser might be. If he or she arrived at the house, Millie said, she would fight—

"Abuse!" Gabriella said. "I am Gabriella Dahl, president and CEO of World Cannabis. No one abuses me."

Millie pulled out another cigarette. Gabriella's eyes narrowed as she lit it. When Gabriella screamed at her to put it out, Millie handed it to Lenny, who took it to the kitchen.

"You obviously have no intention of keeping it," Millie prodded. "What difference is it to you if your drop is a bit smaller than the others?"

"You don't have to want to keep it to want it to be healthy," Lenny said. She turned off the faucet and threw the butt away. "Millie, you can't stay here. Gabriella is already here, and there's only one bed."

Millie looked at Gabriella, whose fingernail slid across her bottom lip as she watched—no, studied—Millie.

"Suppose they catch me?" Millie said. "Suppose they use methods that give me no choice but to reveal I was here? Suppose they discover what you're doing?"

"You told me Exile it isn't as bad as they say it is."

"I did tell you that," Millie said. "However, we—the evaluation class—witnessed a…a presentation. I'm not at liberty to share the details—they exile people for that—but I can tell you it's nothing any one of us would want to survive."

Lenny seemed unconcerned about hiding the silent "I'm sorry" she mouthed at Gabriella, who said, "Well, I understand it, now, at least."

Millie stepped between the two women and faced Lenny. "Carrying is a mere inconvenience to her, but it means everything to me." She petted her stomach. "I want it so very much. Please allow me to stay. You wouldn't want to be responsible for an Exile or prison delivery, would you? Or for them putting my baby in one of the state shelters you're well aware have created plenty of their own Chester Waltons?" She dropped to her knees and presented her hands pressed flat together. "I recognize your limitations and understand you cannot possibly safeguard my future, but I must beg you for one month. Possibly two."

Gabriella, who technically held seniority in the refurbished basement, was granted the use of the only bed. Millie slept on the couch, which did not pull out, for two weeks before insisting on sharing the queen sized mattress with Gabriella. (At first she waited until she heard Gabriella's even breathing before easing herself under the sheets, where she would promptly fall asleep to the sound of Gabriella's dream sighs. If Gabriella awoke and tried to remove her, Millie clung to the mattress. The sneaking and wrestling went on for two weeks until Gabriella agreed to share—Millie sleeping on the sheet, Gabriella sleeping beneath it, and with a pillow between them.)

Because Gabriella screamed and screamed at any smoking in the basement, Millie climbed the stairs multiple times a day for her half-pack habit. She inspected the grounds, then stepped out the living room's back door where she was shielded from everything but her abandoned property. The days passed so slowly that she sped up the hours by marking each ninety minute block with a single cigarette. She stood and she smoked, day after day, noting with disinterest the way the weeds colored the dry, dead field. The grass in the square lawn around her house gradually swallowed her stepping stone walkway, and thick spirals of that infernal, indomitable morning glory wrapped around one front porch column and reached across to the other, roping off her entry with the aid of spider webs that also spanned the width between the columns and swayed with the slightest breeze. There were so many webs that even from as far away as Lenny's back yard, Millie could see them glinting in a certain hour of morning light.

The heat and humidity made Millie's neck and back itch, but during the days she preferred to be where Gabriella wasn't, and Gabriella was never outside. Because neither could leave the house, however, Millie couldn't avoid her entirely, and the more she saw of Gabriella (who, incidentally, Millie discovered was having the occasional clandestine breakfast upstairs with Lenny while both thought Millie was asleep), the more bothered she was that she couldn't identify what it was that bothered her about the woman. She did have an obnoxious habit of noticing herself sideways in the mirror, her months showing without the need for small shirts or clothes pulled tight, but that wasn't it. Nor was it her floating walk or maternal aura, though both were indeed irritating.

Millie waited for whatever it was to come to her on its own while she stood and smoked and watched the vine turn brown with the leaves. The webs broke and withered, but the dried vines held their shape through the winter winds. Millie checked them daily, waiting to find them broken by the only people who would ever approach her front door.

THIRTY FOUR

Lenny squinted at the faint gray outline of Gabriella's face in the dark. Her fine fingernails made short, light strokes on Lenny's left cheek.

"Wake gently," Gabriella whispered. "I'm a friend. Don't be afraid. I'm a friend. Wake gently."

"I'm awake."

Gabriella whispered that she needed Lenny's help finding Millie's cigarettes. No, Millie wasn't smoking in the basement, but Gabriella was just so worried about the fetus. She'd already looked in every bag and cabinet and drawer, and under every piece of furniture.

"They just keep coming, but from where?" she said.

Lenny climbed out of bed and put on socks.

She knew the basement well enough to search it blind, but after exploring every crevice and corner while Gabriella watched Millie for movement, Lenny couldn't find the cigarettes.

Too wide awake afterward to go back to bed, Lenny and Gabriella tiptoed upstairs to the kitchen and ate lemon poppy seed scones at the island.

"You must think I'm a terrible hypocrite." Gabriella spread butter on a bite. "So anxious about what she does to hers, but giving up my own."

"I don't think that."

Gabriella rubbed crumbs from her fingers, then shaped her bathrobe around herself. She looked down at it. "It feels odd, now that I can't help but see it."

Lenny handed Gabriella a clean napkin for her eyes.

Gabriella said, "Do you think I should I keep it?"

Lenny said her opinion didn't matter. The bureau made decisions like that.

"But what do you think?"

"Why, Gabi? Do you want to keep it?"

Gabriella bit her thumbnail and then wiped it on her thigh. She picked up the remainder of her scone and put it down again. She shrugged. She shook her hair over her shoulders. "I know. I'm foolish to think this now, only two months left. I never wanted this. As you know." She laughed. "It was—Oh, those ads!" She put her hands on her hips and stared intently at

Lenny. "'Do you have carrier potential?' And then…Do you know this one? Such happy faces on these fat-bellied carriers standing on the shore of a lovely, lovely beach, their bare sides all touching, here," she said, tapping the sides of her own fat belly. "That one, I always remember: 'Parenthood: the most inclusive exclusive club in the world. Do you qualify?' I should want one to prove I belong, that I 'qualify'? It made me crazy!" She laughed again. "But now, for so long, now, it's just been me, and this," she rubbed it, "and no commercials. I don't hear the pressure, anymore."

Lenny warned Gabriella that keeping it wouldn't be easy. If she wanted to do it legally, she would have to register as soon as possible as an incidental carrier and explain to the authorities why she'd waited so long. ("You'll have to lie. You'll have to tell them you only figured out you were pregnant seconds before you decided to register," she said to Gabriella's shrug and nod.) She would also have to explain why she hadn't replaced her chip. ("I'd find a way to use your past, maybe your mother, as an excuse, and not your feelings about the hormone," Lenny said, to which Gabriella only replied, "Sure, of course.") She would have to find FCP volunteers, too, and go through the evaluation process. And it would all have to work perfectly, Lenny said. A single failed component—failure to convince the board she didn't know she was pregnant, for one—could mean Exile, at worst, and her baby in a state shelter.

"I think…" Gabriella tore her scone. "I think it could easily work if…Is there any reason to hope you might agree to be a secondary guar—"

"No. I'm sorry, Gabi."

Gabriella tore her scone again and set the broken pieces on her napkin. Lenny had never seen a face so sad. She reached out for Gabriella's hand and held it.

"I only wanted to ask," Gabriella said quietly. "It can still be done. I know people who might agree. And I'll do everything else you said."

Lenny explained that it was a big risk to take, that her advice wasn't a guarantee of success. All she had were ideas. To help Gabriella better understand exactly what she meant by "risk," Lenny told her the worst story she'd heard since Chester Walton:

A woman whose neighbor turned her in for being an unlicensed carrier claimed she hadn't meant to carry. She'd been hacked at random, she told the police, and her boyfriend had both raped and forcibly impregnated her before her hormone could be reactivated. The state's attorney said the timing was too coincidental, too convenient, to be believable, and the jury agreed. The woman was exiled one week after giving birth.

Lenny waited for a nod and some version of "I don't know what I could have been thinking." Because Gabriella only stared at her napkin and poked at the scone dough she'd pressed into balls, Lenny reminded her of what Millie had been able to say about the conditions of Exile. She urged Gabriella to imagine being in a place so awful people would be sent there just for talking about it. If it was too hard to imagine a place she couldn't imagine, Lenny said, she should at least try to picture herself in prison, where she would experience...whatever it was that went on there.

Gabriella nodded, but she said nothing.

Lenny looked politely past her, over the breakfast bar and through the living room windows. The sun was only just coming up, and Millie's house was little more than a black peak against a faint purple sky.

"I have to try," Gabriella said.

Lenny stood and grabbed her napkin, then swept up Gabriella's, too, scone balls and all, and brought them to the trash.

Gabriella wrapped her hand around her water glass before Lenny could take it away. "Why are you discouraging me?"

Lenny didn't answer. She understood that people who wanted children could be just as unreasonable as people who didn't, putting anything and everything—including the children—at risk just to have them, but she didn't like it, and the less she talked about it with Gabriella, the better she could pretend to be supportive for the sake of their friendship.

But it wasn't her job to be supportive, she reminded herself. She was there to protect the born child, not Gabriella, who was a boarder, first. A carrier whose baby Lenny was there to protect.

She was so ashamed that she'd almost put her own needs first that she was harsher than she meant to be when she told Gabriella frankly that anyone who would knowingly put their future child in danger of living in a state shelter probably wasn't the kind of person who should keep that child.

"By 'person,' do you mean me?" Gabriella said.

"I mean—I mean anyone. But if that's the kind of thing you would do, then y—"

Gabriella laughed a full-throated, melodious laugh, and then told Lenny she hoped they would stay friends for a long time. Still smiling, she tucked the flaps of her robe more snugly into the belt knotted under her breasts. She stayed quiet for a long time, her smile slowly fading.

Her child would never see the inside of a state shelter, Gabriella said. She would run with the baby in her arms until she found the ocean, and she'd walk them both to the center of it before she would allow that to happen.

"If you took the baby, I know you would choose a safe place, a good place," Gabriella said. "But a child doesn't forget, even then. It never stops wondering why." She flicked her fingers, as if annoyed, when she realized she was stroking her scar. She put her hand in her lap. "From the moment I woke up in front that little animal hospital to the moment I woke up in your basement this morning, I never stopped. I really don't want to quote your friend, but I don't want to do this. I have to."

Lenny remembered Xavier's praise of sacrifice. That Gabriella felt obligated to raise a child she'd never wanted probably meant the licensing bureau would find her more than qualified to do it.

"Do you really believe you'll pass?" Lenny said.

"I'm sure of it."

"If you don't?"

"Do you think I'm going to walk into the ocean?" Gabriella smiled. "I might, that's true, but first I'll run. We aren't so far from Canada, and my car is fast. I can tell you this: We'll be together. Always. Or at least," she laughed, "until it's old enough to want to leave me.—You'll help me, then?"

Lenny made quick mental notes of what that would involve. First, they'd have to go to the drug store for a pregnancy test. The pharmacists should overhear Lenny urging Gabriella to buy it while Gabriella pooh-poohed the possibility of being pregnant. As soon as the positive line appeared in the window, Lenny would drive her to the bureau, whose records would show the date of the test purchase, the time the positive result automatically logged, and evidence that Gabriella had come to register immediately upon learning she was pregnant. When asked to speak, Lenny would go on about Gabriella's irregular periods and say many nice things about her character, and that would be the end of it.

"Okay," Lenny said. "Yes. I'll help y—"

"I remember you, now." Millie, centered in the kitchen doorway in socks and an oversized t-shirt, pushed her wild hair away from her face. "You were the drop who smelled up the van. It reeked for days. Did you know that?"

Gabriella shrugged. "How could I?"

Lenny still didn't remember collecting Gabriella, whose head slanted at an awkward tilt as she looked at Millie.

"Oh! Oh my, yes," Gabriella said. "Yes, yes. I remember you, too! You were the one—You scrubbed your..."—She paused to mimic the motion, smearing her thumb and finger on her hip, disgust on her face—"...to wipe me away. That was you!"

Millie marched into the kitchen and pulled a scone from the plastic bag sitting next to the toaster. "It's so charitable of Lenny to extend her work with drops into their adulthood. Perhaps if I'd been a worthless, unloved discard she'd have been equally enthusiastic about helping me pass my evaluation."

Until then, Lenny had never once been tempted to tell Millie about what her mother had done. It hadn't even occurred to her. It was too low, too cruel. And now, because she was tempted, so very tempted—the sentence was fully formed and ready—she knew she couldn't trust herself to be right.

She thought of her dad, what he would say.

He would say Millie hurts plenty already.

"I helped you as much as I could," Lenny said.

Millie stomped out with her scone. Seconds later, the secret door in the foyer closed hard with a *whoosh* and a solid click.

THIRTY FIVE

Lenny and Gabriella had been gone for seventy-seven minutes.

Millie blew a thick smoke cloud into the shade. Across the field, the dead vines netting her porch entry glowed rich brown, still unbroken. She flicked her cigarette into the drain pipe runoff and lit another.

She imagined them, as she had several times over the last seventy-seven minutes, arriving at the bureau smiling, their arms linked. Lenny would pull open the door for Gabriella and lead her to the receptionist, where she would introduce herself first. "I'm Lenny Mabary," she would say. "Exemplary citizen. Daughter, as you must already know, of the famous author Margaret Mabary and the well-known humanitarian contractor Ernie Aronne."

Gabriella is a good person, Lenny would say. Gabriella is a model carrier. Gabriella is a friend of Lenny Mabary.

However, Gabriella was anything but a model carrier. She was a matured drop and nothing more who until the night before had been prepared to drop her own. The only reason she'd changed her mind, Millie was certain, was that her delivery date was imminent and she was afraid they would discover her once the child was dropped. There would be no evading Exile. Gabriella no doubt believed keeping it would present at least the possibility of freedom.

Fortunately, the evaluators were careful judges (until confronted by a unique specimen, obviously) and would identify her immediately as a candidate for Exile.

Millie spent a good amount of time fantasizing about Gabriella's exile. Because she didn't know the precise procedure or protocol for transporting prisoners, she skipped past that part and placed Gabriella directly inside the facility.

The bureau's presentation hadn't covered apprehension or conveyance, but had, following Eugene's segment, given way to a virtual tour of the facility's interior: its unfathomably unsanitary community waste chamber; the dramatically named Rooms of Eternal Night; deep kitchen pots overflowing with mealworms and mysterious intestines, respectively; and Reflection and Repentance Hall, where—Millie assumed for effect—they had spent the most time.

Reflection and Repentance Hall was a spacious, high-ceilinged cell with painted blue walls displaying rows upon rows of visages of the dropped (as well as those who were differently abused). May Cheney explained that the high stained glass windows streamed "in memoriam" light directly onto certain faces at specific times of day throughout the year. For example, first light on the summer solstice shined on the face of Thaleia Robinson, whose manner of death on June 21 nearly rivaled that of Chester Walton, who received the sun at precisely 2:37 p.m. on the anniversary of his death. And so on.

Only one image was kept separate from the others. The boy was rumored, but not confirmed, to be the younger brother of the facility's overseer, a man known as "the Rectifier." The boy's face hovered in the center of the room and acted as a scanner, recording the arrival of prisoners ordered to make their way to it ("In any way they choose," May Cheney said, "whether walking, crawling, or rolling.") across a floor of retractable, but not retracted, spikes.

"The Rectifier's dedication to punishing those who mistreat children is resolute," May Cheney had told the class, her chin pointed high. "I know the Rectifier personally. Having now seen what is by all accounts a brilliant manifestation of his unique vision, you may be surprised to hear that I deem him to be a sensitive, loving human being. Accordingly, he shows not an ounce of mercy to those rightfully put in his charge."

Millie doubted Gabriella would be compelled to roll across the spikes. According to May Cheney, the Rectifier reserved that punishment for the worst offenders.

She finished her cigarette, took the stairs to the top floor, and looked through Lenny's belongings to pass time. She opened her dresser drawers, which Floyd had never permitted her to do, and found pants in one of the lower drawers and shirts in another. In the shallow top drawer, she found a square newspaper cutout lying atop Lenny's cotton underwear and unpadded bras. It was a portion of a half-off coupon for free range, cruelty free beef, but it had been expired for months. She turned it over.

Governor won't fund hormone alert system despite proven hacks
By Millicent M. Oxford!

The sob that overtook her was so sudden she had no time to put down the article before covering her face, the story a flimsy barrier between her eyes and her hands. She touched it to her wet cheeks, her forehead, her nose to breathe it in, and then held it up and skimmed the damp text for a particularly insightful sentence or clever combination of words that had made Lenny treasure it.

Nothing stood out. The date also held no significance, as far as Millie was concerned.

It was possible, then—more than possible, actually—that there was nothing extraordinary about it at all but for the fact that Millie had written it.

Not since she'd last contributed a piece of writing to the folder hidden in her childhood closet had Millie felt so valued. She returned the article to its spot, patted it down, and slid the drawer closed with a light sigh, then resumed exploring the second floor in a peculiar emotional state, wandering almost drunkenly into to the attached bathroom. She opened a soapstone jewelry box she'd long known held a mere four pieces of jewelry. One of the rings had always drawn her, a smooth, foggy emerald set in a silver water lily. Its individual pointed petals flowered from the band. She slid it on and wore it downstairs to the den (a stack of framed Margaret Mabary book cover prints inside the hutch), the dining room (soft cloth napkins and sparkling silver utensils—to include a set of curious, miniature, three-pronged forks—in the sideboard drawer), and the kitchen (food in the cabinets, wine in the pantry).

The foyer's stone floor should not have been inviting, but Millie sat there comfortably, half-dazed, with a wine glass filled to the rim. She listened for the sound of gravel under Lenny's car tires, the groan of the garage door rolling up the rails. Ten minutes passed, and then twenty. In that time, Millie considered another cigarette, but it was unpleasantly hot outside. She also considered telling Lenny what she'd found, ultimately deciding it would be unwise. Lenny would misunderstand what Millie had been doing in her bedroom.

Millie jumped to her feet at the dull crunch of grinding rocks. She emptied her glass in the kitchen sink and hurried back to the foyer, anxious to hear about Gabriella's arrest—how many had taken her, how they had taken her—and Gabriella's reaction. (She'd likely screamed. Gabriella always screamed about something.) After a frustrating moment of unmet anticipation when the garage door didn't open, Millie heard the slam of a car door. A second one followed.

She marched to the peep hole and slammed her eye socket flat to the wood. The prospect of seeing a triumphant Gabriella bounding up the stairs alongside a jubilant Lenny enraged her.

Two middle-aged figures in dark purple double-breasted suits filled the fisheye lens, one of them—the woman—with an outstretched arm reaching for the doorbell.

Millie took a careful step backward. "Westminster Chimes" flooded the house. Using the sound as cover, Millie ran to the hidden door. She pushed and pushed at the wood panel. It bounced and bounced without opening. The doorbell's melody stopped, and Millie froze. She expected Jenny and Andy to scramble out barking so she could make another attempt, but they were evidently unperturbed by visitors.

A single beep echoed through the foyer and bounced off the high ceiling, and Millie realized she'd been so intent on getting to the basement that she'd missed hearing the arrival of Lenny's car.

The ensuing beeps were entered with painful slowness.

Millie counted seven. There were eight.

Lenny apologized with uncharacteristic volume for the delay in entering her code.

"I declare, I hardly ever forget it," she said on the other side of the door. "Police must make me nervous. Heehee! I sure do hope my dogs don't jump on you when you come in, Officers…?"

Beeeeep.

Millie slipped into the coat closet two seconds (she counted retroactively) before the front door opened. It was a sizeable closet with plenty of room to hide, but to better eavesdrop she concealed herself behind the lightweight jackets hanging closest to the door. If they decided to search, no one spot—behind this jacket, tucked into that coat—would be more or less effective against the aggressive sweeps of determined arms, after all.

"Detective Merriweather, Detective Davis," the woman responded to Lenny's leading question as they invaded the foyer. "Child Welfare and Licensing, Special Division."

They were looking for one Millicent Oxford, they said, and they understood Lenny owned the property listed as Ms. Oxford's permanent residence on her licensing application. Yes, they said when Lenny asked, they'd tried there first. (They must have driven past at the same time Millie would have been outside, had she gone outside. She'd never appreciated a missed cigarette more.) As they interrogated Lenny about Millie—Did she appear to be pregnant? Did she have any known hacker acquaintances? When had Lenny last seen her? ("Gawsh, I reckon it was eons ago!")—their voices gradually quieted as, Millie surmised, Lenny led them away from the door to the basement. Not far enough away for Millie to not hear them from the closet, however, though she had difficulty believing what she was hearing when Lenny asked the detectives if they'd like to search the house.

The male officer, Davis or Merriweather, said that if Lenny said Millicent Oxford wasn't in the house, then Millicent Oxford wasn't in the house. Lenny's impeccable reputation had been confirmed for them when they'd learned she, Lenore Mabary, had just that morning delivered an unlicensed carrier, one Gabriella Dahl, to the Parent Licensing Bureau.

"Oh, pish," Lenny said. "It was a huge ol' mistake, is all. The little chicken had no idea she was pregnant, bless her heart."

"In any case," the female detective said, "we wouldn't think of searching the home of a woman of such righteous action."

"You did more than that," the male detective said. "You said...you said...Where is it? Here, here it is. You said, uh, 'Gabriella Dahl is a person of strong character and unmatched kindness.'"

Millie snorted in the dark, then slapped her hand to her nose.

"I did say that," Lenny said. "It's absolutely true. Gabriella Dahl will be a beautiful parent. If anyone should be trusted to raise a child, it's Gabriella."

"Sal," the man said, "didn't she also give a referral to Millicent Oxford some months ago? You did, didn't you, Ms. Mabary? Before she failed her evaluation."

"Mm," Lenny said. "Hm."

"Yeah, you said...Uh...Now, where is—? Here. Said, 'I reckon she'll be the best mamma imaginable to any little baby.' Any chance you'd help her hide out somewhere? Make sure she's the one who gets to be that baby's mother?"

"Lord, no," Lenny said. "I'd 'a' turned her in in a second if I'd seen hide or hair of her."

"But you did give her that referral," the female said.

Millie wondered if she could get away with smoking. Perhaps, with a jacket stuffed into the gap at the bottom of the door...? No. She would wait.

That referral was months and months ago, Lenny said. Millie had tricked her, Lenny said, but, "I know better, now. Why, I'd be kickin' down your door to give 'er to y'all, given the chance. I can't imagine what that poor child will go through with Millie as its mother."

"She is pregnant, then," the female said.

"Now, I can't rightly say," Lenny said. "But if she's anywhere, maybe y'all should check—Texas, I think it was? I think her ex-boyfriend might 'a' moved there. She really has no one else who cares about her here."

The detectives expressed their appreciation for Lenny's valuable information and took their time leaving. As soon as the door closed, Millie burst out of the closet. Lenny jumped.

Millie popped a cigarette in her mouth and pulled out her lighter. She intended to take a long, harsh, satisfying drag the second she stepped out the back door.

Lenny slapped the lighter from her hand. "Not in here!"

"I know."

Lenny looked at the closet door, and then at Millie. Millie looked at the closet door, noticed she'd left it open, and closed it.

"I had to say those things," Lenny said.

"What things?" Millie said around the filter.

Lenny scratched the back of one hand, and then the other. "Anyway," she said, "it worked. I don't think they'll be coming back."

Millie picked up her lighter.

"I guess you'll be leaving soon," Lenny said.

Millie had said she would leave after the police came looking for her, yes. She'd meant it at the time. However, at the time she'd not given any thought to where she would go.

Hugh was a possibility. She could convince him to take her back, even with a different man's offspring—provided she could show it to him after it was born, when he could be affected by whatever he might personally find irresistible in a baby. In the meantime, staying at Lenny's was her only option. She certainly couldn't live in her own house with all of its rooms accessible via visible doors. What if Davis and Merriweather had lied to Lenny about their trust in her? They might possess the dedication to watch Millie's house for days. Weeks. What if she absent-mindedly turned on a light while they skulked around her property in the dark? What if she needed something on the main level one morning at the precise moment they happened to peer inside her window?

There was, above all, the pregnancy to consider. What did she care about the admiration of those she didn't know in a town she'd never lived in? All this time, she'd been awaiting the day she would walk among the faces that had given no signs of recognizing her work for the *Daily Fact*, faces that would shower her with (deserved) validation in their automatic expressions of awe and envy.

"I'd like to stay," Millie said.

She knew from reading the *Fact* and watching the local news that the names gathered from the Hack House hadn't been released to the public.

Assuming she exercised the appropriate caution, she could still have her moment.

"Did you hear me?" Lenny said.

"It would be three additional months, more or less."

"I said no, Millie."

Millie's surprise was an innate emotional reflex. Before pushing it aside, in a split-second moment of agitation, she almost made a mechanical attempt to reconcile Lenny's rejection with the keepsake article in her underwear drawer, but two decades of trying to figure out her parents hadn't yielded a single rational explanation for their confounding treatment.

"In exchange for safe lodging," Millie said, "I pledge to take care of your cats and d—"

"Ha!" Lenny added, "I mean, that's not—It isn't safe lodging, don't you see? I don't think those detectives believed a word I said."

She went on to explain what Millie already knew about the powers of a warrant. She then expressed concerns about the basement door accidentally being left open, unannounced visits, discoveries and Exile, etcetera.

Millie pulled the cigarette from her mouth. The filter, which had adhered itself to the inside of her lip, ripped off a fine layer of skin. "You don't have to worry," she said, licking the sting. "I discovered that with some minor rearranging of my cigarettes and your abortion aids, I fit— granted, in a tight fetal position—in that small compartment under the bed. If even you didn't think to look there when you and Gabriella were hunting for my cigarettes, it must be safe. Wouldn't you agree?"

Millie couldn't sleep that night, alone in the stale, silent, cavernous suite. She tried the couch and was hot under the blanket she'd pulled from the bed. She pushed the blanket to the floor and was cold. She rolled onto her side, and then onto her other side. When she heard a hint of a creak in the ceiling, she tiptoed up the stairs without turning on a light and sat with her ear pressed to the door, which wasn't quite soundproof enough to entirely muffle Lenny's voice.

"…course you passed! I can't imagine anyone finding something wrong with you. So, now it's the dog tr—? … No dog trial, even a short one? … You must have really impressed them! …" (Laughter) "… Well, you'd have been great with one, anyway. … I'd love to. But I'm busy tomorrow, so, Friday?"

Millie slinked back down the stairs, her face hot, and walked confidently in the dark through the layout she'd become familiar with. She remembered the blanket only when it tangled around one of her feet, pitching her forward into the table she remembered was there a fraction of a second before her cheek bone met one of its sharp edges. Her eye and forehead and nose surging with piercing cold pain, she yanked the blanket off her feet, inspected herself for blood (she felt none), and crawled until she found the telephone.

Lenny was at the shelter—where Millie knew they allowed no television—when breaking news announced the next morning that Gabriella Dahl, wife of the late World Cannabis magnate Ezra Smythe, had been arrested outside of her home in an affluent Haverton subdivision following an anonymous telephone tip accusing her of "willful unsanction-ed pregnancy and intent to drop." Millie watched and listened through the open living room window as police led Gabriella, her expensive white t-shirt stretched taut against her massive middle, from the patrol car to the county jailhouse.

"It isn't true!" Gabriella screamed at reporters gathered at the entrance. "I—I only learned very recently that I was—Please! I passed my evaluation! You must trust the bureau, if not me!" She waved a document in the face of a reporter holding a microphone.

The reporter winced, wiped at his nose with a gloved finger, and tore the paper from Gabriella's hand. "Exile!" he hissed before a hand extended from the camera to tap him on the shoulder. The reporter snapped his attention to the lens. His face flushed purple as he bared his teeth in a winning, objective smile.

THIRTY SIX

The CHESTER'S MOM doll was taking too long to burn. Lenny could smell that they'd added wood, probably to the torso where it would have been easy to hide in the stuffing. They weren't supposed to use wood. They were supposed to use what the staff gave them—thrift store sheets and pillows and ten economy sized bags of cotton balls. The only approved deviation was that each resident could throw one personal item into the fire. The younger residents, before licensing reduced the numbers, used to sacrifice stuffed bears and bunnies and rubber chickens. Now that most of the residents were older, it was usually a pungent sock or a pair of underwear with fresh...soiling, but some didn't want to part with personal items of any kind ("Why should I give that lady my stuff?" said one resident, once upon a time).

Lenny and the other interims continued with their ceremonial clapping as a thirteen-year-old named Denise threw chunks of red velvet "Happy Birthday Chester Walton" cake at Chester Walton's mom's flaming chest.

"She brought you into this world," yelled a small gathering on one side of the shrinking body, "and she took you out," finished the group on the other side.

The staff stepped back for the closing portion of the ceremony, standing by for safety as the residents formed a circle around CHESTER'S MOM to watch her burn.

Lenny looked at her watch. Ordinarily she'd have stayed to try to find out where they got the wood, but she needed to let the dogs out before lunch with Gabriella. This would be her first time skipping the annual post-burning "Compassion for the Abuser" presentation they made the children sit still for. (There'd been a meeting one year about holding the presentation before the fire, but someone had argued the residents would be even less likely to pay attention with all that sugar and CHESTER'S MOM burning to look forward to. No one could disagree.)

She considered feeling guilty about leaving the responsibility to the others so she'd feel better about not being there, then decided there was nothing wrong with being excited to help Gabriella celebrate her passed evaluation. Except for Floyd, Lenny had never had a friend to celebrate with (and Floyd's way of celebrating—getting sick on bags of candy, usually after finishing a challenge of a house—hadn't been as much fun for her as it was for him).

She sped home with barely-stops at stop signs, bent over on her way inside to pick up the *Daily Fact* that had recently started appearing, and rushed the dogs out for a quick walk. It wasn't until she brought them in and set their bowls on the kitchen counter for filling that she saw Gabriella's crying eyes peering over the top of the newspaper's fold. She gave the dogs their food and flipped the pages flat.

Suspected unsanctioned carrier to be freed, police say

HAVERTON—Police say they will release incidental carrier and World Cannabis CEO Gabriella Dahl, 21, Saturday pending no new evidence of intent to impregnate and/or intent to abandon. Police arrested Dahl Thursday in response to an anonymous tip alleging that Dahl had intentionally impregnated without a license and had then made plans to abandon her offspring.

Dahl, a former abandoned whose chip was removed in childhood, told police the removal process had so traumatized her that she was reluctant to replace it. Dahl also claimed she had always believed herself incapable of impregnating and had therefore assumed her abdominal growth was a consequence of "too much pasta and ice cream." One of the arresting officers, Matthew Fence, expressed skepticism.

"She was pretty nervous when we caught up with her," Fence said. "If you ask me, it was damn obvious she was pregnant. She had the telltale weight. Right around here."

Fence went on to say that he would be suspicious of any person claiming to be ignorant of having impregnated, an oversight he called "downright laughable and, I'll just say it, unbecoming of anyone with a uterus." Fence tied his characterization of such a person to Dahl and what he suspected was the motivation behind her alleged plan to abandon.

"Look, she runs the cannabis farm. What more do we need? Everyone knows that anyone with a particular sense of direction— and by that I mean doing anything but everything anyone could possibly do to be a licensed carrier, the only mark of a truly good uterus-bearer—is heinously misguided. Heinously misguided. What's it tell you she never got a new chip? What's it tell you she didn't report herself months ago? I'll tell you what. She's all business. All business. Reprehensible."

Fence's commanding officer, Lt. Penelope Bristol, said that because Fence had had no role in the interrogations he could not comment intelligently on Dahl's circumstances, nor on her potential release.

"Officers with level heads said Dahl was friendly, cooperative, and convincing. She also gave us some very helpful information," Bristol said. She added that Fence was recently relieved of his duties.

Bristol declined to reveal the information Dahl provided, saying only that it was useful to the department's broader search for consciously unsanctioned carriers.

"Millie!"

Dahl's prospective release prompted protesters on both sides of the ongoing licensing debate to march in front of police headquarters as well as in Tinytown's Main Street Park.

"Unsanctioned carrying is child abuse!" one park protester argued. A group of three some feet away chanted, "Whether they love it, beat it, or set it wild, deny no hopeful parent a child!"

Protesters opposing and supporting Dahl said they plan to gather at her residence upon her release.

"Millie!"

Lenny hadn't checked the call log since Millie moved in—no one ever called, not even Floyd. She took it and the phone bud out of the drawer and scrolled through the numbers, but there was nothing from Gabriella's phone and nothing from a police station. (There was, of course, no reason Gabriella should have called. With only one phone call to make, she'd have wanted to contact her lawyer. Lenny doubted she'd have been thinking at the time about how to cancel their lunch.)

"MILLIE!"

Millie had left the door to the basement open—she always left it open—so Lenny knew she could hear her. She spun on the stool to call out again and saw Millie standing in the kitchen doorway. Her hair was flat on one side, and her squinted eyes were swollen—as was her cheek under a colorful bruise. The blue nightgown she wore, which Lenny recognized as one of Gabriella's, gathered on the floor around her feet. The midsection was so loose it was almost impossible to tell she was pregnant.

"What?" Millie said.

Lenny wanted to ask how Millie happened to have one of Gabriella's nightgowns, but she already knew that no matter what the truth was, she would say Gabriella had forgotten it.

"What happened to your face?" Lenny said.

"I fell."

"Are you okay?"

"I'm fine."

Lenny waved her over and slid the newspaper in front of her. Millie's expression gave nothing away as she read it.

"Well?" Lenny said.

Millie sniffed and yawned. "'Studies show child abuse continues its steep decline.' Is that surpris—?"

"Not that."

Millie rubbed her eye. "'Wilma Mezrich, twenty-nine, died of a drug overdose…police found her body in the hallway of a Prospect apartment building'…?"

Lenny hadn't noticed that article. She remembered Wilma from school, her bright makeup and, by senior year, reputation for trading oral sex for THC. They said she spent every Wednesday assembly under the bleachers on her knees, so stoned she was almost asleep. Lenny felt happy for her, now that she was free.

"Don't you see her face in the middle of the page?" Lenny tapped Gabriella's forehead. "Right here?"

Millie folded the paper and placed it face-down. "She's being released. How exciting for—" She winced. She looked down at her belly.

"You don't seem surprised that she was arrested."

Millie slapped at her stomach. "Television media covered it ad nauseam yesterday morning."

Lenny didn't bother to ask whether Millie had been the one to call. "Why?" she said instead. "Do you know how much Gabriella has already been through? Did you think about anyone or anything but yourself before making that phone call?"

Millie plopped a hand on top of her belly and sighed. "Don't be absurd, Lenny. Of course I d—"

"Is that my ring?"

Millie dropped her arm. The sleeve fell over her hand.

Before either of them could say anything else, the doorbell chimed. They looked into the foyer. The bell sounded again, the tune mangled by simultaneous knocking.

Merriweather said through the door, "We need a minute, Ms. Mabary."

"If you have the key to the Oxford house," Davis said, "you can save some time by bringing it to us now."

He, or Merriweather, slipped a folded piece of paper under the door.

Lenny pulled Millie to the opening in the foyer wall and waved her down to the basement, then pressed the door closed behind her.

Lenny put down the camera when she saw Davis and Merriweather leaving Millie's house. She ran through all the rooms on the main level one more time to make sure nothing hinting at Millie's presence had been left anywhere, and she was waiting for them in the foyer when she remembered the ring. Millie had also been to the second floor.

Lenny took the stairs two at a time and sprinted from room to room, but there was nothing. She made it back downstairs just in time to open the door when they knocked.

"Exercising?" Merriweather said.

Lenny smiled and nodded and wiped her forehead.

Merriweather made a point of noticing Lenny's blouse and stiff slacks.

"Gotta do it whenever you can find a lickety minute, these days," Lenny said. "All this being busy nonsense like t'drive me crazy!"

Davis scratched under his nose. "Well," he said, handing Lenny the key, "she's been there. Recently, I mean."

Lenny gasped. "She has?" What could she have so needed from the house that she'd risk being seen crossing that wide field? "I mean—I just mean it seems like I'd have seen her," she said, indicating the living room window. She was embarrassed to notice she'd left the camera on the couch, the lens pointed out the window. Merriweather strolled into the living room, picked up the camera, and looked through the view finder.

"There are some marks in the dust," Davis said. "A fresh cigarette butt here and there."

"You take a lot of pictures of her house?" Merriweather said. She put down the camera and looked around the room.

"I've never seen police investigate anything before," Lenny said. "I watched you. I'm sorry."

Merriweather rejoined them in the foyer. "You haven't heard from her or seen her since the last time we were here, I'm guessing. You'd have called us. Right?"

Her hand pressed to her heart and with all the conviction of a woman telling the absolute truth, Lenny promised that she hadn't seen Millie enter or leave the house in months. She couldn't believe Millie's recklessness. Had the detectives visited at just the right time, Millie would have been taken, her baby dumped in a state shelter like so many others when there were at least twelve perfectly good, privately funded shelters within a hundred m—

"While you're here," Lenny said, "can you please tell me why the bureau won't send collaterals to privately funded shelters? The state-run facilities are…you know. Don't you?"

"That why you're helping her?" Davis said. "You could probably adopt it, if you're worried about it."

"I'm not—This is about your procedures. If you did find Millie, whether here or in…in Texas, or wherever, couldn't you keep her baby out of a state—"

"She's not in Texas," Davis said. "Or Wisconsin. That's where the boyfriend is. Wisconsin."

"Are you pullin' my—Wis*con*sin?"

Merriweather said yes, Wisconsin, and that she was sorry, but they had no influence on "procedure." They investigated; the courts distributed.

"Private shelters don't have federal certification," Davis said. "It takes time and work to make choices, and there are too many private shelters to choose from. Simple as that."

Davis said they were going to have to search Lenny's house, now.

Lenny waited in the foyer throughout their two-hour inspection so she'd be there if they found the door. They didn't.

THIRTY SEVEN

Millie observed no police after two passes on Main Street. She instructed the driver stop in front of a taco restaurant, this time. (She selected a new start point each visit in order to complete the illusion of a woman running daily errands.) She climbed gingerly out of the ancient car, paid cash, and gripped the roof and door for (largely unneeded) support while smiling at passersby and greeting them with "Whew!" and a jolly rub of her pregnancy.

Young people—teenagers and those her own age—sneaked envious or longing looks at her, imbuing her pride and exhilaration that inflated her lungs and warmed her face and chest. To attract the attention of a couple who seemed about to pass without noticing her, Millie looked up to read a restaurant awning and accidentally wandered into their path.

"Oh, excuse me," she giggled breathlessly at them with a hand cupping her abdomen. "I'm so clumsy, these days!"

They smiled and congratulated her.

The next person who attempted to ignore her was treated to her urgent request for physical support while she clumsily fished a fleck of something out of her shoe.

When the clock in front of the jewelry store said an hour had passed, Millie stepped into a consignment store. Under the cold blast of air conditioning, she wiped away the sweat gathered under her large sunglasses and scratched her head at the wig's finger clip, then used the telephone to call a driver. While she waited, she looked for a store she hadn't yet visited. Next time, she would use the phone in the rug store across the street.

She continued the Main Street visits well into the final month of her pregnancy, always circling back before reaching the park, whose regulars had professionally segregated themselves: The homeless claimed the circular granite bench surrounding the flag, whether to use it as a bed or to sit with their backs against it. The laborers and other unemployed scattered themselves in the grass, where they ate takeout and drank Fireball nips. (At least, this was Millie's suspicion, as the sidewalks were frequently littered with empty Fireball nip bottles, and it was unlikely that Main Street attorneys and bankers were sucking on them before morning meetings. The bottles were so ubiquitous in the sidewalk litter clusters that Millie, curious, once bought one of her own and swallowed it in the cab on the drive home. It would have been unmemorable had it not tasted so much like candy.)

The protesters claimed the retaining wall closest to the street, the causes on their signs ever-changing and their opposing positions separated by about six feet of empty space. One day, their signs would support or oppose state-run children's shelters. Another day, they would express outrage or exultation over the IVF ban (or, when shelter levels dropped below the minimum threshold, its temporary lift). They were for or against Exile, for or against licensing, for or against pre-evaluation counseling and the new three-day waiting period, for or against the law requiring shelters to release drops at eighteen years old versus twenty-one, for or against the revival of welfare benefits strictly for released drops, for or against the continued rationing of spices, fruits, and vitamins in an era of licensing, etcetera.

Millie concerned herself with none of that. When she was close enough to read even one sign in the park, she pressed the WALK button and crossed the intersection to delight the other side of the street with her mound, her awkward waddle, and her rosy cheeks. When walking hurt her feet, ankles, and back, she drew even more attention, and if she could safely stay out all day and all night, she would.

In part to avoid Lenny's constant admonitions. She issued them not as a show of concern for Millie, but for the pregnancy. She advised her on what not to eat, what not to drink, why not to smoke ("Where in the world do you keep them, now!?" Lenny once wheezed, flipping over cushions and lifting rugs in the suite and, when she didn't find them there, thrashing unsuccessfully through the upper levels).

Every night before bed, Millie measured herself in the mirror, first with a look at herself from the front, and then from each side, to see what they saw. The more it stood out from her sturdy frame, the wider she smiled and the more she looked forward to her next walk on Main Street.

The only troubling aspect of a late-stage pregnancy was that she would sometimes experience a kick or a punch from the inside. Patting down the offending limb temporarily corrected the behavior, but it did little to ease her mind. She had such trouble sleeping those nights—Did it already hate her so intensely?—that even the pillow in the center of the bed wasn't soothing. So she slept, when she could, during the day, snuggled up in Gabriella's nightgown, lights off in the basement, but with the door open at the top of the stairs so she could hear the comforting sounds of daytime and Lenny's routine.

When even that failed, she hugged the pillow and visualized a deep pink parlor, an elaborate flower arrangement, Millie's picture propped on an easel beside her casket, and—one by one—mourners stepping up to the lectern to share their final, and therefore genuine, feelings about her.

Hugh, with his tie unevenly knotted and his thick brown hair hanging over tear-filled eyes, would say, *I loved her more than I've ever loved anyone, and I'll miss her until the day I die.* Floyd, pockets bulging with his long, skeletal hands: *I shouldn't say it, because Lenny won't like it, but I loved Millie the best. She was different, or.* Lenny, a tissue held to her nose and the sobs making it a challenge for anyone but Millie to understand her: *We were like sisters. No, we were sisters. I'm ashamed of every second I failed to let Millie know I cared, because I did. I will never have a better friend. If I may, I'd like to read one of Millie's articles to all of you here today. I've saved it all this time.* Millie's dad, his dark, wavy hair curling over his ears, a sad smile wrinkling his eyes: *My only regret is that I didn't find my way back to my silly willie Millie before today, though I damn sure tried. If not for that accident...*

Millie had yet to hear the rest of his story before falling asleep.

Millie was sneaking down the front walk to the car waiting at the curb when the contractions began.

She cursed and waved away the driver, then shuffled inside to call the shelter as Lenny had instructed her to. When Lenny arrived twenty minutes later with a strange woman carrying towels and wearing rubber gloves, Millie's breath was fresh from the toothpaste that had removed the red stain from her teeth and two hurried glasses of wine from her breath. (Lenny had warned her there would be no hospital-grade pain medication, and the ibuprofen hadn't been as effective as Millie would have liked.)

Fortunately, the delivery wasn't as painful as she'd anticipated. The baby gushed out on a stream of fluid that splashed into the strange woman's arms. (Mille was sure Lenny had said the woman's name more than once—Paula or Polly or Pauline—but Millie hadn't seen the point of committing it to memory.)

"Well, con...congratulations," Lenny said as the woman handed Millie the baby.

Millie looked at its face and then at Lenny, who didn't seem to notice that, though swollen around the eyes and covered in what Lenny said was Milia, it more than resembled Floyd.

"She has your blond hair," Lenny said.

The baby was less interesting to Millie than it had been as a fetus. It cried and demanded things Millie couldn't identify. Feeding was either painful or tedious, depending, but often both. And she was tremendously bored by the pressure of having to constantly be near it.

She persuaded Lenny to babysit during the day (Lenny owned the shelter, after all, and had plenty of staff beneath her to compensate for her absence) while Millie—purely out of boredom and a need for money—freelanced from a library on a pseudonymous "mommy column" for the *Daily Fact*.

"It won't be much longer," Millie said. "As soon as I have the funds, I'll be on my way."

She'd have asked Lenny for the money, but she wasn't quite prepared to travel with a baby. And because Lenny never offered to give her money to help her leave, Millie assumed she appreciated her companionship.

———

Lenny spent so much time away from the shelter that she missed the residents and was worried they missed her. She'd managed one lunch with Gabriella and her baby, Elmore, but even on a no-wig day when Millie stayed home, Lenny couldn't leave the house. Twice she'd found Millie's baby lying dangerously close to the edge of the living room couch while Millie slept in the basement. One morning Lenny found the baby flailing around under the coffee table after she'd already dropped off the couch, her naturally pale face red from yowling and her fat arms shaking tiny fists. On a night of such loud screaming that it scared her awake, Lenny hurried downstairs to the lit kitchen and walked in on Millie hissing "Shh!" and shooting a stream of breast milk at the baby's face.

There were routine problems, too. Millie didn't change the diaper. She forgot the baby was in the sink during the baths Lenny reminded her to give. She left the baby on a floor in a room full of sharp corners, long wires, or small cat toys, and no amount of "Millie, you can't..." changed a thing.

The days Millie left the house without taking the baby, Lenny fed her the formula she'd brought home from Pauline's infant care shelter and burped her in the foyer. Except for the basement, it was the only part of the house where she could stand and bounce with plenty of room and no windows close enough to see her through.

The only problem with the foyer was that the high ceilings magnified sound. One day, Lenny let Andy inspect the baby on a soft blanket on the foyer floor, and her wide-eyed shock at the big, black nose in her face made Lenny laugh so suddenly and so loud that it echoed off the hard floor and walls. Andy barked and bounced back with his ears down, scaring Margaret (Millie hadn't named her, so Lenny called her that when they were alone). Margaret screamed so loud that Lenny was sure anyone walking on the street could hear her. She picked up the wailing baby and held her until she calmed down, closing her eyes to Margaret's sweet weight and breathing in the musky smell of her neck.

She did try to be patient with Millie. She tried to let her learn her own way. At night, she listened at the top of the stairs for signs Millie was helping Margaret get to sleep. What she usually heard instead was, "Will you *please* be quiet," and once, a confusing, "You interrupted Hugh. Now I have to start over from the beginning!" A few times a week Lenny had to sneak down in the dark to get the baby from the basement and do it herself, rocking her in her top floor bedroom until they both fell asleep.

When Millie said she needed a babysitter so she could write "incognito" for the *Fact* to earn money for her move to Wisconsin, Lenny tried to feel better about things. Millie was trying to be practical, she told herself. And she'd be gone soon. But it didn't make her feel any better. As much as she didn't want Millie in her house, the thought of her leaving with Margaret and taking full responsibility for her, even if only for the time it took her to find Hugh, was...unthinkable.

———

To allay the monotony of supervising the baby—and because people bestowed nearly as much reverence upon parents with infants as they did carriers—Millie flaunted it up and down Main Street, sure to struggle with the oh-so-charming burden on her arm. Because she hadn't thought about what to call it, when anyone asked for its name she would say whatever occurred to her. "Annabelle," she said one Saturday. "Betty," she said the next. On the baby's eighth Saturday, Millie was about to tell a coochie-cooing man the baby's name was Hester when she witnessed Gabriella pulling her baby from the back seat of shiny black AV in a spot near the park.

Millie stopped.

And then she half-laughed at her own foolishness. She was in disguise! She took another step forward.

She stopped again.

They had spent months together in that magnificent basement. If Gabriella possessed any observational skills whatsoever, she would recognize Millie's height, her build, her gait.

Millie had started to turn around when Gabriella announced, just loud enough, "There you are."

They held eye contact through Millie's sunglasses.

Had Gabriella been a true stranger, Millie would already have reacted. It was too late to pretend.

"Exile Dahl! Exile Dahl!"

A crowd of protesters marched briskly toward Gabriella from the park. Following close behind them, a gathering of equal size chanted, "A child is a right! A child is a right!"

Gabriella hurriedly secured her baby in its car seat and looked one last time at Millie. She tapped her ear, smiled (menacingly, Millie thought), and mouthed, "Police," before backing out with a squeal of her tires.

Millie sprinted down the sidewalk, the baby jostling so hard against her chest that its vomit splashed all over her chin and neck. She called for a driver from a restaurant phone and made her plan in the car while gagging and wiping her neck with her sleeve. She would pack her things, contact the *Fact* about the pay she'd asked them to hold until she needed it, and purchase her bus ticket with cash.

The driver circled the neighborhood twice as directed, stopping to let Millie out only when she was convinced it was safe. As she ran to the front door, she felt suddenly grateful for having seen Gabriella. She was tired of hiding, and the people on the street had grown so used to seeing her that the only acknowledgement they seemed capable of mustering was a tight smile or an impatient nod, regardless of how enthusiastically Millie flapped the baby's hand or foot at them in greeting.

———

Sudden, cracking knocks on the front door launched Bertram into a twisting flip before he streaked up the stairs. Lenny dropped the string they were playing with and opened the door. A batty-eyed Millie barreled past Lenny, then spun around and thrust the baby at her.

"Lock it," Millie said, but she threw herself at the door and punched in the code herself.

Lenny laughed when Millie told her Gabriella had threatened to turn her in. She promised Gabriella would never do that.

"She's a good person," Lenny said.

Millie snorted and dashed to the basement.

Lenny bounced Margaret on her hip until she got tired of waiting for Millie to come back. She went downstairs to find her on her knees, jamming clothes into an oversized duffel bag in the middle of the floor.

"What are you doing?" Lenny tightened her hold on the warm, squishy body fatiguing her bicep.

Millie looked up through her mass of frizzy hair. "This was always the plan, as I understand it." She jumped up and ran to the bathroom.

Lenny took Margaret upstairs and paced the foyer. "It'll be all right," she whispered into the baby's velvety ear. Margaret curled her fist against Lenny's shoulder. "It'll be all right," she murmured again and again.

By the time Millie materialized upstairs, red faced and with blond curls stuck to her cheeks, Lenny was sitting at the kitchen island with Margaret's sleeping head on her breast. Millie looked at them, bent over the sink and spit, then stalked over to Lenny and pulled Margaret from her arms.

"Millie," Lenny said, "Why don't you stay?"

———

A primal and profound yearning to stay anywhere she knew she was truly wanted nearly elicited an unthinking, "All right." But being wanted presented an even more compelling reason to leave. What an unfamiliar and rewarding sensation of emotional empowerment to be the one leaving the very person who wanted her to stay!

Millie said no. Even assuming Lenny was right about Gabriella (and she wasn't; she hadn't seen the self-satisfied look on Gabriella's face), it would still, Millie explained, be wholly impractical to hide in the basement for the rest of her life. It would also be taxing to live in a town where the police would never entirely stop being interested in her. She knew that, now.

The baby reached out to pull her hair. Millie craned her neck and shifted her weight to avoid the insistent, saliva-covered fingers.

"Leave her here," Lenny said, reaching for her. "I mean, you...you can leave her here."

Millie spun away and squeezed her arms tight around the baby. "She loves *me*."

———

Lenny wanted to cry for Margaret's soft, new bones trapped in Millie's suffocating hug. She didn't have the power to do anything else.

"Have you fed her?" Lenny said. "She should eat before you go."

With Margaret now flopping on her arm (Lenny relaxed, because at least she wasn't being squeezed to death, anymore), Millie stomped to the sink and spit again. "You can't expect me to anticipate every single thing under such stressful conditions. How long do you think the police will take to arrive?" She rolled her eyes before Lenny could say anything. "How long do you think they *would* take to arrive if they *had* been called?"

"I don't know." Lenny wished it surprised her that Millie didn't seem to care that if the police did come, they'd both be in trouble. But since they weren't coming, the only real person in trouble—which Gabriella couldn't have known when she'd teased Millie like that—was the baby. "Did you pack bottles and diapers?"

"Bottles?" Millie said with a look toward the living room window. "Oh. No. Could you...?"

"What about her toys? Her blanket?"

"Yes, yes, Lenny. I'll bring as much as I can put together in a hurry. Would you like to write me a list before I go?" Millie handed Margaret to Lenny so abruptly that the baby's face scrunched into a knot and she cried. Millie groaned. "Bounce her around, or something, will you, while I—I won't be long."

Lenny followed Millie as far as the living room entry, stopping there to watch as Millie crept carefully to the back door. She slipped outside after looking left and right and started across the field faster than Lenny had ever seen her move.

When she was sure Millie wouldn't turn back, Lenny whisked the baby into the kitchen and yanked open the drawer.

———

The last time Millie had seen the chocolate alligator, it was displayed on the shelf beside Hugh's writing awards. She'd rescued it a mere second before he swept the awards, along with his prized miniature bust of Christiane Amanpour, into a vintage *New Yorker* tote bag. But where had she moved it in the rearrangement? Had she been clear-headed at the time, she'd have set it on a lower shelf, but it wasn't there, so she hadn't. Nor was it on an end table or on the bedroom nightstand or in a drawer or in any of the cabinets or under the couch...

She was finding it difficult to breathe. She had archived not a single photograph. The few pictures she'd had, she'd deleted on the two-year anniversary of her dad's final vacation. One glass of beer later, she'd emptied the recycle bin. She possessed not a single article of his clothing, and he had left nothing else behind—not a watch, a hairbrush, a shoe. Her only remaining evidence of him, the sole object she owned that he had ever touched, was that stale chocolate allig—

There was one more thing. Millie ran upstairs to the linen closet.

The orange towel was worn, with loose threads looped into impossible knots, but it was something. It unfolded when she tugged it from the bottom of the stack, one of the frayed threads catching on the flower petal setting of Lenny's emerald ring. She unhooked the thread and stroked the stone with the very tip of her finger.

It occurred to her that Lenny had seen the ring but hadn't asked Millie to return it.

Millie would take it with her, as well.

She ran down the stairs, the towel a bunched-up bundle in her arm. The door was fewer than six feet from her reach when she looked out the window and stopped short, dropped the towel, and rapidly compiled a visual list of every possible hiding place in her insufficiently labyrinthine home, the spot she would choose if she and Lenny were playing hide and seek.

Millie had been so skilled at being invisible as a child.

———

From where she watched in the living room's darkest corner, Lenny saw the gray car speed down Millie's driveway and brake hard in front of her small, covered porch. (Floyd had said everyone needed a covered place to sit in front of a house, whether the house was a four-room box or a fourteen-bathroom mansion.) The detectives—well, one detective, Merriweather—kicked in Millie's door. She and Davis went inside.

Because Lenny expected Millie to save herself by telling the detectives about Gabriella, she hadn't bothered locking the front door. If they came to her house next, they might as well walk right in. Lenny had enough pills stuffed in her pocket to kill her before her exile, and Margaret, just fed, freshly diapered, and surrounded by pillows in the basement, would be safe until Lenny used her one phone call on Pauline, who was waiting to hear from her.

Millie came out to the porch with Merriweather behind her, but no Davis. Lenny backed against the wall. Merriweather looked over her shoulder, then kicked Millie's back so hard she launched chest first into the brown grass. Merriweather kneeled and put her face to Millie's ear before jerking her arms to stand her up. She turned to Davis as he stepped out the door. She flailed her arms and pretended to fall.

Davis shook his head at her and walked ahead to open the car door. Merriweather shoved Millie into the back seat.

At the kitchen window, Lenny leaned against the counter and bent over the sink to watch the long driveway. She stopped breathing until she saw the car's grille, and then the blue sky reflected in the windshield. Davis's purple left elbow poked out the open window. He didn't seem to be slowing down the way he would if Lenny's house were next.

Lenny almost didn't see Millie slouched low in the back seat, looking up at her as the detective's car passed the kitchen window. Lenny gave her a little wave. She didn't know why. To thank her for not saying anything, or to help her decide not to? To let her know she was there? Millie turned away.

Lenny stood on her toes and stretched over the faucet to keep an eye on the car until it reached the end of Millie's driveway. The brake lights lit and the car stopped. No turn signal blinked.

Had she counted out enough pills? She wondered why she hadn't just dumped the whole bottle in her pocket. It would have been impossible to take too many.

Her hip bones ached from being pressed to the counter, and the balls of her hands stung from holding her weight.

The brake lights flashed off. Lenny waited for the white reverse lights. She made a note to spread the pills around to her other pockets so the bulge wouldn't get Davis and Merriweather's attention.

The car pulled forward and turned right toward Forest Lane.

Margaret was sleeping when Lenny stepped over her for the phone. The plush ball Lenny had left with her was wedged between her bent, bare knees, and her t-shirt, decorated with little red hermit crabs, was bunched up under her arms. Lenny pulled the fabric straight before dialing, thinking it must be frustrating to be a baby, sometimes.

Pauline answered on the first ring with, "That was quick. I guess you're not in jail."

"It'll take me twenty minutes to get her into place." Lenny stroked Margaret's cheek and tried to remember where she'd last seen the note pad. She hadn't planned to write a message, but she couldn't stand to let her go without at least a name. "Can you be there in twenty-two?"

———

Davis drove slowly. Five miles per hour, Millie saw on the speedometer. She looked up at the kitchen window as the car finally approached Lenny's house. She expected her to be there—Lenny had always been watching from her windows—but even so, there was a palpable release of anxious tension the moment Millie glimpsed Lenny's face behind the glass.

She was contemplating the safest way to interact—a wave? a nod?—when a story on the dashboard monitor distracted her. She turned forward to watch the screen.

"...briella Dahl, whose alleged intent to abandon an unsanctioned child inspired protests both for and against her release, has died after being shot in front of her home. Police have taken the alleged shooter, former police officer Matthew Fence, into custody."

"Ha! He finally got one," Merriweather said. She sighed.

"Witnesses saying—What's that?" The anchor held up a finger. "As it happens, a witness, a tourist, got some video that we—we're showing it as is? I guess we're showing it as is. Warning: this is the first time any of us at the station are seeing this raw footage, so please be advised that some of what you see might be upsetting."

In the tourist's exceptionally clear recording, Matthew Fence screamed inches from the back of Gabriella's head as she walked from her car to her front door with a baby in her arms. A crowd of protesters followed several feet behind. It was difficult to decipher above all the shouting what the protesters hoped to communicate, but it appeared they both agreed and disagreed with Matthew Fence's assault on Gabriella, which only escalated when she reached her door. Before Gabriella could enter her code's first character, Matthew Fence used one arm to wrestle away her baby while, with the other, he pulled a handgun from a hip holster and shot her in the chest. As she fell, Gabriella clutched at the air, not quite managing to make contact with the baby in Matthew Fence's arms.

"Look at—Look at her face," the anchor said. "Did you see that? Did everyone see that? Such despair. Can we go back and slo-mo that, please? Back, back, back. There! Stop. Play."

Gabriella fell again, grasped again, slowly. Millie thought her reaction to Matthew Fence holding her baby resembled horror more than despair, but whatever it was transformed into something else entirely as Matthew Fence spun on his heel and tossed the baby at the crowd behind him. Gracefully it sailed, out of his hands and over what appeared to be a holly bush, directly toward at least fifty people who in uncanny synchronicity took one long, slow-motion step backward.

"Oh, I can't—We can't do this part slow, like this. Can we? No. No, we really shouldn't. Should we? No, no, speed it up. Speed it up, please. Now. Now! What are you jackasses doing back there?"

The slow-motion baby glided with delicate, brutal force head-first onto the sidewalk as Gabriella watched from where she lay crumpled on her front stairs, blood spreading a wide stain into her shirt. She struggled to sit up when Matthew Fence ran toward the motionless baby, lifting only her head. It appeared she was focusing not on the police officer, but on the little body on the ground, when her initial horror—despair, Millie still thought the anchor should have said—gave way to an intense stare, the rest of her face blank as she watched Matthew Fence press a finger to the baby's neck. When it was clear there was no pulse, Gabriella smiled slightly, closed her eyes, and lowered her head to the stone step.

"Well," the anchor said. "That was...That was definitely..."

Davis turned off the monitor and flipped to music.

Merriweather said, her face half turned toward the back seat, "And she didn't even manipulate her chip."

Millie said, "Someone hacked me."

"You got scanned," Davis said. "We have the readout."

Millie spun Lenny's ring around her finger. The sharp petals jabbed her thumb. A ball of blood the size of a pin head rose to the surface.

"What'd you do with the baby?" Merriweather turned all the way around.

"I never had a baby."

Merriweather shrugged and faced forward. "Doctor'll be the judge of that, I guess."

Millie wiped her thumb on her pants. She wanted to ask whether Exile inmates were permitted to retain any personal possessions, but she knew the answer. Eugene had had nothing on his person but clothes that clearly weren't his own. She took off the ring, then slid it back on. She carefully pressed the band against the joint on the underside of her finger, and then against the puffy flesh on top, harder and harder until she could see the circular impression. The skin would reform, but she would always be able to recall the sensation of the ring's presence.

She took it off again only when they'd driven far enough away from Forest Retreat Estates for Davis and Merriweather to, she hoped, dismiss as "inconvenient" any thoughts of turning back to question Lenny, who Millie suspected needed a little time. She offered the ring between the front seats as they passed the crumbling remains of Oxford Spirits I, asking Merriweather to please deliver it to Lenny.

"It was a gift from my mother for my first article published in the *Daily Fact*," she lied, and because Lenny was the last person alive who had known her mother personally, she should be the one to have it. (That she should be the one to have it was true, at least.)

Merriweather took the ring and dropped it into her suit jacket's inside pocket. "She's a good friend to help you out."

"I'm sure I don't know what you mean."

"She hid you. Somehow, some way. Right?"

Millie said it had been months since she'd last seen Lenny.

"Mm."

Davis stopped at a stop sign. Merriweather looked at Davis. Davis continued looking straight ahead, but he changed his signal direction and turned right when, if they were going to the police station, they should have turned left.

"You know," Merriweather said, "I like Exile. As a system, I mean. I respect it." They followed a narrow dirt road toward the cannabis fields. "I've taken the tour. All us bureau employees have." She turned to Davis, who confirmed with a single nod. "And, I don't know. I think they're a little too lenient." She twisted in her seat to look at Millie. "Not on what they call the 'worst' abusers, but, you know, on people like you. Now, people like you, you still have a hard time, don't get me wrong, but compared to what the others get..." She shook her head. "You'd be lucky to go there." At a split in the road, she pointed Davis left. Left went beyond the cannabis farm, into a dense expanse of trees leaving only enough room for a single car to pass. "You'd be damn lucky," she said again. "And you can go if you want. We'll take you there. All you have to do is tell me something that'll make it easier for us to do our job. Something that'll tell me you want to do the right thing. Something like, 'Yes ma'am, Lenny Mabary helped me subvert the one system in place that's designed to protect the welfare of innocent children.' You tell me that, and Davis'll turn this car around."

Millie looked at the dashboard clock. They'd been driving for nearly an hour. If Lenny were as predictable as Millie believed her to be, she had every reason to believe the baby would have been dropped by this time, and that Lenny would already have removed all evidence of Millie and the baby from her house.

She ran her thumb over her ring finger. The impression was already gone.

Millie told Merriweather the same thing she had told her earlier. She and Lenny hadn't seen each other in months.

"What if I told you she was the one that turned you in, called us just before we came to get you?"

Then Merriweather would be telling a preposterous lie, Millie didn't say. Lenny was the most loyal person she had ever known.

She told Merriweather she was sorry, but that whatever Lenny might or might not have said or done didn't change Millie's stateme... *testimony*.

Merriweather shrugged and turned to Davis. He pulled over into brush and leaves. Merriweather retrieved the ring from her inside pocket and positioned her hand so that Millie could see her trying it on each finger until she found the one it fit, her sleeve pulling back to reveal a small tattoo on her wrist: *Guardian.*

Davis looked out his side window as Merriweather stepped out of the car and gestured for Millie to join her.

Benny Goodman's "Get Happy" played through the open doors.

Kristen Tsetsi lives in Connecticut with her husband Ian, cats Hoser, Simon, and Sampson, and dog Lenny.

Her previous novels, *Pretty Much True* and *The Year of Dan Palace*, are published under the name Chris Jane.

More information: kristenjtsetsi.com